A Congress of Kings

Talon Series

Book 9

His Coat of Arms

A Congress of Kings

by

James Boschert

www.penmorepress.com

ISBN-13: 978-1-950586-59-2(Paperback)
ISBN :13: 978-1-950586-58-5(e-book)

BISAC Subject Headings:
FIC014000 FICTION / Historical
FIC032000 FICTION / War & Military
FIC031020FICTION / Thrillers / Historical

Senior Editor: Chris Wozney
Editing: Virginia Saez
Copy Editor Catherine Griscom
    The Book Cover Whisperer: Christine Horner:
ProfessionalBookCoverDesign.com

Address all correspondence to:

Penmore Press LLC
920 N Javelina Pl
Tucson AZ 85748
USA

Dedication

To Danielle and Markus, and Simone,
and
my two grandchildren, Sophia and Eva,
who are all very precious to me.

Acknowledgements

My sincere thanks to my wife Danielle Boschert who knows the meaning of patience, Christine Horner and Chris Wozny for their efforts and help with this manuscript.

And to my sources:

Dungeon Fire and Sword by John J. Robinson
Deus Lo Volte by Evan S. Connel
The Crusades Through Arab Eyes by Amin Maaloof
A Short History of Byzantium by John Norwich
Civilization in The Middle Ages by Norman Cantor
Byzantium by Judith Herrin
The Assassin Legends by Farhad Daftary
Castles of the Assassins by Peter Willey
Who's Who in the Middle Ages by John Fines
The Dream of The Poem by Peter Cole

Wikipedia
Google

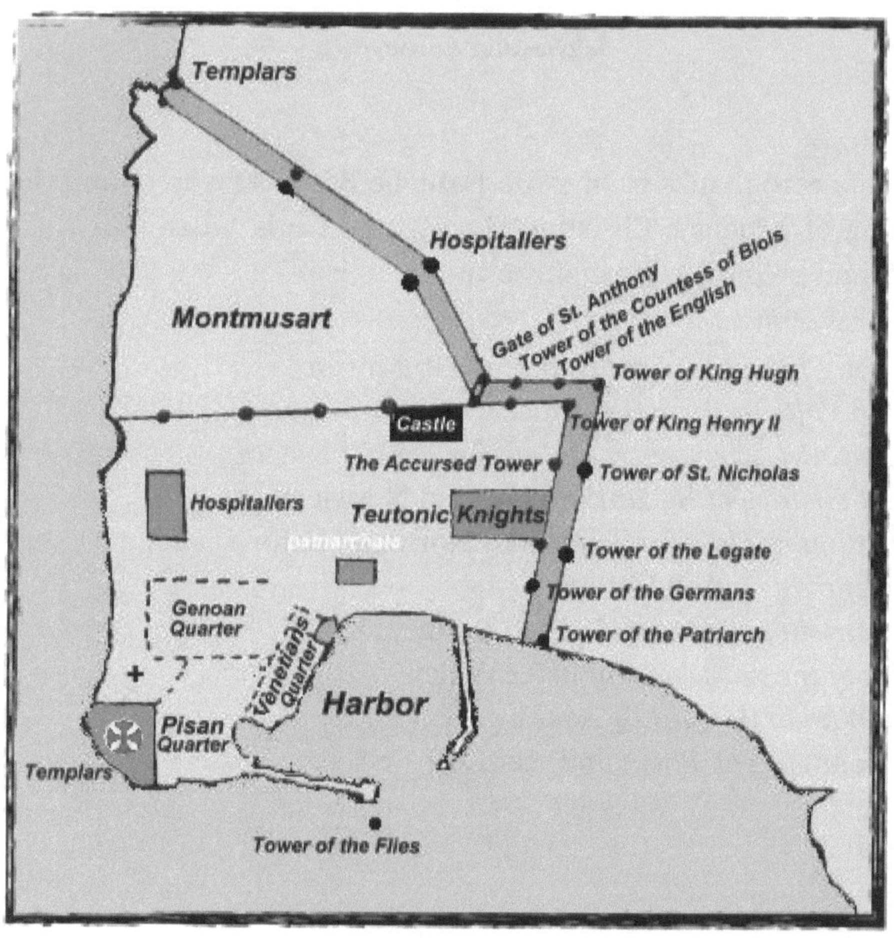
Templars
Hospitallers
Montmusart
Gate of St. Anthony
Tower of the Countess of Blois
Tower of the English
Tower of King Hugh
Tower of King Henry II
Castle
The Accursed Tower
Tower of St. Nicholas
Hospitallers
Teutonic Knights
Patriarchate
Tower of the Legate
Tower of the Germans
Tower of the Patriarch
Genoan
Quarter
Venetian
Quarter
Harbor
Pisan
Quarter
Templars
Tower of the Flies

Many a vanish'd year and age,
And tempest's breath, and battle's rage,
Have swept o'er Corinth; yet she stands
A fortress form'd to Freedom's hands.
The whirlwind's wrath, the earthquake's shock
Have left untouch'd her hoary rock
—Lord Byron

The lone horseman sat his horse on a low rise overlooking the plains in front of the distant city of Acre and stared intently. He could just make out the desperate conflict taking place before, and even on top of, the tall walls of Acre, once again besieged, this time by the Christian crusaders.

Although he was the commander of all the Arab forces in the entire region, from his scuffed horsehide boots to his collar, Salah ad-Din was dressed very much like one of his average cavalrymen, but was perhaps not as patched and stained. The only concession to his rank was his helmet, which was of burnished steel with an inlay of gold filigree patterned around its rim. There was, however, no mistaking the fine breed of his mount, which was a magnificent creature and had come from Yemen. Salah ad-Din, being a Kurd, was a horseman first and foremost. He rested the palm of his hand on the animal's neck to calm it while he scrutinized the events taking place ahead of him. His features were set in a tight, grim expression.

Besieged towns were not an unusual sight in the beleaguered Holy Land, but Acre was a very important city for both the Moslems and the Christians, as it represented one of the main portals to Jerusalem.

In a loose group behind the sultan, giving him some respectful space to be alone, were his heavily armed, mounted escorts accompanied by his brother, Prince al-Adil. They were also staring at the untidy encampment of the Christians and the current assault taking place at the walls of Acre. While they shared their leader's frustration, they also knew that they could do nothing for the city at present. Fervently, they hoped that the defenders could endure until their own numbers increased sufficiently to drive off the Christians and relieve their comrades' suffering.

It was April, and the vast majority of Salah ad-Din's former followers, who had left at the beginning of winter, were still at home, dealing with their own domestic issues: farming, planting and other tribal matters. The vast numbers he could usually muster would not be available until June. Until then.... His jaw tightened and he clenched his fist on the reins. He would clean them out like bed bugs and settle some old scores, including the taking of Tyre which still remained in the hands of Lord Conrad. The count had been a thorn in his side since the beginning of this campaign. *In Sha' Allah,* God willing, it would all be dealt with, this year. He sighed and tried to settle himself more comfortably in the saddle. The recent illness that left him tired and sometimes weak had not improved with the onset of the spring rains.

He cocked his head to listen more closely as the sounds of conflict became louder. The hoot of trumpets, the clash of steel and the cheers of the Christians as they pressed home their attack, could be faintly but clearly heard, even from this distance. He frowned. While there had been many attempts to take the city by ladder, mobile towers and suchlike, this time it really looked as though they might succeed. Christian fighters had managed to climb their makeshift ladders and were now clustered on the battlements, fighting hard to gain a permanent foothold.

Salah ad-Din shook his head angrily. The Christian army was constantly being swelled by newcomers: from Germany—the remnants of the disastrous Crusade by King Ferdinand—from Normandy, Languedoc and other regions with allegiance to France, as well as freebooters and mercenaries on the lookout for loot. The erstwhile king, Guy de Lusignan, had given his oath to Salah ad-Din, after the Arab victory at Hattin, never to fight on this land again. But here he was, the commander of the sizable force below. The sultan wondered whether he had made the right decision when he'd released the man, two years before. Keeping Guy de Lusignan in prison had not kept the crusaders at bay, and Salah ad-Din had released the ex-king because his incompetence was legendary, in the hope that he would die quickly in some stupid skirmish. Now, however, the man was laying siege to Acre, and while his foul-smelling camp was infested with disease and rats, the Christians, despite all obstacles, were still there, taxing his own resources to the limit.

"My lord!" his Prince al-Adil called to him. "They appear to have gained a foothold! What should we do?"

Salah ad-Din turned his head. "Send our cavalry to attack their camp. We need a distraction. Do it now!" he called back. He remained on the slopes with most of his escort while his brother galloped off to lead the light cavalry, who had been waiting for this very opportunity.

Within minutes Salah ad-Din saw a large contingent of horsemen and footmen racing toward the Christian encampment. He noticed, too, that for a few vital moments, their opponents were unaware of the menace. Perhaps this was just the opportunity he needed to do some real damage to his enemy.

*****

Eyes wild with the excitement of battle, Lord Gerard de Ridefort glared out from under his helmet nosepiece. As he placed a mailed hand on the ladder in front of him, a body landed with a loud thump just next to him, blood pouring from a gaping wound in its neck.

Lord Gerard de Ridefort paid the body scant attention, but then someone grabbed his arm and shouted, "My lord! My lord!"

De Ridefort whirled around to see a distraught knight. He shrugged off the man's hand angrily. The knight's face was distorted and he was gesturing wildly behind him, across the heads of the milling knights, who were pushing and shoving to reach the ladders and gain glory on the battlements above. The knight gestured again, insistently, toward the camp.

"What is it, Marcel?" Gerard shouted back. It was hard to see with all the dust around, let alone to make oneself heard over the din of the shouting, swearing men at arms, and the clash of weapons. The screams of dying and wounded men filled the air.

"We must stop them, Lord!" And again, Marcel clutched his arm.

"Unhand me, damn you!" Gerard shouted, wrenching free, but just then, his eyes were drawn to the place where his follower was pointing. There were Arab banners flying high, and they appeared to be much too close to the Christian camp.

"They are striking us from behind, Lord! They bring fire and sword!" Sir Marcel yelled over the noise. "Their cavalry has attacked our encampment. We need reinforcements or we are lost!"

Gerard seized Marcel by his hauberk. "What happened to Lord Robert?" he snarled. "He was supposed to protect our rear while we dealt with this place!"

"D—dead, my lord. Struck down by an arrow! God have mercy on his soul!"

"Saints' robes!" Gerard shouted. "Where is my mount?" Marcel turned away to find his squire, who was hovering on the edge of the crowd of roaring, shoving knights.

Another man had noticed the exchange and paused at the base of a ladder. "Geoffrey, they are attacking our rear, and Lord Robert is dead!" Gerard bellowed.

Lord Geoffrey, the brother of Guy de Lusignan, looked startled and then swiveled his head to stare hungrily up the battlements, where men were struggling for their lives. He had wanted so badly to get up there and slaughter the defenders! Another body hurtled to the ground, landing with a soggy thump nearby. This time, it was one of the defenders. Just to be sure he was dead, a footman spitted the corpse with his spear and promptly began to rummage through its clothes, looking for anything else of value, disregarding the conflict going on all around him. Someone tried to join him but was snarled at savagely and backed off.

Geoffrey yelled at the men surrounding him. "We must protect our camp! Get down! Get back down!" he shouted angrily, his voice full of frustration. Thwarted and enraged, he turned away from his objective to look for his horse. By the time Geoffrey had mounted and called his men together, Gerard de Ridefort had already galloped off, back toward their camp. Shouting to the mounted men to follow him, Geoffrey rode hard after Gerard. As he passed a group of men gathered around Guy de Lusignan, he shouted. "They have killed Lord Robert and are attacking our camp. It is in disarray!"

He and his men, joined now by other horsemen, rode hard, straight through the camp and out of the other side, which faced east. The Arab cavalry had been stopped and then was chased off— but only just—by the rear-guard defenses. The wide ditches and spiked posts presented a hazard of some significance to mounted horsemen, preventing a cohesive assault that could have proved fatal. Instead, their massed charge had been broken up by the obstacles and they were met by spearmen and crossbowmen, as well as mounted knights drawn from the attack on Acre, who formed solid blocks that they could not easily break up.

However, some of the more nimble and reckless riders had still managed to get within the tent area and, with their lances, had 'picked' the tent pegs of several tents, which had then collapsed in a tangle of canvas and ropes. Other riders following right behind had stabbed at the struggling forms within the fallen coverings, creating havoc and pain for their victims. The riders had then made their escape, yelling exultant war cries and brandishing bloody lances.

The gathered Franks were made aware, yet again, that these light Arab cavalries could also inflict much damage from a distance, which they proceeded to do, galloping in, to within thirty or forty paces, loosing their arrows, then wheeling their mounts and galloping out of range of return fire. By the time Redford and his men had arrived, the ground was littered with horses and men—wounded and dying—who had been victims of these skirmishes. Geoffrey and his brother, Guy de Lusignan, stared out at the Arabs with frustration. "Where are our own archers? Get them here and hurry up about it!" Geoffrey bellowed. He turned to his equally angry brother. "A few more minutes and we could have taken that bloody wall! Perhaps even the God forsaken city!" he fumed.

"*He* is watching it all from up there." Guy panted angrily and pointed a grubby finger toward the distant figure. "He knew exactly what he was doing."

"Damn him to hell!" Ridefort raged from nearby, waving his sword in the air. "I'm going after him! When I get to him, he is dead!"

He cast a glance down at the corpse of Lord Robert, two arrows protruding from its chest, and made the sign of the cross across his own breast. He spurred his mount forward in the direction of the shouting Arabs, his face contorted with anger. "I'll kill them all!"

His men followed him, albeit very reluctantly, as he drove his horse recklessly through one of the gaps in the spikes and ditches, heading for the densest group of enemy riders.

"He is really quite mad!" Geoffrey muttered as he reined in his own mount. "Ridefort, stop!" he roared. "Don't be a fool! Do not go out there!"

His words fell on deaf ears as Ridefort charged toward the opposing cavalry. His men had barely caught up with him when the enemy loosed a hail of arrows. Arrows struck several riders and horses and brought them down. More than one struck Ridefort's mount, which staggered and fell to its knees. Ridefort, still a strong and nimble man for his age, managed to disentangle himself and scrambled to his feet, holding his sword.

"For God and the cross!" he yelled, and ran forward, brandishing his sword to attack his opponents on foot. He didn't bother to see if his men were following him. It was not very long before he was well ahead of his men, some of whom had lost their nerve and slowed their forward movement. They watched in horror as Ridefort stood on a low knoll and brandished his sword, screaming, "I shall not retreat. I shall kill them all before I leave." He was quickly surrounded by Arab horsemen and disappeared from view.

Several of his more ardent followers made to go after the enemy but were quickly dispatched by the cavalry, while the others, seeing how futile the effort had become, reluctantly turned away, to the jeers of the enemy who had captured their leader. He was still screaming and struggling wildly as they took him away.

His remaining followers slowly made their abject way back to the camp and their waiting comrades, followed by the mocking yells of victory from their hated enemy.

Guy de Lusignan shook his head. "God protect his soul!"

Geoffrey was a more pragmatic man. He shrugged. "He was quite mad. It was only a matter of time, I suppose. God be merciful, but I fear he is destined for hell."

Guy snapped him a sharp look. "That is close to blasphemy, brother," he chided.

"Gerard needlessly sent many a brave and pious soul to his death. Mad or not, I expect he will spend considerable time in purgatory for that," Geoffrey retorted.

The two men, one who had once been the King of Jerusalem and the other a lord in his own right, turned away from the scene of the skirmish, where men were laying out the dead or escorting the wounded to the dreaded leech tent, and made their way through the camp, followed at a respectful distance by their retainers.

Few even bothered to acknowledge their presence as they passed. These days, disease, suppurating wounds and the gas death caused more death than actual fighting, and few had any illusions as to the future success of this forlorn venture. Guy and Geoffrey were unwashed and unkempt. They ignored the rags, offal and dung piled along the muddy tracks they followed and the audible hum of the innumerable flies that buzzed around the filth in clouds. Not even the rats bothered to scuttle away as the men approached. The stench of the camp no longer assaulted the men's nostrils; they had been in this place for over a year with little to show for it. A gust of wind stirred the rags of what had once been garishly colored banners fluttering above the tents.

"It's going to rain again," Geoffrey sighed, wiping his sweating face and looking up at the dark clouds gathering in the west. They had arrived back at the western edge of the camp and were now facing the walls of Acre once again. The pall of dust that had hung over the previous frantic activity of battle had settled or blown away. The ladders were lying at the base of the walls; some were broken like the corpses of both besiegers and defenders. Only when darkness came would there be any attempt to remove them for burial, and that would only be after their corpses had been plundered for every item of clothing they wore, any jewelry or coin.

Guy wiped a filthy hand across his straggly and unkempt beard and scratched. "Rain brings more plague and... fleas." He glanced irritably at one he had fished from his beard and popped it, leaving a small patch of blood between his fingers. "Ugh!" he grunted. "How I wish for a bath!" Guy had been previously known for his fastidious personal hygiene.

"I hope to God that the king of France, even the king of England will arrive here in time," Geoffrey muttered, ignoring his brother's discomfort as they watched the stragglers from the assault drift back into the camp, some supporting their wounded comrades. "We do not have the numbers to hold him off in the summer *and* complete the siege; God help us!"

"Do we know if they will come at all?" Guy asked. He sounded skeptical. "How long must it take for them to decide to take up the Holy Cause while we fester here? My wife and daughters were martyred in this stink hole. God rest their souls." He sounded as though he were ready to weep.

Geoffrey glanced at his brother with mild contempt. "You should have thought of that before you brought Queen Sibylla here

Brother. It was clear to all that it was a pestilent place from the day we arrived."

Guy shook his head hopelessly. "When that bastard Conrad refused us entry to Tyre, she insisted on being at my side. I wanted to send her to William in Sicily, but he goes and dies, leaving me no choice!" He groaned. His wife, Sibylla, the former sister of King Baldwin IV, had died of the plague, along with her daughters, almost a year ago, and he had been mourning them ever since.

Geoffrey recalled the humiliation of the event outside Tyre. Guy and himself, newly released from an Arab dungeon, had collected Sibylla and made for Tyre, the only city to hold out against Salah ad-Din since the fall of Jerusalem. They had been unable to approach the walls because the causeway to the island city had been cut, but Lord Conrad's messenger had been clear enough. Lord Conrad had denied them entry unless Guy rescinded his claim to the throne of Jerusalem, which Guy had refused to do. Although he had little admiration for his brother, Geoffrey approved of the stance, pointless though he felt it really was. The Sultan, Salah ad-Din, ruled Jerusalem now, but Geoffrey still boiled inside when he was reminded of this additional humiliation.

Guy wiped his eyes with the back of his hand and repeated his question, "Do we have news of the kings?"

"We have word that they have sailed from Sicily, Brother. But nothing else."

*****

Salah ad-Din had remained on the hill all this time. Although he could not see everything that had transpired, he was clear about one thing: his men had accomplished their goal. A horseman came galloping toward him, pulling up in a small cloud of dust before he touched his forehead respectfully to his leader.

"God's blessings, my lord. Prince al-Adil sends his respects and asks your permission to bring an important prisoner to you, Your Highness."

"Who is the prisoner?" Salah ad-Din asked.

"A man called Lord Gerard de Ridefort." The messenger repeated the name carefully, unsure how to pronounce it.

Salah ad-Din's eyes opened wide. "Ridefort?" he snapped.

"Yes, my lord." The messenger produced a scrap of paper from his sleeve, confirming the name. He handed it to his sultan.

"That man has broken every oath of trust he swore to me," Salah ad-Din muttered to himself. He stared at the paper in silence for a long moment, as though reliving the great battle of Hattin, which had destroyed the Christian army, and the subsequent capture of Ridefort and the king of Jerusalem. Both had broken their pledges never to fight his people again. The messenger fidgeted but dared not intrude upon his thoughts.

Salah ad-Din finally looked up. "I do not wish to see him. His head is to be removed forthwith. That is my command," he told the messenger, who nodded, touched his forehead, and called out.

"Your will be done, my lord." He wheeled his horse and galloped back the way he had come.

Salah ad-Din paused for just a while longer, staring hard at his enemy's camp, but then the first drops of rain began to fall. He turned his horse and rejoined his escorts, who were thankful that they might just make it to cover before the deluge.

CARAMANIA
SELJUKS OF ICONIUM
PAMPHYLIA
MEDITERRANEAN
SEA
EDESSA
TURKS OF MOSUL
The Kingdom of
JERUSALEM
with its Environs
at the time of the
CRUSADES
TRIPOLI
DAMASCUS
Mouths of the Nile
EGYPT
ARABIA
AJUBITES OF DAMASCUS

Part 1

Storms on the Horizon

Chapter 1

He clasps the crag with crooked hands;
Close to the sun in lonely lands,
Ring'd with the azure world, he stands.
The wrinkled sea beneath him crawls;
He watches from his mountain walls,
And like a thunderbolt he falls.
—Alfred Lord Tennyson

There were many castles in the region known variously as the Holy Land, the Levant and the Sultanate, under the rule of Salah ad-Din, but some were so deep within the mountains of the lands north and east of the Duchy of Tripoli, bordering on the Duchy of Antioch, that not even the sultan and his army could subdue them. These few castles belonged to a man known as the Master, the leader of a very dangerous sect of people who dealt in murder and extortion, knowing no borders. No one was safe from them.

The three boys who had most recently passed the skills tests of knife and stick fighting were now assembled in a small room in their best clothes. These were simple enough, as the boys were not rich, and their master was not inclined to bestow wealth upon them. Each wore a turban wrapped around his almost-shaven head, and a tunic of washed-out white linen.

They were tense with anticipation, as this was their initiation into the Paradise they had been promised from the very beginning of their training. Their particular class had started out as seventeen boys between the ages of thirteen and fifteen, but now there were only eight of them left. These three were the very best of the surviving group. Their former companions were all dead, having failed, in one form or another, during the training, either losing their grip on a wall and falling to their deaths or making an error when fighting with real knives, or simply having failed to understand the exacting rules of the Master.

Rashid Ed Din—the Master, or the School Master, as he was otherwise known—did not tolerate. These boys were his absolute slaves and would either fight to the death on his behalf or die at his command. It mattered not to him, as there were always young boys to be had from among the population in the towns and cities along the coast of the Levant.

Tonight, the youths were here to receive their reward and to glimpse the meaning of Paradise, as defined by the Great Master, who lived in his remote castles in faraway Persia.

Seated in front of them was a *Rafiki,* one of their senior instructors, who was there to see to it that they were looked after, and to ensure that the process was done correctly, as protocol demanded. The first part of the ceremony began with a servant entering through a door and presenting the boys with tea. The *Rafiki* indicated that they were to drink it, which they did cautiously. As they settled the small cups on the brass tray, they began to feel sleepy. It was not long before the three boys were sound asleep. After, the *Rafiki* lifted his hand and servants entered the small room to carry the boys out and place them on beds, in rooms adjacent to the tearoom.

The rooms were sumptuous by the normal standards of the otherwise austere castle, which was the intent. As the Master watched from his secret place, the boys would wake up and find themselves on a beautiful bed of silk, covered with wonderful embroidered patterns, and a girl in attendance, subject to their every wish, leaving the boys exhausted but with indelible and vivid memories of the foretaste of Paradise. This was all they lived for or died for hereafter.

When the boys woke up the second time, they were back in their familiar surroundings and the Paradise they had experienced had vanished, as though it were a dream, but the memories of the flesh remained an enticing reminder, and distraction, from that moment on.

They were to continue with their final training, later to be joined by the others, and it was then that the Master would pronounce them *fida'iyin*. They were now entitled to wear a cloth cummerbund around their waists with a red stripe woven into it. However, their proper training was not over by any means. Soon the youths would be ready for him to do with as he wished, and to send to wherever he commanded them, to kill or to insert themselves into any city or palace he might choose, assuming the roles of merchants, scholars or poor men, as the occasion demanded.

However the particular task Rashid Ed Din, the Master, had in mind for these three boys was perhaps even more dangerous and fraught with peril than any before. These young killers were to be the point of his barb that would finally finish off the impudent pair who lived in Cyprus, a cobra's strike that would finally kill the man called Talon and his "Brother" Reza, who was also known as the *ghost*. Rashid had not forgotten the last debacle, but he was a patient man and now the time had come to prepare his killers for a final attack on the two renegades who had thwarted him at every turn.

*****

In an equally remote location, within the mountains of Cyprus, the night was quiet and cool. Other than the very distant yap of a fox and the nearby hoot of an owl in the dense woods along the eastern part of the mountain ridge, the silence was complete. An attentive listener might hear the light keen of the wind in the corners of the tall towers of the sleeping castle, or the mice squeaking in the stables as they hunted for grain, accompanied by the occasional snuffle from one of the horses. Otherwise, it was very quiet.

There were only a few clouds in the sky on this moonless night. It was still quite dark and several hours would pass before dawn. The soldiers who patrolled the battlements of the castle of Kantara were alert for any sounds that might herald danger. These men were experienced veterans of many a skirmish and knew the dangers of inattention only too well.

Slowly, very slowly, a hand crept over the top edge of the northern wall, fingers blindly seeking a firm grip on the stone. They hesitated, and then the fingers found and gripped a tiny crevice. Half a pace away, another hand appeared on the cracked and fissured stone. A dark, shrouded head rose and very carefully peered over the edge of the battlements.

Seeing and hearing no signs of danger, the intruder, who had climbed the high north wall of the battlements in the dead of night without alerting anyone, was now able to slip over the top and slide slowly and noiselessly into a dark shadow and wait. He heard the sound of a sentry walking along the stone toward him, but fortunately for him, the sentry detected no danger and walked right past the dark recess wherein crouched the intruder. The sentry, who carried a light shield and a short spear, did, however, stop a few paces further along and peer over the lip of the wall, down at the sharp rocks a good one hundred feet below, then shook his head, muttered something, and resumed walking.

Soon after his departure, the shadow of the visitor moved and drifted silently down to the castle grounds, disturbing neither the hounds nor the horses stabled not very far from the huge bulk of the keep, its doors closed and bolted. He went unerringly for his target. Not one of the patrolling sentries saw or heard anything as the intruder glided through the castle grounds.

The sentries at the castle gatehouse situated on the south side of the fortress did not see or hear anything until the figure touched one of them on his shoulder. The man spun around with a surprised grunt to find a dark, menacing figure, his face covered to the eyes, silently holding aloft a small banner.

The sentry gasped and shrank back fearfully, but the man held out the stick bearing the banner insistently for him to take, still saying not a word. The sentry took the banner gingerly and walked shakily to the gatehouse and the guard commander. The sentry glanced behind him, but the intruder had vanished.

Perched on the walkway above in the darkness, overlooking the meeting between the intruder and the sentry, another man clad in dark clothing and a face covering that only showed his eyes, smiled with satisfaction. Reza was very pleased. He would enjoy telling Talon all about it in the morning. The sentry had reacted as though he was about to drop dead from surprise and fear, even to the point of clutching his chest!

*****

Lord Talon was woken by a sharp knock on the door to his chamber. He stirred and sat up groggily while Rav'an, his wife, huddled deeper into the bedclothes. It was an hour after dawn, and she was tired.

"What is it, my love?" she murmured.

"I think I know what it is. I will deal with it, my Rav'an. Go back to sleep. I shall tell you about it when you are up."

He clambered out of the bed and dressed quickly. Opening the door, he found Junayd, one of the Companions, waiting patiently outside. Junayd ducked his head respectfully.

"Good morning, Lord. I thought you would want to know..." he said, with a half-smile on his lean, dark features.

"Good morning, Junayd. What is it?" Talon asked, but then his eyes widened; he knew. The wall had been climbed!

"The banner presented to the guard commander in the early hours, Lord. Andreas did well! Master Reza witnessed it."

Talon breathed a sigh of relief. It was the requirement of any of the would-be assassins who comprised his and Reza's group of Companions to complete their initial training by climbing the north wall of the castle. It was a dangerous enough enterprise in broad daylight; at night it was doubly perilous. Two years ago, they had lost one of the acolytes on the sharp rocks at the bottom of the walls.

Talon had been the very first to scale the wall when he was scouting the castle for himself, some four years earlier. Then Reza, Talon's comrade of many years, had climbed it to show that he could. After that, all the senior Companions had been compelled by their master's example to follow suit. And so it became a compulsory final test for all would-be Companions. They were few in number.

Reza never told anyone when the attempt would be made by an acolyte who aspired to become a Companion. "People would be giving the game away, especially you, Talon, because you worry about them and would stay up all night; so all would know, including the sentries!" he teased.

The last time, almost a year ago, it had been Talon's son, Rostam, who had been nominated for the climb. Talon had to agree with Reza that they could not exempt Rostam, although Talon knew the risks only too well. Neither he nor Rav'an, Rostam's mother, had been informed until the next morning, when the banner had appeared attached to the doors to the castle keep, placed there by the chagrined guard commander of that particular night. Talon had been deeply relieved, and Rav'an had held her peace, glad that she had not been told, and relieved the boy had survived.

Now Andreas, the new acolyte, had passed the final test of acceptance to the very select group and could call himself a Companion at last. It had been three years since the commencement of his training, under the strict and exacting supervision of Reza, who was known by all as Master Reza.

Chapter 2

Reflections

Always it is a great encouragement
to feel and realize
That the ultimate Truth
Can never, never tolerate
Human deception-night.
—Sri Chinmoy

The castle of Kantara stands high on a mountain ridge, at the northern corner of Cyprus. From its battlements, observers can oversee both the northern coast and the south side of the island. A sentry on its topmost tower can see a ship as far out to sea as twenty leagues. The castle would better be called the Eagle's Nest, or some such name, but its owner and lord, Talon de Gilles, had let the old name stand.

On this gusty but bright sunny day, he rose early, glancing at Rav'an, who was still asleep. She had been up most of the night with their daughter, Fariba, who was suffering from some malady and had a mild fever that needed watching. Rav'an had told him that the child was over the worst of it, when she came to bed, just as the cock crowed down in the main yard, the first streaks of dawn having begun to glow the eastern sky.

Dressing quietly, Talon left the chamber, closed the thick wooden door carefully behind him, and descended the spiral stairs to the main hall. Some sleepy maids were already at work scrubbing and cleaning. They ducked their heads and curtsied as he passed and murmured, "Good morning." They smiled back. "Good morning, Lord!" they chorused. He smiled and put a finger to his lips and pointed upwards.

He made his way to out of the main doors of the hall, which were open to the fresh morning air, down a few stone steps to the paved main yard where there was already much activity. He was on his way to the small but finely built chapel, which had been restored to its former simple beauty. As he walked the fifty or so paces to the little building, he could hear, smell, and see that life in the castle all around him was well underway.

The Sergeant of the Guard, Palladius, was inspecting the day guard, having just dismissed the night sentries, who were hurrying off to the kitchens to grab a bite to eat before going to their beds. To Talon's critical eye, the day guard appeared to be alert and well-turned-out. Palladius was a tough Byzantine, ex-mercenary, who had come over to Talon's side at the time when Talon finessed the castle out from under its former Castilian. Promoted to sergeant, he took his duties very seriously. As soon as he was aware of his lord nearby, he turned and saluted. "Good morning, Lord."

"Good morning, Sergeant. I see the guard is well-turned-out today." Talon responded with a smile, but he didn't tarry.

Palladius nearly burst with pride. "Thank you, Lord. God's blessings." He whirled back to face his men. "You! Brace up! I didn't say dismissed! Stay right where you are until I give the order!" he bellowed. Talon walked on.

Over in another area of the yard, a small group of Companions and their students, dressed in loose clothing in several shades of brown and green, were assembling under the sharp eye of Dar'an, one of the most senior Companions.

They were all armed with light throwing spears, swords, and bows.

Dar'an also took his duties seriously. In this instance, he was about to lead the little group out of the castle and into the dense forest, along narrow paths of the southern slopes. Their work was to ensure that no strange people, least of all, none of the bands of mercenaries who worked for the emperor, were lurking in the woods, perhaps contemplating a surprise attack on the castle. Talon knew that the further out his scouts were placed, the earlier he would be warned, and hence, better prepared. The usurper, Emperor Isaac Komnenos, was always trying his luck, one way or another, determined to regain the castle.

Grooms were hard at work cleaning stalls and brushing the coats of the horses to a shine, maids carried pails of milk from the goat and cow sheds, and small children were running around, some screaming with excitement, as they chased the loose chickens around the yard, while their embarrassed mothers tried to hush them because the lord of the castle was passing by.

Talon, while he was aware of all the activity, barely acknowledged it. However, the men all knew that, had there been anything amiss, he would notice—and none wanted that. While the lord was known as a kind man, he was also stern. The defense of the castle was of paramount importance to him, above most other matters.

The men gathered at the gates were gossiping and joking with one another when Brandt called softly, "Be quiet, you nattering jackanapes. Lord Talon is coming."

Men turned and ducked their heads as Talon went by. He greeted the group with a smile and a raised hand but didn't stop.

"Lord Talon is on his way to the tomb again," one of the Welsh archers, Caradog, murmured.

"Aye, and he's limping a little more than usual today," Dewi, his companion, said in a low voice.

"Never quite got over that wound he picked up in Hattin," he remarked to his other companions.

Brandt nodded. He watched his master with concern. "Must be a storm coming," he allowed. You can always tell that when he is limping more than usual."

"Humph," snorted Junayd, one of the stealthy Companions who was standing with them. "I'll wager there will be no storm today, and I would bet anyone here that he can still outperform us all with the sword. And I didn't see any loss of accuracy with his bow, despite that leg," he told the others, pointing his chin at the departing Talon.

Someone else chuckled. Dar'an was a veteran of many battles alongside his leader and knew that many had underestimated Talon before.

"I agree with Junayd. Nothing wrong with Lord Talon, even if he is limping. Come along now, you Welshmen." He jerked his thumb at Dewi and Caradog. "You need to be off with Junayd and Nasuh to check on the south borders. Take the students with you, Junayd. We've been hearing from the shepherd boys that strangers have been seen in the area. If there are any who should not be around, try to catch them and bring them in, or bring them down, if they flee."

Brandt, a huge Saxon and the commander of the Saxon contingent, turned to go and join the other warriors, who were just beginning to appear from their sleeping quarters. "Breakfast time," he growled. "That is, if those Welsh cattle thieves have left anything for the rest of us poor mortals to eat."

*****

Talon was about to enter the small wooden door of the chapel when he heard voices from within. He could not quite make out the words of the heated discussion, but he was familiar with its content. He sighed. The two most religious and pious beings in the castle, Father Psellos and Brother Martin, were arguing heatedly, yet again, about some obscure point of theology and the finer details of their respective views of Christianity. He had to take a step back as Psellos, their resident Greek priest, dressed in dark, stained and patched robes, stormed out through the door. He noticed Talon standing there, just in time to stop and nod his head and to give Talon the benefit of a short bow.

"Forgive me. I did not see you there, Lord." He gestured behind him to the interior of the chapel.

"That... that man in there drives me to distraction with his ignorance. But I love him like a brother! What am I to do?" His mutilated face appeared even more horrible as he appealed to Talon with a grimace. Years ago, he, among many of the priests in Cyprus, had been mutilated by having his nose cut and his lips slashed by the evil Lord Raynald de Chatillon. Talon was glad that Chatillon had been executed by the leader of the Arab nations at the conclusion of the disastrous battle of Hattin, some four years previously.

Talon tried hard not to grin at the man. He was very fond of Psellos, who was not only well liked in the villages below the castle, but well respected, too.

"Are we not sent here to endure and to love everyone?" he intoned. Psellos rolled his eyes. "Add the words forbearance and patience to that list of yours, my lord. I bid you a good morning. I have to go and see to the schooling of those scamps down by the harbor." He grinned ruefully at Talon as he lifted his hand in a half salute, then ambled off toward the castle gates, where an escort of Saxons was waiting for him.

"Psellos, get someone down in the town to sew you a new tunic! Lady Rav'an will have a word with you otherwise. That one has had its day!" Talon called. Psellos waved to indicate that he had heard and carried on walking, his threadbare tunic flapping around his knees in the light breeze. Talon noticed Brandt standing with Psellos's escort, but guessed he would not be leaving with the priest. He would remain at the castle, unless Talon himself decided to depart.

He shrugged and went into the chapel. While it possessed windows, they were not wide and the light was restricted, but he liked the cool interior of the place. The two men of God, no matter their differences, had made the single chapel into a space where worshipers could gather and send prayers up to God. Talon was somewhat skeptical as to whether God would deign to respond.

Brother Martin, a monk whom Talon had rescued from Acre, after the debacle at Hattin and the subsequent loss of the city to Salah ad-Din, turned from wiping furiously at a copper candle stick with a cloth.

"Ah, there you are, Lord. I was not sure if you would be here today. I shall leave you to your deliberations."

Brother Martin was a small, somewhat rotund man, slightly balding, with a short and straggly beard that could not obscure a kindly face. Today, however, there was a double furrow between his bushy unkempt eyebrows and his brown eyes were flashing, so Talon waited for what he knew was to come.

The monk took a deep breath. "Why is it that we can agree upon so little, but at the same time, agree upon so much?" he asked rhetorically. "I wish I could get that... that priest to see as we, those faithful to our Father the Pope. Those Greeks are such a stubborn lot, but... I love the man for what he does for the people here and the selfless way he works in the villages." He sighed. "What am I to do?" He continued to rub hard at the candlestick.

Talon chuckled. "If you rub that candlestick any more there won't be anything left of it," he observed. "You will continue to work with him, doing all the good you both do so well, and I suppose you will continue to find differences, which you can discuss with, um, "patience and, er, forbearance," he added. "How are the new manuscripts coming along?" he asked, to change the subject.

Brother Martin visibly brightened. "If only I could spend more time with them, Lord Talon! But the days are so full, and I cannot abandon the garden, which my lady Theodora left in my charge. It needs much attention if we are to preserve her good work." He glanced at Talon from under his eyebrows and said, "But I am keeping you, Lord. You need some time alone with Sir Max. I shall leave you be." It was common knowledge that Talon came here from time to time to confer with his former companion at arms. Nobody appeared to find it odd anymore, least of all Brother Martin and Father Psellos.

Talon smiled. "You have only to ask Lady Rav'an for help in the garden and it will be provided," he informed the monk. Brother Martin nodded, then lifted a hand in parting and left Talon to his thoughts. Brother Martin ducked his head and made his way out of the chapel, closing the door quietly behind him. Talon turned to face the altar and walked along the short nave until he came to a stone tomb set just off to the right side of the altar. There, he paused and placed his hand on the stone lid, his head bowed over his hand.

Set along the top of the tomb was a well-cut, stone-carved figure of a man in chain mail and a helmet with a sword lying along his chest. His mailed hands held the sword by its handle with the point of the blade resting near his feet. Talon had hired one of the best stonemasons in Constantinople to create the image.

Max Bauersdorf, Talon's long-time friend, guide, and councilor, was finally at rest. He had died two winters ago of pleurisy, despite everything their physician could do. Talon missed Max enormously; at the time of death he had been devastated, almost falling ill with the same ailment that had taken his companion. It had taken the combined efforts of Rav'an, his adopted sister Jannat, and Theodora's skills to pull him through, and even longer for him to cease mourning the man whom he had considered to be like a father. Today, as on many days over the passing months and years, he came to talk to his long-time friend. The peace and quiet of the chapel allowed Talon to think, and talking to Max helped to bring his thoughts together.

"Hullo, my old friend," he said as he ran his fingers along the shoulder of the prone stone knight. "No news from Theodora, I'm sorry to tell you. She left three months ago and we still have not had any report from her, and I am a trifle worried. She said that she would send word of her safe arrival back with Giorgios." He paused. Giorgios was the shipping agent who had brought the news that Theodora's brother, Alex, had survived the palace torture chambers and the revolution that had swept the Byzantine Empire, and had last been seen in the old family house in Constantinople.

Talon knew the city well. He had spent nearly a year there with Max, getting to know the family Kalothesos and the Greek civilization to which they belonged. Theodora was the younger daughter of the famous Senator Damianus, who had died in those very torture chambers under the mad, cold stare of Exazenos. The senator's wife had died of a broken heart and illness a short time after.

News that Alex was still alive had galvanized Theodora, who had also been grieving the loss of Max. Now she was gone, and there had been no news. The silence from that direction perturbed Talon. There was something wrong with that situation, although he currently knew not what. He might have to send a ship to investigate, if only to know Theodora was in good health.

"Rumor has it that the kings of France and England are about to launch yet another Crusade," Talon went on. He wasn't looking at the tomb now but staring up at the windows above his head. "If that is true, we can expect all sorts of trouble, Max. I hear that the two kings detest one another."

He heard a small, discreet cough behind him and turned his head to see his long-time companion of many years slip into the chamber and walk towards him. Reza made very little noise when he moved. Talon knew the origins of this cat like manner, but many who did not were unsettled by it. Reza came and went like a wraith.

"I decided that if you were not out hunting with the hawks and Rostam, then perhaps you would be with Max," Reza said quietly. "What are you talking to Max about today, Talon?"

Talon sighed, and then smiled with deep affection at his boyhood friend. "I was discussing with Max the rumors that are swirling around this island presently. And my knee is hurting!"

Reza was dressed in a similar manner to Talon, in clothes that might be considered similar to those worn by the Eastern people: flowing cotton robes that were cool in the growing heat of the day. Both men usually wore a loose turban that could be used to wrap around the lower face, to protect it from the sun, dust and wind, or render its wearer unrecognizable. Like Talon, Reza now had some streaks of grey in his well-trimmed beard and at his temples.

Many of their Greek followers, who were either grooms or servants, had followed their master's example, resulting in a colorful mixture of clothing, different from the conservative tunics of the men at arms or the chain mail worn by the Saxons when on duty.

Reza rubbed the polished shoulder of the stone knight with the fingers of his right hand.

"Good morning, Sir Max," he said cheerfully to the figure reclining on the top of the tomb, but then to Talon, "So, if your knee wound is supposed to be telling you that a storm is imminent, then my tits should be aching too?" Talon couldn't help it; he laughed. Reza had been badly wounded in the chest four years back, at much the same time as he. Reza had recovered, but he bore a fearsome looking scar on his right upper chest. Reza chuckled and continued.

"If you mean the rumors of strife on the island of Sicily, the reports, as usual, are confusing," he said, as he perched himself comfortably opposite his friend on a wide, polished wooden rail that had been constructed around the tomb.

"Jannat is getting more pigeons from Dimitri and Boethius than ever before. Visiting merchants, especially from the old Kingdom of Jerusalem, are becoming jittery; they sense something about to happen and are running for cover, if even half of what Boethius says is to be believed. Our Jewish friends have been forced to move ever northward. Not even Beirut is safe anymore because of that pirate, Abul-Zinad, and that siege at Acre isn't helping, either. That Guy de Lusignan friend of yours" —Talon gave an indignant grunt— "is running it badly, which is not a surprise, after what you told me about him," Reza said with a grimace.

"He promised Salah ad-Din that he would not crusade once released, yet there he is, still pretending he is a king, attacking Acre, causing alarm and despondency. If Salah ad-Din gets his hands on him again," Reza made a chopping motion with his hand, "his head will adorn the walls of Acre itself!"

"One can only hope." Talon had no liking for the incompetent Guy de Lusignan. He blamed him, his brothers and his cohorts for the horrendous disaster at Hattin, where more than half of a Christian army, and nearly all of the Knights Templar, had died.

"There is one good thing that has come out of that charade over there," Talon remarked. "Boethius wrote that Ridefort was caught, and Salah ad-Din didn't waste any sentiments on him. His head came off within the hour! He was mad enough when we were at the battle of Hattin, but three years on, he'd become a complete lunatic. Did you hear how it happened?" he asked Reza, who shook his head.

"The Christians were fighting off an attack on their camp. Some ran, but he stayed and yelled—howled like a wolf, if the rumor is to be believed—that he wasn't going to move till the Saracens were all defeated. There he was, brandishing his sword, all alone on a knoll, when they arrived, overpowered him, and took him prisoner. Salah ad-Din didn't even waste a breath on him, just had his head removed. I'm very glad he is gone. He took us from one disaster to another, and now he can answer to the devil for his sins."

Reza shrugged. "I think they are all mad over there," he answered. "I'm glad we are well out of it. As long as Salah ad-Din doesn't decide to take the island away from Isaac."

"Isaac made a treaty with Salah ad-Din, and unlike de Lusignan and his lords, Salah ad-Din keeps his word. Much as I despise Isaac, he was clever enough in that regard. Although I suspect Diocles, his adviser, played a part in that. Very sensible man, that one," Talon responded, his tone dry. "He knew which way the wind was blowing when Jerusalem went down. No, we don't have to worry about Salah ad-Din for the time being. I suspect that whatever bad is going to happen, it will be from Sicily. A new Crusade, perhaps?"

"God help us all if that happens," Reza replied. "By the way, Boethius might be coming to visit. Captain Guy is bringing him with him from Paphos."

"Jannat *has* been busy!" Talon remarked with a smile. Jannat, a princess in her own right, was Reza's wife and the mother of their son, Rostam. She had taken on the responsibility for the maintenance of the pigeons and the intelligence that flew back and forth by way of the numerous birds used by Talon to keep abreast of events on the island. Messages came and went, written in a crude code, from the various towns and villages.

Reza dropped silently to his feet and adjusted his sword to a more comfortable position along his side. "I have to see to the Companions. I'll see you later, Brother. Goodbye, Max!" Reza addressed the recumbent stone figure and then slipped away as soundlessly as he had arrived.

Chapter 3
Training

It's possible I am pushing through solid rock
in flintlike layers, as the ore lies, alone.
—Rainer Rilke

Several mornings later, Junayd and three other Companions, Khuzaymah, Maymun, and Nasuh, were leaning on the low wall that enclosed the courtyard below. They were watching Talon and Reza instructing their two most senior Companions in the finer art of swordsmanship.

Talon and Reza were facing off against Dar'an and Yosef, respectively, and the four were playing one of their favorite sword games, one Talon and Reza had learned in China from a superb swordsman called Fang. Two men with wooden swords, very like the real Nippon swords they had been given a long time ago, faced off against one another just within reach of the tip of each other's weapon. Their weapons were coated with enough grease to allow them to be drawn easily from their sheaths, because this game was all about speed.

As the men on the wall above watched, there was a shout —a blur of movement—as Yosef and Reza each reached for his sword, drew it from its scabbard, and then struck at the other. Despite the incredible speed that Yosef displayed, it was Reza who had the tip of his sword against Yosef's neck before Yosef was able to bring his up more than half way. While the swords were absolutely rigid, their clothing was still swirling around the figures, to settle in place as they stood. There were quiet sighs of astonishment and appreciation from the onlookers, as they shook their heads in awe. They were now joined by the commander of the Saxon contingent, Brandt, and some of his Saxon men who ambled along behind him.

"How in the 'effing world does he do it?" one of Brandt's men exclaimed. "Oi never even saw it!"

"Those masters scare the shit out of me," another rejoined. "I'm glad we are on your side!"

"Watch Lord Talon. He will be next," Junayd murmured with a jerk of his thumb.

"And don't swear so loudly, you peasants, or you might find yourselves down there, being done over," Brandt warned his men with a scowl. He could not believe how fast the two masters still were, and yet they were older than anyone else. There were chuckles of amusement from his warriors. Brandt often swore as loudly and fluently as any of his men, but in his role of a commander for Lord Talon he had moderated his language because, as he himself said when confiding to Brother Martin, "I would hate to forget and curse in front of the Lady Rav'an or the Lady Jannat. I'd never forgive myself for such fucking disrespect!" The wives of the masters were venerated by the watching men. The penalty inflicted by Brother Martin, meted out for that one slip of the tongue, had been wearing to Brandt's knees.

Even as he spoke, both Dar'an and Talon exploded into action, but it was Talon's sword that stopped on the right side of Dar'an's neck. Again, no one had actually seen either man draw, or the wooden blade strike. To the spectators, it was as though both men had gone from one very still position to another with no movement in between. The only indicator that there had been motion was their still swirling robes. Dar'an stood back, smiling and shaking his head ruefully as he rubbed the spot on his neck, after Talon removed his sword.

"You are getting better, Dar'an. I want you to teach that boy of mine," Talon remarked. He smiled at Dar'an with the fondness of a father for his son. Both Dar'an and Yosef went a long way back with Talon and Reza.

"Rostam certainly has the making of a swordsman, Lord," Yosef remarked. The four had been working with their swords at one exercise or another for over an hour, and their thin tunics were damp with sweat.

"He has," Reza agreed, "but there is still much he can learn from either of you two. Make sure he doesn't get a swollen head,"

Both Dar'an and Yosef ducked their heads with amusement. "Don't worry, Master Reza, we can make sure of that." Dar'an spoke for both of them.

Yosef had suffered a severe injury to his throat while in China, so he was economic with his words, but it was clear he agreed.

"Very well, I shall leave it up to you two to bring him along so that Master Reza can *finally* say he is up to standard," Talon sighed, theatrically, "which might not be in my lifetime."

Reza snorted a laugh as the other two grinned. "He'll get there one day, never fear, Brother. Now, Dar'an, call those other seniors loafing on the wall to come down here for some fighting with cane weapons. They need to show the new Companions how good they are."

Junayd and his Companions needed little persuasion; they knew how valuable this kind of training could be. The masters, along with their families, Yosef, and Dar'an, had been to China some years before and had brought back with them knowledge of sword play that only a very few in the world they now lived in could match. All the younger Companions were more than passable swordsmen, but with Master Reza—and sometimes, when his other duties permitted, Talon—mentoring them, their swordsmanship had achieved another level.

"Cane swords today, men," Talon called. "Be sure to wear those light helmets we made, too. I don't want an eye poked out for no good reason." Then he and Reza placed the newer Companions against the older, more experienced men, and the combat began. The tightly bound, stripped sugarcane reeds closely resembled the practice weapons Reza and Talon had first learned to use in China at a dojo. Many were the painful hours the two had spent there, but they had come away with a keen knowledge of how to use their Nippon swords, which they would never have learned otherwise. They were determined to teach their own men as much as they could.

Talon stood back and watched as Dar'an and Khuzaymah went at it in a blur of snapping blades and shouts as they struck at one another. The men were confined to a rough square that the combatants were not allowed to leave without losing the bout. Dar'an continued to prove that he was exceptional, and made Khuzaymah work for every foot, while Yosef chased Junayd around with his wicked speed. Everyone, without exception, was going to have bruises and welts afterward, Talon surmised. Leaving Reza to supervise the combatants, Talon decided that he could do with some practice of another kind.

He walked across a sand-covered space filled with combatants and men practicing against wood pillars, to arrive at another wooden target, a crude torso carved out of a soft wood, depicting an armless man from the waist to the head. The whole contraption was held on a post dug into the ground, bringing it to the normal height of a man. The target, front and back, was pitted with the marks left by blades striking all over its surface. There was another one nearby.

Rostam, his son, was busy with another young acolyte, throwing wide-bladed knives at the target. Rostam was by now a lean, fit, well-muscled young man with a light-colored mop of hair, who now topped his father by a good half hand. He turned to Talon and grinned.

"Hello, Father. Are you going to show us?"

"Is it going well?" Talon asked Rostam in Farsi, without answering the question.

"I think so," replied the boy in the same language. He turned to the trainee. "Show my father how you are doing, Andreas."

"You did very well on the wall," Talon informed Andreas.

The youth was about Rostam's age. He looked embarrassed, but hugely pleased with the compliment. Talon did not give out praise very often. Andreas went over to the target, retrieved a number of blades stuck close together in the wood, and walked back toward Talon and Rostam. He ducked his head respectfully.

"Should I throw them, Lord?"

"Yes," Talon said.

Andreas positioned himself carefully about ten paces from the target, took one of the steel blades in the fingers of his right hand and then, with a burst of speed, he lashed out with the knife, releasing it hard. His body was leaning into the strike with his leading, front knee bent. The blade whirred briefly and then struck the target with a solid thunk just below the base of the neck. Two others followed in quick succession. He turned toward Talon and Rostam, looking pleased with the result.

"Give me one of those," Talon demanded.

He took the blade and, almost casually, from more than twelve paces away, hurled the knife. To the watchers, it appeared to be barely aimed. The blade struck the middle of the throat of the target. Its impact made the target shake and a tiny splinter of wood flew into the air.

"Always better to go for the throat, and never give your enemy any indication as to what you are about to do. The chest has bones that could deflect a knife," Talon admonished the youths. "Rostam, it's your turn, and don't forget to focus."

He watched critically as Rostam threw several knives, and nodded. Rostam was becoming very accurate at knife throwing and was, according to Reza, even better at fighting with them. His thrown blades came very close to those of his father's. After all three had spent some time working on the inoffensive targets, Talon pointed toward Reza and the other men. "Andreas, you need more practice with the unarmed fighting. Come over to the grass dojo." He called the padded grass square a dojo, in honor of his former teacher.

Andreas and Rostam followed Talon to the mat, where they took off their belts and boots, leaving them with bare feet and dressed in just loose shirts and pantaloons.

"You first, Andreas. Come on!" Talon called from nearly the middle of the dojo. Talon insisted upon the obligatory bow, but then it was time. Andreas knew from experience how fast his lord could be. He knew too, that on the dojo, no one was lord, so he struck as fast as he could for Talon's midriff. His blow never landed. Talon, from a deep, low stance, blocked and returned the strike. Andreas almost blocked it, but strong fingers seized his shirt at his chest level, and before he knew it, Talon had whirled inside his guard, ducked under and away from him, and he went flying over his lord's head, to land with a jarring thump on the mat.

"Ow!" he exclaimed, rubbing his arm as he sat up. He reached for his loose turban, which had fallen off when he fell.

"Come on, young fellow. You have been taught how to fall, and you won't need that while we are on the mat," Talon told him, indicating the discarded turban. "Try again, it's only me," Talon smiled. It was one of those smiles that all the acolytes had come to know only too well. It spelled some rough handling.

Andreas tried again, only to meet the same fate. As did Rostam, but then Talon set them against one another and lectured them on how to deal with an opponent.

"Everything is a weapon, from a sword to a small stick, and even your fingertips," he told them, and demonstrated by striking them none too gently in the solar plexus. Both youths gasped, but grinned ruefully and listened respectfully as they rubbed the bruised area.

Finally he told them, "You are both getting better, but remember to use your speed and to seek every opportunity, whether you are on horseback or on foot. Surprise! Your opponent must not see your blow coming." The sweating boys nodded agreement.

Talon scooped up one of the knives lying on the ground and threw it in one fluid motion at one of the targets. It landed with a loud thump, exactly where the Adam's apple would be.

"Both of you go and let Uncle Reza beat you up," he told them. "He is going to be much less kind than I am."

His ears didn't fail to pick up the comment made by Andreas to Rostam as they walked away. "Does Master—I mean, Lord Talon, ever miss?"

Rostam shook his head and laughed. "I've never seen him miss. But Uncle Reza is always saying *he* is kinder than Father." They both snorted with rueful laughter.

Watching them walk toward the others, Talon shook his own head. He felt he was definitely slowing down and it bothered him, but he consoled himself with the thought that the Companions and those foul-mouthed Saxons, whom he proudly and affectionately called his own *Veragnians*, were the product of his and Reza's hard work, now a formidable force to be reckoned with.

They had gathered around them men who were loyal to the death and very capable of inflicting great pain on any enemy who might be bold or foolish enough to try for Talon's or Reza's lives, or those of their families. The two men had, at least, been able to pass along a knowledge that would keep the next generation on its toes, and thanks to their training in China every bit as dangerous—perhaps even more so— than the infamous *Bātinis*, who lurked in the mountains of the Alborz and in Lebanon serving Rashid Ed Din

While they were well known within the precincts of Kantara and its lands, they were phantoms anywhere else on the island of Cyprus. Talon and Reza intended for this to be so, for it kept their many enemies at bay, surrounding the castle and its lands in an aura of mystery and menace to all outsiders.

Talon walked over to where Reza was preoccupied with Dar'an and another would-be acolyte.

"I have to go down to the harbor and sit on the court today. Are you coming with me?" Talon said.

"No, Brother, you go. You are, after all, the lord of the castle," Reza smirked. "I know that you enjoy the role." Talon scowled in pretended annoyance.

"And you know me," Reza continued, "I'd rather be honing the skills of our Companions, anyway. They are doing well, but we have to keep them busy. Don't we, Dar'an?" he said, turning to their senior Companion, who nodded soberly.

Don't forget that there is to be a ceremony tonight for Andreas, who has passed all the tests, including the final climb," Reza added with a grin." "I watched him arrive and it looked as though he was going to give the sentry a heart attack!"

The Final Climb, as Reza called it, was the most severe tests of an acolyte before he was accepted into the brotherhood of Companions, who were ruled by Reza with an iron hand. The story of Talon's entry into the castle, before he had finessed it from under the nose of the emperor, had passed into legend. The reward for this endeavor had been, ultimately, the acquisition of the castle of Kantara with almost no bloodshed.

"I should be able to arrive back at the castle in time for the ceremony, Brother," Talon stated as he got up to leave.

"We cannot have it without you, Brother. So, deal with those petty criminals, drunken sailors, and adulterers, then get back as fast as you can."

"Arg! The duties of a lord!" Talon grated, as his right leg took his weight. "Neither of us is getting any younger Brother, and I spend an inordinate amount of time dealing with petitions, quarrels, and petty criminals. But today, we have a more interesting case. Do you know about it?"

Reza looked puzzled. "I don't think I know about this. What is it all about?"

"I only heard today, via one of the pigeons sent up by Henry's man down at the harbor," Talon stated. "One of our lookouts, a goat herder on the eastern side of the town about a league along the coast, found a small boat in one of the very narrow calanques, not advanced quite as far as the inlet where the pirates arrived last time. The boat was deserted and quite well hidden, but he was sure it had not been there long. And now we have a prisoner. A man has been arrested and is being held. Henry says he and his two companions were making for this boat when they apprehended them. Two were killed from what I have heard, leaving one who is now our prisoner. I am to go and look him over. *Now* would you like to come?" he teased Reza, who suddenly looked thoughtful.

"Only the one man, you say?" he asked slowly.

Talon gave him a sharp look. "Only one left. If they were *Bãtinis* then it comes not as a surprise that the other two preferred to die rather than be captured, but I don't know the full story. If you are thinking what I am thinking, then you had better come along with me and help me to decide who this is and what might be going on."

Reza nodded agreement. "I shall have to tell the others to go without me but—" he paused, "perhaps they should stay nearby. My nose is telling me something is not quite right about this."

Talon felt the hairs on his forearm tingle. "I have never had any reason to distrust your instincts, Brother. We should keep at least some of the Companions on heightened alert and close to the families up here. It cannot do any harm to be careful. We will have an escort of Saxons to take us down to the harbor, so I am not worried about that. So, I can expect you to join me there?" he asked.

Reza nodded soberly. "Yes, I shall be there. In the meantime, I shall send a couple of our more senior Companions to the location of the boat to try to find out more."

Chapter 4

Uninvited Guests

This being human is a guest house.
Every morning a new arrival.
A joy, a depression, a meanness,
some momentary awareness comes
as an unexpected visitor.
—Rumi

Talon stifled a yawn as he sat through the long-winded accusations and excuses of misdemeanors by members of the villages and the crews. He knew most of the petty offenders by name by now and they, for the most part, knew what to expect from him when they were brought before him. The behavior of the accused varied from subservient to cheeky, and sometimes downright outrage at being accused, but no longer was anyone insolent. That had always ended in severe punishment, and people had learned that their new lord, while fair, was not to be trifled with.

Seated on a makeshift dais in order to give solemnity to the occasion, which was built twice a month for this express purpose, he would listen as either one of the captains or village headmen pressed charges. On other occasions, the accusations came from individuals. Those cases were primarily marital or inter-family related, and he found these to be the most irksome. Then the air became charged with emotions which Reza, in private, would somewhat scornfully point out, were very Greek; little was provided in the way of factual evidence. Sometimes Talon found it hard to disagree with his brother, but they were now his people, so he forced himself to remain inscrutable while emotions were played out in front of him.

The cases of drunkenness and petty theft were more easily disposed of. Drunkenness was summarily dealt with by turning over the hungover culprit to his chief, either a captain or a village headman. While theft, anywhere else on the island, would be rewarded by hanging, Talon preferred to dispense stern justice by confinement to a ship, chained, working as an oarsman, whether that man knew how to row or not. The crimes were seldom repeated by the same offender, as neither the crews nor the ships' captains were sympathetic. Finally, the court procedures were brought to a close, but the one matter remained, and Talon sat up and looked around.

"Where is the prisoner?" he demanded of Brandt, who gestured off to their right in the direction of the crew's barracks and storerooms.

Reza, who had been absent for a while, reappeared. Just behind him were two burly Saxons, and between them was a single disheveled-looking man. Behind the trio stalked another of Reza's watchful Companions.

They halted at the base of the dais and Reza strode up to join Talon, who stared down at the manacled prisoner. He was still being held in a tight grip by his Saxon captors.

The man looked tired, and his clothes had known better days; there were rents and stains. His hands were a giveaway to Talon, but he didn't react.

"Do we know anything about this man?" he murmured to Reza.

"He is definitely not one of Rashid's little boys," Reza responded from the corner of his mouth.

Talon nodded in agreement. This was no *fida'i* from Lebanon. "Seen his hands?" he inquired of Reza.

"Yes, this is no peasant, but he does know how to fight. He put up a struggle," Reza said. "Rodosthenos can tell you more. He was there when it all happened. I learned it from him an hour ago."

Talon beckoned to the man named Rodosthenos, the town headman. He walked forward and took a knee. "My lord?" he asked.

"Tell us what you know, Rodosthenos," Talon said, indicating that he should rise. The man stood. Although his name meant strength and power, the slim, wiry man did not project that image. However, as Talon knew very well, appearances could be deceptive.

"Our boys were herding over to the east of the town when they saw this small boat tucked into an inlet, one of those very thin ones. As you have instructed, Lord Reza, the boys sent one of their members back to find help, and that boy brought back three off-duty archers, who were by the harbor. They brought some of the sailors with them, and it was just as they arrived that three strangers were seen trying to leave, Lord." He paused.

"You mean, they were trying to escape?" Reza demanded.

"It looked like it, Lord," Rodosthenos replied.

"What happened then?" Talon asked.

"The men thought it was suspicious, Lord, and shouted at them to stop." Rodosthenos glanced at the man. "We meant them no harm, Lord, but they refused to stop, so we chased after them, shouting at them to halt or we would shoot."

Rodosthenos opened his hands and shrugged. "They continued running and had made it to the beach when one of our men decided to shoot at one of them. It wounded him grievously, and his cries made the other two turn back to help him. Our people had arrived, and then the fighting began."

Rodosthenos looked again at the prisoner, this time with frustration and anger written on his lined, dark features. "We told them to surrender, but they would not. We did not wish to harm them, but they fought back fiercely so that our men had no choice. They wounded one of our people before we killed two of them, before this man surrendered, Lord. I am sorry for it if we did wrong, Lord. They were determined to leave despite our calling to them to give themselves up."

Reza nodded at this. "I have talked to the men who were there, and it happened just as Rodosthenos stated, Brother. I do not think they did anything wrong."

"Take the wounded man to the castle where Lady Rav'an can treat him," Talon ordered.

Rodosthenos looked relieved. "At once, Lord"

Talon nodded then stared back down at the prisoner, who had been forced to his knees by his captors. He tried Greek. "Who are you, and where do you come from?" he demanded.

The man looked up. Although he had clearly been roughly handled, there was still some defiance in his hazel eyes. "Ah, someone who speaks Greek the proper way, unlike the barbaric accent of this island. Do you mind if I stand? It's uncomfortable here on my knees."

Talon leaned forward and said with an edge to his voice. "You will stay right where you are. But Greek isn't your native tongue, now, is it? You will learn just how barbarically we treat spies in this land if you do not answer my questions, and quickly." Talon glared. "I have other things to do today."

"Like watch a polo game," Reza muttered from nearby, in Farsi.

Talon suppressed a grin and put on a stern scowl for the benefit of the prisoner.

"Furthermore, I dislike your tone."

The man hesitated.

"Answer me!" Talon roared. The Saxons didn't yet speak much Greek, but even the imperturbable Brandt blinked. The guards almost took a step back. The prisoner appraised his captor with wide open eyes, as though he had not expected this approach.

"I... I am from Venice," he said.

Talon sat back in his chair. "Ah. And what might a man from Venice be doing with two others in a small sailing boat on this coast?" he demanded. "You are a very long way from home," he added.

"'I was er... investigating," the prisoner replied.

Talon gave a sigh. "Give me your name and the real reason you are here. Where is your ship? You didn't sail all this way in a small fishing boat."

"No, I didn't. May I have the honor of knowing to whom I speak?"

"I am Lord Talon, and this is Lord Reza," Talon replied briefly. "You may stand," he told the prisoner. He gestured to the guards to allow the man to get to his feet.

"My name is Cristofo," the man said as he struggled to his feet with evident relief. He even rubbed his knees with his manacled hands. "We were on our way back from Alexandria... er, Lord. There was a storm, a bad one. We only just managed to avoid being thrown onto the shore, not very far from here. But we did sustain some damage. However, there are bad stories about this island, and I didn't want to land and find myself in a dungeon. The emperor has a reputation, you see."

"I am aware of this," Talon said dryly.

"I wanted to investigate the lay of the land before bringing my ship in for repairs. The thin inlets along this coast would have been ideal for us to rest and recuperate, but then your people discovered us and we were desperate to get back to the ship. I am a merchant and I look for trade, not trouble, so I decided to leave the vessel out at sea in this calmer weather and investigate. There is too much damage to allow us to sail all the way back to Venice."

"All you had to do was to sail up to our harbor here and announce yourself," Reza snapped. His tone was skeptical and caustic at the same time.

"Er, yes, my lord, but you see, we Venetian people have become wary. Not so very long ago, the emperor of Constantinople, a Greek like yourselves, allowed his citizens to massacre our people. I was simply being careful." He grimaced, as though at a bad memory. "We are, however, tenacious merchant people. Our existence depends upon trade. I am sure that there are other of my people who have visited this island, but certainly not recently."

"You might be right there," Talon nodded his agreement. "Our emperor here is not welcoming to the Greeks of other lands, and he harbors an unreasonable dislike of other foreigners, for his own reasons, I dare say."

Cristofo had looked resigned to whatever fate lay in store for him up to this point, but now his expression brightened. "I feel I should humbly beg for your forgiveness, my lord. Had I known better, I should not have been so lacking in discretion."

"Your recklessness has cost you two companions," Reza remarked dryly. "We are not yet decided as to whether we should believe you or not."

Talon, who had been watching Cristofo, noticed how crestfallen he became at this news.

"I do not know what I can say to prove that I am innocent of intended harm to your people," he said carefully.

"Then why did you flee?" Talon demanded. "Why did you fight?"

"Because, Lord, we were interlopers, and the reputation of this island is well known -- your emperor and his people, as I said."

"Then count yourself lucky that you survived this encounter," Talon told him. "You picked the worst place on the entire island to try to spy out the land, but by the same fate, you might just live, while we think on it. You are not free to go, but we will consider your words. Where is your ship at present?" he asked.

Cristofo looked out to the sea. Before he could say anything, however, something happened to make all eyes swivel toward the distant castle. A rocket had climbed silently into the sky, leaving a thin trail of smoke. It was too far away for anyone to hear its hissing sound. Cristofo gasped, but it was no surprise to Talon and his men. The watchmen on the roof of the castle keep, trained to the task, had lit the fuse to one of the signal rockets, which Talon had installed on the roof of the castle keep, and sent it high into the sky.

"What is it?" Reza called over to Dar'an, who was already on the quay of the harbor.

"It's a ship, Lord. Henry is alerted." Dar'an called back. "He is on his way out already!"

Dar'an's light coloring drew attention to the fact that he was a Kurd. He had known Talon since their days in Jerusalem, when Talon had rescued him as a young, starving boy from a doubtful life on the streets. He was now a superb horseman and very skilled in the art of stealth and weaponry. Talon and Reza had seen to that.

Now the three watched in silence as Henry, one of the ship captains, conned his galley rapidly out between the two small towers that had been built to guard the channel into the harbor. The sleek, warlike vessel slipped out to sea to intercept another vessel that they could observe some leagues further out. The small rocket had warned Henry's men that there was an approaching craft, and he had responded exactly as Talon wished. He nodded his approval and glanced at Reza, who smiled back.

"Henry didn't waste any time at all!" he commented.

Dar'an, who had the sharper eyes, pointed and exclaimed, "I see not one, but two ships!"

The others stared hard, and then they, too, realized that there were indeed not one, but two ships that Henry was approaching at speed. One without doubt belonged to Guy, but the other was a mystery, and it looked in far worse shape than Talon's vessels. In fact, it was being assisted toward the harbor by Guy's ship, using a tow line.

Talon had a thought.

"Bring the prisoner here," he ordered.

When Cristofo was brought before him, he pointed to the three ships. "Is that ship yours?" he asked.

Cristofo darted his eyes toward the incoming vessels, and a shifty look came over his youthful features. "I've never—" he began, but he was cut off.

"Don't lie, Cristofo. That would be a very poor beginning," Talon snapped.

His tone was ominous.

Cristofo sighed with resignation. "Yes Lord. That is my ship. Will you be merciful to the passengers and crew, I beg of you?"

He pointed to the after deck of the ship that was being towed. "That is my sister who is standing there, my lord," he stated with a pleading look at Talon and Reza.

"You have nothing to fear from us at this time as long as you tell the truth and do not try to escape," Reza assured him.

They all turned their attention back towards the two ships which were now maneuvering towards the quayside.

There were several ladies on the Venetian ship and from what he could tell one of their number was one dressed in the fine clothes of a noble woman. Talon realized that Cristofo was very concerned for their safety. He shook his head but then said, "We will protect you as our guests,

Cristofo. You need not fear for your womenfolk. We are not barbarians. However you will be guarded until I decide otherwise."

Cristofo appeared to accept this verdict and then waved to the women on the after deck of his ship. There was a wary response from his sister.

"Her name is Armilia," he told them. "May I go and speak to her? She will be confused and worried, my lord," he asked Talon, who nodded.

"Yes, go," he told the young man.

"Now this is becoming interesting," Reza remarked with a gesture towards Guy's ship.

"Indeed," Talon agreed as he glanced up and recognized Irene, the daughter of Boethius the merchant from Paphos. He gave a sober nod. "I think we need to provide an escort for the ladies on both ships, one that will protect them on the dangerous journey to the castle." He half smiled. "This gets more intriguing by the minute. Boethius has sent his daughter instead of coming himself! I wonder why?

"You go with them, Brother, and take young Rostam with you. Make sure *everyone* behaves themselves," he finished with a half-smile at his brother. "I want to talk to Guy and hear what news he has before he goes and gets drunk."

Guy had much to tell. After he had seen to the anchoring of the ships and the transfer of the passengers and the foreign crew to shore. He gave Talon a bear hug that nearly broke his ribs, shouting with pleasure as he always did when he came back from a voyage.

"Well met, Lord!" he bellowed. "We have a cargo and some guests as you can see. The wine and copper sold well in Alanya."

"Well met again, Guy. I see you appear to be well. Any pirates?" Talon demanded as he pulled his robes back into place.

"One gave chase but after we sent a harpoon into his bows he became more interested in staying afloat, and we left him behind with no difficulty," Guy responded, rubbing his huge hands together as though relishing the memory.

Talon smiled and placed a hand on his captain's broad shoulder. "I'm very glad of it, Guy." There appear to be more pirates in these seas than ever," he said.

"Boethius would agree with you on that score, Talon," Guy growled, "which is why Irene is here with us. He may well take advantage the next time we visit. The emperor is taking an unhealthy interest in the city again,"

"Ah but come; you and your men should eat and rest," Talon told him.

Later Talon sat with him as he and his men wolfed down a meal of fresh fried fish and turnips, along with huge chunks of bread, washed down with wine that Talon ordered to be provided. He considered his men to be worth the expense, although he could sell his wine for a good price almost anywhere these days.

"Tell me first, how is Boethius?" He demanded of the hoary old mariner. Guy spoke with his mouth full, which was quite normal.

"The word is that the pirates of Beirut are becoming a menace, Talon. They have become brazen and attack small harbors all along the coast, including here on the island, which I am sure you know all about. Boethius is of the opinion that unless that man Abdul ... er..."

"Abdul Zinad and his brother Ibn al-Bannā Makhid," Talon finished for him.

"Yes that's them. They need to be stopped, somehow!"

"I wonder why Salah ad Din is not doing anything about them. It cannot be good for trade inland?" Talon mused.

It was late in the evening before Talon and his tired escort arrived back at the castle.

Chapter 5

Chogan

The Ball no Question makes of Ayes and Noes,
But Right or Left as strikes the Player goes;
And He that toss'd Thee down into the Field,
He knows about all—HE knows—HE Knows!
—Omar Khayyam

By the afternoon small white clouds had scudded in from the south, driven by a cool, fresh breeze. To the great relief of everyone, there was no immediate sign of the storm Talon's knee had foretold.

Tents were lined up on either side of a main marquee on the south side of the freshly mown chogan field. For three days, villagers and crewmen had mowed the new grown grass to a tight green pelt, erected the tents and tied colorful pennants to their poles. Today the area was crowded with spectators, their attention riveted on the game that was proceeding apace.

Seated in the shade of the marquee were Talon, Reza, and their families. To a person, other than perhaps the two restless young children, the family members seemed avidly engrossed in the wild and noisy game taking place on the field. They were surrounded by not only their own servants but some of the Companions, whose eyes never stopped

42

scrutinizing the crowd, and a solid phalanx of Saxon warriors, who, being foot soldiers, were fascinated by the display of horsemanship taking place on the field. Cristofo and his sister were seated nearby, under the watchful eyes of both the Companions and the Saxons. While he had not yet decided if he trusted them, Talon felt confident his men could deal with any stupidity, should they misbehave. He saw no reason, therefore, not to let them witness the festivities.

The game was drawing to a close, but the crowd was still cheering as enthusiastically as they had at the beginning. Not only were horsemen from the castle playing, but a few of the more adventurous youths from the two villages had become enthusiastic, and even talented, players. Their friends and relatives were eager to see how they would manage in this fiercely contested and hazardous sport.

There had been one incident that had caught the attention of everyone when the game had only just begun. The pony that Maymun was mounted on was a stallion. As they lined up, the animal began to get very restive. Maymun, who was an excellent rider, kicked it into place just behind another member of his team, Nasuh, who was riding a mare. Just as the ball was flung into the middle of the two lines, Maymun's mount gave a growl-like snort and tried to mount the animal in front of him. As men and horses converged, shouting and hacking with their sticks at the elusive ball, Maymun and Nasuh were trying frantically to disengage themselves from the very embarrassing situation. Maymun's stallion was determined to ignore his rider in the pursuit of his own desires.

It was only with the use of the whips and much spurring and shouting that the two horses were separated, but by this time, everyone on the sidelines had noticed. Talon suspected that the roar of mirth could be heard all the way to the castle on the mountain.

"What on earth is going on over there?" he demanded, craning his neck to see better.

"I'd have thought it a little obvious, Brother." Reza smirked and grinned at Jannat, who put her hand in front of her mouth as she, too, laughed. There was no lack of ribald remarks from the assembled spectators, even the Saxons, ostensibly on duty, were puce-faced with suppressed mirth.

Eventually, the cluster of players had disengaged, and the game proceeded in earnest. The purpose of the game being to hit the ball into the opposing team's goal while trying to ensure they failed to score, Rostam led one team while Yosef led the other, and there was little in the way of quarter given while the teams battled it out on the large field.

Now there was a light click, and the small, white ball flew high into the air, lofted with a seemingly lazy strike by Rostam, who chased after it on his pony at a flat-out gallop. Rostam's head was tilted back, and his eyes were locked on the flying object. He rode instinctively, unmindful of the other players galloping hard only a few paces behind him. The ball landed and bounced on the short grass, but it was not Rostam who took it on the rise. Yosef beat him to the ball by riding into him and driving his pony off the line, so hard that it staggered. Rostam gave an indignant shout of surprise as he fought to regain control. He had not seen Yosef coming and had almost lost his balance.

Yosef laughed and struck the ball with a skillful, sweeping backhand from his pony's off-side that abruptly reversed the ball's direction and that of the game. Then both he and Rostam concentrated on turning their ponies, to avoid being run down by the pack of riders hard on their heels. The shouts of the excited riders, the drumbeat of hooves, and the click of sticks being used more like weapons than they should have been were encouraged by noisy shouts from the crowd of onlookers, who appreciated the skill of the players in this dangerous game.

Within moments, the ball had been picked up by one of the riders on Yosef's team who was able to lean out and skillfully tap the bouncing ball toward the goal, despite being ridden into brutally hard by an opponent's pony going at a gallop. But then Dar'an managed to sneak a tap that pushed the ball to the side, whereupon he brought his own pony into an impossibly small circle, tapping furiously at the ball and forcing yet another change of direction.

"On me!" screamed Rostam, who had observed the successful result of this maneuver and was racing his pony to be well ahead of the strike to come. Members of his team had split up; some were harassing Yosef and his players, determined to keep them from tackling Dar'an, while a couple of others raced after Rostam, yelling for Dar'an to send the ball their way. The crowd cheered happily.

Dar'an took his time, evading the flying sticks of the opposition players long enough to set up the ball, and then he threw back his right arm, swept it forward, and struck. But almost immediately there was another click. The ball was intercepted by Maymun, who had been waiting, as though in ambush. The youth shouted with glee. The ball ricocheted off his mallet head and whirred straight up into the air. There were shouts of approval from his teammates, and one of them, with a display of superb horsemanship, reached up and struck the ball mid-air, back toward Rostam's goal. Once again, the entire pack of men and horses whirled in a flurry hooves and clods of earth, then set off in hot pursuit of the flying object.

In the stands, Talon gave a grunt of approval. "That was nicely done! Maymun seems to have his randy pony back under control," he remarked, turning toward Rav'an, who smiled back at him. "Are you enjoying the game, my Talon?" she asked sweetly.

He gave her a brief scowl. "Reza and I should be out there, showing them all how to play!" he growled. Earlier in the week, Rav'an and Jannat had conspired to prevent either Talon or Reza playing in this match. "Its fine when you are practicing, my Reza," Jannat had argued, tilting her lovely head with a stern look, "but this is a game the younger men should be allowed to play, and on this day especially."

"What do you mean by that! D'you think we are too old?" Reza had exclaimed, sounding indignant.

"No, of course not, my Prince, but because you have to show some dignity... both of you. There is time to play like reckless and irresponsible youths, but then, at a time like this, you have to behave like *adults*."

Rav'an had joined in. "You are the lords of this land and you should act like lords. In other words, you will preside over the match and let others break their necks playing that insane game. This is the match of the year, and we all should be there to, well, encourage the younger men to show us what they can do."

"We are both perfectly capable of riding rings around every one of them," Talon grumped.

"Yes, and both of you were badly wounded some time back and we do not have Theo here at present to patch you up, should your old wounds re-open." Rav'an responded. Her tone was tart.

"You know what she told you, Reza. Not to strain that chest wound," then she turned to Talon, "and you still limp about, my Talon."

"I do n..." Talon was about to retort but then caught the glare that Rav'an sent his way and snapped his mouth shut. He knew she was right. His wretched leg wound, garnered at the battle of Hattin might have healed well enough, but it could betray him at any time especially when there was a storm about to show up. He tried another tack; the pleading look approach instead but the pursed lips, wide eyes and raised eyebrows dared him to question her. Not for the first time could his beloved wife force her will upon him without a single word!

"Let those others play, my Reza, Talon. The people expect you to be, well, lordly," Jannat pleaded and gave a short laugh. "Whatever that means," she added to the world at large and pretended to look vacant.

Talon and Reza both snorted with indignation, but neither could help but be amused at her expression. The battle was lost before it had begun, Talon told himself with a rueful shake of his head.

"I do a lot of lordly things around this place. I sometimes get a little tired of being one, and wish for some... recklessness," he retorted.

"And... what do I do all day, eh?" Reza demanded, pretending to scowl at his wife, whom he adored.

Both women gave them looks that should have turned them into blocks of salt, but said nothing. Instead, they waited their men out.

The two friends had grumbled, but it was really for form's sake, and they finally agreed to preside over the games instead of taking part in them. Both Rav'an and Jannat were aware of what a sacrifice this was, but they were relieved that their not-so-young husbands had listened for a change.

The match was nearly over, as indicated by the sand clock —a Byzantine treasure of glass and bronze that Talon had found on one of his voyages. It had already been turned five times. The pack of men and horses came charging right by the spectators in a thunder of hooves and shouted calls. The spectators howled with excitement as Maymun, who could do incredible things while on a horse, tapped and even carried the ball with him briefly on the end of his mallet in a frantic charge for the goal belonging to Rostam. Money had been placed on this game, and it was evenly matched at four goals each with the outcome still uncertain.

One of Rostam's riders hammered his pony repeatedly into the side of Maymun's stallion, but he could not cause Maymun to lose the ball. Just a little further back in the shouting and yelling pack, Rostam was trying desperately to get free of two of the opposition players.

Yosef had very cunningly arranged for not one but two of his men to interfere with Rostam, so that he could not get into the lead and perhaps take the ball, while Yosef himself had ridden off another of Rostam's players. Now he edged his pony to the front to take the ball, should Maymun lose it, as the barging and hitting were becoming quite heated at the front of the pack. Sticks were flying and hacking, but not with malicious intent. Both Talon and Reza had been very firm about that. No deliberate injuries or the offender would answer to them, and no one wanted that. Talon and Reza had played their fair share of ugly and dangerous games in their time and wanted none of it on their watch. The game was treacherous enough without the insertion of malice.

All the same, chogan was a rough and violent game, and many in the crowd gasped at the aggressive play they were witnessing. Finally, Maymun was driven off the ball by his opponent. Rostam gave an excited yell and again tried to slip away from his minders, but without success. They remained glued to his sides, preventing him from getting anywhere near the ball. However, one of his team players managed to hook the ball and, for a moment, it looked as though the direction of the game was going to change, yet again.

The keen-eyed Yosef was watching, however, and he smacked the man's mallet out of the way while hooking the ball back under control, all at a flat out gallop. Yelling at Maymun to get up field, he stroked the ball in one long hit, lofting it high into the sky toward the goal. Maymun evaded his marker and raced his pony to catch the ball in mid-air and, with an overarm swipe, sent it through the posts. The man stationed there to watch for the ball ducked as it flew by him and waved his small flag high in the air while the crowd roared approval.

The panting players slowed their blowing and sweating horses, then turned and made their way back at a trot toward the center of the field, where they gathered to await another ball. This would be thrown in by a man standing in the midline of the game field. As soon as he had thrown it, he would run for his life toward the safety at the edge of the field, and battle would commence again.

Just at that moment, however, the sand ran out. A servant who had been charged with watching the clock waved to another man, and a trumpet blared. The game was over.

As the players rode their tired, sweat-drenched, and blowing mounts slowly back to the horse lines, they joked, laughed, and slapped each other on the back, all of them covered in sweat and dirt.

"Well, that was a very good game. Only one goal between them," Reza commented.

"There don't appear to be any hard feelings either," Rav'an murmured as she scrutinized the laughing and chatting group for any signs of ill temper.

"That Yosef is a cunning player," Talon chuckled. "He kept Rostam out of much of the game. The boy must have been furious! Yosef did the right thing, though. If Rostam gets the ball, he is unstoppable. Despite the best efforts of Dar'an, who is an excellent player, too!"

"You always say it is a game of war, Talon," Rav'an remarked. "Our son is a very good player, but today, Yosef outwitted him, and Maymun is incredible!"

"Yosef is a keen student of the martial arts and not to be underestimated," Talon replied, "and he is a good teacher. Rostam is learning a great deal from him."

Cristofo got up from his seat and ambled over to the family. He bowed politely to the women and then addressed

Talon and Reza. "I have not ever witnessed a game of this kind before. Magnificent!" he exclaimed. "It was like watching a... a battle! They are incredible horsemen, Lord Talon."

"Our young men can play without killing one another and still learn the skills required of effective light cavalry," Reza informed him, with not a little pride in his voice, then he grinned. "If you think that was a battle, then Talon and I have some stories for you!"

Talon nodded. "Yes, we have played in very high stakes games where deep malice was involved and lives were on the line. My brother and I always insist that our people keep the game clean." He paused. "Then you do not play this game in the city where you come from?"

Cristofo shrugged. "If it were possible to play this game on water, we would. Perhaps they play on the mainland."

"Can you then ride, yourself?" Reza asked.

"Yes, I can ride, as can my sister, but we were taught on animals that were larger, and nothing as nimble as these beautiful creatures," Cristofo commented as he gazed at the animals walking by.

"Then you have not lived!" Reza told him. Jannat wagged a finger at him, then focused her attention on their little boy, who was about to run onto the field.

"Firuz! Don't go onto the field. It's not safe just yet," she called out and turned to the nurse. "You should not let him get away from you, Marianne," she admonished the nurse.

The chastened young maid nodded. "Yes, Madam, I'm sorry." She ran out and swept the struggling boy up in her arms and brought him back, to deposit him next to Jannat, who curled an arm around him. "One day, my pet, you can play with the big boys, but not today. Stay close to Papa and myself."

Armilia now came over to join her brother. She murmured in his ear and gestured at a well-guarded trophy that had pride of place on a stand of its own. There were two stolid, armed Saxon warriors standing just behind it.

"It is magnificent!" Cristofo exclaimed, his eyes wide.

The trophy was truly a beautifully crafted item, and a source of wonder for all who beheld it. It depicted two fierce-looking creatures cast out of pure silver. On the left was a dragon, while the animal on the right was a lion. They appeared to be locked in mortal combat; the long tail of the dragon was looped around one of the back legs of the lion, the lion's own tail lashing the air high behind it. Both creatures were standing on their back legs, grappling with one another on a flat expanse of silver ground, creating a large arch with their bodies. Their fangs were bared in gaping jaws as if they were about to strike at one another, tooth and claw.

The creatures were so finely crafted in every detail, from the lion's mane to the scales on the dragon, that Talon always felt that one could almost see them breathe. Their claws and their fangs had been carved out of ivory. One of the eyes of the lion was missing its gemstone—a blank space—but the other still held a sapphire, set deep in its distorted, rage-filled face, while those of the dragon were of pure, deep ruby red, and glared malevolently back at its adversary from under the protruding bones above its eyes.

Beneath the struggling beasts were two other figures: two men on horses, playing the game of chogan. They rode small, fine ponies and were dressed in noblemen's clothes, cloaks flying, wearing turbans, and wielding mallets raised high above their heads, with which they were about to strike. The ponies were galloping toward the small ball, which rested in the very center of the ground upon which the two players rode their ponies.

The handspan-high chogan players were very finely crafted of gold and silver. Clearly, they were men of high rank. Their eyes were intent upon the ball in front of them, and they seemed oblivious to the mighty conflict taking place just above their heads.

The foundation for this struggle for domination was an oblong plinth of cracked and fissured black marble. Every time Talon held the heavy item in his arms, or even touched it, he was certain he could hear the game of chogan being played.

Legend had it that this trophy had been made in Isfahan, hundreds of years before, and won in a spectacular game by the Chinese, who took it back home with them. However, neither the winning team nor the trophy had ever reached China. Somewhere along the perilous route, the entire embassy had disappeared—vanished without a trace—and the trophy had become a myth, until Reza had discovered it among the loot accumulated in the palace of a pirate lord, off the coast of Malaya.

It was now the trophy that the players fought so hard to win. Although it resided in Talon's room, high up in a tower of the castle of Kantara, the act of receiving the trophy as winners was considered a huge honor. Yosef and his team would hopefully hear the game being played when they, too, touched it, when Talon presented it to them.

As Talon waited for the disheveled and dismounted players to form up in front of him, two servants carried the heavy trophy with its plinth, to place it just in front of him. When they had bowed themselves back, Talon turned to Reza and beckoned him over. "Brother?"

Reza jumped to his feet, only too willing to join him.

The two men reached out and touched the lion and the dragon. They both grew very still. "Can you hear it, Brother?"

"Oh, yes!" Reza breathed with a look of great satisfaction on his dark features. "It makes the hair on the back of my neck rise!" He laughed delightedly.

"It still holds its magic," Talon murmured, and smiled with the pleasure of the feeling and sound.

He turned to the men in front of him. "A good game, and well played by all. The winners will be first, but then all of you may touch the prize," he told the tired, but excited, youths in front of him. "Yosef, you as the captain of your team, shall be the first."

Yosef walked a couple of paces forward and stood in front of the magnificent object. Very tentatively, he reached out and touched it, only to snatch his hand away immediately.

"Put both hands on it and don't pull away, Yosef. Stay with your hands on it for a while," Talon told him, knowing at once that Yosef had heard the game. Yosef reached forward again with a nervous expression on his sun-darkened features, and this time, he kept the tips of his fingers on the shoulder of the lion. His face betrayed his wonder. "I hear the game, Lord!" he whispered. There was awe in his voice.

"You are fortunate, my friend," Talon told him. "Not everyone does. Congratulations on a good win."

One by one, the players came forward, and each was rewarded with the chance to touch the precious trophy. They heard the game being played elsewhere in time. Rostam, who had touched the trophy many times, was less surprised, but he, too, was awed by the magic that seemed to emanate from the strange object. "I hear it every time, Father, Uncle Reza," he whispered to them, "but I never cease to wonder at it."

Talon and Reza both embraced him, and then the players withdrew. The crowd, which had been hushed, not fully understanding what was going on, cheered them. This was the opening event in a day of entertainment and demonstrations of skill.

Chapter 6

The Games

And yet we trust the notch to know
the whereabouts of the bow,
and trust the tail or fletching
of each salvo to astonish
the target as soon as it gets there, to make its point
within its nest of Os and Os and Os.
—Stephanie Burt

The game of chogan now over, the crowd's attention was drawn to lesser spectacles of skill, which were nevertheless entertaining. Talon and Reza had worked hard with their men to put on a demonstration of arms and skills for their villagers and crewmen, which entertained them and also challenged the youths.

Targets were set up at one end of the field, whereupon the archers gave a display of their skill. Caradog and Dewi had been charged by Talon to teach several of the local villagers and crewmen how to use the deadly longbows they employed with such skill themselves. The young aspiring archers demonstrated their newfound abilities without disgracing the two Welshmen, but then it came to their turn, and the crowd hushed as the two men took up station and prepared to show all and sundry how it was really done.

A distant twang, and arrows hissed quietly in shallow trajectories along the length of the polo field to land one hundred and fifty paces away in straw targets. There were awed murmurs from the crowd as every arrow found its mark. Talon was pleased. Although he was too far away to hear them, he could see two of the Welsh archers waving their arms around and pointing toward the targets. He smiled. The Welshmen could never agree on much, and were yet again disputing their marksmanship in voluble Welsh.

"They are at it again! Do you want me to go and bang their heads till they stop, my lord?" Brandt asked out of the corner of his mouth. He had sidled up to stand next to Talon. The huge hound that accompanied Brandt everywhere nosed Talon's elbow. He absently stroked its ears and received a grunt of pleasure in return.

Talon pretended to consider. "There are times... but no, Brandt, they will soon stop and send a few more arrows to make their respective points, and it will be over."

"They are getting restless, as are our other warriors. Been peaceful recently."

"Be careful what you wish for, my friend," Reza commented from Talon's other side.

"I agree with you," Brandt addressed Reza respectfully. "The games are a good way to let off the pressure. I am going to prepare for wrestling. Please excuse me. May the dog stay here with you, my lord?"

"Of course, he can, Brandt!" Talon told him.

Brandt admonished the dog to stay and then gave a short bow to them and another to the women. "My ladies," he said politely; then he turned around and set off to join the Saxon warriors, who were waiting for him.

"Good fortune, Brandt!" Rav'an called.

"Thank you, my lady," he responded, going red from his ears to the base of his thick neck, and his voice becoming gruff. Brandt was always embarrassed when spoken to by either of the two women of Talon's family.

"That man would march straight into hell to protect us, but he would be as red as the furnace itself while doing so," Jannat said to Rav'an in Farsi.

Rav'an smiled with affection at her sister. "That he would, and we should count ourselves lucky we have those Saxons with him," she answered.

After the Welsh archers had completed their demonstration and Reza had checked their targets, they left to cheerful applause from the crowd, and the Companions demonstrated their skill with bows while galloping at full speed along a line of targets set up in the middle of the field. Once again, it was a success, and Reza was happy. This was his program, and he'd had great expectations. He was not disappointed.

Reza and Talon both watched with keen interest as a pole was raised, roughly fifty paces in front of the stadium. This next was a sport at which they both excelled. Two pigeons were attached to the top of the pole by strings tied to one of their legs. The strings allowed the pigeons freedom to fly, but only within eight paces from the pole. A circle fifteen paces in diameter was marked on the ground around the pole by some servants. Jannat, who was fond of pigeons, looked unhappy.

The first contestant to come out on a beautiful Turcoman-bred horse was Yosef, who looked tense. The pigeons had settled down on the top of the pole, which was the height of two tall Saxons. He cantered slowly toward the pole and then circled it outside the ring of bales, watching the birds while fitting an arrow to his bow, and then loosing it in one smooth gesture. The arrow thumped into the pole just below the birds, which took off, alarmed, fluttering desperately to get away.

His next arrow missed, but the third struck one of the birds and killed it. He was only allowed to use three arrows, and none were left. There were cheers from the awed crowd, but the chagrined Yosef had to halt his horse and salute the watching crowd, then walk it slowly back to the lines while other men replaced the dead bird with another frightened one.

"Yosef must be having a bad day," Talon commented. "He rarely misses."

"Here comes Rostam," Rav'an said.

Rostam cantered his favorite horse slowly toward the pole, and kept his animal at the same pace as he circled the pole. His horse had its head tucked into its neck and was well collected, allowing Rostam to move comfortably with the motion of the animal. The agitated birds fluttered off the pole top and flew hard in circles of their own. Rostam loosed two arrows in quick succession, and both birds were struck dead.

The crowd clapped and whistled their approval as he saluted and left. The pole was taken down. Talon could hear incredulous comments from the Venetians nearby. They had never seen a display of horsemanship like this. He smiled to himself with satisfaction.

"Our boy is coming along well," he murmured to Rav'an.

"He will soon be beating both you and Reza at your own games, my love," she murmured back with a wicked smile.

He snorted derisively. "That'll be the day!"

Reza gave a snort of his own. "We can still show those whippersnappers a thing or two, I can tell you, my sister."

She merely smiled sweetly at him, and cradled her daughter deeper in her arms.

After a short interval, the wrestling began, with the Saxons, including Brandt, taking on all comers.

The roar of the crowd filled the air as one after another Brandt's challengers were sent flying across the small space marked out by willow wands. These were used because, should a man —or a boy— be flung onto them by one such as Brandt, the wands would bend and not skewer him.

The next challenger, one of the braver and larger crewmen from one of the ships in the harbor, landed face-down, and those close by winced. Friends hastily ran into the ring and picked up the dazed, bleeding, and now gap-toothed victim and carried him off, while the huge Saxon, bare to the waist, put his hands on his hips and roared fiercely at the spectators.

"Any more of you goat turds want to try me out?"

The crowd loved these displays of strength and skill, along with the abuse that the Saxons spiced their speech with. The men laughed their approval while the older womenfolk clucked their tongues at the bad language and covered their children's ears. The wrestling, as well as the archery, had become a yearly event. The crowd laughed at Brandt's pretended fierceness, and many shouted praises for their hero, who had remained unbeaten for two years now. But challengers kept on stepping into the ring to try him out. Even his Saxon comrades still felt compelled to try to take him down a peg or two. This was their one opportunity in the year when it would not be viewed as a disciplinary issue.

Finally, Psellos, the priest who was the unofficial umpire, stepped into the ring and called for silence.

"I pronounce our Saxon, Brandt, to be the champion of the game for this year of our lord eleven hundred and ninety-one!" he shouted. "Lord Talon will present the prizes!"

He walked up to the sweating and grinning Brandt and clasped him by the forearm. "Well done, Brant!" He held Brandt's huge hand in the air and the crowd cheered. If it were possible, Brandt went an even deeper red with embarrassment, but he was hugely pleased, as well. He and the other Saxons had become very much a part of the community over the last few years, and he was proud to be there. His native companions, dotted among the spectators, cheered their approval and slurped their beer and wine. There were even a few blue eyed children running about these days.

The wrestling ring was quickly dismantled, for there were other displays for the crowd to watch today.

The field was a project dear to Talon's heart. It had been completed the previous year, after much work and planning, for the two men yearned for a space upon which they could play the game of chogan. This year, their efforts had been rewarded.

"If Brandt keeps on demolishing our eager young men, there won't be any left, either to row the ships or plough the fields," Rav'an remarked.

"Those lads need to be toughened up a little, and they all continue to volunteer," Reza countered with a grin.

"Wait until you see the shield wall demonstration," Talon warned. "Brandt and his men have been hard at work, training townsmen and villagers alike for the last few months. This is going to be a competition to remember."

"No one is going to get hurt, are they, Talon?" Jannat asked. She sounded concerned.

"Well...," he hesitated, "Reza and I have watched them practicing, and sometimes it can get a little out of hand," he admitted.

"It's about war, my princess," Reza told her. "Brandt and his men know what they are doing, but yes, it can get rough. It's becoming a competition now, you see," he added with a grin. "The sailors against the inlanders. Twenty men on each side."

"Are the Saxons going to be involved?" Rav'an asked. "That might make it very uneven!"

"No, they are going to encourage their respective teams. Brandt is neutral, but Aedwalt and Hrodulf oversee each of the teams, with help from Oswine and Cynemaer."

"Talon offered to pay one gold bar to the Saxons of the victorious team and a purse for the men," Reza said. "So there really is an incentive to win."

"Why does it have to be a gold bar?" Jannat asked with a puzzled expression.

"Because, being Saxon, they will melt the bar down and display their prize as a gold band. They call them arm rings, of which they are very proud," Reza explained. "They are badges of battles, but also awards, and a sign of wealth."

"The townsmen and crews will go at it and fight it out, but when they are done, the Saxons will put on a display of their own. They will do a demonstration of how they perform in battle," Talon told them. He lifted his daughter, Fariba, from his wife's arms and onto his lap. "I just hope it isn't the full battle display!" he murmured into his four-year-old daughter's dark hair.

Reza laughed.

"What are you laughing about, my prince?" Jannat asked him.

"I shall tell you later, Princess," he assured her.

They watched as men walked out into the field to wedge four thin stakes into the ground, in line with the stands and separated by forty paces.

"Those represent the line. Each side must drive the opposition across to win," Talon told them, pointing to the willow wands. More men followed, all of them well-muscled, yet a discerning eye could distinguish the corded muscles and strong hands of men who alternately rowed at the oars or handled the ropes of masted ships from the men who worked the fields, who were for the most part natives of the island, hence not as tall. Each man carried a big round shield, while some carried short staves and others held longer staves. They trotted across the field and formed two double lines of twenty men. Brandt reappeared with his Saxon contingent, all fully armed, their chain mail hauberks and gold arm rings gleaming in the early afternoon sun. They were not carrying shields, but immediately began shouting at the men.

Talon had little doubt that the language was very Saxon, but the competitors appeared to be eager to comply with the bellowed commands, and two double lines quickly formed. It was a colorful display, for the shields were painted in many shades of red, blue, and even yellow. The center bosses were made of burnished bronze, riveted to the wood behind.

After the desperate time when pirates had attacked the town and the village, Talon had resolved that their inhabitants should be able to defend themselves until help arrived from the castle. He had invested in expensive hauberks for the leaders, and paid for lesser armor for the rest of the men, some of whom were clad in brightly dyed leather on which were sewn metal rings or small metal plates. All wore helmets. Brandt had insisted that each man be instantly ready to go to battle, should the call go out. Now they were going to show their lord what they could do.

One of the Saxons barked a command, and the men fell silent. The crowd hushed expectantly.

Brandt and two of his men marched to the front of the group, and he raised his sword in the air. He called out a command. The men behind him raised the rims of their shields up to chin-height, and then, on another shout, the whole mass of men marched straight toward the stands where Lord Talon, his family, and other Companions were seated. Brandt was in the lead. As the two groups approached, there was another roar from Brandt, and the advancing men began to yell battle cries and beat their shields with their sticks, making a menacing drumming sound that stilled all conversation within the excited crowd gathered all about the stand.

Although Talon could not hear it, there was another command from Brandt, and the warriors crashed to a halt right in front of him. He stood up and stared back at the men gathered in front of him.

Brandt brought his sword up in a salute, and then lowered it so that its point nearly touched the grass at his feet. There was total silence all around.

Talon cleared his throat. "Today, you are going to demonstrate to everyone here that your training was not in vain and that you can, when needed, fight effectively for your families and homes, to hold off an implacable enemy until help arrives from the castle."

He knew that the attempt by pirates, almost three years ago, was still vivid in people's minds, so he drew upon that.

"People of the towns and ships of Kantara! You have seen how useful a shield wall is. Many of you were there on that fateful day and remember it well. Every man and boy aged fourteen and above must have this training, but the best amongst you are here today, to fight for possession of a purse and the standard." He indicated the flag that had been embroidered by Rav'an and her waiting ladies to display two golden towers set on a ringed wall with a ship in the middle. The banner was fluttering in the breeze above his head, alongside his own standard. This bore the image of a ship and a castle on its red and gold background.

A spontaneous cheer erupted from the crowd, and grew to a roar of approval. Talon lifted his hand for quiet and the noise subsided.

"Let the best team win!" he called out. "Commander Brandt, the field is yours."

The crowd cheered wildly again while the competitors faced and marched back to the center of the field, where they moved into position, into two rows of men, the front row in line with the willow stakes so that the men were separated by about twenty paces. Their shields were up; they were braced for the start of the competition. Brandt was watching Talon, who stood up with Rav'an at his side.

"You have the honor as always, my lady. You were the one in command when the pirates came last time. It is now our tradition." He smiled at her and handed her the large, white scarf, which she took with a smile of her own and held aloft.

There was a long pause and then she released the scarf, which fluttered to the ground.

"Now!" roared Brandt. The four Saxons howled their war cries and screamed at their respective teams to move.

"Get over to them, you lame maggots!" Aedwald yelled. "Beat your shields and walk, do not run! Not yet, do you hear me, you sons of dung beetles?" he bellowed at several over-eager men surged too far ahead.

"When I say run, you run, you pig's bladders on sticks! Hear me!" he rapped one of the men on the helmet with the flat of his sword.

"Close up! Close up! Damn your worthless hides!" another of the Saxons shouted, but the men needed little persuasion. They wanted that coveted flag even more than the purse, which, while useful, was not the point.

The lines of shield men closed in and walked forward. "What have I always told you turds? Close your shields up, right edge over left edge. Do it now!" Another Saxon yelled into the ear of the man on the extreme right end of the line.

Aedwald glanced up at Brandt, who nodded. "Now run! Charge! Cut their balls off and kill them!" screamed Aedwald. His two lines promptly began to run toward their opponents, yelling insults and obscenities at the other team, which had also begun to run toward them. They met more or less in the middle with a crash and a rattle of sticks on shields and opposing helmets. The men roared and struggled, pushing and shoving, poking at one another with their short sticks, while the Saxons danced around the edges of the struggling men and shouted encouragement and advice.

The crowd of onlookers shouted themselves hoarse with encouragement, and then some began to chant a war song.

Before long, the hills echoed with loud raucous singing, mainly from the sailors, who sang rowing songs and obscene ditties, while the townsmen's supporters sang their own songs, accompanied by a medley of musical instruments, which always appeared during the games. Drums were pounded by eager men and boys, and the whistle of flutes competed with the screams of encouragement.

Jannat put her hands over her ears and looked pleadingly at Rav'an. "Do men always have to make such a noise?" she asked.

"Men always make noise when they are trying to kill or hurt one another," Rav'an retorted, and then gasped. Everyone was caught up in the excitement of the moment as they watched the struggling lines waver and realign.

"Or because they are scared silly. Those men out there are not scared of the enemy. Not yet, anyway. They are more terrified of Brandt and his giants," Talon observed. "It is not much fun to be in a shield wall, but it is the only place to be if you are fighting a murderous mob of pirates."

Talon glanced around him out of habit. The caution was ingrained in him, as it was with Reza. He was aware that among the crowd were his other men, the older Companions and their trainees, there to make sure that he and his family were always under protection. By now, some of the youths who were natives from the harbor and even the village further inland had also been recruited.

After several minutes of panting, the shouts from the struggling men had died to a grumble. Suddenly, the crowd saw an unmistakable movement in one direction, as the men from the ships began to give way to the townsmen. At first, the front line wavered a little and then, despite the roars and threats coming from their Saxon coaches and the crowd of supporters, the line began to buckle. Finally, with a roar of triumph, the townsmen pushed through the center of the sailor's line and struggled toward the line of willow sticks. As soon as the first man arrived, he raised his arms into the air and yelled his triumph to the sky. His sweating and disheveled companions hoisted him up upon their shoulders, and with yells of triumph they trotted toward the stands, where Talon was now standing, waiting for them.

Both he and Reza waved at the men, and the crowd howled its approval. Kostos was a large man, almost as large as Brandt himself. He shouted with delight at his friends as he was brought toward the stands, and then he ran forward and dropped to one knee, still grinning, and bowed respectfully to Talon, who walked forward. After he had placed a bright green and white sash over the proud man's shoulder, he said, "Stand, Kostos; you and your men have earned the purse. I hereby give you the prize." He embraced the delighted Kostos and turned to Reza.

"Lord Reza will present the banner, which you will keep well until the next time you meet on this field."

Reza took the banner down from its place and presented it to Kostos, who bowed deeply and then kissed the banner, thanked them both, stood back, and waved the banner for all to see. His team shouted and the crowd cheered. The disconsolate losers straggled up to join them, having allowed the winners their moment of victory.

There was one more event about to take place, a demonstration from the Saxon contingent. During the presentation, Brandt and his leaders had mustered the rest of the Saxons, who normally stayed close to Talon and his family during these events.

The Saxons were wearing polished and gleaming hauberks, silver and gold arm rings, and bearing large shields with Talon's emblem painted on the front: a single tower, a ship, and below that, a dagger with a blue background. The warriors wore boots and iron greaves, and helmets with face guards that made them look menacing, which was the intent. Talon spared no expense when it came to armoring his Saxons.

They formed up as two lines of fifteen, and then on a quiet command, they turned as one and faced the stands. Brandt gave another command. Their swords hissed out of their scabbards and they began to trot toward the stands. There was no mistaking the menace of their approach. The shields were up, covering only the warriors' chins. Their silver inlaid iron helmets had been burnished to a shine, as were their shield bosses. The cheek and nose guards hid most of their faces; the large men, some with blonde hair flying behind their shoulders, screaming battle cries and hammering their shields with their swords, presented a sinister sight that was truly frightening.

Many in the crowd shrank from the onrushing warriors, but Talon stood his ground, facing the charging men, who came within six paces of him. Brandt, who was in the lead, raised his sword high and bellowed a command that halted the warriors in their tracks. There was a stunned silence from the onlookers. Some small children, frightened by this ferocious display of arms, began to cry, only to be hushed by their mothers. Brandt dropped to one knee and bent his head.

Talon took two paces forward, held both hands out, and lifted the Saxon to his feet. "You are our Veragnians, my faithful warriors, and I and my people thank you!" he called out loud. The crowd had, by now, recovered itself enough to cheer, but Talon waved to two men behind him, who carried a small chest out to place it next to him.

"As we have done for the last three years, Brandt, I am honored to present you and your men with the arm rings," Talon stated as one of the servants opened the chest. There, nesting together, were thirty-one gold arm rings that he presented to the Saxons every year. "Well earned, Brandt," Talon said solemnly.

Brandt ducked his head. "Thank you, Lord."

There had been several skirmishes with mercenaries from the emperor's palace in Famagusta over the last few years. Isaac Komnenos had never fully accepted the loss of the castle of Kantara. But each time, the Saxons had appeared in all their fearsome glory, had attacked with their customary ferocity, and the enemy had fled. Their reputation was now known from one end of the island to the other, which suited Talon very well.

"I thank you for sparing us the, um, fullness of your battle tactics," Talon told the giant in a low voice.

Brandt turned red and look sheepish. "No, Lord. Not in front of the ladies."

Reza joined the two of them and laughed. "Thank you, Brandt. That was as good a display as we have ever seen. It's now time for the celebrations to begin. "Try to keep your men from deflowering every maiden in the town tonight, and please leave us with some sailors to man our ships, in case of trouble."

"I shall, Lord. Have no fear; they will behave." Brandt grinned. He and Reza got along very well.

"There is wine and ale for all in the barrels over there. Winners and losers, go and enjoy the feast!" Reza called to the gathering in front of him.

No one needed any further encouragement. The men sheathed their swords, piled their shields on the side of the field, took off their helmets, and made their way toward the barrels and the laden tables, where they were greeted by excited families and furtive glances and giggles from young women.

"The inns and the whore house in the harbor are going to be very busy tonight," Reza observed to Talon, as they walked the short distance to join their own families.

The Greeks knew how to enjoy themselves. Rhythmic music began to fill the air, and the younger couples among them began to dance, while the older and the very young clapped their hands in time with the rippling music. Before long, everyone was singing.

Talon glanced up at the sky and then off to the south. Storm clouds were gathering in a dark line just above the ridge of the castle. There would be rain tonight.

It had not escaped Talon's attention that, while the Saxons were all on the field, Reza's Companions had moved quietly into place, nearer to the stands. The protection was ever there, and he was content for it to be so.

Chapter 7

Storms and Unwelcoming Shores

So blow, ye tempests, blow,
And my spirit shall not quail;
I have fought with many a foe,
I have weathered many a gale;
And in this hour of death,
Ere I yield my fleeting breath...
—Charles Mackay

Much later in the evening of the same day, Talon was seated at the table in the untidy room he called his Sanctum. In effect, it was his study, where he could read undisturbed, which was not often enough these days, and where he could work on the numbers for his merchandising enterprises, which were considerable, even in these uncertain times. His ships plied the sea between Cyprus and the mainland, including Egypt and Constantinople.

The much-anticipated storm had struck; however, the chamber was calm enough, and Talon ignored the noise outside. All around him were his memories, as he liked to call them. His favorite among them all was the white stone dragon that stood almost waist high, which he had been given by Hsü, a lord he had known in China. Behind the dragon was the chogan trophy.

Suddenly, the outer shutters of the window in front of him were flung open with a crash that made him sit up with a jerk. The gale had come up from the south with great speed, and the wind keened like a banshee just outside the thick stone walls. Having won the first round, it appeared determined to demolish the inner shutters as well, which rattled furiously and threatened to break loose from their hinges. The several candles in the room were blown out, leaving a single lantern, protected by horn sides, to flicker feebly while the untidy piles of papers on the single desk and piled-on shelves rustled nervously.

Talon smacked his hand down on several documents, which were about to fly off, then put a weight on them before rising to his feet and hurrying over to the window to do something about the wooden shutters before the wind could smash them to splinters against the stone walls outside.

From his lofty study in the high north tower of the castle keep, he peered out at the storm that raged all along the coast, ignoring the stinging rain drops, noting the lightning flashes and the dense cloud mass that appeared to be almost level with the castle of Kantara. A flash of lightning, closely followed by a very loud clap of thunder, told him that the storm was right overhead. Despite himself, he flinched; like everyone else, he knew lightning was a mysterious and dangerous force that sent bolts of fire to the earth and, as often as not, left a fire to rage, especially in the dry forests.

While he wrestled with the shutters, he cast a glance north toward the harbor and the village on the coast, wondering, even as he seized the handle of one of the shutters, if all was well down there. Even at this distance, he could tell the sea was very agitated. He heard a call behind him, and then Reza was next to him, shouting over the noise of the wind and the slashing rain. Talon could barely hear him, but between the two of them, they managed to haul the heavy wooden frames closed, and then the wind, as though peeved at their success, slammed the shutters hard shut against their frames. Lifting the latch, Talon dropped it back into place and, in the quieter moment, grinned at his longtime companion, who was shaking the rain from his hair.

"Phew! That is a real storm out there! What did you say, Brother?" he asked.

"I said," Reza wiped his face, "God help anyone out at sea in this weather. This is one of the worst we've had this year. That wind was trying to smash those shutters to pieces! I could hear these banging away from downstairs. It managed to do, so down at the great hall. There will be some repairs to make after this."

Talon reached for some linen cloths on a table nearby and tossed one over to Reza.

"The last storm was only a week ago," he observed, as he dried his face. "I only hope that Rostam and the captains down at the harbor have secured the ships. I hope he is not in the middle of all this bedlam."

"I am sure he is all right, Talon. He knows how to look after himself," Reza assured him. "The family is downstairs, Brother. Come and join us. You have been cloistered up here for hours and they are beginning to wonder what you are up to."

"I've been doing some thinking, Brother. The reports coming in from all sides are disturbing," Talon countered.

Reza rolled his eyes. "Thinking again. Always a bad habit, but come on down and have some wine. Rav'an is asking for you, and it's time for the children to go to bed."

*****

To the south of the island of Cyprus, off the coast of Limassol, the sea raged, and in its grip were ships.

Captain Willimus hurriedly swiped the rain from his eyes and bearded face with one hand while he gripped hard onto the large wooden tiller of his bucking vessel with the other. He peered forward, trying desperately to see into the darkness of the howling night. Torrents of rain slashed at his exposed face, half blinding him. He and his unhappy steersmen were drenched to the bone. Rain drummed on the wooden deck with an ominous rattle, sending streams of water across his boots. The wind made it hard to hear shouted commands. The captain was sickeningly aware that his ship, *Seynte Mariecog*, was in danger of foundering, right beneath his feet. They were perilously close to the island of Cyprus, lying in wait out there, somewhere to the north in the raging storm. Their dubious safety lay in being well away from land on a night like this.

He turned and stared to the south, in the vain hope that he might see the lights of the other vessels that accompanied his ship, but the darkness gave him no clues. Muttering a prayer for the other vessels, he turned his attention toward his own ship's bows and tried to guess their position, but there were no stars to aid him on this terrible night.

There were few others on deck, only those crewmen who were forced to remain, in case the skimpy sail failed yet again. They crouched under whatever cover they could find, roped to either the mast or some metal ring on the ship's side to prevent themselves from being washed overboard. An hour ago, the main sail had been shredded by a sharp gust of wind that was inexplicably warm. No matter where it came from, it had demolished the sail, leaving the soaked and frightened crew to struggle with another, smaller sheet and haul it into place, so that it might keep them moving eastward and prevent them from drifting too far north.

The ship pitched and yawed like a drunken creature. One minute, its bows were pointing heavenwards, and then with a shudder and a twist that caused its strakes deep inside to groan noisily, it dipped downward to bury the bows deep in yet another huge wave that reared menacingly above them. Foaming sea water would tumble down onto the forward deck and a wave would rush back along the main deck, sweeping away anything left to break free before it crashed into the walls below the upper steering deck, sending spray high into the darkness. The ship staggered and then wallowed like a whale as it became temporarily submerged, after which it struggled to rise, water pouring in huge streams out of its scuppers. The captain knew full well that the strain was opening the timbers to unstoppable leaks. If they survived the storm, they might well sink anyway, due to the bilges being too full to bail.

Men who had been clinging for dear life to the main mast reemerged from the black tide, gasping and choking for air, praying out loud for deliverance from this monstrous sea. The captain noted with a sense of growing despair that, each time, the ship wallowed for just that much longer.

He wondered how his passengers were doing. He was carrying people on this voyage, not cargo. These were knights and horses, destined for the Holy Land.

Lightning flashed, a jagged line of glaring white light, illuminating the sea for miles around. The lightning appeared to linger for a long moment, like a jagged fork from hell, and the frightened men on the steering deck all saw the one thing they dreaded most of all: the unmistakable darkness of land, and it was far too close!

The captain felt his stomach churn as the men around him pointed, one of them screaming into the wind, "God save us! It is land! We are dead men!"

Captain Willimus could not disagree with him. How they had been driven this far north, he could not say. A previous storm had driven them, along with several other ships, far to the south, away from the main fleet, which had been steering for Acre, but now they were about to fall prey to the deadly rocks of Cyprus! However, the captain was a courageous man who had been to sea for many years and was not prepared to give up just yet. He leaned all his weight against the tiller, trying to move the vessel to starboard in an easterly direction, and shouted at the other men to help him. Soaked by the rain and numbed by the battering of the cold waves, they moved to obey, but they were men in a daze of exhaustion and fear. Some had clearly given up already as they called out prayers to the unheeding wind.

Now, even in the darkness around them, he could see the dark loom of land and knew with a chilling certainty that nothing he could do for the plunging ship would avert disaster. Nonetheless, he struggled to move the vessel far enough to enable them to sail in a more parallel direction to the coast, which was coming closer at an alarming speed. Despite their combined efforts, the ship was being driven by the current and the wind, inexorably toward the coastline and the black fangs of its jagged rocks.

As the landmass became clearer, his eyes searched desperately for a beach where they might be able to run the vessel aground. He knew there were beaches along this coastline, but there were also treacherous, rocky outcrops that would destroy his ship, should they be driven onto them. He could now make out tall cliffs ahead and knew with a certain despair that the wind would drive them where it chose and that there was nothing he could do. They were less than half a league from the coast now. Lightning continued to flash, followed by the deafening crash of thunder, but now more distantly, as the storm moved north. They could clearly see the white contrast of the surf as the waves flung themselves against jagged rocks, sending spray high into the dark sky.

The panic of the crew had communicated itself to the passengers below, and they began to appear on deck, risking the danger. They were promptly drenched by the spray and the water breaking over the transom. All too quickly they realized their peril. Their cries of dismay and fear were heard by others below deck, who struggled up the heaving gangways to join them. These were no sailors; most had emptied their stomachs long ago, but they still retched, and some even wept as they realized their peril. Many were praying. lords, knights, their squires, and their attendants peered through the slackening rain toward the dark coastline.

Then a crewman shouted and pointed, "Captain! Captain! I see lights on the shore! There is help waiting for us! God be praised!"

Captain Willimus, a fervent Christian, believed that while God preserved those whom He wished, it was up to the individual to assist God in that endeavor. He could just see the distant flickering lights, and noted that there was, indeed, a beach almost ahead of them, but the sea and wind threatened to take his ship past it and drive his vessel onto the terrifying jumble of rocks beyond, unless he could do something about it. He roared at the numb crew, and managed to have the sail hauled around just enough to bring the wind to bear, right behind them. Then he and his steersmen leaned all their weight on the tiller to bring them to port. If they had to strike land, let it be a sandy beach and not some deadly rocks.

Slowly, very slowly, the bows of the vessel turned, but it would not be quite enough. While the vessel responded, it was too low in the water, too slow to respond to their desperate efforts. Captain Willimus could judge the distance and speed of the sluggish boat well enough. They might get lucky and be driven onto the junction of the beach and the outcropping rocks, he prayed. There was nothing left to do but watch, make their peace with God, and hope.

He could make out flickering torches on the beach more clearly and knew, with some relief, that while they might crash onto the rocks ahead, there would be help waiting to fish some of them out of the water and provide shelter.

"Dear God, let it be so!" he muttered and wiped his face again. It was still raining, but nowhere near as hard as it had been. The ship was yawing less, but the waves were still high, and he knew without a doubt that they would have a hard landing. He peered down at the now-crowded main deck. The men among the passengers, young and old, were clustered on the port side, staring and waving as though the people on land could see them. Fools! All that would be seen of the ship would be a dark shape about to crash into the coast of Cyprus.

He braced himself for the impact as a wave came up behind the ship, lifted its stern, and carried it straight toward the black teeth of some jagged rocks, which became exposed as the sea withdrew temporarily, before rushing back in with its victim firmly in its watery grasp. As he stared in horror at the onrushing catastrophe, the captain could hear wails of terror from all around him. The cries of passengers were then drowned out by a splintering crash, as the bows were carried hard against the teeth of the rocks.

The shock threw everyone on the steering deck off their feet, clutching at whatever they could to avoid being hurled down to the main deck. Willimus clambered to his feet and watched with fearful fascination as the front of his ship disappeared in a welter of spray. Large, fractured sections of splintered wood were swept back to tumble into the crowded main deck, to kill and maim many. He hung on for dear life as he and the other men on the steering deck witnessed the horror and destruction just below. The main mast gave a loud crack, and then slowly fell, like a tired, old tree to the starboard side, in a tangle of ropes and stays. It then rolled and crushed even more people to death.

Many, sure that help would be waiting for them on shore, took their chances with the boiling sea and began to jump overboard. It was not far to go, but the ship was already sinking, and many who did jump into the water were caught up in the swirling currents near the rocks. They could not swim, so they perished. Others struggled to keep afloat, seizing onto bits of wood or sections, and allowed themselves to be carried off, wailing and crying.

Meanwhile, the time had come for the captain and his steersmen to abandon the vessel. No man among them could swim, but there was now much in the way of flotsam, barrels, and spars aplenty.

Captain Willimus and his crewmen levered a hatch off the opening on their deck and heaved it into the water, which was now almost level with the deck itself. Without further ado, they scrambled onto the bucking platform and hung on desperately, to avoid being thrown into the water and certain death. A few terrified souls remained on the ship, wailing and praying. They could not face the sea, not even the chance of succor only a hundred paces away on the beach, and so they, too, perished, as the ship settled on the sand and rocks below the turmoil of the waves and surf. Glancing up from his prone position on the grating, which he clutched at for his very life, the captain could tell that, when the sea had calmed, the ship would be clearly visible. Perhaps it would not break up, and something might be salvaged; but then the waters around him and the present danger took his focus off the ship and back to his own survival.

Wind and wave propelled them towards land, and soon they were close enough to the shoreline to be able to stand and then to stagger—soaked to the bone and cold—through the surf, toward the welcoming torches on the now crowded beach. Captain Willimus had time to send a prayer of thanks heavenwards. He noted that others of his crew had also made it to safety and he was thankful. He and his three crewmen called out to the approaching figures, expressing their gratitude, but there was something not quite right about the figures coming toward them.

These men, as he could now see, were armed. Their torches played light that gleamed off chain mail, helmets, and spears. The men who came up to the captain called out something in Greek, a language he was familiar with, although he was not fluent. Like all captains who sailed the Middle Sea, he could understand several languages and make himself understood.

"I am the shipmaster of the unfortunate vessel," he called back, feeling apprehensive. Something was very wrong. The men were not welcoming, and, in fact, some had their spears pointing at him and his bedraggled crewmen.

"You are our prisoners," the leader of the men nearby called out in bad French. "Do not try to escape or you will die!"

As if to emphasize this, he pointed down the beach. The storm had slackened considerably, and there was dim light of dawn beginning to grow in the east. It provided just enough light for the appalled captain and his men to see members of the armed group spearing to death other survivors who had made it to the beach. The cries of hope and joy were changed to screams of terror. Some of the survivors tried to put up a fight, but they were no match for the dark killers, who dispatched them ruthlessly, one by one. Those who had the energy to flee were chased and cut down, or shot with crossbow bolts.

"Stop this, in the name of God! What are you doing?" Captain Willimus shouted.

He received a back-hand blow across his face for his trouble, which knocked him down. A man stood over him with a spear, poised to ram it into his recumbent body. "Halt!" the leader called out. "We take him and some others prisoner. They can tell us what was in the ship."

The spear was withdrawn, Captain Willimus was hauled to his feet; his hands were jerked behind him, then bound with leather cords. He and his exhausted men were driven up the beach to the grassy border by their rough captors. He noted that the slaughter on the beach had stopped, leaving only a small cluster of prisoners who, like the captain, were bound and then driven up the slope of the sandy beach to join him.

The prisoners were beaten into a rough line and then driven onto a track that led along the coast. Glancing back, Captain Willimus noticed that their captors were plundering the bodies of those who had died. No doubt, they would do the same for the drowned bodies that drifted onto the beach and then concentrate their greed on the remains of the ship.

"God curse these people!" one of the prisoners said out loud. Captain Willimus recognized one of the knights who had been a passenger on his ship.

"Who are they? Why did they do this to us?" another called out.

"Shut your mouths or you will die!" bellowed one of their captors, and he beat the prisoner with the haft of his spear.

"They belong to emperor Isaac Komnenos," Captain Willimus muttered to the knight. "He employs mercenaries, from what I have heard."

"But we are knights in the service of King Richard!" the knight exclaimed, indignantly. "We cannot be treated like this by fellow Christians!"

The leader of the mercenaries seized the knight by the front of his soaked tunic and hauled him out of the line, which came to a ragged halt, exhausted men blundering into one another and cursing.

"Are you a knight?" he demanded loudly.

The man drew himself up proudly, "I am Sir Forder. I am a vassal of King Richard of England. You would do well to treat us a good deal better than this!"

He got no further; the leader struck him in the side with a long dagger.

"What need have we of English knights?" he asked the world at large, as he let his gasping victim fall at his feet. He withdrew his bloody dagger from the still-writhing body, wiped it on his dying victim's wet tunic, and sheathed it; after which, he motioned the line of prisoners to continue. The shocked captain and the others staggered on in silence, leaving Sir Forder lying on the sand behind them.

Two more of the survivors, one old and one a mere boy, died along the way. Exhausted from their ordeal at sea, they fell to the side, where they were dispatched without ceremony by the mercenaries. The remainder of the survivors kept their peace and moved along, encouraged by the spear points of their captors. Eventually, as the sun came up over the eastern approaches of the island, they arrived at the outskirts of a walled town.

The captain learned its name was Limassol, from what little Greek he could understand from their escort. In some respects they had been lucky, because to the east of this town there were high cliffs and a rocky coastline almost as far as Famagusta, where, from time to time, he had docked his ship in the past. They would have been totally destroyed had they drifted further east. *Small comfort in that*, he thought to himself ruefully.

After being admitted through the gates of the town, the prisoners were paraded through the streets, heading in the direction of the harbor. Limassol was just waking up. The curious citizens came to their doors and gaped at the ragged prisoners who stumbled by, splashing along what passed for a main street through muddy puddles left behind by the storm, too worn out to care who might be watching them. The captain noted that there had been quite a lot of damage to many of the houses and huts that lined the road. Thatch had been torn free and scattered around. Several houses had lost tiles. Even some trees were down, partially blocking the side streets. The locals chattered in their rough Greek dialect and pointed.

When one of them called over to ask who these people were, the guard replied that they were pirates who had just been captured. Whereupon some of the men and boys picked up stones and mud and hurled them at the weary prisoners, calling them names and spitting. The mercenaries laughed but didn't pause; they drove the prisoners on toward a small fortification overlooking the harbor, then down into an underground dungeon.

As the doors slammed shut on the prisoners, they fell to the floor. Some wept while others sat against the stone walls in silence, appalled and bewildered by what had transpired. Others, Captain Willimus included, promptly sought to untie each other, and then groaned as the blood flowed back into their numb limbs.

The captain rested his head against the wall and thought about what he had just seen. He had reflexively observed the shipping in the harbor and the bay, and had been surprised to note that three of the ships that had accompanied his from Sicily were now anchored in the middle of the bay. He was sure one of them belonged to King Richard's sister, Queen Joanna, daughter of Eleanor of Aquitaine. He was very glad that she appeared to have survived the storm, and a small glimmer of hope grew in his mind.

"How many are we?" he called out to the groaning crowd in the darkness.

He had to repeat himself, as most of the men in the cramped chamber had fallen asleep, almost where they fell.

"We are maybe twenty," someone called out in the darkness.

"Did anyone notice the three ships in the harbor?" Willimus called back.

The response was a mixture of groans and snores.

He lapsed back into silence, thinking. Finally, he, too, drifted off into a troubled sleep.

The prisoners were woken by the crash of metal on metal as the bolts to their cell were thrown open. Two of the mercenaries stood at the door with drawn swords. The men in the cell either clambered to their feet or cowered against the walls, fearing that they were to be murdered. The example on the beach was uppermost in their minds. Starting up, Willimus could hear shouts and cries came closer. Then, to everyone's surprise, even more prisoners were herded inside the already-crowded cell. The flickering light cast by the torches held by the mercenaries illuminated the worn and haggard faces of Norman knights and a few attendants. None wore armor nor weapons, and many were bound.

The doors were slammed shut again, plunging the dungeon into darkness. Willimus moved forward to try and find out more about the newcomers. There was a babble of calls and shouts between the two groups and he had to bellow for silence. Although there were probably men here who outranked him, he was presently acknowledged as their leader.

"Which ship did you arrive on?" he called out. He noticed that the dark of the chamber was not so dense now; a patch of light above their heads heralded the dawn.

"The caravel *Marie La Belle*," a gruff voice responded. "Is that you, Captain Willimus?"

He recognized the voice. "Aye it is. Get over here, Drury."

A form materialized before him, and Drury said, "I am still tied." Willimus went to work on the thongs, and then the two men embraced. Drury was the first mate on the *Marie la Belle.* They knew one another well. Holding Drury out at arm's length, Captain Willimus asked the question, "God be praised that you are alive, but where is your captain?"

Drury wiped his eyes in a tired gesture, "He argued with them, demanding succor. The bastards rewarded him with a sword in the belly. God curse all of them!" he spat.

Willimus nodded in the gloom. "They are a ruthless crowd for sure. But did you notice the three ships in the harbor, by any chance?

"I did, but I didn't believe my eyes!" Drury exclaimed. "So, I was not dreaming? Those ships belong to the queen?"

"Aye, I am sure of it," Willimus responded. "We must escape and tell them of our plight."

"That sounds easier said than done," his friend replied. "Perhaps they know already and will negotiate on our behalf?" Drury asked tentatively.

Willimus called out to the murmuring crowd. "Who among you is a lord or senior knight? I am Captain Willimus and I want to talk."

There was more muttering, and then several men clambered to their feet and moved toward him. One of them called out. "We all serve King Richard, but I am Lord D'Onston, and some of these men serve me."

The tall Norman walked up and stood in front of the two burly seamen. He was still rubbing his wrists. Their bonds had been tight. "How many of our ships went down?" he demanded.

"We do not know. But right now, you need to know that Queen Joanna's ship is in the harbor, along with two other vessels, Lord D'Onston," Willimus responded.

He heard a gasp from both the men in front of him. As word spread, a murmur of surprise and astonishment came from all sides.

"Dear Lord, above!" exclaimed Lord D'Onston. "Are you quite sure?"

"I noticed them on our way in, Lord," Willimus said with some confidence.

"By God, but this is good news!" Lord D'Onston exclaimed. "It won't be long before the king himself arrives. He won't let her be taken by that swine, Komnenos, I'll swear by it."

"In the meantime, my lord, we have to be on our guard because we have seen how these people treat prisoners. I have no reason to trust them not to commit even more crimes," one of D'Onston's men murmured.

Willimus nodded his agreement. For all they knew, the upstart emperor might decide, upon a whim, to kill them all rather than ransom them or use them as hostages.

"Has anyone got a weapon of any kind? A knife? Anything?" he called out.

"You don't think," D'Onston stared hard at the captain in the gloom, "that they could come and kill us all in here?" He sounded incredulous.

"That is exactly what I think, m'lord," he replied, "unless they have something just as unpleasant in mind for us."

Chapter 8

Messages

Arriving late sometimes and never
Quite expected, still they come,
Bringing a folded meaning home
Between the lines, inside the letter.
—Muriel Spark

The messages began to arrive with the dawn. The first pigeon to settle on the window sill came from Famagusta. Jannat took its tiny-wrapped note to Talon in his study, where she found the two friends poring over a letter.

Talon stood up to greet her with a smile. "Hello, Lady Jannat. What news?"

"Dimitri tells us that there has been much activity in and around the palace, and many men left last night, riding hard for Larnaca, or perhaps beyond to Limassol. Very unusual, he says. He asks what he should do?" she responded, handing over the small piece of paper with the hieroglyphic writing on it. By now, Jannat could read the messages as though they were in clear writing, rather than code.

"What is going on?" she asked both men.

"There might have been some ships wrecked on the coast between Larnaca and Limassol, my love." Reza responded.

85

"That would get the emperor going very quickly, plunder being his main motive."

Talon nodded his head in reluctant agreement. "I hope instead it was a pirate ship that foundered. They are a plague upon our shores," he said, "especially along the southern coast."

There was as soft knock on the door, and Rav'an stepped in. "Are you having a conference?" she demanded with a smile.

"No, but it might be a good thing to start the day with one." Talon smiled at her. "We can go downstairs to the Solarium where we will be more comfortable, if you like."

Rav'an and Jannat nodded agreement, whereupon they all trooped down the narrow steps of the tower, along an echoing corridor and into the large room they had dubbed the Solarium.

The storm had passed, leaving in its wake some damage, but not, Talon was glad to note, to the castle, other than a few shutters. However, messages were coming in from the two villages of trees down and some dykes damaged, and not a few of the precious grape vines torn up. Many roofs would need repairs, but otherwise, they had escaped the full fury of the storm during the night, as it had come in from the south; hence, the mountains had sheltered the villages and the harbor. The ships inside the harbor and those within the protection of the stone walls had suffered no damage.

However, there was something more pressing, which Talon wanted to talk about. He summoned his most senior retainers, Yosef and Dar'an, who brought with them the huge Saxon, Brandt. The archers were already out in the woods scouting for any unwelcome visitors, accompanied by several of the younger Companions.

When everyone was settled, Talon spoke up. "There appear to have been some shipwrecks on the southern coast, and while that in itself is not so unusual, there appears to be something different about these ships."

When the exclamations had died down, he glanced at Reza and nodded. Reza rose to his feet and addressed the assembly.

"As you know, we have, with the help of Dimitri in Famagusta and Boethius in Paphos, established spies in both Larnaca and Limassol. They have been taught to be observant and inconspicuous. They also keep pigeons." There was a general chuckle at that. Jannat had her hands full these days with courier pigeons arriving so often.

Reza continued, "What we are hearing is very disturbing. There were two, maybe even three, shipwrecks in the vicinity of Limassol and Larnaca. But these are no merchantmen." He glanced at Jannat and Rav'an. "They were full of men and horses."

There was a startled silence, and then everyone began to speak at the same time. "Is it an invasion?" Brandt growled; the obvious question. Talon shook his head and held up his hand for silence.

"No Brandt, but it is a good question. At first, we thought the Byzantine Emperor had sent yet another fleet. Our informant in Limassol, however, tells us that the survivors speak a language which they cannot understand. One note told us that these were tall men with light-colored hair."

Brandt's brow furrowed. "Men, Saxons, like me?" he queried.

"It is possible, but I suspect they are Normans," Talon responded. "These ships might have come from Sicily. What we are puzzled about is that the emperor's mercenaries slaughtered many of them on the beaches where their ships foundered, but then took some prisoners, who are now being held in the Limassol prison."

"I thought Isaac had an alliance with King William of Sicily," Rav'an spoke up.

"As did we," Talon confirmed, "but with this emperor, treachery is his first instinct. Perhaps he has disregarded that alliance and was just looking for plunder. We need to know more."

There was another long silence after this, as everyone looked at the two leaders.

"What do you want to do, Lord?" Yosef spoke up. His lean dark features were eager. He and Dar'an were veterans of many assignments. Talon smiled warmly at Yosef.

"We were discussing whether we should send out a scouting party. There is some urgency to this, but whoever goes must not be discovered by the emperor or his minions."

Yosef grinned and glanced at Dar'an, who grinned back. He nodded. "I understand, Lord. We will leave at once."

"Dar'an, I will need you to remain here, in charge." Talon smiled at the crestfallen expression on Dar'an's face. "I should not have to point out that the castle has to be protected by someone of your caliber, Dar'an. The Lady Rav'an will want it to be so." Dar'an reluctantly nodded, but he was clearly disappointed.

"Dar'an, Lady Jannat and I will be honored to be under your protection. It is no small responsibility that Talon has imposed upon you," Rav'an chided him gently with a smile.

He shifted uncomfortably, but then grinned, mollified by her compliment. "You are right, my lady. It is I who am honored."

Talon glanced at the young man. "Good. We rely upon you to protect, not just the castle, Dar'an, but to watch for trouble down at the villages, too."

"Yosef, take two of the other Companions with you, Junayd and Khuzaymah, and take good, fast horses," Reza said. "We should not be too far behind you, but we will be heading for the forests to the north of the town if we miss each other."

Talon nodded. "I shall be bringing Brandt and his Saxons with me."

The two men were gone in an instant, leaving the rest to ponder the situation.

"Brandt, take a seat and have some tea," Rav'an told the huge man, who looked hopelessly embarrassed. He lowered his bulk onto a huge cushion and took a small bowl of tea from her. It seemed like a thimble in his huge hand, which trembled. He worshipped Rav'an, but was hopelessly awestruck in her presence, no matter what she tried to do to make him feel at ease.

"You would never think this man a great warrior in battle, would you?" Reza said to the women, in Farsi. "He is terrified of you, my princess."

"Reza, be nice," Jannat said with a sweet smile at Brandt. Either of the two women could have asked Brandt to jump out the window, and he would not have hesitated.

Talon turned to the Saxon. "Brandt, it is no secret that neither you nor your men like these people, but if, indeed, these are Normans, we have to go and take a look at them. We will leave before noon and then wait for Yosef and the others just outside of Limassol. So now I want you to muster the entire Saxon Guard and have them prepared to leave at a moment's notice. I have an uncomfortable feeling about all this. While you are at it, I would like to have some support for your men from amongst the trained footmen that gave us such a good demonstration the other day."

Brandt had slurped his tea in one gulp, wincing because it burned his tongue. Now he struggled to his feet to tower over everyone. "I shall go immediately and get them ready, Lord." He appeared desperate to leave this unfamiliar world of domesticity.

Talon let him go. "Thank you, Brandt. Also, send off a boy to find those two Welshmen and their men. We might need them too."

Brandt nodded, trying not to scowl, and left. Talon smiled inwardly. The rivalry between Brandt and the two mischievous Welshmen was a source of amusement to everyone. But Talon had never had to intervene. Somehow, the three men rubbed along comfortably enough, despite their loud arguments and insults, usually instigated by the Welshmen, who could not resist poking fun at their friend, as well as everything and everyone else.

"He is so bashful, that man." Jannat said to the others with a wide smile. "Yet, you tell me there is no one to match him in battle, Talon."

"At Hattin he could clear a path with that ax of his like no one else!" Talon gave a dry laugh at the memory, but then became more serious. "If these are Normans from Sicily, then I am curious as to why they have come here. There has been much talk of the king of England and France making another Crusade. I wish I knew more!" he lamented.

He had only a few solid contacts outside Cyprus since the demise of the Kingdom of Jerusalem. Salah ad-Din and his people were everywhere and, while they were not brutal to their conquered people, no one wanted to be caught spying. The Jews, whom he had earlier been able to rely upon, were trickling back into the cities, but not in large numbers—a few merchants only, and, like all merchants in the region, they were skittish and prepared to leave at the first sign of danger. Few merchants thrived in warlike conditions.

"I think we should take some of the village soldiers with us, Talon," Reza said. "I agree, the Saxons are a formidable force, but the emperor has many more men. I'd like to think that if we do run headlong into him, we can fight our way out of trouble."

"I agree," Talon nodded soberly. "That will give us some of the Companions, the Saxons, and the Kantara footmen. It should be enough, if we also take the archers with us."

"You will not leave us helpless to defend ourselves?" Rav'an demanded sharply.

Talon shook his head emphatically. "No, my dear. I will leave Dar'an with you, most of the Companions, and Palladium, who, as you know, has only to smile and dragons faint away! Dewi and Caradog can decide who stays here from amongst the archers." He paused and thought. "At the very first sign of trouble, send up the rockets and bring as many villagers in as possible, then lock the castle down. Dar'an will know what to do after that."

*****

In the harbor of Limassol to the south of Kantara, the three ships anchored, well out of bow shot in the bay, tugging gently at their anchors. One of the ships was very low in the water. It was sinking, which caused much concern and not a little panic among its cargo of knights and soldiers. After much frantic activity, the ship's boats were lowered into the water and the crew and the passengers--lords, knights, priests, and attendants--were ferried from the stricken vessel to the larger remaining ship.

Standing on the steering deck, Queen Joanna contemplated the disaster with dismay. They watched as the men from the other ship clambered aboard her own vessel, carrying whatever they could salvage of their belongings.

"I hope that our vessel is not so threatened?" she demanded of the captain.

"No, my lady, we are in good shape in that regard, thank God. Although, I have to admit, I am surprised. The storm was one of the worst I have encountered at this end of the Middle Sea," he replied respectfully. "However, the mast and that spar up there," he pointed to the tangled mess high above them where men were busy, "is in need of urgent repair. We cannot sail in this condition. It would be too dangerous to venture into the deep seas before I have shored it up.”

The captain was in awe of this fine lady who, until recently, had been the queen of Sicily. Her long blonde hair was tidy and coiled, and it framed a still young and very beautiful oval face, wherein were set piercing light blue eyes and a firm but sensuous mouth, above which sat a somewhat aquiline nose. At this moment, Joanna was frowning, displaying two small creases between her brows.

“God’s grace!” she muttered to herself. Then, she took a folded and sealed letter from her sleeve and handed it to him. “I have written a letter to my brother, the king,” she told him, “telling him where we are and saying that we are safe for the time being, but to come quickly. I do not wish to be detained here for any longer than I must. The Usurper has a reputation.”

The captain touched his forehead with his knuckle. “I shall have it taken at once to the caravel over there and order them to sail immediately, my lady,” he told her.

Within half an hour, with the letter safely delivered into the hands of its captain, the caravel hauled anchor, raised its sail, and began to move out of the harbor, driven by a brisk offshore wind. Joanna watched it go with a prayer on her lips.

She heard a hesitant step coming up the gangway behind her and turned to greet a young woman, who dropped her a short curtsey and asked in a low voice, “God’s grace, Lady Joanna, I am so very glad to be in one piece. Will we go ashore to rest? I am tired of the sea and its moods. I cannot remember the last time I was so sick.” She sounded exhausted and her tone was plaintive. The speaker was Princess Berengaria, Richard’s betrothed, a dark beauty from the Spanish court. She was very young. Her black tresses were bound up under a smudged wimple that had once been white. Her clothing had suffered considerably from the effects of the two storms and the long confinement in their cabin. She was to be the future queen of England. Joanna considered her pretty, but timid as a mouse.

Joanna was made of sterner stuff; she was, after all, the daughter of Eleanor of Aquitaine, the former queen of England and Richard's mother. She turned away to stare at the increased activity between the stricken ship and her own. The shore beckoned and she, too, longed to be on dry land; the last couple of weeks at sea had been a very unpleasant ordeal. However, this was Cyprus, ruled by a usurper named Isaac Komnenos, who had a foul reputation. She seriously doubted that it would be wise to disembark just yet.

Just then the lookout shouted down to the deck that they were about to receive a visitor. A boat was pulling away from the wooden jetty of the harbor basin and heading in their direction.

"We shall know, soon enough, what kind of reception we are to receive," Joanna told her young companion. The captain, Adalgrimus, was alerted. He ordered the ship's crew to stand by, and the crossbow men to load their cumbersome crossbows and be ready. Several knights took up station to greet the visitor.

The boat hailed the ship and a short man, who had a balding head and a beautifully embroidered coat with wide sleeves and silk slippers, asked permission to board, speaking in accented French. Thereupon, he clambered up the steps to arrive breathless on the main deck, where he paused to look around. His demeanor was haughty and arrogant, which caused Joanna to dislike him immediately and feel wary. A Byzantine was a Byzantine, she decided.

The official addressed the captain, who stood in front of the cluster of curious knights. Even drawing himself up to his full height, the official only came up to the shoulders of most of the knights, who were of solid Norman stock, and he was clearly somewhat intimidated. His French was halting, but clear enough.

"You are intruders within the lands of His Most Gracious Majesty, Emperor Isaac Komnenos. You must surrender your ships and put yourselves at his mercy. Failure to—" he didn't finish.

A sharp clear voice from above interrupted, which made him stop and peer up at the steering deck with an astonished expression on his plump, smooth face.

"You!" Joanna called down from the steering deck rail. She spoke in fluent Greek. "I am Queen Joanna of Sicily, wife of the late King William. Is this the way you treat your allies? Go back to the emperor and tell him that I refuse to submit to his outrageous request and I shall remain here on my ship until its repairs are made, after which, I shall leave for Acre, where my brother, King Richard, awaits me—King Richard of England. You *do* understand?" she added, pointedly pursing her lips and lifting her chin while staring down at him, as though daring him to dispute her words.

The Cypriot official might have been far better dressed than anyone else on board with all his silk and finery, but there was no doubting the authority of the woman glaring down her nose at him. He gurgled and went very red with embarrassment, but then collected himself and bowed low.

"Forgive me, my lady!" he called up at her in a high-pitched voice as he bowed deeply again. "I had not known. I shall inform His Majesty at once." He glanced back at the forbidding stares of the tall, bearded knights standing in front of him, and shuffled backwards, feeling for the opening in the side of the ship with one hand. He nearly missed it, and would have fallen overboard into the sea, had not the captain seized him by the sleeve and steadied him. After another nervous glance up at the queen, the official scrambled down to his boat and was rowed furiously back to shore.

"God damned eunuch!" someone shouted to the departing boat.

"What's a eunuch?" a younger voice asked. This elicited raucous laughter from the men on the main deck, followed by vulgar explanations accompanied by rude gestures. The buzz of conversation continued as everyone on board watched the unfortunate official disappear, but then an event occurred which silenced then all. The ship that had accompanied Joanna's from Sicily, already very low in the water, gave a loud groan, then subsided slowly into the harbor waters with a hiss of escaping air and the gurgle of seawater rushing into its bowels. As the vessel settled out of sight into the depths of the bay, the only thing that remained visible above water was the very top of the mast.

Joanna wondered if this might be an omen, but then turned and watched as the caravel disappeared over the horizon, heading for Acre. There was still hope. Richard, once he knew where she was, would come for her at once. She prayed it would be soon. They now had far too many people on the ship, and they were low on fresh water.

*****

The visit by the official and the sinking of a ship had not gone unnoticed by an individual standing on the walls of Limassol. He casually walked away from the excited guards and loiterers who were still gawping at the remaining vessel in the harbor and hurried to his home. Very soon, a pigeon flew away and, after circling for a minute, began to fly northeast toward the mountains.

Chapter 9

Rescue

We, the rescued,
From whose hollow bones death had begun to
*   whittle his flutes,*
And on whose sinews he had already stroked his bow—
Our bodies continue to lament
With their mutilated music.
We, the rescued.
— Nelly Sachs

Talon and Reza crouched just inside the border of the forest of trees that came down from the low hills behind them to within two hundred paces of what passed for a highway in Cyprus. To their right, they could clearly see the walled town of Limassol, while, to their immediate front, opening to the south, was the bay. The road was a well-worn track that, some time long ago, had been paved with stones by the Romans. Now, with most of the flags gone, it was dotted with pot holes and muddy puddles from the storm.

They watched the activity taking place on the other side of the road nearest to the sea with interest. From their point of concealment they could see men on horses supervising the work of a gang of prisoners laboring in the hot afternoon sun to construct what appeared to be a low dyke.

The armed men were brutally free with their whips and abuse, as the unfortunate prisoners carried rocks and barrows of sand and dirt to form a wall that stretched from the walls of Limassol for some distance along the borders of the bay.

Talon and his men also noted with interest that there was a large, strange ship lying at anchor in the middle of the bay. This was the ship that the message had briefly described. The ship's banners denoted some high-ranking person, but no one knew who it might be. The men overseeing the work on shore were also observing the ship with some intensity, and seemed in a hurry to complete as much of the wall as they could before darkness fell, within roughly three hours' time.

"Why are they building a wall? It's just a dyke, and they are tearing up what is left of the road to build it," Reza commented as he peered out from the dense undergrowth. Crouching alongside were their Companions and the Saxons, with the Welsh archers close by, ready, on Talon's orders, to shoot should the need arise.

"It is almost as though they are expecting an invasion," Junayd observed. Their voices were slightly muffled because Talon insisted that all the Companions, including the archers, cover the lower part of their faces whenever they left Kantara. Emulating Talon and Reza, most of them wore a loose turban and a *shemaugh*.

"Even that coward of an emperor should be able to deal with a single shipload of enemies," Yosef commented scornfully from his position next to a large tree. "But see! Those poor men building the wall are not Greeks. They look more like Brandt and his men, Lord. Except they are in very poor condition," he finished, sounding doubtful.

Even as he spoke, one of the prisoners tripped and fell, dropping the large rock he had been carrying. Even at this distance, the men hidden in the trees could see that he was unable to regain his feet. One of the guards dismounted, strode over to him, then kicked him in the side, but to no avail. The observers then saw the guard draw his sword and drive it into the back of the prisoner, who jerked as he died. They could all hear the choked-off scream. The man who had committed the killing shouted at the other prisoners as he wiped his blade on the dead man's rags, and the whips cracked. The work began again.

The man who had killed the prisoner decided to relieve himself, and it was while he was doing so that Talon decided he had seen enough.

"Reza, I suspect those unfortunates are the survivors of the shipwrecks we have heard about. If this continues, there won't be any of them left! I don't believe they are pirates either, or they would look more like the people of this region, and I imagine that the emperor ordered this."

As he spoke, Maymun called out in a low tone. "Lord Talon! A horseman comes, riding hard from Larnaca."

Sure enough, a rider was galloping along the road, splashing through the puddles, his horse's hooves throwing up a spray of muddy water. The rider hauled his horse to a halt in front of one of the guards and a lively discussion ensued, with much arm waving and pointing, both at the ship and the prisoners.

"It would seem that things are about to become livelier," Reza commented.

"That is what is worrying me," Talon responded. "They don't appear to have much regard for their prisoners, which tells me that something bad is going to happen to them before long, unless we do something about it."

"Well, Father, the gates of Limassol have just opened, and a lot more of those mercenaries are coming out, along with many citizens," Rostam stated, pointing toward the town.

A group of well-armed men were now approaching, leading a large crowd of citizens armed with a mixture of spears and swords. Not many had shields, and even fewer wore helmets.

Talon realized that, if he wanted to save the prisoners, he might be too late. His own little army, while very well armed and experienced, was considerably smaller than that mob. He noticed with concern that the prisoners were being herded into a group and surrounded by their mounted captors. There was an ominous look about the men who were watching the prisoners. It was time for a decision, and he felt strongly that he should intervene, if he could.

"Do you think they are about to kill the prisoners, Brother?" Reza asked the question that was on his mind.

"Father! I think they are about to do so," Rostam called. "Look! Their swords are out!"

"Dewy and Caradog, take down those men on the horses. Do it now!" Talon ordered. His archers had been ready. Almost on the instant, he heard the twang of his archers' bow strings, and arrows arced out of the forest into the afternoon sky. From where he crouched, Talon watched the slim dark streaks as they descended upon the unsuspecting victims.

There were seven men on horseback guarding the prisoners when Talon gave the order. Six of the horsemen were struck; of the men on foot, the one who had killed a prisoner and five others were slain by arrows.

Easy work for the Welsh, Talon thought, but he was impressed that their new recruits had done so well. All the men had been tumbled off their mounts and remained motionless, while the one remaining rider gave a shout of surprise and fear, but then reacted very quickly. He hauled his horse around as an arrow meant for him hissed by. He crouched in his saddle, put spurs to his horse, and raced off, back towards Larnaca. Dewy sent an arrow after the man and cursed as it missed.

"Should have let me do it!" Caradog stated with a nod in the direction of the fleeing man. Dewy shrugged, annoyed, and would have tried again, but Talon called, "Leave it, Dewy. We have to deal with that mob over there. Everyone, out of the woods and form up on the road! Quick as you can! Brandt, lead with the Saxons! We have to put ourselves between the prisoners and those people from the town! I will not have a massacre taking place under my nose!"

His men needed no further orders. The Saxon contingent rushed out of the woods and ran hard the two hundred or so paces, to place themselves in a double line on the grassland just to the inland side of the road. The surprised and shocked prisoners huddled together and fearfully watched their arrival. First, their tormentors had died under a hail of arrows, and now, these light-haired men were charging out of the woods.

Talon and his companions, meanwhile, remounted and cantered their horses out of the woods behind the archers, who were chasing after the Saxons. He and his small army turned their backs on the prisoners and faced toward Limassol and the hundred or so citizens of that town, who were led by a solid group of mercenaries, clad in their bright bronze armor and gleaming weapons.

"Hmm, this might have been just a little rash, Brother?" Reza murmured as he loosened his sword in its scabbard and drew his bow from under his left thigh. The noisy mob drew to a halt about fifty paces away.

Talon swallowed. He, too, thought he might have been too impulsive, but they were there now, and committed. "I do not think we have much choice in the matter, Brother. I am sure Rostam was right. They were about to kill the prisoners, now that the work has, for the most part, been completed." Talon gestured toward the wall. "That is the way of this emperor of ours."

He cast a look behind him and motioned for the prisoners to stay where they were. Some had had the presence of mind to seize the dead men's weapons and were about to join his men, but he didn't want to have to worry about that bunch of scarecrows while he was dealing with an angry mob, which might easily, if well led, overwhelm his little army.

Angry the Greeks certainly appeared to be. The shock of witnessing the slaughter of the guards appeared to have worn off somewhat, and their leaders, having recovered, now began to harangue them and point scornfully at the deceptively small group of men, huddled behind large shields, standing in their way.

"D'you think they were coming to join in the killing, or were they being brought to man the walls?" Reza asked.

"I think they are expecting something to happen over there," Talon pointed with his chin toward the ship.

He looked over at his Saxons, formed into two lines of fifteen men each, the one right behind the other in the configuration of a small shield wall. On each side of the Saxons were more of the Kantara foot, who had been trained by Brandt and his men. Brandt called out several names, whereupon four of his Saxon men detached themselves and joined the Kantara men, who gave a low cheer. Talon nodded his head with approval. Now they had solid leaders supporting them. This was, for the Kantara villagers, their first real test in battle. A good number of them were probably scared silly, but the calm of the Saxon veterans, who had all been in many engagements, reassured them.

"That man who escaped is going to bring the hornets back with him, I imagine," Junayd commented, his eyes locked on the noisy mob before them, engaged in jeering and waving weapons in a threatening manner at the ominously silent strangers.

"Which is why we must deal with these people quickly," Talon replied. "If we don't, we will be squashed like bugs between that angry crowd and the emperor's soldiers. Brandt," he called out over the shouts, "are you and your men ready?"

Brandt gave him a grin, pulled his helmet down more firmly onto his head and tightened the straps of his cheek guards. "Ready, Lord!" he called back. "Anytime you'd like." He shouted in his own language to his men, who greeted him with a roar.

Talon didn't need to tell Dewy and Caradog where they and their archers should place themselves. These men swiftly took up position behind the Saxons and prepared their bows and quivers.

The thirty Saxons and twenty Kantara men, ten on either side of the Saxon van, were now drawn up, facing the soldiers and citizenry on the road to Limassol.

"They certainly don't look very friendly," Reza observed to Talon.

"These Saxons will put the fear of God into them. You mark my words, Brother," Talon replied.

The noisy Limassol citizens, who were being joined every minute by others, anticipated an easy victory over this odd-looking group. However, Brandt had something in mind that would change their point of view very quickly.

"You, archers!" Brandt bellowed over the noise. "Be ready when I give the word!"

"Aye, Saxon, we'll wait for you," Caradog shouted back. He muttered something to his group, whereupon, they all knocked an arrow and then waited in silence.

Brandt shouted to his men, who roared something very rude, whirled around, and bent over to pull their tunics up, baring their backsides to the enemy. There was a stunned silence from the Limassol citizens and their mercenary leaders as they saw this strange and unsettling vision.

Talon rolled his eyes and clutched his forehead with his right hand. Although his voice was muffled by the *shemaugh* he wore, everyone heard him say out loud, to the world at large, "Do I deserve this? They don't really belong to me!"

Reza snorted with laughter. "I am terrified, and they are not even showing their asses to me!" he gasped.

"Hey!" Dewy shouted. "You could have warned us, Saxon! We want to see your lovely asses, too!" He cackled with laughter and nudged Caradog. "There are some good-looking bums in that lot!" Caradog snickered.

Rostam and the others were bent over their horses' necks, choking with laughter. The situation was very serious, but the Saxons had just taken everyone by surprise.

"I cannot think of a sight more calculated to bring about alarm and despondency," Talon observed.

The Saxons, having displayed their backsides to the enemy, whirled back to face them. Their large round shields clashed together to interlock and form a perfect shield wall. Then they began to shout imprecations and insults at the stunned-looking, and now not-so-noisy mob.

Threats and the crash of weapons hammered on shields was just the opening move; the line of Saxons surged forward. They stamped each pace, striking their shields with their swords as they did so. Their long hair fanned out behind them.

"Reza, you hold the right wing with Yosef and Maymun. I'll be on the left with Rostam and Junayd." Talon turned in the saddle to address the other horsemen, who were a mixture of their own townsmen and the Companions.

"Our work is to ensure that no one gets past the Saxons," he called. "Half of you with me, and the other half with Reza. Those with bows, use them well. Quickly now!" He urged his horse into a canter to arrive on the left wing of the Saxon phalanx. "Keep pace with Brandt!" Talon called to the horsemen with him. "No one is to get ahead and risk being cut off!" While he was confident that the roaring Saxons, backed by their yelling Kantara footmen, would crush any opposition to their front, there might be some courageous mercenary who would take down a lone horseman, should the opportunity present itself.

The Companions on horseback and the archers were already inflicting casualties on the enemy as the gap closed. The first to go down were the crossbow men, cut down before they could reload their cumbersome but deadly weapons, by the longbow archers under the charge of Dewy and Caradog.

Then arrows began to hiss and land in the bodies amongst the Greeks with a thump, in this or that person. The next to fall were some of the more demonstrative mercenary leaders, which demoralized the mob. As more arrows began to find their marks, the remaining mercenaries began to look uncertain and noticeably less confident as they cowered behind their small bronze shields. Seeing their leaders going down one by one served to alarm and confuse the townspeople all the more.

The range shrank to less than thirty paces, so it was hard to miss their targets. Brandt, upon a wave from Talon, shouted another command, and the men of the shield wall smoothly formed a wedge, with Brandt, Aefstan and Eadwine positioned at the center. These men brandished long-handled axes, which they could use to hook a victim and haul him into the range of a spear or sword, where a Saxon could finish off the screaming man or youth.

Talon saw the Greeks waver under the rain of arrows, and decided that it was time.

"Charge them, Brandt!" he called to his commander. "We'll take the wings to make sure none of that rabble gets past you!"

Brandt waved to indicate that he had heard and shouted another order. The Saxons broke into a trot. Still bellowing their fearsome battle cries and rattling their swords on their shields, they closed the gap very quickly. So fast were they that they took the citizens by surprise and smashed into the disorderly ranks, taking down many men. Those who survived the initial charge were utterly terrified, and desperately tried to get away from this awful machine-like mass that killed whoever stood in its way. Some even tried to climb over their own comrades as they attempted in vain to get away from the deadly shield wall.

"Brandt, try not to kill them all! Just go for the mercenaries!" Talon bellowed, as he hacked down a soldier who had stood his ground. His Japanese sword cut through the mercenary's shield, taking his arm off. The man went down with a scream. Next Talon whacked a Greek townsman, who was already fleeing, on the back of the head with the flat of his sword. The man tumbled to the ground with a cry, rolling around and clutching his head.

"Don't kill them all, Lord?" Brandt inquired, as he ducked a savage swipe from one of the mercenaries. He almost cut him in half with the casual back-handed blow of his huge ax. By this time, there were few mercenaries standing, so the Saxons gleefully went after the Greek citizenry, who could not run fast enough, and beat to the ground those they caught, with the flats of their swords. There were those who made the mistake of trying to defend themselves; they were slaughtered. There was much blood, and the Saxons roared loud enough to be heard within the distant town walls.

Brandt turned his attention to another larger man, who appeared determined to try his chances against him. The luckless soldier lunged with a spear that Brandt casually took on his shield, brushing the other's shield aside, leaving his attacker wide open. His ax came down on the man's shoulder, and cut so deep that the arm was severed from the body. There was a spray of blood and a roar of satisfaction from the Saxon, as he hauled his ax away and went after more victims.

Talon had barely anyone to fight. Rostam and Junayd, flanking him, appeared have taken it upon themselves to kill or disarm anyone who was foolish enough to come anywhere near Talon.

"Will you and Junayd stop flailing about in front of me and let me *do* something!" Talon snapped irritably to his son, who laughed back. Junayd looked sheepish, but Rostam responded.

"Mother told us to look after you, Father," he called over his shoulder. He then turned away a clumsy thrust from one of the few remaining mercenaries and spit the luckless man, sliding his sword between the metal plates of the jerkin. The man looked surprised and then choked before he sagged to the ground. Rostam and Junayd appeared to be enjoying the battle and dispatched several other victims in quick succession.

On the other side of the shield wall, Reza hacked at whatever came his way, but not many wanted to engage him. His sword flickered in the waning sunlight, turning red as he dispatched one man after another. Talon scowled. He had been looking forward, at the least, to a little battle, he thought to himself morosely. Now his wife was telling his own son to keep him out of trouble. Even so, he was quietly very pleased with how quickly his men were turning the attack into a rout.

The citizens of Limassol, having lost most of their mercenary leaders and many of their own, realized that they had no hope of stopping this juggernaut of screaming, blond-haired, berserker warriors, deadly archers, and wickedly agile horsemen. The men in front were pushing against the men behind, with the Saxons and the Kantara soldiers hacking and stabbing at their backs. Panic ensued. The shouts of abuse they had thrown at the tiny army they had formerly sneered at changed to wails of fear and screams of agony. The citizens of Limassol broke and then fled for their lives, toward the shelter of their town.

It crossed Talon's mind, briefly, to take the town. It would be something of a prize, but he knew he could not hold it, and wasn't inclined to loot it. Furthermore, he suspected the emperor was not far off. Instead, he edged his excited mount nearer to Brandt and called out.

"Just chase them off, but don't follow them, Brandt. I want to deal with the prisoners!"

Brandt waved his bloody ax to show he understood and bellowed another order. As smoothly as a greased wheel, the shield wall became a line again, which trotted forward another thirty paces. The Saxons dispatched any of the mercenaries who had not left the field. Those citizens who were wounded and in the path of the big men were trampled on, regardless, their wails adding to the general din. Some of the citizens were taken prisoner. The pathetic huddle waited to hear their fate, as Talon and Reza rode up.

"Go home," Talon called out in Greek. "Get out of here and *don't* come back."

Reza nodded to the Kantara horsemen who had rounded them up. "Let them go," he ordered. The citizens took off for the town as fast as their legs could carry them, followed by the jeers of the Kantara men.

Talon, rode forward, ahead of the shield wall. "Let them all go home!' he called to the Companions, who were still chasing some of the citizens about.

"Reza, let's take a look at the Normans. Rostam!" he shouted, over the groans and screams of the wounded. "Help Brandt rescue our wounded. Dispatch any of the mercenaries."

"Yes, Father," Rostam called back, and dismounted with his companions to go and help the Saxons with their grisly task.

"He has to learn some time that it's the aftermath of a battle which is the really ugly part," Talon said quietly to Reza, as they made their way back across the former battlefield towards the huddle of ragged men, who were clustered near their work site. "How many did we lose?" he asked.

"You might not believe this, Brother, but from what I can tell, we have one twisted ankle—one of the Saxons slipped on something—and two lightly wounded Kantara men at arms. Amazing!" Reza said with an incredulous shake of his head.

Talon and Reza stopped their mounts a few paces away from the two dozen or so prisoners and stared down at them. They were mostly taller than their captors had been, and certainly a good deal more pallid. Most were, in fact, not unlike the Saxons who served Talon. Having already surmised that they were probably Normans, he couldn't help but wonder how they had arrived in this predicament.

Part II

War comes to Cyprus

Chapter 10

Normans

*"The Saxon is not like us Normans. His manners are
  not so polite.
But he never means anything serious till he talks
  about justice and right.
When he stands like an ox in the furrow—with his
  sullen set eyes on your own,
And grumbles, 'This isn't fair dealing,' my son, leave
  the Saxon alone!"*
—Rudyard Kipling

Talon and Reza contemplated the prisoners in silence; finally, one of the prisoners walked forward and stood in front of Talon. He bowed respectfully and spoke French. Talon understood; Reza, however, unused to the accent, found it somewhat more difficult.

"You have just won a great victory!" the man remarked with a wry grin. "I doubt I could have faced such a terrible sight."

Talon laughed. "They are Saxons. You are Normans, if I am not mistaken, and if my Welsh archers are correct, there is no love lost between your people. I'd be very polite to them, if I were you."

The man bent his head and smiled. "At this moment, I simply thank God that you and your Saxon warriors appeared from nowhere, and we are at least saved from this slavery. What do you intend to do with us? Are you... are you Greeks or Saracen?"

"This is Lord Talon de Gilles!" said a strong voice near Talon. He glanced down to find his commander, Brandt, standing next to his horse. "You would do well to mind your manners!" He was glowering at the prisoners. The fact that he was a huge man and armed with a bloody ax and a large round shield that was covered with other men's blood enhanced his menacing looks.

Talon sighed and said, "This is Brandt, the leader of the shield wall. He has no love for the Norman kind. You may thank him for your deliverance, however."

"I certainly do, Lord," the man gave Brandt a polite duck of his head. "I am Captain Willimus of the ship, *Seynte Mariecog,* that was driven onto the rocks east of that town." He gestured toward Limassol. "Two days ago, Lord. I—we are all so very grateful for your help. God be praised that He brought you to save us!"

By this time, Rostam and his companions, Junayd, Yosef, and Maymun, had joined them, along with the other Companions.

"One or two of you should ride toward Larnaca and find out where the emperor might be," Talon murmured to the riders. "I don't want to be surprised by any of his nasty people. These prisoners don't look capable of defending themselves from a more disciplined army, and we are too few to have a confrontation with him out in the open. Furthermore, we cannot take these men back with us."

Maymun and two other Companions immediately broke away and galloped off in the direction of Larnaca to keep watch for any trouble from that quarter. Talon returned his attention to the prisoner.

"Did you come from Sicily?"

"We came through Sicily, from England. Do you know who is in that ship over there, Lord?" Captain Willimus turned and waved his hand toward the bay where the large ship was anchored.

"My lord, as surely as I stand before you, I could swear that the ship is that of the sister of King Richard of England, and she is taking Princess Berengaria with her to the Holy Land."

Talon and Reza glanced at one another with surprise. "How do you know this, and for that matter, what brought you here to Cyprus in the first place?" Talon demanded.

"King Richard of England is sailing to Palestine, Lord. We are on a Holy Crusade. The storms took us off our course." The captain sighed. "There were two big storms. The one sent us off course to the south and the other threw us onto the rocks of this cursed coast. That Queen Joanna of Sicily and her ward survived can only be due to God's mercy. But I am very sure, Lord. That is her ship; I have seen her pennant at the mast head."

"How many of you are there here?" Reza asked.

"We are about three dozen, we who survived the wrecks and then the slaughter that followed after, on the beaches," the captain replied bitterly. "They are barbarians, those people! They murdered our men when we came ashore!" He waved angrily in the general direction of the town.

"That sounds like the emperor's mercenaries to me," Reza murmured. "The townspeople are too craven to have done so on their own."

Talon glanced again at the ship anchored in the bay. The sun's rays were reflected on the still agitated waters of the bay, as there was still a brisk breeze, and the ship appeared to hover on the water like a mirage. He searched the beach and found what he had hoped to find. There were a number of fishing boats drawn up on the sand.

"Are you and your comrades able to row or to sail out to that ship?" he asked, pointing towards the vessel. By this time, the other prisoners had drawn near and they heard him. "We can row back to England if we have to!" one of them called out. The others sighed wistful agreement. Many had blood-stained bandages wrapped around their limbs and were in poor condition, but Talon knew the only way to protect them was to send them to the ship and hope that the captain knew what he was talking about.

"Then you have your chance. There are some boats on the beach, Captain," he addressed the leader. "They will have to suffice. Go, and be quick about it." He glanced off to the east where he could see his own people, who were already racing back toward him. "My scouts are coming back in a hurry, and that is not a sign of good news. I cannot protect you here; we are too far from my castle, but God willing, the emperor will not be inclined to resort to piracy and abduction where the king's sister is concerned, so the ship is your best option."

"First, tell me from where *you* have come, Lord?" the captain demanded. "I must know!"

"Why, we have all come from the castle of Kantara. That is Lord Talon's keep, and the emperor hates us for it!" Rostam interjected.

"You had better go now. We cannot protect you further at this time," Talon told the prisoners. "Go with God."

The Normans needed no further persuasion. "Run!" one of them shouted. "Thank you, Lord. God send you a thousand blessings!" someone else shouted, as the excited Normans rushed for the beach, which was only a hundred paces away.

"You saved our lives, Lord." Captain Willimus said. "I shall make it known to the king's sister, and the king, himself, if God permits." He turned and ran off to join his companions, who were struggling to push the heavy boats into the water.

Talon noticed one of his men, the limping Saxon, being helped along by his comrades and called over to his riders.

"Put Hereweald and the other two wounded men on horses, Yosef. Then detail three of your men to escort them back to the castle. When they get there, they are to round up fifty more men, fully armed, to come back as soon as possible. I don't think we are done here yet."

"Very good, Lord." Yosef immediately gave orders for mounts to be found, and the wounded were soon heading toward the woods, where they would find paths that led to the castle. Talon was sure they would be grilled by a curious Dar'an when they arrived, and men would be sent, but he was not sure what would occur next. Time was running out. He and his men needed to disappear before they were caught out in the open.

He glanced down toward the beach, where the Normans were struggling to launch the fishing vessels. "Better give them some help, Brandt," Talon suggested. "Use our Kantara men at arms to assist your own men."

Brandt scowled, but then he grinned. "Very well, Lord. Come on, men, let's get rid of these fucking Normans, eh? Push 'em out to sea, and may the sea gods gobble them all up!"

He and his men joined the Normans in heaving and hauling the heavy boats into the water, and then pushed them off. Oars were found, and even a sail of sorts, so that before long the crowded boats full of Normans were rowing hard and moving steadily out into the bay.

"May the lice on your heads go south and eat your balls off!" shouted one of the Saxons. There was a laugh and an unintelligible reply from the rowers. Then one of the Saxons decided to bare his backside, to the roars of laughter from the other Saxons, but Brandt raised his arm and put a stop to any more demonstrations of affection.

Talon clutched his forehead with one hand. "Oh, God, forgive us!" he groaned.

Reza laughed. "I hope your Saxons don't do this in front of the Norman king, if he ever shows up," he remarked.

"*My* Saxons, now, are they?" Talon growled.

Reza laughed, then asked, "Do you know this queen, Brother?" he asked.

"No, but I know of her. She is married to William the Norman, who has just died, if the rumors are true. I had no idea that she was on her way to Palestine I did meet her brother Richard once, however," he said ruminatively, remembering the encounter. "It was a very long time ago. It might well be that there really is another Crusade in the making. I do not see that as the best of news."

By this time, Maymun and his two companions had ridden up on their blowing horses. "You were right to send us to watch, Lord," Maymun said, and pointed to the east. "There are horsemen and infantry, and they are hastening toward us. There have to be several score of them, perhaps even several hundred, and they are less than half a league away. That Greek who escaped must have warned them."

Reza raised himself in his stirrups and shouted toward the beach. "Brandt! Get your men back up here, and hurry! The Greeks are almost here. Where are the archers?" he asked, looking around, and then spied the Welsh and their little group hastening toward him.

"Make for the woods over there, Dewy!" Reza shouted, and waved them away. "We will join you. Be ready for trouble!" Swiftly, the archers about faced and trotted off toward the woods. Dewy waved acknowledgement without looking back. Talon nodded to himself. They would be ready for anything by the time the emperor's men arrived.

In a very short space of time, the Saxons and Kantara men were grouped around Talon and his followers. He pointed in the direction from which the emperor and his army were going to approach. "More than a hundred better-armed Greeks are coming to investigate," he informed them. "It's time we disappeared. I certainly do not want to be caught in the open. If they pick up our scent, then we can lure them deeper into the forest and ambush them."

The happy and bloody Saxons and Kantara men at arms clattered off in a chattering group, loping off toward the shelter of the forest, loaded with loot they had managed to pick up from the dead mercenaries. Talon and Reza, with Rostam and the Companions, trotted their horses behind, keeping a wary eye on the eastern road.

"I am beginning to think that we have to provide blood for those Saxons from time to time, just to keep them cheerful," Junayd observed with a grin at Rostam.

"I'm just glad they pointed their arses at the enemy," Rostam responded.

Reza frowned as they arrived at the edge of the forest of stunted oaks and larches. There they spread out, keeping well undercover, waiting for the arrival of the emperor's army. Talon's archers were already in position to inflict much pain on anyone inquisitive enough to investigate the forest edge.

*****

The lookout on the queen's ship shouted from the cross trees, high up the mast. "Alarm! There are men in boats coming toward us! 'Ware below!"

Joanna was below deck, resting from the blazing sun with Berengaria in their stuffy cabin that still reeked of sweat, unwashed bodies and vomit, when the shouts of alarm sounded. Soon after, she heard the thumping of bare feet on the deck above, as the sailors ran to their stations, and then more shouts and the sound of boots pounding the deck, as the armed knights and crossbow archers took up station along the ship's sides. She hurried up on deck with Berengaria and their maids, to be greeted by the captain, who was squinting at something in the direction of the shore, his hand shading his eyes from the sunlight glittering off the water.

"What is happening, Captain?" she demanded.

"Some boats are approaching, my lady. I would caution you that we do not know at this time if they are friend or foe. There are three boatloads crammed full of men, so it might become dangerous. I beg that you go below, my lady. It would be safer."

"I most certainly will not go below until we have made certain of who those people are," Joanna responded sharply. She did not want to go back into that stinking cabin. "I suspect it is another attempt to inveigle me to shore, where the emperor awaits to hold us for ransom," she declared forcibly. "The last emissary was a sniveling little man who couldn't have scared a crab. No, I shall wait on deck and we shall see."

The captain sighed. "Yes, my lady. We will see soon enough, I dare say, but if there are arrows, I beg that you take cover below."

"Very well. In that case, we will take your advice, Captain. Now, who is it that is coming?"

The boats were approaching with some speed, with men straining at the oars and the small sails full. There were shouted commands on the ship, and a group of crossbow men made haste to load their weapons with quarrels and set them to half cock. Then they headed for the bows of the ship and waited. The buzz of conversation grew as the boats approached. There were more shouts between the captain and the lookouts, several seamen perched high up in the cross trees.

"It's very odd, my lady," the captain commented. "Only a few of the men in the boats appear to be armed. They look decidedly ragged, too. My people don't know what to make of it!"

But then there came a shout from the leading boat. To everyone's surprise it was spoken in French. "Hold! Do not shoot! We are King Richard's men. We have escaped. Bring us aboard!"

There was a collective gasp of surprise from everyone on board. "State your name!" someone in the bows of the ship shouted.

"Lord D'Onston and Captain Willimus, with survivors. Permission to come aboard?"

The captain gaped. "Yes... yes, of course! Bring them aboard at once. What in God's name happened?"

Joanna's mind was a whirl. What had happened to the other ships? Had they wrecked, and had the treacherous emperor imprisoned the survivors? How, then, had they escaped?

The boats pulled alongside, and their passengers clambered aboard. They were a sorry looking group. Some were wounded, with crude bandages wrapped over bloody gashes. All were in rags; a far cry from the colorful and confident knights who had left Sicily. To a man, they looked exhausted. One even fell to his knees. The knights who had gathered exclaimed, and several rushed forward to assist him.

One of the knights shouted up to the steering deck, "They are our people, my lady, and some are near dead from exhaustion!"

The last man clambered aboard to be greeted by the captain of her ship. "Well met, Willimus. I did not think we would see you again after that terrible storm. Thank God for your preservation!" They embraced, but then the new arrival stood back—it was more of a stagger—and said, "We would not even be here were it not for the help of a strange man who killed our captors and helped us into the boats."

"I am Lord D'Onston," another ragged man claimed. "The captain is quite right, we were saved by some strange people, thank the Lord."

Joanna was instantly intrigued. "Come, Captain. See to it that all these men have water and food. And I wish to talk to Lord D'Onston and Captain Willimus to find out more."

Both men made their way through the crowd to the steps and were helped up by eager hands to stand in front of Joanna and Berengaria. Lord D'Onston was not in as good shape as the captain, but still managed to perform the semblance of a bow to the ladies. Joanna lifted her hand.

"Find stools for these men! Lord D'Onston, I had almost lost hope of seeing you again. God be thanked that you are alive, but you look weary." She smiled at the man, whom she had known well in court. An ally even, during difficult times. "Bring wine for these men," she commanded. "They are about to fall over. And bring chairs for me and the princess," she added.

When the two tired men were seated, Joanna and Berengaria, surrounded by their followers and other curious knights and lords, listened with keen interest to their tale. Eventually, Lord D'Onston finished his story, and then indicated that the captain should conclude it. Captain Willimus had gulped down the meager ration of bread and stale cheese that he had been provided.

"So you see, my lady, there is this lord who holds a castle on the island. One of his men called it Kantara. He is called Lord Talon de Gilles, and he is about the same age as Lord D'Onston here, a little younger, perhaps. He had, I'd say, around fifty men in all. They came to our rescue, despite overwhelming odds." He paused. "There does not appear to be any love lost between him and the emperor. But he spoke fluent French, although he commanded a savage band of Saxons, and other darker, more sinister-looking men on horses, who appear to be more like Saracens. We could not see their faces, for they were covered to the eyes. Even this Lord Talon was dressed as the Saracens do. However, thanks be to God, they chased the enemy off, with as interesting a tactic as I have ever seen."

The moment Captain Willimus said this, he regretted it.

"How so? What kind of tactic did these Saxons employ to drive off the Greeks?" Joanna asked with a raised eyebrow.

"Er... ahem, well, my lady. Well, umm," he hesitated. His weather-beaten features went red with embarrassment.

"Spit it out, man!" Joanna demanded, looking impatient and puzzled at the same time.

"They... er, they bared their behinds to the Greeks, my lady. And then they spun around, gave a great shout—some were even laughing—and began slaughtering anyone who got in their way," said Captain Willimus with great discomfort. Lord D'Onston nodded his agreement. "It's true, my lady. Bless my soul. Never seen anything like it before! Must have been terrifying for the enemy." He put on a lugubrious expression and grimaced theatrically.

He was rewarded with an incredulous snort from Joanna, who had to place a hand in front of her mouth to hide her amusement. Princess Berengaria gave a small squeal of laughter and put both hands to her face. The knights and attendants, being less inhibited, laughed aloud, and some doubled over with mirth.

"Saxon behinds, eh?" Joanna asked, looking as though she was about to lose the battle with her self-control.

"A truly terrible sight, my lady. The Greeks were utterly demoralized," Captain Willimus assured her solemnly, while trying to keep a straight face himself. His comment caused even more splutters of laughter from all those who could hear. Before long, everyone who had been close enough to hear what was said was recounting the tale to others on the main deck.

"Let us pray that when my brother arrives, which I am sure he will soon, they will continue to be demoralized, and that we can punish the usurper properly," Joanna said.

In an aside to one of her knights, she murmured, "Please remember that name. I will talk to my brother about him when the time comes."

Chapter 11

New Arrivals

The sellers of glass worked in peace
And paid no attention to the sounds of the mouse,
Until to protect them they bought a cat—
Who shattered all their wares when he pounced.
—Yitzhaq Alahdab

As Talon and his followers disappeared into the forest, the leading riders of the emperor's troops appeared on the road from Larnaca, having ridden hard to protect their erstwhile comrades. They realized soon enough that they had come too late to help them. Their shouts of anger and dismay at what they discovered could be heard by the concealed watchers. The cavalry arrived in a bunch, well ahead of the units of infantry, but they spread out as they sought the bodies of their dead comrades.

The escaped prisoners could be seen rowing hard toward the lone ship in the mouth of the bay. Several horsemen rode down to the beach and waved their fists at the departing Normans, threatening them with all manner of painful deaths if they should catch them. Others riders looked around with more discerning eyes. They knew well enough the prisoners had not accomplished this massacre on their own, but it remained a sinister mystery as to whom. While some of the younger mercenaries and those who had lost friends in the massacre were hot for revenge, others eyed the darkening forest apprehensively. Their leader rode slowly back to Isaac, who sat on a splendid white horse, looking numb.

The bodies of the slain were piled two or three high in places, among them his precious mercenaries, alongside peasants and townspeople. All very dead.

The leader addressed his emperor deferentially. "My lord, whoever the mysterious attackers were, they are not here now. Perhaps they sailed away with the prisoners in those boats. We should ask the citizens of Limassol," he finished with a scowl, "if they had anything to do with this—" he didn't finish.

Isaac fidgeted in the dusk. Seeing the dead all about, he wished very much not to be out here in this desolate area with them as company, but safely behind sturdy walls.

"We will go to the city and demand answers," he ground out, failing to hide his anger and his fear. "I shall spend the night there," he added, to stop his attendants from reminding him that he had a tent to the east of the town, where he had previously intended to spend the night. The town was a more secure place than a tent out in the open.

Who could have done this? Isaac wondered; but lurking at the back of his mind was the enigmatic castle of Kantara and its sinister occupant. "God curse that man," he muttered to himself. "Will I ever be rid of him?" He all but ground his teeth, he was so enraged at what he was contemplating.

The commander of the cavalry, Gôsakos, a veteran of some battles and many skirmishes, restrained himself from showing any expression. He doubted if his leader had the stomach to do anything more this evening, with the sun setting over the low hills that led to Larnaca.

"Very well, my liege," he bowed from the waist and shouted some orders.

The riders, who had been drifting around the battlefield checking for life among their comrades, were called in and, once again, formed up to ride toward the town, the gates of which were already opening to admit the emperor.

*****

Hidden in the bushes and trees of the forest's edge, Caradog eased his pull on the string of his bow and gave a small sigh. One of the riders had come close to the edge of the woods. He had paused for a long moment, staring straight into the shadows of the trees, but then had come a shout, and he'd turned away to canter his horse toward the other horsemen.

"I'm glad you were not tempted, Caradog," Talon murmured from two trees away. "Very well, they are not in the mood to investigate tonight, so we will go deeper into the woods and see what tomorrow brings. Yosef, the word to all the men is to leave as little trace as possible." He turned and walked back to where his horse and those of the others were being held by Kantara men.

"There is an open space half a league from here, Father," Rostam told him.

"I know of it," Talon responded. "Ask your uncle to post sentries at the edge of the wood and to change them out regularly." Reza knew what to do and would ensure that the Companions were suitably employed.

"We make no fires tonight," Reza ordered. "There is bread and smoked meat enough for one night without a fire. Rostam, come with me," he called out.

With Rostam beside him, Reza walked to the edge of the forest, overlooking the battlefield. "We need to recover all the arrows we can." He pointed to the sprawled corpses bristling with arrows. "Tell the men you send out there to gather as many as they can without being noticed from the town walls, and tell them not to tarry. But wait until it is darker. They will be jittery over there." He indicated the walled city with his chin. "If they thought they could get away with it, their horsemen would sally out and cause problems." He waved toward the town again, where torches were lighting up the gate area and men could be seen in the gloom, standing on the battlements. The walls of the town were not high, and Reza, looking at them, had a thought.

Rostam was eager to comply. "I will send some of the Companions, Uncle," he answered, but then asked, "Should I not go with them, Uncle?"

"No, I want you for something else tonight, Rostam."

Rostam nodded, puzzled, but strode off to get his men, while Reza gazed at the walls reflectively. He barely heard the silent approach of another, but said, "I wondered when you would arrive, Brother."

"Are you thinking what I am thinking?" Talon asked quietly.

"What if," Reza sounded reflective, "what if I went over those walls and killed the emperor? Would it make a difference?"

"We could kill him, but we might end up with someone even worse from the ranks of those mercenaries, and certainly no one as stupid," Talon remarked.

"It's not *we,* Talon, it's *me,* or one of our people. You are in command, and I won't have our commander in that kind of danger. Please, do not argue this point, Brother. I cannot let you go there. Remember the chess board? Well, as far as we are all concerned, you are our king, and you don't go into danger of *that* kind anymore."

Talon snorted. He was annoyed. "Are you telling me I am too old for this now, Brother? I might remind you that we are the same age!"

Reza snorted in response. "You are older by a month or two, old man!" he chuckled, and was silent for a long moment of companionable silence. "What if we send Junayd or Yosef, and we wait here?" he asked.

"To do what, exactly, when they get in there?" Talon demanded. There was no question in his mind, or that of Reza, that their people could scale the walls and achieve entry.

"Kill Isaac, or something like that. He is a serious pain in the backside to everyone."

"We don't kill him, Reza. We scare the shit out of him, and that should send him packing. Then we wait and see what happens to that ship. If he stays around and threatens those Normans, we will go further with this; that I do promise."

"Who do you suggest for the mission?"

"Yosef or Junayd. The best of the best, other than—" Talon left it unsaid.

"Hmm, I agree. All three, then." Reza said. "He needs to know how to do it for real, Brother."

Talon scowled. "Didn't he do it for real in Famagusta against that idiot from Constantinople?" The curtness of his reply told Reza much.

"He dallied and then placed himself and others in great danger, because he was sniffing around that concubine in the palace," Reza retorted. "Bedded her, just like that, from what Junayd told me, with the whole place in an uproar all around them. *That* took some nerve!"

"It will be very dangerous," Talon remarked, his tone reluctant, but the corner of his mouth twitched.

Reza took his arm and faced him. "I love the boy, too, Brother, but this is what you and I trained him for. The other two will make sure that he makes no mistakes. Not this time. Let him go."

Talon looked down and shook his head, but before Reza could say anything, he looked up again at the dark shadow of his brother standing in front of him. "Very well, but I don't know what I shall say to his mother if anything goes wrong."

Reza gripped his arm a little harder. "Be of good faith, Brother. We trained him well."

Talon knew he wouldn't sleep a wink while they were gone, but this was an opportunity to frighten the emperor again, and perhaps something would come of it. Talon hoped that it would drive the man back to the comfort of his palace and to leave the ship alone.

Reza disappeared into the darkness to find his men, thinking furiously. For some years now, his own people had been close bodyguards to the emperor himself. Perhaps it was time to bring them home.

*****

Dawn came slowly to the island of Cyprus and, with it, terror in the emperor's quarters. He had been woken up by one of his eunuchs, hysterical with fright, who pointed with a shaking hand to a plain looking dagger protruding from the pillow, right next to the emperor's head.

The emperor himself was scared out of his wits. He thought he was going to faint, his heart was beating so fast, but he now knew without any doubt, that the battle outside the town walls had indeed been fought by that dreadful magician, Talon, with his fearsome companion, Reza, and their men. He felt like vomiting.

That the intruders had managed to get into the city and past the numerous guards, and then into his room, was terrifying enough, but when he screamed for the two guards who should have been protecting him and there was no answer, Isaac went cold all over. The eunuch wrung his hands and babbled incoherently, then stammered out that they had vanished, no one knew where. Isaac screamed for his other guards and kept on screaming for a full five minutes, with spittle flying in all directions, as he vented his anger and fear upon the luckless men.

"I shall have you flayed alive when we return to the palace, in full view of the entire population, to teach you to do your work properly!" he shrieked, as he kicked an inoffensive chair to pieces. "I shall make an example of you, you worthless, useless worms!" He went on in that vein until his commander, Gôsakos, hurried in and put a stop to the tantrum with his calming presence.

"Get those useless pigs out of my sight! Put them in irons. What do I pay all of you for when you cannot even protect me in my own bedroom!" Isaac screeched.

Gôsakos, himself shaken by the news, waved his hand to dismiss the men, and then spent half an hour trying to calm the hysterical emperor. He knew it had not even been Isaac's intent to sleep in the palace in Limassol, but the sight of the corpses had unnerved him enough to forgo taking his ease in the luxurious tent prepared for him several leagues to the west of the town. There, an encampment had been set up, in customary extravagance with, no doubt, a girl waiting in his bed. Gôsakos wondered how the intruder had known to come here instead. There did not appear to be any safe place on the island from those dreadful people from the castle of Kantara.

The night before, while he was gobbling a lavish supper, Isaac had commanded that people be brought before him to explain the catastrophe of the escaped prisoners. The inhabitants who had taken part, and some who had been spectators on the walls, had told him and his lieutenants of huge blonde men who resembled the Norman prisoners, and the aftermath of the brief but savage encounter in the field. His commander told him, in a low voice, that few of the mercenaries sent from the town had lived to tell the tale. Those who had survived were cowed and frightened men.

Now there was this terrible warning; without a word being spoken, his very life had been put on notice. He was sick with worry and wanted only to go back to the comforts and dubious safety of his palace in Famagusta.

"Prepare the army; we are leaving!" he shouted at his officers. He was disheveled and pale, his toiletry eunuchs, who would normally have been hard at work on his makeup, curling his hair, powdering his face, and trimming his eyebrows, cowered nearby. The former objective of seizing the ship and taking the queen prisoner was quite forgotten, until a mercenary came rushing in with more bad news. He stammered out his report, that several more ships had been sighted out in the bay and were approaching the lone vessel that had been anchored there for almost a week.

It took a good hour for the commander to persuade the very reluctant emperor that he should at least deploy his men along the low wall and wait to see what developments took place off shore before they left for Famagusta.

"It would be a mistake to leave now, Your Grace!" Gôsakos insisted. "We cannot let them come ashore, whoever they are. We are, by far, the more powerful force, should they contemplate such madness. We will slaughter them on the beaches and before the dyke, before they can gain even a foothold!" He was desperate to persuade this dithering idiot who was his leader.

Isaac placed a lot of faith in his commander, so he stopped tugging nervously at the hem of his coat with fidgety fingers and began to listen. "You really think we can stop anyone coming ashore?" he inquired.

"Of course we can, my lord! We will sink their ships if they dare approach! We'll kill all who have the temerity to set foot on your shores!" Gôsakos boasted.

"Who...who do you think they might be?" Isaac asked.

*****

It was the dawn of the seventh day since her arrival at the bay of Limassol when help arrived for Joanna, her ward Berengaria, and the now-very-crowded ship in which they had been confined for so long. Clean water was almost gone, bread was going moldy, and even the smoked meat was beginning to rot in the stifling heat.

Clothing, even that of the ladies, was foul with dirt and vomit stains from the storms. The men were beginning to look gaunt. The lookouts, posted at the masthead to watch for trouble from the shore, pointed, instead, out to sea when they called the alarm. They began to scream with excitement, and this mood communicated itself to the crew and men at arms, for they recognized the pendants flying from the lead ship's top mast.

Joanna fled the stinking, suffocating cabin with Princess Berengaria and their maids at her heels, to arrive on the overcrowded deck, where men were shouting with glee, pointing out to sea and slapping each other on the back.

"What is it, Captain?" she demanded as soon as she reached the top deck, but she was sure she knew.

"My lady, it is the king! King Richard has arrived, all praise be to God!" her captain bellowed, almost in her ear. He was grinning broadly, displaying his broken teeth. "Your faith was justified, my lady! The messengers got through to the king and he is here with his ships! Look!" He waved in the direction of the approaching vessels. "Dear God, what a sight!" he exclaimed.

Joanna allowed herself a feeling of huge relief, and even bestowed a warm smile upon the exuberant captain and the smelly men clustered about her. Her eyes searched the approaching ships for evidence of her brother. Behind her, Princess Berengaria was exclaiming and one of her maids was weeping. Perhaps their ordeal was finally over?

There was no mistaking Richard; he had ever stood taller than most men. There he was, standing proud on the upper deck of the closest ship, a cloak billowing around him, and waving at the roaring welcome he was receiving from Joanna's ship.

Soon after, a boat bumped against the starboard side of her vessel, and her brother boarded, to stand on the main deck, looking well and fit and very kingly, with every man around kneeling before him, but his eyes were searching for her. She came and stood by the rail.

"I am here, Brother. Praise God, but you are *such* a welcome sight!"

"By the saint's toes, I am right glad to see you, too, my sister!" Richard exclaimed. His previously grim expression evaporated and was replaced by a great smile and, big man though he was, he almost danced up the stairs to stand towering over her, still beaming, with his arms outstretched.

"We thought you had perished!" he exclaimed, as he swept his sister into a bear hug before everyone. "There we were, resting in Rhodes after the storm, when our ships intercepted the vessel you sent for me. God himself had a hand in this, I swear! Had they not met the messenger when they did, he would have sailed on to Acre and there would have been a much longer delay. The messenger told us of your plight. Are you all right, Joanna?" he demanded, as he released her and held her at arm's length. "You look tired."

"All is well, Richard," she responded after catching her breath with a ragged smile of her own. "You recall Princess Berengaria?" she added, somewhat dryly. Richard had not even glanced in the princess's direction, even though she was standing right alongside Joanna.

"Oh, yes, of course!" he responded looking put out. He bowed inelegantly over Berengaria's proffered hand.

"I trust you are not hurt, nor too discomforted from your ordeal, my lady?" he asked solicitously, but barely seemed to hear the soft reply. Joanna could see that he was distracted.

"What is this I hear about the usurper? The messenger asked me to make haste because that serpent was trying to take you prisoner?" he demanded, staring at the shoreline.

"He did, indeed, send an envoy out to request that we land so that he could provide hospitably, but I was wary, and I told him we would stay here until you arrived. He then proceeded to deny us any fresh water, so that we are down to the last water butt. And he has committed many crimes and outrages toward our other men, who were dashed ashore by the very storm that brought us here," Joanna told him.

"I want to hear all about it, Sister." Richard grated. His scowl returned, and his voice took on an ominous tone.

A good hour later, after she had presented Captain Willimus and Lord D'Onston to the king, they had told their stories. There was a long pause. Richard had listened attentively and roared with laughter when he heard about the Saxon attack. "This I wish I could have seen!" he exclaimed to the tittering attendants.

Joanna finished with the comment, "So, you see, Brother. This man who owns Cyprus is no better than a pirate and cannot be trusted. These men were very lucky, indeed. Had it not been for this Lord Talon de Gilles, they would all have been murdered on those beaches over there."

Richard was silent for a long moment, squinting at the distant shore. The sun was now high in the sky and the water glittered, making it hard, at this distance, to discern any activity taking place on land. No one spoke, but it was not long before Joanna realized what he might be contemplating.

"Richard! You are not thinking of going there, are you?" she demanded of her silent brother.

"Indeed, I am, Joanna," he growled. "It is perhaps time someone taught that pirate a severe lesson, and finished the work done by this strange fellow you are all talking about."

"But should we not be sailing for Acre, my lord?" asked one of the lords, carefully.

Richard stood up and glared around at the assembly on the deck and snarled, "Not until we have punished this usurper for shaming my family and killing my people. To arms, and prepare to go to the boats. I see you have several tied to this ship. Who is willing?" he demanded.

His words were greeted with a roar from everyone on deck and he smiled. It was the smile that Joanna had become used to over the years. It meant trouble for whomsoever he was hunting.

"Time to go, Sister," he said over the din of men calling to the other ships. "I shall see you before very long." With a wave of his arm to his sister and Berengaria, he climbed down into one of the boats and was rowed across the dividing water, back to his ship. He quickly reemerged fully armored in chainmail that gleamed, wearing a helmet with a gold circlet denoting his crown, and carrying a shield and an axe.

In less than an hour, a small flotilla of boats crammed with armed men was heading for the beach, with Richard standing tall in the prow of the leading boat.

*****

Talon was woken by a light kick to his boot from Yosef. He had been dozing in the shady forest camp. It had been a long night, but eventually his son and his henchmen had returned like wraiths, to report that they had had a successful night.

"What is it, Yosef?" he asked, wiping the sleep out of his eyes. "Have the reinforcements arrived yet?"

"They are close. Our scouts have gone to meet them and bring them in, Lord. Master Reza thought you might want to see this," Yosef said in a low voice. All around them, men who had been resting were up, hurriedly seeing to their arms. Talon struggled to his feet, now wide awake, and followed Yosef to the edge of the woods that overlooked the new dyke and the bay.

There were now many men gathered behind the wall; they were spread out along its length, but the main concentration was to the east. As the wall was only several hundred paces from where his men were concealed, the Greeks could be seen clearly, and they were all staring and gesturing toward the bay. Three new ships had arrived, but what Talon found more interesting was that there appeared to be a small flotilla making its way directly toward the beach in front of the dyke.

"What do you make of that, Brother?" he asked Reza, who was staring intently at the approaching boats.

"While you were lazing about and getting some rest, we watched those new ships arrive. There was a lot of activity, after which those boats started for the beach. I suspect that your King Richard, or someone who is well-known to the queen, has arrived and decided to mount an attack, Brother!"

Reza sounded incredulous, but he grinned as well. "The emperor might have stirred up a hornets' nest with his bad behavior. Whoever it is that is coming is dead set on punishing him, if I am not mistaken. The sheer gall of it is astonishing!"

Talon had, by now, assessed the situation for himself and concluded that, unless the men who were landing had some help, it might go badly for them.

"Dewy, Caradog, come quickly," he called.

Soon the two Welshmen were standing next to him, looking out at the men on the dyke. "Can you do harm enough from here to distract those people?" Talon asked.

"Just over two hundred paces, I'd say," Caradog murmured.

Dewy sucked his teeth. "Well over; nearly two hundred and ten, if I am not mistake'en," he argued.

Talon rolled his eyes at Reza, who grimaced with amusement. "Can you hit anyone?" Talon pressed, his tone sharper.

"Oh, yes! Of *course* we can, and our apprentices can, too, you will see."

"Then bring them all here and spread them out along the forest edge. As soon as those madmen in the boats land, I want you to start shooting at the emperor's men, who will be facing the invaders."

It didn't take very long for the longbow archers to get into position. Talon had his Companions stand guard nearby, to prevent any attempts at a counterattack, which could occur once the mercenaries realized the menace behind them had not gone away.

"Brandt," Talon called softly, "I want you to have the Saxons ready in case we have to go and assist those people." His commander waved a hand and strode off to bring his men together behind the archers and await orders.

"Someone has to guard the back door, and we are the ones to do that. If we can prevent the emperor from returning to the town of Limassol, it will be an achievement of sorts," Talon told Reza, who nodded agreement.

"Rostam, prepare the horses. We might need them," he said. Talon watched as his son vanished into the gloom of the forest behind him. The three of them had done well, he reflected, but he had not slept a wink until they'd reappeared to report on what they had accomplished.

*****

Isaac's army—augmented by unwilling recruits from the town—had filed out of the gates of Limassol, with the emperor closely surrounded by his armed guards. When the last footmen had passed through, the gates of the town were promptly slammed shut with a crash. The citizens of the town, having had a frightening enough time the evening before, did not want to repeat the experience.

There was an unnerving period when the conscripted citizens and the mercenaries passed the corpses still lying out in the slopes between the wall and the forest. The more experienced could not fail to notice the ominous sign that most of the bodies were stripped of any armor. None of the former victims of the bowmen still had any arrows protruding from their bodies, either.

Many were the apprehensive glances cast toward the thick, inscrutable woods to their left, as they rode along the road. The commander ordered the men to spread out along the entire length of the dyke. This was done with some reluctance. The troops shared the emperor's strong desire to leave this ominous place and head for home in Famagusta as fast as their legs or their horses could take them. Morale was at a new low.

Commander Gôsakos and his officers were worried. The newly arrived ships had, thus far, made no attempt to enter the harbor of Limassol, but had instead anchored very close to the ship of Queen Joanna. One officer, who had some knowledge of emblems, pointed out a pennant flying proudly from one of the ships.

"It is the lion of England, sir. It may be the king himself who has arrived," he told the commander, whose eyes narrowed. Even if the new arrivals included King Richard, they could not just leave now; they occupied the position of strength.

"Then we must persuade the emperor not to run away, just yet," he muttered to himself, and cast a glance over to where Isaac, who still looked as though he had just climbed out of bed, was staring fixedly at the ships.

Just at that moment, one of Isaac's men on horseback shouted and waved.

"My lord! There are boats coming this way from those ships!"

Everyone standing along the wall stopped what he was doing and stared out to sea. Sure enough, there was a small flotilla of boats rowing hard, directly for their positions.

"The fools are coming to fight us, Lord!" Gôsakos said to Isaac. His tone was incredulous. "They offer themselves to you as prisoners and hostages! We can slay them as they come ashore, and even take their ships, my liege," he added confidently, watching Isaac out of the corner of his eye. It would prove disastrous if the emperor cut and ran for the safety of his palace in Famagusta at this crucial time.

"Prepare to face the enemy!" Gôsakos roared, more to prevent some craven command from Isaac, who looked pale, than it was to alert his men to the impending skirmish, which he truly believed was all it could be. Nonetheless, being a cautious man, Gôsakos then told his attendants to take the emperor to the far end of the wall, just in case things went wrong.

The Normans landed in the low surf, greeted by yells of defiance from the Greeks and a hail of javelins and bolts from the crossbowmen. Some men went down, but others used their shields to protect themselves while wading thigh-deep in the surf, as they struggled to gain footing on the beach. There were shouts and yells in reply from the invaders, as they followed a large man brandishing a huge axe and bellowing battle shouts. There was little doubt that this man was the leader, and Gôsakos realized this might indeed be the English king. Would it be better, he wondered, to kill him or to take him prisoner for the ransom?

Just when all the attention of the mercenaries was focused on the landing Normans, something terrifying occurred. Arrows began to fall among the Greek ranks, but these did not come from the Normans. The whispering death came, instead, from the edge of the forest. Gôsakos heard screams and saw his men falling. It took a little time for the Greeks to understand that they were also under attack from behind, and more men went down from the silent killers that sped out of the sky to strike them with tremendous force.

Hidden in the foliage of the edge of the forest, Talon and his men had a grandstand view of the arrival of the Normans.

"That must be him," Talon remarked to Reza and his men. "The king of England is not, it would seem, one to stay in the rear of his army."

It was an act of reckless courage to assault the beaches with Isaac's men well protected by the wall, but now, it was time to make the wall as untenable as possible. "Dewy, Caradog, do your work," he called out.

The archers needed no persuasion. Bows twanged and arrows sped away into the sky, to descend into the ranks of the Greeks. The reaction was just what Talon wished.

"We shall keep this up and wait until the Normans have gained the beach; then we will show them the Saxons," he told the men gathered around him. "Prepare yourselves, and someone bring my horse. We are going to roll the Greeks up from the town side and see how they like that!"

Reza and his Companions joined Talon at the edge of the forest. As he handed Talon the reins, Reza grinned and said,

"Hurry up, Talon, or there will be no one left."

"Brandt!" Talon called.

"Yes, Lord?"

"Form up your men over there, to our right, where you can see things, and then, on my command, go straight at the men on the side nearest to the town. Don't wait for anything,

Brandt. Surprise is important. Attack them, and we will then help you to sweep them up towards Larnaca!"

The demoralized and bewildered Greek soldiers, who had been cowering from the deadly hail of arrows, now had another peril confronting them. To his own consternation, Gôsakos saw strange men begin to file out of the woods. Then, to his horror, he saw the large blond men form into one of their notorious shield walls, and this group of men, attended by horsemen and other footmen carrying long spears, charged directly for his men, positioned nearest the town. Their battle cries and roars could be heard all along the line.

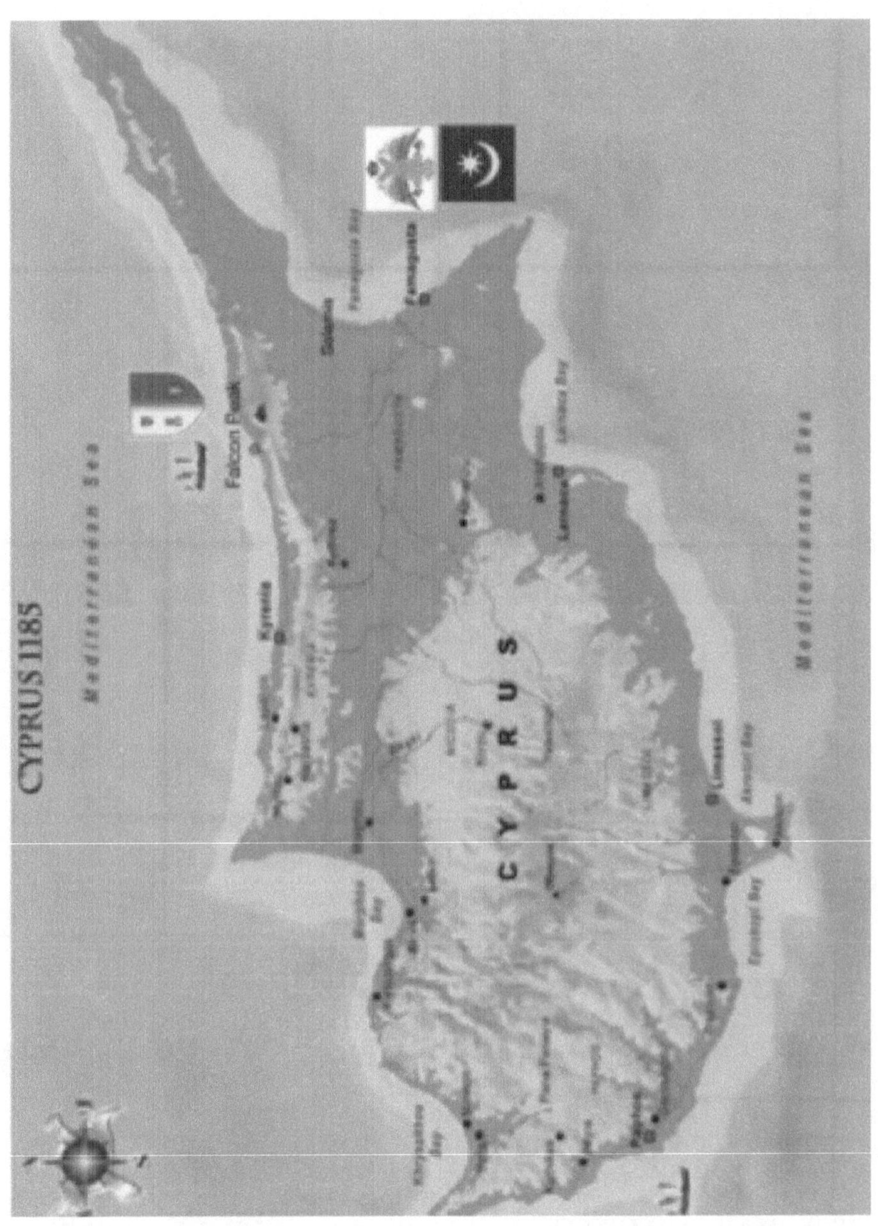

CYPRUS 1185
Mediterranean Sea
Mediterranean Sea
CYPRUS
Falcon Peak
Famagusta
Salamis
Kyrenia
Limassol
Famagusta Bay
Larnaca Bay
Akrotiri Bay
Episkopi Bay
Khrysochou Bay
Morphou Bay

Chapter 12

Invasion

Come with the buckler, the lance, and the bow.
Trumpets are sounding,
War-steeds are bounding,
Stand to your arms, then, and march in good order;
England shall many a day
Tell of the bloody fray,
—Walter Scott

Talon felt the familiar tightening in his belly as he mounted his horse. "Come on, Jabbar," he muttered to his mount, as he settled deeper into the saddle and reached for a lance that one of the Kantara footmen was holding out to him. "Time we were back in the fray!"

He shrugged off the uncomfortable feeling that this maneuver was just as reckless as that of the Norman king and tapped the hilt of his Japanese sword.

The weapon, when cared for, was formidable. Talon, while he knew the basics of how it had been forged, was still astonished by how it could cut so deeply, even through steel rings, as though they were only made of leather. He and Reza frequently practiced the unconventional fighting techniques they had learned in China from a ruthless instructor, and

140

they nursed their swords as though they were extensions of themselves. Now, as he felt its weight on his hip, Talon felt more at ease. His lance would only do for one, at best a couple of victims, and then it would be time for the sword to slake its thirst for blood.

It was clear that the Saxons were also keen to draw blood again, from the excited growls from that quarter. He glanced around to see how ready his cavalry was, and his eyes met those of Reza.

"It's time to go, Brother." Reza gave him a tight grin. The other horsemen held long, wooden, shafted lances brought from Kantara. Talon nodded and raised his sword. "Now!" he called out.

His call was greeted with a great shout from all his men, including the replacements. Nasuh had brought some of the deadly canisters with him, but they could not be deployed against a mixed scrimmage of attackers and defenders. Now it was simply time to charge and get it over with. The Normans were having a hard time on the beach. All the advantages of speed and momentum, not to mention dry clothing, were with the Greeks.

"Charge!" roared Brandt, as he brandished his axe. Talon and his men crashed into the exposed rear of the Greek army and the slaughter began. Among the Saxons were men who could hurl a short axe some distance. As they came within a dozen paces, the axes flew and hammered into the confused and shocked enemy.

The Saxon shield wall smashed into their opponents, but Talon and his horsemen struck first with their lances, and then with their swords. The roars and battle shouts of the Saxons mingled with those of the Kantara men, as the screaming enemy tried to dodge and flee back to the town gates.

"Drive them toward the east!" Talon roared over the din of clashing shields and blades. By now, there were wails of despair from the Greek wounded and dying. Brandt and his men altered their formation to sweep up the confused enemy and drive them onto one another. When the mercenaries tried to form up to resist Talon, his hacking, screaming horsemen rode into them, split them apart, and forced them to scramble backward toward the center, where the fighting against the Normans was the most fierce. The defenders at the wall continued to be threatened by the rain of deadly arrows.

Talon glanced over to his left and was gratified to see that the Normans had finally gained a foothold on the beach, and that some had even reached the wall. They were battling fiercely with the mercenaries, as they tried to fight their way over the makeshift obstruction and up onto the road. It was proving to be a hard struggle.

Talon shouted over to Reza, "Come with me, Brother, and bring our horse archers with you!"

Leaving Brandt's Saxons and the Kantara infantry to roll up the enemy from the Greek flank, he turned his horse away from the fighting, and pointed to the center of the struggling mass of men at the point of the invasion from the sea.

The tight group of horsemen galloped along the grassy field between the road and the forest, their horses' hooves tossing up dried mud and clods of earth as they went. Relying upon Dewy and Caradog to know when to stop shooting, he galloped headlong toward the point of most resistance for the Normans, loosing arrow after arrow straight into the backs of the men who were trying to stop the invaders. Throwing a look at the forest, he saw that Dewy had taken the initiative and was now running with his archers and their protective shield of Companions to harass the enemy at close range.

The mercenaries were well aware of their peril, should they remain where they were, caught between not just two, but three, groups of determined opponents. To their right, there were the dreaded berserker Saxons, sweeping up their comrades and coming ever closer. Their own comrades were crowding into them as they fled the howling blond menace; arrows were still coming in from the woods and taking a terrible toll, while the Normans were fighting like madmen, led by a champion who apparently knew no fear and laid about him with an enormous bloody axe!

Many of the Normans carried axes, like the Saxons, and protected themselves with large, pointed shields; but the sand was soft and the climb from the water to the base of the wall was difficult to accomplish with the weight of their armor and shields. The top of the wall was at head-height and bristling with crossbowmen and spearmen. They needed some help to get over it. Talon noted with respect that the king could be seen at the center, hacking furiously at anyone in front of him. There was already a small pile of dead scattered about his person. His men stayed very close, and some were even trying to drag the screaming Greeks from their perch on the walls to slaughter them whenever they could.

Then Talon and his men drove into the back of the fighters with their horses. The shock of the attack was enough to distract the defenders, which, in turn, allowed the first of the Normans to clamber over the wall and clear a space for themselves. All the while, Talon kept an eye on the Greek horsemen, who were clustered to the east of the fighting, not having taken part in any action up until now. However, they appeared to be forming up; an attack from that flank could prove disastrous.

"Reza!" he yelled, gesturing frantically at the ominous-looking group. "Over there! We must turn and face them!"

Reza shouted something back at him, and then screamed at Rostam and his men to turn and join Talon to confront the new threat. At the same time, Dewy and Caradog noticed the danger and raced to close with Talon and his horsemen, who were woefully outnumbered by the enemy cavalry.

"Shoot at them!" Dewy shouted at his men. He hesitated for a moment, but then shouted.

"At the horses; kill their mounts." He was clearly unwilling to issue such an order, but he realized there was little choice. A hail of arrows flew directly at the charging mercenaries. Their aim was true.

"They flinch, Lord!" Caradog shouted. It was true the archers had done much damage, bringing down horses and men, but there were still too many, and they appeared intent upon taking revenge; they looked undeterred. Talon, however, had no intention of allowing the Greek cavalry to destroy his archers.

"Form up on me!" he bellowed to his horsemen. Within a moment, the thin line of the Kantara cavalry and the Companions had placed itself in front of the charging Greeks. Talon's heart almost quailed. They were going to be destroyed!

The Normans, still shouting themselves hoarse and hacking away with swords and axes, had cleared a widening space at the top of the wall, and the soldiers who had formerly held them back, lacking clear leadership and unable to regroup, became dismayed. It appeared to them that they were being attacked from every side, so the less brave among them began to look for ways to escape from the trap. The retreat from the Saxons became a rout, and the fear very quickly communicated itself to the other men, struggling against the Normans and the relentless archery. The mob began to run for the dubious safety of the eastern highway, their only avenue of escape.

In doing so, they fanned out. The space between the charging Greek cavalry and Talon's men filled with fleeing mercenaries and citizens. Talon had not yet given the order to countercharge, but the emperor's cavalry was thundering toward them. Stunned Kantara horsemen and archers watched in astonishment as horsemen bore down upon the soldiers who were fleeing for their lives. Too late, they tried to haul their horses to a stop, but not before they had run down many of their own people, knocking them over and trampling them. The charge petered out as screaming men and horses tumbled to the ground or were trampled to death. To Talon, it was too good an opportunity to waste.

Slipping his bow into its sheath under his left thigh, Talon drew his sword and pointed it at the confusion right in front of them.

"Charge them!" he bellowed, and led the way, to crash into the milling crowd, hacking and stabbing as he went. His men followed, with Reza shrieking something unintelligible at his side, Rostam and his Companions on either side of the two men. While they, too, were determined to make the most of the opportunity that had presented itself, they were just as interested in making sure that Master Reza and Lord Talon survived the madness. The fight moved faster and faster toward the east, as the Greeks gave under the pressure of Talon and his men.

The Saxon fighters, having sent Greeks running for their lives, reached the Norman line. They paused for breath, as did the Normans, who were exhausted from their run up the beach and the struggle for possession of the wall. All eyes were on the milling mass of men and horses, almost a quarter of a league down the road by now.

*****

The Normans and Saxons regarded one another warily, in the silence that grew as the noise of battle drew away. They were covered in blood, mostly that of their enemies, but there were wounded men on both sides. All around them was the detritus of war, the groaning wounded and silent dead, draped one upon another in places. Abandoned weapons and shields lay strewn around on the blood-soaked ground, where their former owners had abandoned them.

Finally, King Richard, who had been staring hard at Brandt, strode forward and stood in front of him. "By God, but your arrival was timely!" he called out. His voice was hoarse from yelling.

He pointed to Brandt's weapon. "You carry an ax as large as mine! Are you the Lord Talon de Gilles I have been hearing about?" He panted and leaned on the long handle of his own bloody axe. Men all around were doing much the same, but even as they leaned on their own weapons, the Saxons still held firmly to their formation, staring back at the Normans as though sizing them up for a fight.

Brandt's chest was heaving so hard he had no breath for words; it had been a struggle to arrive at this point. He could see that Richard was viewed with respect by all the Normans around him. He only just understood what the king was saying. He shook his head and pointed off toward the east, where the mounted conflict appeared to be almost over. There were no more standing enemies in sight; they had fled the field. There were only the dead and wounded. Now everyone could see that Talon and the archers were making their slow way back toward the group clustered around the king.

"I am no he, Lord. That man over there is Lord Talon. I his servant," Brandt stammered in broken French.

Richard laughed. "If you are his servants, then he is well served to have such warriors who fight so well. I thank you from my heart, nonetheless." There was a ripple of agreement from the Normans gathered about him, while most of the Saxons, who could barely understand him, merely stared.

"He is coming, Lord," Brandt stated and pointed again toward Talon, who led the way with his men. Talon lifted his hand to Brandt.

"Good to see you and my Veragnians, Brandt! All well?" he called. Then he recognized Richard as being the man in charge of the Normans, and guessed he was the king of England.

"All well, Lord," Brandt replied, and then indicated Richard. "The king, Lord Talon."

Talon dismounted somewhat stiffly and gave the reins to Rostam with a nod, then limped over toward the king. There, he eased himself down onto one knee and said, "Welcome to Cyprus, my lord king."

*****

As Commander Gôsakos hurried from the battlefield, he carried with him a sense of bewilderment and outrage. How had his army, which outnumbered the combined forces against him, have fallen apart so easily? He and a tight-knit bunch of his cavalry had extricated themselves with difficulty from the chaotic melee. His perfectly timed charge had been utterly disrupted by his own infantry, who were running for their lives from the ferocious Northmen: Normans and Saxons alike. He, himself, had run down two of his own soldiers before he could haul his horse to a halt and try to take stock.

By that time, a number of sword-wielding, yelling madmen had charged straight at him and his men, and set about them with bloodcurdling screams and flailing swords. Their horses were a good deal nimbler than his own cavalry and danced around the blundering infantry, to appear right in front of his luckless horsemen and cut them down. The footmen, already panicked and disoriented, had begun to scream and had run, if anything even faster, to get away from the maniacs who were intent upon cutting up whomsoever got in their way.

Gôsakos realized very quickly that these expert riders were intent upon striking directly at the heart of his own units. He hauled his horse around and put spurs to it. The animal jumped away as the spurs bit, and he beat his animal with the flat of his sword until it began to gallop as fast as it could carry him, away from the screaming mass of enemy horsemen and panicked footmen.

His own followers, observing his departure, needed no further encouragement. The arrows from the forest that never seemed to stop, the determination of the Norman invaders, and now this reckless and insanely mad attack by the strange people from Kantara was enough to demoralize anyone, but it was the hasty departure of their leader that settled it. The cavalry beat its way through the still-running infantry and fled the field.

As Gôsakos drew abreast of the startled emperor, who had been watching aghast but with paralyzed amazement at the chaos around the Norman invasion, he called out.

"My lord, we must leave immediately. There are too many and we have been outflanked. For your safety, we must *leave!*"

Isaac needed little persuasion. Wide-eyed with confusion and fear, he could see for himself that the blond warriors had crushed his flank. The Normans now held a large portion of his wall. His men, their weapons and shields abandoned, were fleeing along the road past him, literally brushing past his horse with barely a glance in his direction, ignoring the calls of his attendants. He wrenched his horse around, sending the slaves who normally held it for him staggering, and took off after Gôsakos and his flying cavalry. He wanted so badly to return to the safety of Famagusta. His departure was just in time, because those accursed horsemen who had inflicted so much damaged were not far behind Gôsakos. They looked very intent upon capturing him, should he dally.

Commander Gôsakos intended to gain some space on more open-level ground, where he could regroup and perhaps counterattack the combined enemy forces. It proved a vain hope. Although he and his men tried hard to stop the fleeing infantry by riding among them and beating them with the flat of their swords, the terrified men continued to stream past. The emperor's encampment was nearly four leagues from the battlefield, but Isaac was in no mood to pause here and repeat the humiliation. When Gôsakos tried to persuade Isaac to stop and allow him to reassemble his motley army, Isaac whirled on him.

"*You* said we would 'drive them into the sea!'" Isaac screamed at him, mimicking his general. "*You* said we would beat them easily and that would be that!" he shouted, his voice climbing several octaves. "No one said anything about that cursed dog from Kantara getting involved. Bastard!" Now he was foaming at the mouth. "We go back to Famagusta and we go *now*!" he shrieked, and began to gallop off along the road toward the distant city, his silk coats flying in the wind.

Gôsakos shook his head in disgust, but he had no choice. "We leave," he called to his men. As a body, they scurried after the emperor, who was already out of the other side of the camp and on his way to Famagusta. Gôsakos cast a look of regret back at the tents they were abandoning and shrugged. Too bad Isaac was more interested in saving his skin than preserving his possessions. There was much plunder that would fall to the Normans, when they came after them.

*****

"So, *you* are the Lord Talon de Gilles I have been hearing about!" Richard exclaimed.

Talon bowed his head and nodded. "I am, my lord. And you are now the king of England," he smiled.

"Why do I get the feeling that we have met before?" Richard asked, as he took off his helmet and handed it to an attendant soldier nearby who, in turn, provided him with a cloth. Pushing back his leather under-cap, Richard wiped his perspiring forehead and bearded face. Talon remembered the face of the king. He had slightly long features dominated by a sharp beak of a nose. Richard shot a glance towards the Saxons, who were still formed up. Other than the gold circlets on their arms, and their different shields, there was little to distinguish the Saxons warriors from the Normans. With few exceptions, they were big men, compared to their Greek enemies. The Saxons had blond or red hair instead of the darker hair of the Normans, and blue-colored eyes. All wore chainmail hauberks, which, after the battle, were in various stages of disrepair. However, to his discerning eye, it was not hard to note the better quality of the linked coats the Saxons wore.

"Phew, but that was close, and it is hot!" Richard grunted with a smile.

"We met in France some fifteen years ago, my liege," Talon responded. "You were in some danger and I managed to give you a warning." Talon also took off his helmet and smiled up at the king.

"Stand, Lord Talon, while I think about that," Richard said with a puzzled frown. "It would seem that We have to thank you, not once but twice, for your help. My sister and her people told me about the first incident, for which we are grateful. I would hazard that, then as now, your help was very timely."

Then he snapped his fingers. "I remember now!" he exclaimed. "You were the... the youth who placed a note on my pillow and scared the shit out of me; then we met at the chapel." Richard paused to examine Talon more closely. "Yes, I remember. Your eyes, and that scar on your face. You appear to have garnered another under your eye, Lord Talon."

Talon grinned. "That was received in a sea fight, some time ago now, my liege."

They were interrupted by the high-pitched wailing of some of the wounded enemies nearby. It was so loud that Richard scowled, but Reza signaled to Brandt to deal with it. After a low, murmured command, three Saxons broke ranks and, within a couple of minutes, the screaming stopped abruptly. The Saxons returned to their own company without a word.

Richard and his Normans were clearly somewhat taken aback at the ruthlessness of the action, but then he shrugged it off. He cast an interested look about him at the assembly, and spent a few long moments examining the silent horsemen who had accompanied Talon. They all had their faces covered. He shook his head. "I doubt that I have ever seen such a menacing group of people," he remarked. "These are all your men?" he asked, almost rhetorically.

Talon nodded. "Yes, my liege. They are my men." He couldn't keep the pride out of his reply. He paused, then said,

"I hope I am not too forward, my lord, but I would suggest that we follow up on our victory here and take advantage of the enemy's departure by chasing after them, to prevent them from reorganizing. My scouts have told me that their encampment is only four or five leagues away. If we can drive them out of their camp, then the only place the emperor can go is back to Famagusta."

Richard's head went up. "We'll need horses," he replied, and turned to one of his men. "Sir William, send messages to the ships to come in much closer and to unload all our horses. We need to be quick about it, before it is dark."

The man hurried off and very soon after, the boats that had been beached were rowing back, now empty of warriors, toward the distant ships. Talon glanced up at the sun. It was well past noon, but there was plenty of daylight left for an attack on the camp. He turned to his own men and said to Yosef, "We need to have scouts out and ready. I don't want to walk into an ambush at this late stage. Send three of our Companions to find out what is going on near the camp and have them report back, as soon as they know the disposition of the enemy."

Yosef dipped his head. "I'll go with them, Lord, just to make sure." Yosef and three other horsemen prepared to depart.

After they left, Talon said to the king, "My men will keep us informed as to the whereabouts of the enemy, so that we don't run into any trouble, my lord."

Richard watched the men canter off. "Beautiful horses," he commented with a shake of his head.

"I would consider it an honor if you would accept one of my remounts for the time being, my lord," Talon said and gestured to Junayd. "Bring the best of our remounts for the king and his men, Junayd. I am sure he would prefer to be mounted at this time."

As Junayd disappeared toward the woods, Talon said, "Better to wait for your horses to arrive, my lord. We can provide some, but it would not be wise to chase after the Greeks on foot. The more level ground will favor them east of here, and we could find ourselves outnumbered and outpaced."

Richard, who appeared to be already chaffing at the delay, nodded reluctantly. "So be it then, Lord Talon. We can wait for a while, but not for too long. I am eager to teach this usurper a lesson he will never forget."

Most of the Normans were, by this time, either seated on the low wall taking their ease or attending to their own wounded. Talon murmured to Brandt, "Stand the men down, Brandt. I need to know whom we have lost and how our own wounded are doing. I think it is safe at present to do so."

Brandt barked a command and the Saxons broke ranks to spread out and join Rostam and his men in a search for Kantara men who might have been wounded in the confusion of the battle. As everyone knew everyone else, it would not be so hard for them to find their people.

While this was going on, Talon waved Reza off his horse and presented him to the king.

"This is Lord Reza, my brother, my lord. He is known better as Master Reza, as he is the leader of our Companions."

Richard was a big man, almost half a head taller than Talon himself; standing in front of him, Reza looked very slender; as he was not as tall as Talon, he had to look up at the king. He went down on one knee and bowed his head respectfully, however.

The king gave him his hand and lifted him to his feet. "We owe you and Lord Talon here a great many thanks. You are warriors to be reckoned with, Master Reza," he said with a grin. "I was impressed with how your horsemen rode in and out of the melee with the Greek cavalry. "Incredible horsemanship!"

"That is because our horses are used to playing chogan, my lord," Reza responded with some pride. He noticed the puzzled look on the king's face and went on to explain, in his basic French, how the game was played. The king and the men around him seemed to be impressed. Talon, who was familiar with the kind of horses he expected to see from the ships, said, "In this part of the world, light cavalry is better for covering rocky ground, but I suspect that the destrier is your mount of choice, Lord."

Richard nodded vigorously. "It is, and when they are in good condition, there is nothing that can stop them when they charge!"

Talon agreed. "No, my lord. Not when their riders are well led, then it is true; the Saracen on his lighter horse is at a disadvantage, but it should be remembered that, at Hattin, these heavy mounts were countered by Salah ad-Din, whose generals have learned how to deal with reckless charges by the Christian heavy cavalry." The disastrous events of Hattin were still the stuff of nightmares for him. It was still hard to keep the bitterness out of his tone when he talked of that battle.

Richard gave him a sharp look. "So, you were at Hattin?"

"I was, as were Brandt, my commander of the Saxons over there, and Yosef, who has gone off to scout, my lord. Few survived."

"I want to hear about it; we have a little time, I believe," Richard suggested with a glance at the busy activity surrounding the ships, which had drawn closer.

"The Christian world was very badly led, my lord," Talon began. "Had the king and his lieutenants listened to people like the late Duke of Tripoli and others, who have lived in the region all their lives, then we would still have had a kingdom and still be in control of Jerusalem."

The king scowled. "Explain to me why?" he demanded.

Talon glanced about. The recent battle had been a bloody disaster for the mercenaries and their Greek followers. The area stretching all the way along the road, to within a few score of paces from the gates of Limassol, was littered with the dead and wounded. The low wall resembled a charnel house. The dead were strewn about with gaping wounds and covered in blood, while the victors themselves looked more like butchers than men at arms. The Greeks had fought hard to stop them, but while they might have defeated the Normans, they stood no chance against the ferocity of the Saxons on their flank and the arrows striking them from behind.

Talon and Richard walked some short way toward the east, leaving behind his Saxons, who were still warily keeping one eye on the Normans, to a quiet place where they could talk in relative peace. Talon was to discover, during the next hour that, while Richard listened to what he had to say, he did so with detachment.

Talon told the king as much as he could about the fiasco at Hattin and who had been responsible. Richard didn't comment much at first, but appeared to be paying close attention, and was absorbing the information and storing it away.

Talon was curious as to how Richard would react to the present situation, now that he had a foothold on the island. Conquering Cyprus, after all, not been his original objective.

Richard must have had Isaac on his mind as well, because after he looked around, he turned back to Talon and asked, "So, who is this man, the usurper, Isaac? Will he be back?"

"He has lost many men who cannot be replaced easily, my lord. Most of the people lying here are mercenaries who have come from every city on the coast of the Levant. Many were Byzantine, and experienced enough, when it came to suppressing a population such as we have here on the island, but they met their match today, and that is very significant."

"What do you mean?" Richard demanded.

"I think he will, at first, negotiate and try to gain time. We should definitely be on our guard, Sire. His people will inevitably see how small your army is, and he might think he can win it all back."

The two men were interrupted by a shout from Rostam, who pointed to the east. "Someone comes, Father!"

Yosef and two of his men halted their horses in front of Talon and the king. He spoke in Farsi to Talon.

"Lord, the Emperor has abandoned the camp. There is no one there at all. I am sure he has fled to Famagusta. Larnaca is far too small to hold his forces. We searched for any signs of their presence some of the way to the village, but the farmers told us the army rushed right past them."

Talon looked thoughtful and replied in Farsi. "So, what did you find in the encampment, Yosef?"

"It is quite large, Lord, and looks as though they left everything!"

By this time, Reza had joined them. "Nobody at all?" he demanded. Yosef nodded with a quirk of his mouth, as though he knew what was on Reza's mind.

Reza turned to Talon and lifted his eyebrows. "The scavengers will be there quickly enough, Brother."

Talon pretended to look very serious. "Which means that a contingent of our cavalry must hasten to the camp and take possession, but," he glanced toward the king, who was standing a few paces away, "not led by you, Brother. This must be seen as proper, and the king has met you. Yosef, take a good dozen of our Kantara cavalry and several Companions. Invest the camp, but with caution. I want you to load the others with as much as they and their horses can carry from the tents, and tell them to leave for the castle. The king's men will certainly loot the site when they get there, and I want our share."

"You don't trust these men?" Reza grunted, looking as though he was about to laugh.

Yosef looked as if he, too, was having some trouble with his expression.

"Brandt doesn't, so I am going to base any trust I might have on his example; and in this case, I think we can assume that, unless we first take what we can, they will take it all," Talon murmured. "Take coin and gold, nothing bulky, and then send word to Lady Rav'an that we are all alive and well. Get going, Yosef. You and your scouts should meet us at the entrance to the camp when we arrive and give us the good news. The others should be long gone to Kantara by then."

Yosef saluted solemnly and urged his horse away while Reza and Talon turned back to the king, who was observing them with no little impatience.

"What are you talking about in that strange language, Lord Talon?" he inquired a little huffily.

"I apologize, my lord. We speak that language amongst ourselves," Talon responded. "My scouts informed me that the enemy seems just about to leave his camp. Apparently, he is intent upon retreating to Famagusta as speedily as possible. My man here is going to keep an eye on the army to make sure there are no surprises and to determine if, indeed, the emperor has decided to leave." He glanced at the beach where horses and more men were disembarking. "I see the animals are here, and I'd like to present you with a fresh mount for this sally."

Yosef and his men were already almost out of sight, galloping furiously toward the enemy camp. And Junayd had arrived with horses from Talon's own reserves.

"Let us make sure as many of your men as can be are mounted before we leave, Sire. Then we can make our way to Larnaca and see what the emperor intends."

Richard looked delighted with the mixed breed Arab-Turcoman horse that Junayd held toward him. "I shall ride this one for today. It is a beautiful animal!"

"It is called The Sound of the Wind, Lord," Reza informed him. Junayd murmured something to the animal as he handed it off to the king. It calmed enough for Richard to mount, but it appeared to be as eager as the king to be moving.

Richard was clearly impatient to be gone after the usurper, but common sense appeared to prevail; so while he mounted along with some of his other men, they waited until all the animals from the ships had disembarked. It took several hours.

To Talon's eye, the horses were in a sorry state, which was hardly surprising after several months on a pitching and heaving ship. It took another frustrating hour before the horses were saddled and the men who were to accompany

Richard and Talon were all mounted and ready to leave. By this time, the sun was almost on the horizon, displaying a deep red in the sky

"We should hurry!" Richard muttered. "If they leave in haste, there might be some spoils to be had, and I intend to have it."

This comment served to confirm Talon's belief that, whatever they did find at the camp would all go to the king. He glanced at Reza, who nodded affirmatively.

****

The camp was deserted when they arrived. The large silk tent of the emperor was surrounded by abandoned wagons, fallen tents, food and gear, all the signs of a hasty departure. There were donkeys wandering around, looking lost. One was even braying.

Yosef greeted them at the entrance with two of his men and, after saluting the king, he addressed Talon and Reza. "They are gone, my lords. We carried out your orders." He rolled his eyes northwards. "We chased away some curious citizens from Larnaca."

Reza lowered his eyelids in acknowledgement while Talon turned to the king. "Our caution was justified, Sire. There were some of the enemy here, but when they saw my people, they broke and fled. The camp is yours!"

Richard nodded. "Good. I don't think we could have handled another pitched battle, in any case. Lord D'Onston!"

"Yes m'lord?" D'Onston edged his mount closer to the king, smiling at Yosef and Talon.

"I take this encampment in the name of the Crown," Richard announced loudly. "All within its bounds, prisoners and booty, belong to the Crown. See to it that my orders are obeyed."

D'Onston ducked his head and began to issue orders, while Richard cantered his mount toward the large silk tent in the middle of the camp.

"By God's teeth! This looks like rich pickings!" he muttered, more to himself than to Talon who, along with Reza and several of the king's guards, were keeping pace with him, wary of any unwelcome surprises. Talon knew perfectly well that there would be no danger of that sort. Yosef had seen to it, but caution and a show of caution were the right approach.

When they arrived at the tent, Richard dismounted, tossed the reins to an attendant rider, and stalked into the tent. He stopped abruptly at its entrance and simply stared. To Talon, the interior of the tent was not that remarkable. He was well used to elaborate and overt displays of great wealth, but to these rough men from the North, it must have appeared sumptuous. Richard didn't even bother to hide his awe.

"We will stay here for the night. Post guards and let's have a look at the place," he called back to his men, who laughed and dismounted hurriedly, eager to see what their king had won.

Talon and his men watched and noted as the Norman contingent strode about, seizing everything that could be moved. The king and his aides unearthed much in the way of silver plates and gold drinking vessels, along with trays and gold coins, which Yosef had prudently left for them to find. Talon was in no doubt that the larger portion of coin would find its way to Kantara with his men.

While the king, his lords, knights, and now his foot soldiers were thus preoccupied, Talon greeted Brandt and his men, who had brought up the rear of the small army, as Talon had ordered. King Richard knew little about the people he was fighting, unaware that their preference for ambush was common knowledge in these parts. Talon was not about to allow that. He dismounted and beckoned Brandt over.

"Yosef found a good place with some water for our men and our mounts, Brandt. It is on the north side of this camp with good access to the woods."

A rising din came from the Norman contingent, as they discovered some wine and set to drinking it.

He sighed. "It will fall upon us to be alert and to post sentries in case we're surprised. I doubt if any of these men will be worth anything before too long."

"I see they are busy plundering everything they can find, Lord," Brandt remarked in a dry tone. His eyes rested somewhat wistfully on the looters.

"Hm, yes, but Yosef, as you know, was here first and took care of our entitlement. We will keep it amongst ourselves, but I can promise you, there will be plenty to go around."

Brandt gave him a sharp look. He had not been aware of the orders given to Yosef. Now he grinned and nodded, looking very pleased. "Very well, Lord. I will see to the guards. He really is the king of England, then?"

"Yes, he is, your country, I believe."

"Not one of these people speaks my language, Lord," Brandt said, scornful.

"They don't speak Saxon English?" Talon demanded.

"Not a one of them, Lord."

Talon looked surprised. "But they took the country over a hundred years ago," he protested,

"They conquered our land, Lord. They never felt the need to talk to the Saxons about much at all, after that." Brandt's disgust registered on his grim face. He touched his forehead. "I'll take care of the guards."

He turned and issued an order, whereupon the Saxons marched toward the northern extremity of the camp and began to settle in. Talon was left to ponder his remark.

The night passed relatively quietly. Men were exhausted from the previous day's fighting, and those who had drunk too much wine soon were asleep, almost where they lay or fell. In the tent of the king, his followers found some food and set to with a will. After months of sparse—even bad—food and conditions at sea, they now found themselves in a place some of them could only have dreamed of. The king stuffed himself. He, too, was exhausted and soon fell into the great silk bed and slept like a log. Tired though they were, Talon and his men kept watch.

Chapter 13

Home...for a while

Of all sweet birds, I love the most
The lark and nightingale:
For they the first of all awake,
The opening spring with songs to hail.
—Pierre Vidal, End of Twelfth Century

Talon and his small army arrived at the gates to Kantara the day after the battle for the beach and the English King's arrival.

They had left quietly in the early hours, leaving the Normans to recover from their hangovers, and hopefully, no intrusions by the usurper, Isaac Komnenos. Leaving three unhappy Companions behind to keep watch just in case, they traveled as quickly as they could for home. Their arrival was greeted with much enthusiasm by everyone who had been left behind, all of whom were starved for news.

The men were very tired, caked in mud, dust, and dried blood, but they were exuberant and very happy to come home, even if for only a while. Talon and Reza were sure that they would be back on the road very soon, so there was some urgency to obtaining good food and rest.

As they were admitted to the bailey, Talon glanced around at the very familiar surroundings and gave a sigh of satisfaction. The ground had been swept clean, the new dragon of fire squatted in the same place as its predecessor, glaring directly at him as he rode under the main archway. The former dragon's breath he and his men had devised had disintegrated upon being fired, but it had done its deadly work, nonetheless. This one was made of bronze and, he hoped, would prove to be far more robust.

Talon and Reza ignored the cheers and shouts of welcome and turned their horses to face the tiny army of warriors who shuffled to a halt. The gates crashed shut, followed by a short silence. He addressed his men.

"You are home now. No better group of men could I hope to lead, no men could have done better." He smiled at them with pride. "Go to your homes and rest. Sergeant Palladius and his men still have the castle, so you will have time to yourselves and your families. We will find places for those from the villages and the ships to rest today, and tomorrow we will escort them back down to their homes. Those who wish to go home now, may do so. Remember the signal that will recall you to the castle, as that will mean we are leaving within the day."

The men cheered and there was a rush for the entrance that led to the main castle grounds and the keep. It was a little while before Talon, Reza, and their Companions were themselves able to gain entry. The Saxons were in front of them, growling happily in their guttural language. Brandt made sure that Talon was fine with his men dispersing. Talon dismounted and handed his horse over to one of the eager boys who came running out to take them, then clapped his friend on the shoulder. "Our mission succeeded because of the discipline of the Saxons, Brandt. I am grateful and very proud of them."

Brandt ducked his head and smiled back. "It was a good fight, my lord," he growled. He lifted his head to look around as though looking for someone.

"If you are looking for the two Welsh bowmen, they were amongst the first through that door, Brandt," Reza laughed. It amused both Reza and Talon to note the relief in the huge Saxon's heavily mustached features. "Cattle thieves, but they have their uses," he growled. "They are probably heading for the kitchen."

He turned away just in time to find himself being attacked by a huge, grey, wolf-like creature that had wriggled past multiple legs to throw itself with an excited yelp at its master. Tail wagging furiously and reaching eagerly to lick Brandt's face, the hound, Harold, greeted his master with unreserved enthusiasm. Brandt seized its head in his huge hands and shook it gently from side to side, clearly very happy to see the excited animal.

Leaving Brandt and his men to be taken care of by their families and attendants, Talon, Reza, and Rostam, closely followed by their closest Companions, walked toward the main castle.

Rav'an and Jannat met their men at the top of the stairs. Both women were accompanied by their children and their hovering nurses. Dar'an, smiling from ear to ear, stood by. The first to greet Talon, however, were the two hounds that he had, more or less, inherited when he took the castle, some years before. Both hounds were getting old and brindled. Just like me, Talon thought ruefully, as he stooped to greet the frantic, tail-wagging creatures.

Talon raised a grateful hand to Dar'an as he climbed the steps to greet Rav'an. He kissed her and they embraced. He breathed in her clean scent and, at that moment, knew he was home. Rav'an, on the other hand, pulled back after he had crushed her to him.

"My Talon, you nearly broke all my ribs! And you need a bath!" She laughed, but she held onto his hand very tightly as they turned to walk into the bailey. Reza and Jannat followed them, chattering happily as they walked.

Talon glanced at Dar'an and nodded. They would speak later and exchange information, with an accounting of what had been and what was to be next, now that the arrival of the Normans had changed everything.

When they were fed and refreshed by much-needed baths, the family and their closest Companions assembled in the Solarium. Talon noted that their guests, Cristofo and Armilia, were absent, but Irene, the daughter of Boethius, stayed close to Jannat, who appeared to have taken her under her wing. Talon smiled at her, noting that she seemed to be blooming into a beautiful young woman. He sent a sideways glance at Rav'an, who appeared to read his mind and smiled at him. Then she deliberately rolled her eyes at Rostam, who was being very attentive to Irene. They both smiled, like a pair of conspirators.

Tea was served, and wine was to hand. Talon and Reza were happily enjoying their first drinks in nearly a week, savoring the dry, slightly heady wine from their vineyards.

"Ah, but I have missed this," Reza sighed as he sipped his wine. "The Greeks call it the nectar of the Gods, and I have to agree with them." He smiled at Jannat, who was seated on a cushion very close to him. Their boy, Firuz, had fallen silent for the first time since he saw his father return. His eager questions had given his father little rest until Jannat, who was eager herself to be alone with Reza, told the nurse to find the boy something to occupy him. Firuz was banished to his favorite place in the castle, the aviary, where the huntsmen welcomed the boy and allowed him to pamper his favorite hawk.

Talon and Rav'an's reunion had been similar, but soon, ever sensitive to his state of mind, Rav'an had suggested that they all congregate in the Solarium and discuss events, before the feast that was to take place that evening. Given the now-fluid situation on the island, they needed to be prepared for any eventuality. There was also the conundrum of the Venetians, and what to do about them.

Dar'an and Yosef were there, as was Rostam. Talon, as was customary, presided over the informal gathering. There would be more meetings where Brandt and the other Companions would be involved, but for the time being, only the inner circle was present.

After their adventures outside Limassol were recounted, Talon directed the conversation toward the implications of these same events.

"You all appear to think this man from England is a very powerful person," Rav'an said, after one of the short silences.

"I don't think any of us doubt that, my lady," Yosef said, "but there is something else about him." He looked to Talon and Reza.

"He is a courageous man, but given the circumstances, things could easily have gone very badly wrong for him and his men. The landing could have been a complete disaster," Reza commented thoughtfully.

"We have a very powerful man who is unafraid to use small resources in a big way. I don't doubt his courage, but as Reza pointed out, he is not above impulsive actions, either," Talon said.

"What do you think he will do next?" Rav'an demanded.

"Much depends on Isaac, our great emperor, I suspect." Talon commented, smiling at the derisive snorts of contempt his comment elicited.

"You don't think he will cower in Famagusta until this Norman leaves?" Rostam asked, as he helped himself to a small beaker of wine and offered Reza some more. Talon noted with amusement that Irene appeared to have eyes for no one else but Rostam.

"When he comes out of his funk and realizes how small the army of Richard is, he might be tempted to try something aggressive. That would end very badly, but whether for the king of England or the emperor of Cyprus, who can say? My hope is that the Normans feel the pull of their Crusade and leave as soon as possible. Richard has saved his sister's honor and the princess, so there is nothing more to keep him here."

"Isaac has ever been one to act stupidly, so I shall not bet on a reasonable outcome," Reza muttered darkly.

"Very true, Brother, but I suspect that, should he decide to take this further, this king of England will not be any easy nut to crack. According to one of his lords, he is not one to be intimidated. We've seen that for ourselves too," Talon paused. "Also, he is greedy for the riches that go with a Crusade. He is focused upon his own personal gain, and that could spell trouble, not just for Isaac."

"The king took all the loot from the encampment for himself; he was not inclined to share it," Rostam murmured.

This elicited surprised looks from those who had remained behind in the castle.

"Then, explain how we came about all the riches that your men brought to the castle before you arrived," Jannat demanded. "There were four horses staggering under the weight of it all!"

"Ah! That, my dear princess, is because our fox here," Reza indicated Talon with a wave of his hand, "must have suspected something, and asked Yosef to ride ahead to the deserted camp and see to our share, before any of the Normans arrived." Reza chuckled, as did Yosef.

Dar'an smiled. "Yosef most certainly did. It was not a trivial portion. We are still counting the coin!"

"I just took precautions," Talon stated. He looked up at Dar'an. "To change the subject, how are our Venetian guests behaving?"

"Cristofo behaves himself, my lord. He didn't like being locked up at night, but those were your orders, so that was done. His cell was not uncomfortable."

"His sister is well behaved," Rav'an told him. "She spends most of her time with him during the day, and they talk in their own language. They have a Companion hovering nearby every minute, so they have made no overt effort to leave the castle. I think they realize it would be futile. She, too, stays in a locked room at night. However, she is pleasant enough with us all." Rav'an added.

"Then, when we have completed our own business, we should bring them to the feast and find out more about them. I am interested in what might come of this unplanned visit of theirs."

"Do we see an opportunity here, Father?" Rostam asked.

"Yes, Rostam, I do, but we must tease it out and see where it leads," his father responded. "We are traders, and I fear that our market is to be threatened in the near future. Perhaps we need to look beyond Palestine and Byzantium."

"Your father has a point, Rostam," Reza pointed out. "Trade is never comfortable with the threat of war in the air, and I, too, suspect that war is coming, although perhaps not here on this island. You are right, Talon, that we should be looking further afield than just the eastern seaboard."

*****

"Hey! Where are you two rogues going in such a hurry?" Brandt called to the two Welshmen as they brushed past him.

"Hello, Harold!" One of them said cheekily, ignoring Brandt, and he patted the huge dog on the shoulder as they went by.

"Lord Talon has invited the Greek musicians to come up to play!" Caradog called back. "I love their music!"

"And enough of calling us rogues, Saxon. Didn't we just save your worthless h'ides at the battle? Hadn't been for us skilled archers now, none of you would have surv'ived, I tell you. As it is, I don't know why we did it!" Dewy laughed.

"Skill, that's what is was, Bach. Skill!" Caradog bragged.

"Bollocks! Go and eat them both!" Brandt commanded Harold, with a push in their direction. Harold charged at the two men, but when he arrived, all he did was wag his tail and wriggle around the two laughing men.

"See, Brandt! He's still properly grateful we didn't eat him when we was all a-starv'ing in that Tyre place," Caradog called back.

Brandt rolled his eyes. 'That dog embarrasses me more and more,' the big man sighed to himself.

"But more importantly, the word is out that, tonight, Her Ladyship is going to play for all of us! Come along, Saxon, it will be good for your educa'ytion." Dewy called back, as they headed for the main hall to join a growing crowd of attendants, servants, and men at arms, all heading in the same direction.

Brandt's head jerked up. Her Ladyship would be playing? Before he came to Kantara and served Lord Talon, he had never heard of the lady of a castle playing to a crowded hall of retainers and servants. Even here, it was not a common event. When she did, there was almost no room, even to stand in the hall. Barely a person in the castle wanted to miss the performance, and many even made the journey up from the villages to hear her. Although Brandt, his Saxons, and the Companions had pride of place, with their benches nearest to the High Table, Brandt knew that, commander or not, he would have to hurry to get the best place to sit.

It was just before sunset and the castle was settling down for the night. The grooms were hurriedly completing last minute tasks with their horses, which were contentedly munching their feed. The huntsmen were checking their birds of prey and talking to the hounds. The guards were mustering for night duty, and those who were now relieved were hastening to the hall, both to eat and to be well placed for the entertainment to come.

The sun finally disappeared below the distant jumble of mountains to the west of the castle. There were quiet murmurs and the more muted sounds that go with the onset of dusk, as the servants and retainers finished their daily tasks and made haste for the main hall. Tantalizing smells from the kitchens drifted out into the yard. The cooks would be kept busy this evening.

Brandt increased his pace, while the two archers almost ran up the steps to the main door. "Bugger!" he muttered to himself. "I'm hungry!" He set off in pursuit of his friends. "Come along, Dog!" he called, and gave a low whistle.

Harold, who had wandered off, bounded back up the small lane between the stables and the chapel to join him, wagging its tail and bouncing about. "Don't get in my way!" Brandt yelped, as Harold nearly tripped him up in his excitement. He patted the hound affectionately on its ribs with a huge hand. The dog grunted happily and sped off.

*****

The meal provided that night was organized by a man named Rizardo, who Boethius, the merchant spy in Paphos, had sent to them. "He is a magnificent cook my Lady," he had explained to Rav'an in a letter, "but he has incurred the unwelcome attentions of Isaac, and might lose his feet, should he be captured by the emperor's men. If you can find a place for him, however humble then I am sure he will be grateful."

Rizardo had proved to be very grateful but also very talented and from that time on he had changed the nature of the food provided to the family and their retainers.

This evening had been no exception; there were the usual pies of course, filled with mouthwatering stews of mutton and pork. There was roast lamb and venison from the forests for those who desired it. There was even a boar's head in the place of honor at the high table. The grilled fish and vegetables were garnished with herbs from Theodora's garden, where very often Rizardo and Brother Martin would huddle like a pair of conspirators as they discussed the merits of the effect of this or that herb upon this dish or that. It was clear that Martin was filling out well from this rich diet, too.

The creamed fish roe was placed in jars on every table along with olives floating in oil and huge loaves of bread alongside. Vine leaves stuffed with ground meat and herbs were plentiful for all. But it was with the pastries that Rizardo came fully into his own. Baclava, Talon's favorite, fine pastry rolls stuffed with ground pistachio nuts and raisins soaked in honey were distributed all about. He made quite sure that only the best and lightest pastry went to the high table. Rizardo glowed with pleasure when Talon and Rav'an made sure he knew how much they appreciated the food

The wine flowed freely and the talk grew loud as men talked about the battle with one another or informed those who were not there; there was not a little bragging going on as to how it had gone. Caradog and Dewi took center stage and the shouts of laughter at their jokes and descriptions of events filled the hall. Then it was time.

*****

The remains of the food were cleared away by servants, to be replaced by jugs of good red wine and beer. Conversations fell silent, and the air filled with anticipation as Lady Rav'an finally took up the four-stringed instrument that she called a tar. She settled herself on a high stool near the steps, leading down to the tables, where were gathered Lord Talon's retainers. She smiled at the crowd, which hushed expectantly. Some, who'd had a few cups more than they should, were poked into silence by others, who were determined to have quiet the better to hear. A noisy hound near the entrance to the great room was cuffed. The crowd waited, attentive, and then she began to play.

The first tentative notes thrilled high into the warm evening air and ensured absolute silence. Even the hounds stopped quarreling over their bones and appeared to listen. Then music danced away from Rav'an's instrument, as her fingers moved over the strings as though caressing them. Nevertheless, the notes were crisp and clear. A general sigh of contentment rose from the crowded benches.

Tonight she had started with an old Persian song, which she had told a serving girl was called "Butterflies." It seemed to the rapt listeners that each note from the tar was reflected off the stone walls of the hall, tripping into the cavernous darkness above the crowded benches to dance among the great, dark, smoke-blackened beams, high above the candlelit tables, then to drift back down to once again envelope the enthralled audience with its magic.

She would play a small ripple of notes and then pause very briefly on a high or a low note, then repeat the previous ripple, leaving a wistful note in the air before her fingers continued with their skilled work and the song moved on.

"She makes it sound like the flowing of water along a *dingle*!" Caradog whispered in awe. "That's a small stream to you ignorant Saxons," he added.

"How does she play like that?" Dewy whispered, wiping a tear from his eye. "I swear, she is be'tter than Llewellyn himself. I can feel the music reaching deep into me bones."

He received a glare from Brandt, seated nearby, who pursed his lips and put a thick forefinger in front of them.

Seated on the dais and overlooking the assembly, Talon rested his chin in his cupped hand and listened as raptly as anyone else. He half closed his eyes and let his mind drift with the familiar music.

"Your music often takes me to a shore, from where I can see a distant castle shimmering over an island in the middle of a lake," he had told her once, and had been rewarded by the tinkle of her laughter. "We have no lake, my darling. But there is much else to be thankful for," she'd informed him, and she had stood on tiptoe to kiss him.

Rav'an played many tunes that evening. They were in much the same vein, reflective and wistful—even haunting—holding the audience in thrall as the very last note faded into the darkness of the roof above the tables, until, finally, while no one dared to breathe, there was silence. Talon wondered if there was a dry eye in the whole hall. Hardened warriors—Greek, Welsh, Saxon, and Arab alike—were very quiet, avoiding each other's eyes, lest they see each other's tears, while young maidens were openly weeping. Psellos, the priest, was sobbing into his sleeve, Brother Martin patting him on the back, gently trying to calm him.

Talon slowly stood up as Rav'an walked back to her seat next to him.

"You have bewitched our people yet again, my lady," he murmured, taking her hand in his. Then he called out, "My lady has finished for the evening, but we have the players from the villages here with us, and they will entertain you further. I bid you all good night."

The musicians, who had been silently waiting at the side of the hall, stepped forward and began to play their instruments vigorously, playing the fast and exciting music that was unique to the island. Talon liked it, too, but he was ready to leave the revelers to their enjoyment, as he could see that Rav'an was tired. He and his family took their leave.

*****

The days passed quickly; too fast for Talon, who found he was tired when he returned to the castle at the end of each day. Although busy with land affairs, he was still persuaded to take time for his children, at the insistence of Rav'an, who told him on the third day, "If you keep this up, they will not know who you are, and won't let you read stories to them. Then where will we be?"

He responded with a kiss. "This evening, then. I will be there with all of you, and I shall bring a story."

That evening they gathered in the Solarium. Talon seated himself and handed a roll of paper, held closed by a red ribbon, to his daughter, who was watching him with a solemn expression on her oval face, framed by her light-colored hair. Not for the first time, he remarked to himself how like her mother Fariba looked. Except for her hair, she could have been a small replica of her beautiful mother. Her huge grey eyes were focused on his face with an expression of intense concentration, but there was also an air of anticipation as she took the roll of paper and went through the little ceremony they always had when it was time for him to read a story to her and her little companion, Firuz.

"Which story is it, Uncle Talon?" chirped Firuz. He eagerly watched Fariba pull the ribbon off the paper and unroll it. Neither child knew yet how to read Greek, but their parents had discovered that both children liked the ceremony that was part of an evening's entertainment. It delayed the going-to-bed part, which the children would do nearly anything to avoid.

Talon smiled at Firuz and glanced at his mother. Jannat had the boy in the curl of her arm. "That will be revealed as I read it," he stated, and took back the long and wide paper document his daughter held out to him.

"I hope it is about Sulieman the Great King!" Fariba squeaked and snuggled back into Rav'an's arms.

The fire crackled in the hearth, and the audience prepared themselves, enjoying the anticipation of a story and the warmth of the fire. The evenings were still cool. The servants in attendance, two maids and one young servant boy, were just as eager to hear the story, because it was to be recited in Greek this evening, although the document itself was in Arabic. They moved closer, unobtrusively, to hear more clearly. The two Saluki hounds solemnly stared down their long noses at Talon and crossed their paws as though about to conduct an audience.

Talon pretended to examine the writing on the paper very carefully, as though he had never seen it before. He even turned it upside down once and peered myopically at it as though he was unsure what to read.

"Papa!" exclaimed Fariba. "You must stop doing that and read the story!" she insisted.

He lifted the paper to read it more clearly in the candlelight.

"There was once a great king!" he began.

Rostam grinned. Everyone was enjoying the performance. Firuz spoke up. "I know this one!" he exclaimed with huge satisfaction.

"Then perhaps you will allow those of us who do not know the story to listen, my darling," Jannat murmured and ruffled his hair. "Now, quiet, and let Uncle Talon read the story!" she admonished. Firuz subsided, and Talon again began to speak in a clear voice.

"As I said, there was once a great king. He was very wise and, indeed, he was also a magician."

"A magician!" both children breathed in unison.

"Yes, a magician. They do exist, you know." Talon insisted, looking stern.

"This sultan was known far and wide as a very wise man who, although he was a magician, was careful not to use his powers very often, except for the benefit of his people." Talon paused and looked around. His audience was riveted.

"The sultan, being a sultan, had many, many wives, and sometimes their demands upon his time would tire him. They would quarrel and then expect him to decide in favor of one or the other for very trivial matters."

His daughter could not remain silent a moment longer. "How many wives did he have, Papa?"

Talon glanced up. "Oh, about nine hundred, I should think," he said, trying to sound solemn.

"Nine hundred!" the children shrieked, accompanied by the laughter of their parents. "Hush, both of you!" Rav'an laughed, to quiet the squeals from the children and the giggles of the maids.

"Now then, children, if you cannot remain silent while I tell this story, then we will never reach the end of it." Talon remarked, while his wife and Jannat rolled their eyes in amusement.

"In order to find peace and quiet, the sultan, whose name was...?"

"Sulieman!" Firuz and Fariba chanted.

"Sulieman would escape the tiresome duties of his office —and, it must be said, the clamor of his wives—to a beautiful garden near the palace. He refused to use his magic to quell the noise because he didn't believe in showing off. The only person he would permit to be with him on these occasions was his favorite wife, whose name was Balkis. She alone, of all the wives, knew when to allow him space to reflect and be on his own for a while. He relaxed on the bench, waiting for her to appear, in due course.

Talon continued reading. "The great sultan had other talents to go with his magic. He could understand what animals and insects were saying—which could be just as annoying as the endless chatter of his wives. Especially the ants. They gossiped about everything and everyone! On this day, however, the sultan found peace and seated himself on a bench to enjoy the evening and the quiet of the extensive garden.

"But then he was jerked out of his reverie by a little noise —more of a tiny chatter—coming from a bush nearby. He cocked an ear and began to listen. Not very far away were two butterflies, and they were having an argument. The sultan smiled to himself. There were occasions when eavesdropping was a diversion.

"The young male butterfly appeared to be irked by the other, a female, who was clearly not afraid of him and wouldn't let him dominate the conversation."

Jannat glanced at Reza, who grinned mischievously. "Is there a moral to this story?" she inquired innocently.

Talon smiled and continued. "Finally, the male butterfly said to his wife, 'I could stamp my foot and the huge palace and this garden would *all* disappear!' Then he flew off in a huff to land on the arm of the king. 'You know how women are,' he told the sultan.

"Sulieman found this very amusing and asked the butterfly, 'Why did you lie like that?' but before the insect could answer, he said, 'But I shall help you, if you decide to do this.'

"'You really would do that, Lord?' the butterfly asked him. His antenna fluttered, and his large eyes grew even wider than they already were with surprise.

"Meanwhile, Balkis had walked into the garden and she also overheard the conversation. She slipped over to the butterfly's wife. 'Why did you challenge him?' she asked, very amused.

"'Oh, he thinks he should be master of the world. You know how men are!' the little creature responded.

"Balkis laughed and told her, 'You should dare your husband to stamp his foot, as he must be fibbing. Then you can argue with him again.' In reality, she was hoping the disappearance of the palace would shock the sultan's noisy wives into silence. For Balkis had noticed the conversation taking place between the sultan and the other butterfly, and she guessed correctly as to what it was about.

"Balkis retreated and waited while the female butterfly thought about it. The male butterfly eventually flew back to her. When she demanded that he show his power and stamp his foot, he told her the sultan had called him over to ask him not to do so, because he, Suleiman himself, was afraid of the butterfly.

"'You say you are hugely powerful and the sultan himself fears you!' she challenged him. The listening sultan detected a petulant tone in her tiny voice that reminded him of some of his wives.

"'Yes, I do!' retorted the other, 'and I can tell you that, if I go and ask him for a favor, he will listen to me and do what I ask. For if not, if I stamp my foot, the palace will disappear and there will be," he lowered his voice, "*darkness* everywhere!"

"'Humph,' she snorted." Talon paused.

"Can butterflies snort?" he asked the room in general. After the laughter had subsided, he continued.

The butterfly's wife then said, 'You have to prove that to me,' and she glanced over to where Balkis was hiding. 'I do not believe you!'

"The young male began to prevaricate. 'Well, I don't think the sultan would like it,' he replied, 'but I could, you know!'

"'Very well, then, go on and prove it! He is right here, sitting on that bench.'

"The butterfly glanced apprehensively over his wings and regarded the sultan seated on the bench. He appeared to be gazing appreciatively at the flowers, but he winked at the male butterfly, who then said, 'Very well, I will!' But there was a trace of uncertainty in his voice.

"'There he is. Go and ask him,' the butterfly wife insisted. 'You're just boasting as usual.'

"Whereupon he flew back to the king, and explained his predicament. Sulieman tried hard not to look amused, but told him to go back to his wife and stamp his foot. So the little creature came back to his wife and frowned at her.

"Butterflies can frown," Talon stated for the benefit of the audience. "He said, 'The foolish sultan refused to grant my wish!' Then he lifted one of his little feet, and stomped.

"Abruptly, the palace simply vanished, as did most of the garden, leaving only a small space, wherein were the sultan, Balkis, who was holding her sides with amusement, and the two butterflies.

"This made the butterfly's wife very scared, and she promised never to argue with him again, as long as he promised to bring it all back. This left Sulieman in fits of laughter.

"Now, when the palace had vanished, taking everyone inside with it Sulieman's quarreling wives were deathly afraid. They believed that the king was dead, and the very heavens were mourning his passing.

"But when the sultan decided to bring the palace back into sight, Balkis went to them, exclaimed that a butterfly was angry at his quarrelsome wife, and Sulieman with his power and majesty made the palace and garden vanish until she promised to never quarrel again. Then they wondered what, if the king would do this terrible thing for the sake of a tiny butterfly, would he do to them, who have been making him miserable with their quarreling? And they, in turn, become scared of Sulieman's powers, and were nice and quiet from then on.

"And that is the end of this tale of two butterflies," Talon said, and rolled up the paper, to the groans from his children and the sighs of the servants.

"I believe it's time for bed," he stated.

Chapter 14

The Venetians

There were still many pieces on the chess board, after slightly less than an hour of playing, between Talon and the Venetian. Talon had lost a pawn, a knight and a bishop, which he had just sacrificed in order to place his queen just where he wanted and to distract Cristofo from the knight he had buried in among Cristofo's pieces. Cristofo moved his black castle forward one place, hesitated, then moved it two squares, knowing it was well protected by his own knight.

He smiled at Talon. His teeth gleamed in the candlelight as he contemplated victory. He knew he was within three moves of a checkmate, and he was sure his opponent didn't realize it. However, Talon had other ideas. He moved his own white bishop halfway across the board in what appeared to be an evasive move, to get away from Cristofo's knight.

Sensing victory, Cristofo moved his queen into line behind his castle. Clearly, he planned to sacrifice the castle if necessary, but his queen would finish the game.

Nearby, watching the game with a glint of amusement in his dark eyes, was Reza, who smiled openly when Talon moved his queen forward and took a pawn. The move placed the queen right next to Cristofo's king; she was covered by the bishop and the knight that had been lurking in among some pawns.

"I believe it is my game," Talon murmured. Cristofo, taken completely by surprise, blinked and gaped at the board while Reza chortled.

"You are not the first to be taken by surprise, Cristofo!" he laughed. "The only one amongst us who can beat Talon is Lady Rav'an!"

Hearing her name being mentioned from the other side of the room, Rav'an glanced up at the men, and then back at her young visitor, Cristofo's sister, Armilia.

"Many have tried to get the better of Talon," she murmured with an amused smile, "but few have succeeded."

Armilia smiled back, but she caught the warning, too. Her impressions of the castle and its inhabitants were mixed, but she was impressed, despite her reservations.

"I—I feel as though I have just been mentally stripped naked and tossed in the midden!" Cristofo exclaimed. "You literally handed me that bishop! I know that is what deceived me."

"Ah yes, I never had much time for bishops," Talon remarked. "The good part about that is that you won't smell like a midden," he added with a smile. "Have some more wine," he offered, after the general laugher that ensued.

"That I will, sir!" Cristofo stated. "I need something to help me recover from that rout! This is excellent wine," he commented, as he sipped the deep red liquid appreciatively. 'Tell me, where on the eastern seaboard can one find a wine like this? There is none to be had in Beirut, and certainly not Alexandria. Perhaps it is from Constantinople?" he offered.

"I once knew a senator who could have competed very well with this wine," Talon remarked thoughtfully.

"Grown right here on our land," Reza interjected with pride.

Cristofo's eyes widened again. "You are a people who are full of surprises!" he exclaimed. "This is much better than I might have expected from this island, better even than most I have tasted in my native land," he added.

"Then perhaps we could discuss trade?" Talon said with a glance at Reza, who nodded thoughtfully. Talon had been thinking along these lines ever since the Venetians had arrived. Dar'an and his men had inspected the vessel very carefully from top to bottom, and had brought back to the castle information that had interested Talon and Reza greatly.

There had been a small cargo of salt, carefully contained in well-sealed boxes, which, Talon assumed, had come from Egypt. He knew all about transporting salt. It was difficult, but there was none to be had in Palestine in the amounts and quality Dar'an had found on board the ship. Talon's memories of Al Fayoum, where he and Max had spent many months, had come back to him with a rush. The best salt to be found in this side of the Inner Sea came from that great lake. He thought he might buy it from Cristofo, should he be willing, as there was a great need of salt by the Christians in Palestine.

There was some gold in the vessel, also from Egypt, he assumed, but not much, as well as olive oil, which was at a premium these days. The incessant wars produced warriors who deserted their armies, and then went for the easy pickings of caravans.

They had also found dates, figs, and some barrels of copper ore, which was, according to Dar'an, of poor quality compared to Kantara's mine. He had even brought a very small sack of it to give to Talon and Reza for examination, along with another small sack of gold. "It is not a well laden vessel, Lords," he had stated. "Our ships are always full when they come home."

Talon and Reza had looked at one another. "Perhaps an opportunity, Brother?" Reza had inquired.

Cristofo sipped the wine again and looked very interested. "So you grow the grapes that make this wine?" he asked.

"We do, and we trade it, too," Reza said.

"What do you sell when you come to this end of the sea?" Talon asked, in order to keep the conversation going where he wanted.

"Why, we have tanned goods, grain, millet and wheat, crafted goods such as armor, and, of course, wine. Then we can deal in ships, which we build, and… slaves."

"And you buy salt, which is from Al Fayoum." Talon said, ignoring the suggestion in Cristofo's tone.

"I have ceased to be surprised at what you know, Lord Talon," Cristofo said. His tone, already respectful, became markedly more so. "Yes, indeed, we do buy salt from Egypt, but I have never been to this place you mentioned. They have an agent who deals with foreigners in the port of Alexandria. But there are discoveries in our own land, where salt is being found of late, so that trade might dwindle."

"You also seek copper?" Talon inquired. "Dar'an," he called over to his longtime Companion. Dar'an, who had been playing the game of Go with Rostam, looked up. "Yes, Lord?" he asked.

"Do you still have that little sack of gold that you found on their ship?"

"Of course!" Dar'an got up and walked over to join Talon and Reza. He handed Talon the little leather sack, which

Cristofo immediately recognized. Although his eyes widened, he said nothing; his mouth tightened, and he looked worried.

Talon thanked Dar'an, then tossed the little bag over to Cristofo. "Don't worry, nothing has been taken. My men here were concerned about its security while the ship was in our port. Not from our people, but perhaps from your own?"

Cristofo had the grace to look down. He nodded. "I will admit that I was worried, as was my sister." He looked up. "I thank you, Lord. Your men did the honorable thing." He glanced up at Dar'an to thank him, but Dar'an had already left to rejoin Rostam.

"I hope you didn't sneak any stones in while I was over there, young master," he said with a pretended frown, as he settled himself down opposite Rostam, who rolled his eyes. "I can beat you at this game, without cheating either, Dar'an."

Dar'an pretended to count the stones, then pointed to one on the periphery of the mass of black and white stones. "So how did that one get there then, Lord?" he inquired with a surprised look on his face.

Rostam looked indignant. "I absolutely did not sneak one onto that board! Mother, did you see me do anything untoward?" He appealed to his mother and Jannat, who were seated nearby.

Rav'an looked up. "Dar'an was just checking to see if you were paying attention, my darling," she remarked with a smile at Dar'an, "which, obviously, you were not."

Dar'an grinned at the women in a conspiratorial manner. "Come on, Master Rostam. Let's see if you can manage to win this time."

Meanwhile, Talon and Reza, accompanied by an attentive but silent Yosef, found themselves in an ever-deeper conversation with Cristofo, who was giving them his full attention now.

"What is it that brings Venetians to this end of the sea? Tell us, because we are interested," Reza asked him.

"Our city, the lands behind us, Lombardy, want pearls and gems, spices, precious metals, medicines, carpets, other fabrics, and lacquerware. All kingdoms need healthy horses, weapons, and armaments. Silk, while it is produced these days in the Arab world and has spread to Lombardy, is still in demand, as there is never enough, nor is the local stuff of such good quality."

"And I believe, sugar cane, ceramics and perhaps even gold?" Talon added.

Cristofo took another sip of wine, but his eyes never left those of Talon.

"These are all of interest," he nodded. "They sell in Venice, but also further inland, as well. The lords of Lombardy, when they are not skirmishing with the Byzantines, are always in need of these things."

"Your family? They are nobles?" Talon inquired. He knew that Rav'an was talking with the young girl at the other end of the room, so he didn't feel the need to inquire too deeply.

Cristofo nodded again. "We are a family of consequence in Venice," he agreed. His tone was cautious.

"Since the er... unfortunate incident in Constantinople, we have not seen too many Venetian ships these last few years," Talon remarked, as though it were an aside. But he knew immediately that he had hit a nerve.

Their guest's eyes flashed with anger. "We have been at war ever since the horrendous evil that was committed by those... those Byzantines. My cousin, God rest his soul, was one of those murdered in the massacre," he ground out.

Talon was well aware of the tragedy that had occurred in Constantinople, and while he was clear in his mind that the citizens of the city were very wrong to have committed such a horror, it had come as no surprise to hear of it. The Venetians and their counterparts, the Genoans, had become exceedingly arrogant toward the very people who had made them rich. Their behavior, up to the time when they had been massacred, had been reprehensible. He did not, however, elaborate on what he knew. It was clearly a very sensitive subject.

"A terrible tragedy for you and your family. Please accept my condolences," Talon said, but then added, "A financial catastrophe of huge proportions, too, no doubt."

Cristofo's lips tightened under his mustache, but he could only nod his agreement. Then he said reluctantly, "We are still recovering from that disaster." He stared at Talon with a question in his eyes. "How do you know all this?" he asked.

Talon gave a very small shrug. "We have eyes and ears in many places. I understand that, even though relations have not been restored between your people and the Emperor of Byzantium, the Pisans and the Genoans remained there; hence competition is fierce." He gazed up at the roof as though contemplating the beams. "However, perhaps your family and mine could come to some kind of arrangement," he murmured. "To our mutual benefit. You understand?"

Cristofo shook his head as though in disbelief. "You are very well informed, Lord Talon. I have never encountered a noble of the land who cared much about trade," he added. "Few of the nobles on the mainland care for it. It is beneath them!"

"Then surely, that is to our advantage. Your father and his father were merchants, I assume?" Talon offered.

"Yes, my grandfather founded our family in the city. We are not of noble birth, but...."

"Your family is wealthy now and resides within the city of Venice, so they *are* nobility, am I not right?"

Cristofo nodded his agreement. "The city of Venice depends on families such as ours for its wealth. We are sea traders, as there is no land to speak of, and we cannot depend upon the mainland for anything much, other than treachery. We are indeed the new nobles. My father is on the council, which advises and reports to a *doge,* who is, in effect, the prince or lord of the city," Cristofo stated with some pride. "I was sent on this journey by my father to attempt to reopen trade with merchants in Beirut and other cities, but most of our agents have gone, or died in the chaos. Beirut is controlled by a pirate, so we barely escaped with our lives." He finished with a shrug. "As you have, no doubt, verified for yourself, Lord Talon, we came away somewhat lean."

"Something will have to be done about that pirate, Ibn al-Bannā Makhid," Reza growled.

"I think it is his cousin, Brother. But yes their time will come." He turned his attention back to Cristofo.

"Then, I think we should talk some more, Cristofo, and see if we can forge some trade ties that are of mutual benefit," Talon told him. "Would you like some more wine?"

*****

Nearer to the fire, the women were seated on cushions, and while Jannat was engaged with Irene in conversation, Rav'an was taking the measure of her young guest.

Armilia was in her late teens, and pretty. Her wide-set bright blue eyes were intelligent, and her slightly pursed lips were set in a firm line as she studied her hosts.

"You must tell us more of your home, about your city, which is surrounded by mysteries and tales of wonder," Rav'an prompted.

"Are the streets paved with gold, as we hear they are in Constantinople?" Jannat asked, having just heard her comment. Both she and Irene began to listen in.

Armilia and her brother had heard rumors aplenty while in Famagusta, but the people of the castle did not appear to be the menacing ghouls described by rumor. No one had the stink of sulfur about them, and the magician, Talon, while he presented a formidable appearance, had been very civil. The women were kind to her and, she remarked to herself, beautiful, although older by some years. They also, she noted, appeared to be very refined.

Seeing her hesitate, Jannat smiled and said, "You have nothing to fear from us, dear. We will not bite."

Armilia smiled back. "We are a city built out at sea; we have very few paved streets."

"Built on an island?" Jannat asked.

"On many islands. I am told that, long ago, it was just one, in a huge marsh," she responded. "All our houses are built upon wood."

"Wood? Why not rock or clay?" Rav'an demanded.

"The islands are of sand and clay, and houses built directly on the ground sink and settle. Venice is sometimes known as the Floating City, built upon trees that were placed in the marsh."

"What brought your people to live on this strange sounding construction?" Jannat asked.

"The barbarians sacked Rome, and our tribes relocated. Today we are traders, as you can see. But some of our family were caught up in the terrible events in Constantinople, and we were hurt because of it."

"It was very courageous of you to embark upon a voyage. It is one thing for a man to, but you decided to go along with Cristofo and endure the dangers, too?" Rav'an interjected.

"I love the sea and the distant lands that promise much," Armilia responded with a deprecating smile."

"That makes you unusual, in and of itself, Armilia," Jannat said. She stopped just then because they had heard a groan from nearby.

"You've done it again! Dar'an, I don't know how you do it!" Rostam exclaimed, sounding annoyed. He stared at the board of white and black stones, as though trying to divine what had completed his demise. "Mother, I do not know how he does it!" Rostam complained, shaking his head.

Rav'an smiled. "It is called finesse, my dear, and you still have some learning to do in that area. Besides, you will learn more by losing to one such as Dar'an than by winning against a lesser opponent," she told him.

"Dar'an learned from an old man in China. It was the gardener, wasn't it, Dar'an?" Jannat said.

"It was, my lady. While the young master and his friend were playing with kites, he taught Yosef and myself. May God be kind to his soul, for I am sure he has gone by now." Dar'an replied. Rav'an watched with amused affection as Dar'an began pointing out the weaknesses in Rostam's game. She turned to find Armilia watching her.

"You talk to your servants as though they are your family," she remarked with some surprise. "I do not speak your language, but even to me, a stranger, it is clear that it is so."

"He became a member of our family many years ago now, and I—we all trust him implicitly. Talon took him off the streets of Jerusalem, a starving urchin, about to be hung for the petty crime of stealing fruit to save his sick father," she told the Venetian girl. "He has repaid that debt many times over. He was directly responsible for saving this very castle and all in it from the predations of some very unpleasant people, not so long ago."

Rav'an did not miss the interested glance Armilia sent Dar'an's way.

*****

Later that night, Talon and Reza were in Talon's study, sipping some arak, which was also produced on their lands. They were discussing the Venetians.

"I fear that Cyprus is not going to be a good source of trade, if Isaac continues on the course he is on at present," Talon stated.

Reza nodded in agreement. "Since Diocles retired, Isaac has had no sensible advisers. The only one is Gôsakos, who, while he might be a veteran mercenary, is no administrator. I wonder how Gôsakos is faring after this latest debacle? Without any good advice to rein in his impulsivity, Isaac believes he can simply take what he wants, and it is only a matter of time before he confiscates one of our ships on some pretext or another, and then we will have to kill him. I don't know why we haven't, before now," Reza told him.

"Because Brother, neither you nor I would wish to rule this disordered island! It is full of Greeks!" Talon laughed. "Why, even now, there are food riots in Paphos and Larnaca. They are complaining bitterly about the taxes, too. Look how much trouble we have within our own small villages! They quarrel endlessly, and I often get tired of listening to them. Although, I suppose, I love them dearly."

"There is a lot to love about them," Reza agreed. "I love their music, and the wine they help us produce." He kept his council about ruling the island, however. He was very sure that Talon could rule the island and restore its rich heritage, but his brother seemed disinclined to expand their land ownership.

Talon was continuing. "Cristofo told us of things we were only partially aware of, west of here, in the Latin world, where they have a Prince of the Church, who appears to be very powerful. They call him the Pope, and that is significant. The Templars report to him, not the bishops, which galls them no end. If we had trade contact with a family, such as Cristofo's, in this strange sounding city on the edge of the Latin world, then we might be better off. Information is an important asset, as the Arabs have many times demonstrated, and we both know that."

"Then we could load his ship with what we have to hand in our store houses and send him on his way," Reza said, as he sipped the fierce drink reflectively. "But how do we know he will come back and deal with us honestly, Brother?"

"I think we could send one of our number to make sure he does, and to establish some kind of foothold which, ultimately, would be ours alone," Talon murmured.

"You or me?" Reza inquired.

"Hmm, perhaps, but I have something else that I think is important for you to do for us all, Reza. While I may be worrying unnecessarily, I fear that all is not well in Constantinople. Rav'an is also concerned, and I would be happier if you could investigate. We can decide upon someone, perhaps one of our trusted men, to go to Venice to represent us. I cannot leave, as long as the English king is still here. I want to keep an eye on him."

Reza nodded. "I agree with that, Talon. But are you so concerned about Theo?" Reza asked.

"We should have heard something from her by now. I am worried that Theodora and perhaps her brother, might have fallen into some kind of difficulty. I ended up liking him very much, so yes, I am concerned."

"We could send Rostam to Venice," Reza said with a smirk. "I have seen the way that girl watches him."

"He is our best navigator, and he would learn more of the routes than the Venetians are likely to realize," Talon said thoughtfully. "But you would consider going to Constantinople, Brother?"

"Theodora saved my life, Talon. Of course I shall go and see what is going on. It is probably all good and she is back in charge of the family villa, living high," Reza said firmly. "Perhaps I can steal some of the vines to bring back and graft with some of our own," he joked.

"Then we shall drink to that." Talon smiled at his longtime friend as he poured another small beaker of arak for each of them.

Chapter 15

The Wedding

They ride in glittering gowns of silk,
He harnessed like a lord;
There is no gold about the boy,
But the crosslet of his sword;
The rest have gloves of sweet perfume,
He gauntlets strong of mail;
They broidered cap and flaunting plume,
He crest untaught to quail.

—Sir Walter Scott

The welcome the English king received in Limassol appeared, on the surface at least, to be enthusiastic. The gates of the town were thrown open, and the leading citizens prostrated themselves, as was the custom for their emperor, on either side of the road, as the king and his men rode in triumph through the portals. The Normans wore bemused expressions on their bearded faces as they marched into the city. They had not expected obeisance.

No one had liked the "Usurper", as Isaac was now being named out loud. Formerly, it would have meant instant imprisonment, and even death; but now that the tall, fierce-looking Normans were in charge of the town, the Greeks began to demonstrate how much they detested the man. Effigies were burned in the square; some mercenaries, along with those who had cooperated with them and who had not been quick enough to flee, were beaten in public or lynched by a vengeful mob.

*****

Watching the noisy crowds milling about in the streets from one of the palace balconies, Princess Joanna said to Lord D'Onston, "It reminds me of Sicily all over again. My brother arrives, all is chaos for a while, and then we leave."

Lord D'Onston didn't fail to note the cynical tone, and smiled to himself. While Princess Joanna would defend her brother vehemently in public, she had few illusions as to his character. At this moment, Richard was dispersing the plundered wealth from the usurper's encampment among his lords and knights, while boasting of what he was going to do to Isaac, should he dare to show his face again.

"Our soldiers have a fine appreciation for the Greek art and decor," she continued in an acid tone. "I hear that his men are even digging the small gold-plated tiles off the walls with their daggers! The fine frescoes and images of Greek heroes mean nothing to them. My brother encourages them. He thinks this is a rich little island."

"It once had that reputation, my lady," D'Onston answered. "When we spoke together, Lord Talon de Gilles told me that the emperor, I mean the usurper, stole from everyone when he first arrived and taxed many of the merchants out of business. There is not so much in the way of pickings left."

"Not by Greek standards," was her dry response. "Remember, Lord D'Onston, England sees little enough of gold. Even in its palaces, we have silver coin, but not much else to boast about. These men have never seen such riches before. But it will only whet their appetites for more. I rather doubt that the majority of them are so pious as to overlook the opportunity to plunder when they can, even when it comes to the Greek churches."

D'Onston nodded his head. "We had to put an armed guard at the doors of the chapels because our men thought that, because they had round domes, they were mosques and should be burned!"

"Speaking of Lord Talon, where is he at this time?" Joanna asked. "I am intrigued by this man. Tell me what you know, Lord D'Onston."

"He and his men were not to be found the next day at the encampment, my lady. They just vanished during the early hours. Lord Talon did leave word that he would be back, once he had ensured that all was well at his castle to the North." Lord D'Onston gave a shrug that was more of a small shudder. "None of us is quite sure where that is, but I think the Greeks know. They are like ghosts, those people of his, even the Saxons move quietly. But they fight like demons, and I, for one, am very thankful. They not only saved my life, but we are lucky that we had their help the second time, or we might well have failed to gain the beach. Lord Talon and his close friend, Master Reza, keep their men on a tight rein, and all are very courteous. Our people could learn some manners from them," he finished with a rueful grin.

Joanna nodded and smiled back. "My brother praised them, which is rare enough. I must meet this man. Would it be possible for him to come to the wedding, perhaps?"

D'Onston shrugged again. "None of us knows where to find him, my lady. But he left three horsemen with us for that very purpose. If we want to send a message, one of them will carry it to him, I am sure."

She thought back to the day she had come ashore to find an exuberant Richard distributing the loot from the camp, from which he had just returned.

Berengaria had excused herself almost immediately, saying that she wanted to clean up and have a bath.

"I hope you don't mind, my lady," she asked timidly of Joanna, who wanted nothing more than the same, but Richard was beckoning her from across the crowded room.

"Go, and I shall join you as soon as I can," she'd replied.

"Hello, my sister!" Richard had called in a loud voice,. "Come over and sit next to me. We are going to teach this usurper a lesson he will never forget, but first, I have some presents to hand out! And here is a feast to make you welcome. The food is a lot better than that pig's swill we have lived on aboard ship!" he exclaimed, popping a grape into his mouth, as she was seated by an obsequious Greek servant.

All around were trays made of gold, loaded with meats and fruit, and silver cups full of wine. Some silver utensils were lying in a pile just behind the king, along with rich cloths and bejeweled belts and hats. There were even a couple of buckets of pearls.

"Congratulations, Brother, on your magnificent victory." she told him.

Richard almost preened. "It was hard fought, but we overcame the odds, and now we have Isaac on the run," he grinned.

"I thought it was just a little impetuous of you, Brother, but then I heard that you were assisted by the stranger, Lord Talon," Joana remarked. Her tone was just a little dry.

Her brother glanced at her from under his brows. "Yes, that's right, we did have some assistance from that Lord Talon and his men. They've vanished now. I have no idea where they could be, but I will admit, they were useful in the scrap. They have missed getting a share of the winnings, but then, to the victor go the spoils," Richard said casually.

He waved a gold tray toward a kneeling knight. "Here, take this, it will buy you more than a few acres in Shropshire, if you survive the Saracens and get home, that is." The king chuckled at his own wit as he handed the item over.

"I've met this Lord Talon before, you know."

Joanna was intrigued and stared at him. "You have? Where? It could not have been here, and I hear he has spent his whole life in this part of the world."

"It was a long time ago; you were just a child then. In Auch, you know, Aquitaine. I was there with Lord Harold de Mays, who was a loyal knight then. He saved me some serious grief with our father at the time. This Talon of ours appeared and told me that Sir Guy had been murdered, and to watch out for more trouble. He gave me an important message from the Count Raymond of Carcassonne. I had Lord Cumberland hanged for it, the traitor." The king neglected to tell his sister in what manner the young Talon had managed to rivet his attention.

"So, now you owe him a second time," she remarked.

"Well, let's not be too hasty. I admit, he did help, but we Normans know how to storm a beach." His tone was a little defensive.

"I would like to invite him to your wedding, Brother," Joanna said clearly.

Richard squinted at her. "Wedding?" he asked, his tone uncertain and wary.

Joanna remembered her mother's admonishment. "He must get married as soon as you arrive in the Holy Land, Joanna. He needs an heir, and I want grandchildren." Joanna had winced at that, for she was childless and very vulnerable to any suggestions about the lack of offspring between herself and William.

"Yes, Richard, wedding. Within the next few weeks. Princess Berengaria is here with us, and for decency's sake, if nothing else, you should marry her. There is a very nice chapel—Chapel, of St. George, I think—near here, which would be perfect for the occasion. This would be an opportunity to take stock of the Greeks. We must make sure that those Cypriot nobles who want to side with you are here to demonstrate their newfound loyalties, and this should include Lord Talon." She smoothed her dress on her knees and then said, "The twelfth of May will do nicely; it is only a few days away."

"I'm not getting married by one of those heretical priests of theirs. It has to be one of our own chaplains," he retorted, looking just a little hunted.

*****

There were not as many people to witness the marriage as Richard might have liked. The island had not yet, after all, been fully conquered, and it became clear that many of the island's nobles were seated on the fence, waiting to see which way the wind would blow. However, there were his loyal followers and the former Norman prisoners. Even Lord Talon appeared from nowhere, with his glowering Saxons and sinister-looking guards. There were several Greek nobles who had committed themselves, as well as the curious townspeople, who formed a respectable audience and cheered when he appeared, riding on one of the magnificent horses provided by Lord Talon. The bridle was studded with silver, as was the beautifully made saddle. The saddle cloth was of deep royal blue, which offset the king's own attire to perfection.

The marriage ceremony was held in the small Greek chapel of St. George, just as Joanna had suggested. It was a warm day in late spring. The storms were gone, the sky was blue, swept clear by a cool westerly wind coming in off the sea, and the sun was shining down upon all who were gathered outside. The Norman knights and their attendants found the climate here in Cyprus much warmer than most of them were accustomed to, and they sweated copiously under their heavy hauberks. Talon wondered how they would feel once they arrived in Palestine, where there would be little in the way of sea breezes to cool them.

There was barely room to breathe inside the chapel, and only Talon, Reza, Rav'an and Jannat were able to gain entry to observe the proceedings, and even then it was only because Lord D'Onston was there to make sure that they did. Rav'an glanced at Talon and wrinkled her nose at the smell of unwashed people. Jannat looked a little pale from of the lack of clean air.

Before entering the chapel, Reza posted his Companions at strategic points outside, with the Saxons within easy hailing distance. Confident that their men could handle anything untoward, Talon, Reza, and their wives were able to concentrate on the ceremony. This was performed in front of the altar by a burly Norman priest, who bellowed out the bans and the words of the marriage vows. Despite the fact that many had lost their possessions to wind and storm, it was a colorful display. Everyone wore whatever finery they could muster, regardless of clashing colors and ill-fitting clothing.

The king himself wore a tunic of luxurious and heavy ruby-red samite, a silk fabric of a twill-type weave, which included gold and silver thread in the pattern of flowers. His sword and scabbard, which were encrusted with gold and precious stones, hung from a heavy belt of tasseled Sicilian silk. With his well-groomed beard, his oiled hair, and his tall, striking appearance, Richard looked like everything one might hope from a conquering king.

Beside him his bride, Berengaria, paled in comparison, despite all that Joanna and her maids could do to make her look regal. Talon felt, unkindly, that she resembled a diminutive and timid ghost when she stood beside her future husband.

The service was perfunctory by comparison to any Greek ceremony, which seemed to suit the impatient king, who fidgeted through most of it. When the priest completed his part, the Bishops of Bordeaux and Évreux moved forward, determined to regain control of events on their terms. While Évreux placed a crown on the head of the kneeling princess, Bordeaux called out prayers to God to protect the union. Richard then drew her to her feet and kissed her in an absent-minded manner on both cheeks. Berengaria was now the Queen of England.

At this point, the solemn occasion became a celebration. The king led his pale wife out of the chapel, to the cheers of the Norman men at arms and the Greeks, although they had been kept at a distance from the chapel by spearmen. The enthusiastic Greeks were clearly looking for the king of England to relieve them of the tyrant, once he had his domestic affairs in hand.

"That was a short affair; they don't waste any time with long chants and ritual, do they?" Reza commented to his Companions. "Father Psellos would have been appalled!" he laughed as they followed the throng out into the open air. They all blinked as they emerged into the bright sunlight. Around them, men, knights, lords, and ladies were cheering the king and his bride, or tossing flower petals at them as they walked slowly toward their beautiful mounts.

"She is but a young maiden," Jannat murmured. "I see little in the way of love in that match."

"I agree, Sister," Rav'an rejoined. "She looks more like a hostage than a queen going to her marriage bed."

"I gathered from Lady Joanne that the match was made by her mother, Queen Eleanor," Talon murmured. "The king was not thrilled by the idea, but it cements in place a treaty with someone in Navarre, which means, I am told, protection for the southern borders of Eleanor's Duchy of Aquitaine."

"This mother of the king has much power?" Rav'an asked Talon as they mounted up on their own animals.

"Oh, yes! From what I have gathered from Princess Joanna and the Lord D'Onston, she does." Talon remarked with a wry smile. "She is something of a legend in her own right. I am surprised she is not here, leading the Crusade herself! She came to the Holy Land once before, when she was the wife of the king of France, before she became the wife of Richard's father, King Henry."

They turned their horses away from the slowly moving throng, their mounted Companions in a protective ring around them. Talon glanced off to the side and caught the eye of Princess Joanna, who beckoned him.

"Where are you going, Lord Talon?" she asked, when he had ridden up and saluted her. "There is to be a feast and much celebration today. Will your family not join us?"

She looked up at him and noted with approval that he did not look in the least subservient, as did so many of the people who attended her, but neither did he appear arrogant. Instead, he appeared to be attentive. The gaze from his piercing green eyes was steady and, did she dare admit it, somewhat unsettling. He reached forward just a little and stroked the neck of the beautiful dun-colored horse he rode.

"We leave for my home, my lady. With the usurper still at large, I have responsibilities to my family and people."

"Where has he gone, Lord Talon? Is there danger? Are you going to abandon us all in this strange land?" she asked with a small quirk of her lips.

Talon smiled back and shook his head. "Not at all, my lady. I have sent my scouts out, and we know where he is. He has removed to Famagusta, but he could move quickly, and his cavalry still carries a sting, especially on open ground, so I am making sure that he surprises neither you nor your king. But he must not be allowed to take advantage of my absence from my own home, which is not so far from Famagusta."

Joanna smiled ruefully. "I had hoped to be able to talk to you and your beautiful wife and learn more about you, Lord Talon. I have not yet had the opportunity to thank you for the exquisite silk and the patterned cloth you gave to Queen Berengaria and myself. I have never seen cloth to match this, and the intricate patterns are very beautiful. The Queen would thank you as well, Lord Talon."

"The silk is from China, my lady, and the pattern of the cloth is known in Persia as *pashmina*, but I believe it originates from even further east, in the mountainous regions of northwest India." He smiled as he said this, and Joanna decided that, despite his formidable reputation, she liked this man.

He glanced behind him toward his waiting people, then back to her and bowed from the saddle.

"Fear not, my lady, there will be time for discussion, but first we must deal with Isaac Komnenos. He is a slippery one, and he still possesses a large enough force to be troublesome, but I will ensure that you have plenty of warning, should he attempt treachery. Andreas over there will keep you safe; my word and his life on it."

Joanna turned to see whom he named. A youth, who looked somewhat familiar, gave a short bow, and lifted his hand to Talon. She realized that this young man had been in the near background for several days. She'd taken him for just another attendant, though less obtrusive than most. Another of those cats who belonged to this enigmatic man, she thought to herself.

"He is your guard, my lady," said Talon, raising his hand in return.

She smiled. "Very well, Lord Talon. I shall not keep you. God be with you, and I hope we will meet again soon."

"God be with you, my lady," Talon said, and turned his horse away to canter after his own people.

Joanna watched him as he rode away, moving easily with the motion of his horse. Then Lord Talon and his entourage were gone. She turned away, her eyes searching for the youth, but he, too, had disappeared. She felt reassured that he was somewhere near, as she walked off to join her brother and his bride. She sighed. This was not going to be a match made in heaven, she thought to herself. But if Richard could get his wife with child, then it didn't really matter, did it?

She began to plan just when she would extricate Berengaria from the feast, and then pry her brother away from the drinking, in order to get him to perform his duty as a husband, as soon as possible. The first thing to do was to have the bedchamber aired and cleaned up. Richard was none too particular about tidiness and cleanliness, nor were his squires, who should have seen to it.

*****

Three days later, an envoy arrived from Isaac. It was the same eunuch who had spoken to Joanna on board her ship. The man arrived with a small escort of horsemen in brightly burnished armor, which made an impressive sight, although the effect was marred by the envoy's obvious discomfort; he did not appear to be any sort of rider himself.

He was brought into the presence of King Richard, who was seated on a makeshift throne, attended by his new wife, Berengaria, with Joanna seated nearby.

The envoy was nervous and, although the day was not very hot, he repeatedly wiped his forehead with a fine linen cloth as he approached the throne. Then he fell to his knees and presented a rolled-up document with both hands and waited with his head bowed.

A man who spoke Greek took the document from the envoy, whom Richard bade rise. "What is your name, sirrah?" he demanded, and waved the translator to proceed.

"Oh, great... Lord King. My—my name is Alekos Stavropoulos, and I am an ambassador for His Most Gracious Emperor, Isaac Komnenos, who awaits your response to this missive I have presented... Sire," he added.

Richard scratched his beard and stared down at him with his piercing blue eyes.

"Now he sends me a wriggling, pretty-colored caterpillar with a letter. I feel uncomfortable with this thing creeping around at my feet," he said out loud to Joanna, clearly of the opinion that the envoy would not understand French. Joanna noticed immediately that the colorfully dressed envoy certainly did speak the language, for his eyes widened at the insult and he shuffled backwards a pace or two. Richard either did not notice, or did not care. Instead, he turned to the translator, who nervously unrolled the parchment and began to read it, his lips moving with the words. He paled and hesitated.

"Get on with it, man. What does it say?" Richard demanded impatiently.

"It says, Your Majesty, that the emperor gives you two days to go aboard your ships, and leave the island of Cyprus immediately thereafter." The man hesitated and glanced apprehensively at the king.

"Go on, man, I'm listening," growled Richard. "Or is that all he has to say?" He looked around at the attending knights and the two bishops, who were leaning forward, paying close attention to the translator and the king's expression, which began to look thunderous.

"Er... no, my lord. It goes on to say that, if you do not obey, he will destroy your army of pirates, and then imprison you and wreak vengeance upon all your people, who have invaded this island."

The knight stopped translating and stared at the king. Richard was watching the envoy, who was now cringing under his wrathful stare.

"Well, now! It appears that this usurper failed to learn from his mistakes." Richard's tone was low, but it was full of menace. "Count yourself lucky, envoy Statappopolotus, or whomsoever you say you are, that I am in a benign mood today. I was just married, you know. You will leave this place with your head attached to your shoulders, instead of severed and rolled up in this effusion. You will inform the usurper that I am coming after him, and he will be the one contemplating the inside of a dungeon. Go!"

Ambassador Stavropoulos groveled his way out of the chamber. When he was gone, Richard beckoned to Lord Bedford, who strode over and bowed.

"My lord?"

"We leave as soon as possible, Lord Bedford. In what condition are the horses? Methinks we will have need of them."

"Some died, as they were too far gone, but most are well on the way to recovery, my lord," Bedford responded. "And lord... er—"

"Lord Talon?" Joanna interjected, with a raised eyebrow.

"Yes, my lady. He left nearly twenty of his horses with us, so we will be well mounted."

His words were greeted with a harrumph from the bishop. "I would not trust that man any more than the Greeks of this city," he grunted, his chins wobbling.

"That man, as you call him, came to the aid of our sailors who were prisoners, Your Holiness, and then assisted my brother in gaining a foothold on this island!" Joanna snapped.

Richard glanced at his sister. "Granted, he did help, but we would have managed on our own, Sister."

Joanna glared at him. "We should, I think, be thankful that he was here, nonetheless, and neither should we be denigrating an ally. They are rare enough when we need them." She directed this last at the bishop, who went red with anger, but had the sense to refrain from answering.

Richard was looking thoughtful.

"Hmm, I would prefer to have our own destriers for the next encounter. I doubt very much that those Greeks will be able to withstand a charge by our larger mounts." He glanced at Lord D'Onston.

"My lord, you have talked with this Lord Talon. Do you know where he might be, and whether we can get a messenger to him or not?"

Lord D'Onston bowed and said, "My Liege, I believe he went back to his castle. It is called Kantara. There are two messengers he left behind for just this purpose, my lord."

Richard nodded. "Does anyone know how far it is to Famagusta?" he asked the general assembly. Lord D'Onston reached out and took a squire by the sleeve.

"Go and find the messengers, now!" The boy scampered off as D'Onston turned back to the king.

"Lord Talon's messengers can lead us to it, my liege. I have sent for them."

Within a few long minutes, Nasuh and Andreas were ushered into the presence of the king. The gathering of knights and attendants made a pathway for the two Companions as they were led toward the throne. When they were within ten paces, they stopped and bowed their heads. Their behavior, although polite, raised eyebrows from those near the throne. Unlike the groveling envoy, these two young men, dressed in loose, comfortable cotton clothing, riding boots and loosely wound turbans, were not much more than youths, yet they carried themselves with dignity and pride.

"By the saint's toes, but those two are a dangerous looking pair," Richard muttered aside to Joanna.

"They are like wild cats," she murmured, as she gazed at the two Companions. "They might look young but—"

"Do you speak French?" Richard demanded of the two youths, interrupting her.

"Aye, a little French," Andreas said clearly.

"You are to find Lord Talon and inform him that I march on Famagusta by week's end, and he is to meet up with me as soon as he is able. Do you understand?"

Andreas bowed. "I understand, Lord. I go at once."

"How far is it to Famagusta?" Richard demanded.

"It is two days." Nasuh held up two fingers. "Good marching, Lord. I go with you and show best road."

"Very well. You stay with me, and you," he pointed at Andreas, "go and find Lord Talon. Bring him to Famagusta."

Richard waved them off. The youths bowed again and glided out of the room, watched by everyone until they vanished.

Back in the chamber, Richard rose to his feet. "I think it is time we taught this insulting usurper one final lesson," he stated for all to hear. His knights seemed very pleased by this prospect.

Joanna sighed. "What should the queen and I do while you are charging around the island, my brother?" she asked.

"I think you will be safe here in Limassol, my dear. Don't worry, I shall leave guards to protect you. Ships are arriving every day now; the word is out that I am here with you. Three ships yesterday and two more today. I'll have an army in less than a week, and then we'll see how he likes that."

"I am not worried about *my* safety," she replied.

*****

Andreas and Nasuh went to find the spy whom Reza had planted in Limassol, well over a year before. Soon two pigeons were on their way to the castle with news of the imminent departure of the Normans for Isaac's lair. Andreas appeared to leave the city gates within an hour, per his instructions from the king. However, he did not intend to go very far. Talon and Reza had made it very clear that one of the two Companions had to stay and ensure the safety of the royals, which meant the king, the king's sister, and his queen. If the king decided to decamp, then Nasuh would be with him at all times, but if the women did not wish to leave the city and retire to the ships, then Andreas would stay and follow his master's instructions.

Within a matter of hours, Jannat, who was in charge of the pigeon message system, found two of the grey-winged birds perched on the entry point to the pigeon house. With great care, she gently captured the new arrivals, removed the copper tubes secured to their legs, and placed them with the other birds to feed and rest. After she deciphered their messages, she went down the stairs of the tower to present the information to the others.

"Well, now we know the intent of the King of England," Rav'an said to the assembled family. "It is nothing less than the conquest of the island of Cyprus!"

The king has ordered me to attend him at the gates of Famagusta, so I must comply," Talon said. "But it will take him two full days to reach the city, and he is still assembling his army, so we have a little time before we leave."

"I shall come with you, Talon," Reza stated, but Talon shook his head. "No, Brother, not this time. As we agreed, you should make haste to depart for Constantinople. There has been no news from Theo for many months now."

Rav'an sighed. "It is very unlike Theodora not to send a message by Gregorios or some merchant to Paphos, to let us know how matters stand," she told them. "She knows full well that Boethius would immediately send the news on to us. Who knows what is going on in that city these days?"

"I'm worried," Talon stated to the room at large. "It has been too long since we have heard from her. So I am asking Reza to go up to the city and find out if all is well." He turned to face Reza directly. "Henry or Guy can take you, under the pretext that we are still trading with the city and have a cargo of goods to sell, which we do. Take the emperor's papers with you, of course; they might still honor them. Your main objective, however, will be to find out how the family Kalothesos is doing. We do, after all, owe them a great debt for helping us establish trade routes.

"I shall make preparations immediately," said Reza. "Who should I take with me?"

"I suspect Yosef would be pleased to go with you," Talon commented. "He has often talked about going back. He knows a little about the way the city is laid out. That might be useful."

Reza looked at Jannat, who appeared apprehensive. "Jannat, Talon and Rav'an are right. It's not like Theo to fail to send a message back. I, too, am worried, but this will simply be a trading journey and nothing more. I will bring back good news, of that, I am sure."

Jannat touched his arm. "Just remember where your home is, my prince, and come back home safe to us," she told him softly.

"What do we do about the Venetians, my Talon?" Rav'an asked.

Not for the first time, Talon regarded his wife with respect. She liked to have things tidied up before everyone went about their own business.

"That young fellow could hardly stand by the time you and Reza had finished with him," Jannat laughed.

Reza chuckled. "It was the arak that did it."

Jannat turned to Rostam, who had remained silent during this exchange. "What do you think of him, Rostam, my dear?" she asked.

"Father and Uncle Reza squeezed a lot of information out of him before they sent him off to bed, Auntie. I doubt if he realized what they were up to," he responded.

Later that night, Rav'an lay close to Talon.

"You have been watching those two Venetians, my Rav'an. What do you think? Should we trust them?" he asked her.

"The boy is intelligent, but the girl... " Rav'an hesitated, "there is something calculating about that one."

Talon traced his fingers from her throat down to between her breasts, moving very slowly and deliberately, downward.

"My prince," she sighed.

"What is it, my love?"

"I was wondering when you would come to the conclusion that you had a wife as well as a counselor."

"Hmm, in fact, it had never entered my mind to think otherwise, but... you are to blame, my princess, because of your insistence upon all these well thought out and weighty plans. They take time away from... some other, umm... important things."

He was interrupted by her exclamation of surprise and pleasure.

"I shall give no more advice tonight, my darling. You appear not to need any." She growled like a hungry being and rolled on top of him. "Just be careful of that king of yours, for I do not trust him. And that princess, Joanne. She likes you, you know."

Chapter 16

A Fleet

The ships seemed old and storm-beat,
Their canvas was in strips,
The rust of smoke and ocean spray
Hung on the cannons' lips,
And in the lull, the fleur-de-lys
Hung drooping o'er the ships.
—John Hunter Duvar

The city of Famagusta reflected the mood of its emperor. Fear and uncertainty were pervasive. Upon his return, Isaac sought refuge in the arms of his concubine, Tamura. It didn't help his mood that his arousal required assistance and some imagination on her part.

Later, when he was enjoying a massage in his own room, he had time to contemplate his situation. It was hardly reassuring, and he was still aghast at the results of his confrontation with those barbaric Normans. His rage increased, even as the skilled fingers of the masseuse eased the tight muscles on his neck and back.

He abruptly rolled over and sat up, throwing off the oily hands of the masseuse, and called out, "Tell Gôsakos to come here at once!" he shouted, reaching for a robe.

Gôsakos found his leader waiting for him, seated at a table laden with grapes, bread, and olives. Isaac always ate when he was upset, which did nothing to reduce the rolls of fat that were forming around his middle. Gôsakos marched in with an impassive face. He was very worried. The emperor was clearly in a state, and this could mean punishment for him. Having meted out many punishments at the orders of the emperor, he wondered if, finally, it had come to his turn.

As it happened, that had been on Isaac's mind, but if he lacked almost every talent bestowed upon most men, he still retained the cunning of a rat. While he had contemplated what awful things he would like to do to Gôsakos, he had come to the reluctant conclusion that he had no one else to turn to. The mercenaries who ostensibly owed him their loyalty were probably more loyal to their commander than their emperor, and they would not happily comply with any order that threatened the well-being of their leader.

He, therefore, made his commander stand while he deliberately popped some grapes in his mouth and slowly munched on them, all the while staring with his slightly protuberant eyes at his intended victim. The burly, bearded, and scarred mercenary commander withstood the scrutiny impassively, which only increased Isaac's wrath.

"You have let me down. You have betrayed me and allowed those—those barbarians to get the better of our own army, which, need I say it, was much larger than theirs!" Isaac's voice dripped sarcasm. "Tell me why I should not have you impaled?" This final word was screeched, along with much spittle, in Gôsakos's direction.

The soldier would not quail, although he knew well enough how agonizing a death that would be. He took a deep breath and was about to reply when Isaac bellowed, "How is it that a few hairy-arsed Normans can get ashore and defeat our army? Well? I'm waiting?"

"My Emperor," Gôsakos began, "we were attacked from the rear and the wings. In that confined space, our main asset, our cavalry, could not maneuver, and then that cowardly group commander, Giorgios, allowed the Saxons to roll us up, just when we were about to drive the Normans into the sea! I will have him executed by sunset." He began to speak forcefully. "Your Highness, if we had only waited for them on the plain between Limassol and Larnaca, we would have destroyed them. They were, for the most part, unmounted, and those treacherous assassins were not numerous enough to have made a difference. We can still beat them and drive them off the island. That is your wish, is it not?" he asked. His tone became just a little sly.

Isaac stopped eating and stared at him. "Of course it is, you imbecile. Are you quite serious?" he demanded, as the words sunk in. His tone was incredulous.

Gôsakos drew himself up and gazed right back at the emperor, who was again stuffing his mouth with grapes in a kind of reflexive action. His mouth full, Isaac mumbled, "You really think so, eh?"

"If we waste no time, my lord, we can attack them, and it will be done."

Isaac swallowed. "You said that before. And what about those damned archers of that heretic up on the mountain?" he asked, his tone skeptical. "Your people are scared witless of them."

"We did not bring many of our own crossbow men with us when we took them on last time, my lord," was the cool response. "Our archers can outshoot theirs."

There was a long silence as the emperor continued to stare at his commander. He came to a decision. "Very well, we will send a delegation to them and tell them to get off the island. And if not, we will destroy them." His tone became menacing. "You had better be right about this, or your head will decorate the gates of this city, after I have impaled you! Do you hear me?"

Gôsakos nodded and gave a half bow. "Whom should we send to speak to the Normans, my Lord?"

"Why, the same man we sent to talk to the whore on the ship, of course!" As his commander turned to go, Isaac could not resist having one last word.

"You have failed me once, Gôsakos. Do not fail me a second time!" he grimaced and shook his fist in the air.

*****

In the harem of the palace, Tamura was seated at a low table, sipping some delicious red wine, and thinking hard. The wine came from the enigmatic lord of the castle on the mountain, but since Diocles had retired to a tiny village on the coast, the supply had dwindled, and now each cup was precious. She didn't even allow Siranos to put it out when the emperor paid her one of his not-so-frequent visits.

Tonight, she was pensive and worried. Isaac had not been forthcoming as to what had actually occurred near Limassol, but Siranos and Martina, between them, had been busy piecing together the fragments of gossip, and it was not reassuring. Isaac and his men had been roundly trounced in a fight and had left everything behind to seek shelter in this city.

"The citizens of Famagusta are very frightened, my lady," a worried Siranos told her.

"What does your friend, the spy, say?" she asked him.

"I have not yet heard from him, my lady. Nothing at all."

Tamura deemed this tidbit of information to be ominous. Hitherto, their contact, the spy from Kantara, had been quite informative, as that fellow appeared to have his finger on everything that transpired around the island.

"Find out what you can from him," she ordered.

"He is frightened, you know," she said to the world at large, after Siranos had departed. She was referring to the emperor.

Martina, standing nearby, nodded her head. "It is like the plague, my lady. Fear is everywhere; I cannot remember when it was this bad. I, too, am very afraid," she whimpered, her eyes huge.

"These days, I never know what he will do next. He says one thing, and then he goes and does the opposite. It is all very confusing," Tamura muttered to herself.

She didn't add that she wanted to escape this stifling place, which was full of eunuchs who watched her every move, as well as heavily perfumed women, both young and old, who hated her for her position with the emperor and were eager to settle scores. She had made many enemies; one misstep and she could tumble all the way to her death, especially if any of her multitude of secrets were discovered and exposed. Isaac was a vindictive man.

The execution of the commander outside the city gates had horrified her, but instead of a lingering, tortuous death, the unhappy victim had died suddenly, from two arrows shot by some daring riders, who had appeared out of a small grove of olive trees. Two more arrows had killed the man who was being flayed alive. The emperor had been livid, but also very scared.

*****

For Talon, the morning had not been peaceful. He and his men were tired after a forced march that had brought them to the edge of the forest near the gates of Famagusta. One of the sentries posted by Brandt had noticed a lot of activity taking place on the battlements of the city, which were just less than four hundred paces away from the copse. He immediately brought it to his commander's attention, who, in turn, sounded the alarm. It was possible that someone had noticed the men lurking in the woods, and the Greeks might be getting ready to sally forth and attack.

But that was not the case. Instead, people gathered on the parapet and looked down as the gates opened. The watchers saw a little procession of armed men dragging two prisoners along with them, to stop just outside the gates on the side of the road, in plain view of the spectators on the parapet.

The prisoners were bound and naked. The armed men drove stakes into the ground and stood back while others dragged the struggling men toward them.

One of the prisoners was then impaled on the spiked stakes, and the other had skin removed from his back while he writhed against the restraining chains. The prisoners convulsed in agony, their screams carrying to the woods.

"Dewy! Caradog," A very angry Talon roared. "Horses, Rostam, immediately!"

The two archers were at his side in an instant. "Get up behind me and Rostam, we are going out there!" Talon snapped. He leapt onto his horse and hauled Dewy up behind him. Rostam, who had been very quick to respond, did the same with Caradog.

"Now grip with your knees for your life, Dewy. Tell me when we are close enough, and then kill the prisoners! Rostam, we move now!" Talon called, and set spurs to his mount.

They covered the ground at a flat-out gallop with the two archers hanging onto their bows and clutching at the riders' belts for dear life.

"Here, Lord!" Dewy shouted, as they came within about one hundred paces. The crowd gathered on the parapet had noticed them but had not reacted, other than to point out the charging horsemen to each other. There was still time. Talon and Rostam hauled their horses to a sharp halt in a cloud of dust. At the same time, Dewy and Caradog slipped off the horses, ran forward several paces, and drew their bows. Two arrows sped on their way. Both arrows stuck the prisoner who was impaled. He jerked very briefly, and then fell limp. "Now, for the other!" Dewy called. Two more arrows flew, and the other prisoner died.

Dewy and Caradog were not finished. Two more arrows were sent toward the crowded parapet above the gates, and two people fell back, with arrows protruding from their chests. There were shouts of alarm and fear. The two Welsh archers fell to arguing as to who had had the most accurate hits, completely ignoring their peril.

"Stop arguing, for the love of God! Come along, you two, get back up!" Talon shouted. He and Rostam rode up to the two archers, who woke up to their danger, hooked elbows with the riders and swung up behind them.

"Wish I'd known who they were up there," Dewy called out, as they galloped back to the shelter of the trees. They dismounted and joined the other archers, who were now fully alerted. Everyone waited with bated breath for a counterattack, but nothing happened. The guards had fled to the safety of the city and closed the gates. Sentries peered carefully over the edge of the parapet, but nothing else occurred. The gates remained firmly closed, and there was relative silence. The men at the edge of the woods stared back at the blank walls and shook their heads.

"They have no stomach to come and get us," Brandt commented derisively. "You took a bit of a chance there, Lord," he commented to the grim-faced Talon, who stood nearby.

"He does this kind of thing regularly," Talon said. "It is foul, but his mercenaries do his dirty work, and he keeps the population in thrall with these barbaric acts. I could not let this one go without doing something. Besides..." he grinned, "Those two are in need of practice!"

Brandt slapped his thighs with amusement while Dewy and Caradog who had overheard Talon glowered at the absurd notion and pretending to be very hurt.

"Prac'tice we need now, is it?" Dewy grunted rolling his eyes at Caradog.

*****

Several days later, just as the sun was appearing over the horizon, Isaac Komnenos was rudely awakened by one of the slaves, who actually had the temerity to shake him.

"Wake up, Your Majesty. Please wake up!" the frightened man called as he looked over his shoulder at Gôsakos, who was standing at the doorway with his helmet tucked under his left arm.

"Wake him up, I don't care how!" Gôsakos growled. His tone was urgent.

Isaac struggled awake, protesting, and shook off the slave. "What are you doing, you scum! Why are you touching me? What is going on?" The last sentence was delivered with a shout of indignation and rapidly mounting rage.

Gôsakos strode forward. "There is a fleet approaching the port, Your Majesty." he said without preamble.

Isaac's eyes popped wide open, and his jaw dropped. "Wh—what?" he gobbled. "A fleet? Is it merchants? Pirates? Oh, God, preserve me. What is happening?" he cried.

"Whoever it is, they will outnumber us. There are many ships. Their banners are definitely not Greek, but neither are they those of the Sicilian merchants."

Gôsakos had not anticipated an attack from the sea. He had been shocked when a messenger had clamored to see him and then bade him to come and view the sight from one of the towers.

"I want to see this for myself!" Isaac shouted.

They were soon on the seaward side of the palace walls where they had a good view of the harbor, and more importantly, what was beyond the untidy pile of water-breakers.

A fleet of ships was indeed approaching, and the banners flying from their masts were becoming more clearly displayed, but they were not those of the English king. Isaac sagged in relief, then whirled about and pointed his finger at his commander. "Who are these people?" he shouted.

"I think they are more Latins," Gôsakos murmured uncomfortably.

A soldier ran up and went down on one knee in front of them. "Oh, what is it this time?" Isaac shouted. His features had become contorted with worry.

"His Grace, the bishop, told me I was to tell you that we know who those people are now, my—my liege," the soldier stammered. "The bishop has people who know the signs and banners. These belong to the other Latin king. The one called King Philip of France."

Isaac became quite still. The blood drained from his face, leaving his normally dark features looking quite pallid. "Then —then they are no friends of mine," he muttered. He wiped his sweating brow and shot a venomous glare toward Gôsakos. "We are leaving for Nicosia. There, on the plains, '*you* can defeat them because *we* have the cavalry.' That's what *you* told me! We leave now!" He charged off before anyone could reply. He even lost a slipper in his haste to get away.

Gôsakos sighed to himself. Not for the first time, he wondered why he was still here on this pestilent little island, with this halfwit of a tyrant. But it had been very lucrative, so he had only himself to blame now. He was determined to take what he could of his own hard-earned loot with him.

"Prepare everyone to leave the palace. Tell the lady Tamura to be ready within the hour. The troops to assemble with all their gear. We are going to Nicosia."

"What about the other women in his harem, sir?" one of his officers asked, with a smirk. Gôsakos wanted to slap off his face, but this was not the time.

"Leave the whores behind, and leave those damned eunuchs with them." he snarled. "They will slow us down, so we cannot take them, but the emperor would never forgive me if we left his favorite behind." *And*, he thought to himself, *she is the only one who can keep her wits and not go into a fit of hysterics.*

Chapter 17

Famagusta

And having answered so I turn once more to those
who sneer at this my city,
and I give them back the sneer and say to them:
Come and show me another city
with lifted head singing so proud to be alive
and coarse and strong and cunning.
—Chicago

It was late at night when Talon and his two companions arrived alongside the base of the walls of Famagusta. In the dim light of the myriad stars above, the walls were stark black shapes against the sky, with the occasional silhouette of a sentry walking along its parapets.

"I am curious as to what might be going on inside the city," Talon told Brandt and the Companions. "I shall go have a look for myself."

"Father!" Rostam protested. "Uncle Reza would not allow it, were he here. Send someone else, please."

Talon didn't mention that it was precisely because Reza was not there to stop him that he was going into the city uninvited.

"At least take me with you, Father!" Rostam whispered vehemently.

Talon hesitated, and Dar'an chimed in. "Master, take me and Rostam. We can help." Dar'an didn't add that he was concerned that, if Talon did get into trouble, he wanted to be there to ensure he escaped.

"I am only going to see Dimitri," Talon protested. "I am not going to do anything foolish, like go to the palace," he added.

"Then Brandt and Junayd can take charge out here, and we will accompany you, Lord." Dar'an's tone brooked no argument, and Rostam was looking rebellious, so Talon shrugged resignedly in the dark and agreed. His men would not be denied, and would follow him anyway, even if he told them no.

"We go in, see Dimitri, find out what the numbers are, and leave at first light," he told them. "Junayd and Brandt, you have charge of the men. See to it that they are well rested. We might be in for a fight tomorrow or the next day."

He received a grunt of acknowledgement from Brandt, who turned away. "I think Lord Talon is quite mad to attempt those walls," he muttered to Junayd. "I know, I know, that is what you people do, but I am still concerned. He was badly wounded at Hattin, and that knee of his is not back to where it should be."

Junayd clapped him on his broad shoulder. "If it is any consolation Brandt, I, too, am concerned, but Dar'an and Rostam will be with him. Now, we have to settle everyone and the horses. Come along, my friend. We shall pray to God that they will be safe."

*****

Talon and his two Companions had to crawl part of the way towards the base of the walls. They were very conscious of the fact that it was a bright starry night and any quick movement would be easily detected. However it was not long before they arrived at the base, where they found some darkness to hide in while they scrutinized the parapets for lurking sentries. The walls were made of limestone, which, over time, had hardened and crumbled. This offered both advantages and perils. They would have to be careful to avoid the rotten areas. Talon was afraid that they would find themselves halfway up and in the middle of precisely that kind of stone. Just in case, Dar'an carried a rope coiled over his shoulder.

The wind changed direction and brought with it an all too familiar stink of something dead. Isaac and his general had left the corpses as a lesson for the Normans, when they arrived. There were also piles of trash heaped against the walls where citizens had dumped their refuse. Talon shook his head in disgust.

Dar'an touched him on the arm and pointed upward. The dark figure of a sentry was moving in their direction. The three men huddled even deeper into the shadows at the base of the wall. The sentry stopped and peered towards the line of trees, then drifted past without reacting to their presence. But the man seemed to be simply idling along and not paying much attention to what was going on around him. In fact, he appeared to stop walking along the parapet, so they assumed he was down behind the walls somewhere.

Their scrutiny resumed. Rostam pointed to their right. "That area has good hand holds, Father. We could try there," he whispered.

"Very well, we go up there." Talon was about to start up when Dar'an held his arm and whispered, "I go first, Lord, then you, and then Rostam,"

Talon rolled his eyes with exasperation, but reluctantly gave way. "Go," he whispered. "I follow."

Talon watched critically as Dar'an climbed the wall just as Reza would. *Like a spider*, Talon thought to himself. Dar'an eased himself over the top and vanished. Talon and Rostam waited in a silence that lasted long enough for Talon to wonder what Dar'an might have encountered, before one end of the rope was thrown down. Talon looked up to see Dar'an's head silhouetted against the stars, and one hand gesturing for them to ascend. Talon seized the rope and started to haul himself up. To his dismay, his knee would not behave, and it became an effort. But he gritted his teeth, and kept on climbing. He was within six feet of the top when he became aware of a scuffle taking place above him. There was a low groan, and then silence. He froze, wondering what was happening, out of sight on the ramparts.

There was a scraping sound, and just to his left, the limp body of a man was pushed over the ramparts, to fall loosely past him. He even felt the wind of its passing. The body struck the ground with a soggy thump and remained spread-eagled and motionless. Dar'an leaned forward and signaled frantically for Talon to hurry. Talon quickly joined him, although his knee was hurting fiercely. Now they had a dilemma. The body could be seen, should anyone peer over the walls in this place, even at night; and when it became day the guard's body would certainly be discovered, and the alarm raised.

Thinking quickly, Dar'an hauled the rope up and, leaning far out, gestured to Rostam to leave. With great presence of mind, Rostam ran over to the body, hauled it over his strong shoulders, and loped off, back toward the woods.

"It was the only way, Lord," Dar'an explained to Talon.

"Rostam will be very disappointed, but you are right, we could not let them find the body. What happened?" he asked.

"The man was a sentry, but he was asleep, right where I arrived!" Dar'an whispered. "He began to wake up as I came over the wall and I had to deal with him, or we were lost."

"Come along. We must get to Dimitri before we run into anyone else," Talon whispered. Despite his knee, which was aching painfully now, he managed to keep up with Dar'an as they moved silently along the battlements and down into the streets. As they penetrated further into the convoluted streets of Famagusta, they began to encounter more and more people. The Greek soldiers were restless, drinking, and nervous. They, too, knew there was to be a reckoning, and their last experience had not reassured them that the next would be any better. For now, they were secure behind tall walls, so many were carelessly drunk. Talon and Dar'an decided that they should not be slinking around. Instead, they took off their turbans and walked casually past the drinkers, hoping none would challenge their passage, and before too long, they were at the entrance of the house that belonged to Dimitri. Talon knew the rough looking doorway set deep into a stone wall could withstand a determined assault. Over the years Dimitri had made certain changes and reinforcements to the property.

Dimitri's guards were wide awake. so it was mere moments after a knock from Dar'an before the grill on one of the massive doors was slid open and one of his alert guards peered out at them. The guard recognized Talon and, although very surprised, he opened the door enough to allow them to slip inside; then it was bolted firmly shut.

A beaming Dimitri came barreling out of the house upon being informed of their arrival and gave them both bear hugs. "Come inside," he said. "That you are here, tonight, means I will not need to send messages in the morning. Come! I have a certain wine for you to try." They shared information for the next few hours, while the city finally had enough of drinking and went slowly to sleep.

It was early the next morning, just as Talon and Dar'an were preparing to leave, that Khuzaymah and his men arrived, somewhat out of breath, to tell them of the presence of a fleet of foreign ships, which had arrived at the entrance of the harbor.

"This could change everything," Talon said to his friends. "Before I leave, I want to know who this is. Richard might have sent his ships around the cape to attack from both sides."

Their surprise was almost as profound as that of the emperor's when they deciphered the emblems on the banners streaming from the lead ship as it entered the inner harbor. By this time, the entire population of Famagusta was awake, and many, fearful of what lay ahead, were loading donkeys and carts, preparing to leave in the wake of the emperor, who had already departed, but whose baggage train and attendants were still struggling to get out of the crowded gates to chase after him.

"Dimitri, keep low but keep watch, and I will come back as soon as I can," Talon told him. Then he left the house with Dar'an. "Our best opportunity is to leave with the mob. I want to be with my men, even if it is the King of France at the entrance to the port. There is no telling how difficult it will become to leave after he has landed."

They trotted off and joined the noisy crowd of citizens who were pushing and shoving their way out of the city, along with the remainder of the emperor's soldiers. The guards had left their posts to catch up with the fleeing army, so the area around the gates was disorderly and unsupervised. It was hot work getting through the crowd, and on more than one occasion, they had to use elbows and kicks to get past slow citizens who didn't feel in the least like giving way to two more men, no matter how dangerous they looked.

"I suppose I could have met Philip at the quayside, and told him I owned the city!" Talon said to Dar'an, but prudence informed him otherwise. Philip didn't know him, and without his men, Talon would mean nothing to the invading French. They staggered out of the press of burdened, panicked people and moved under the shelter of the trees, to find several of Talon's Companions waiting for them.

Rostam started forward at the sight of them, his face lighting up with relief. "I was just coming to rescue you! What have you done to cause all this excitement, Father?" he demanded. "I wish you had let me come in with you," he added reproachfully. But then he embraced Talon with a grin, who laughed.

"There is nothing to brag about, Rostam. We joined Dimitri and then, this morning, the excitement began. We had nothing to do with it." Talon continued, "This is Famagusta in a state of abject panic. You must have seen the emperor on his way out."

"Oh, yes, we did, Lord," Brandt called out. "We sent two of our people to follow them at a discreet distance, to find out where they are going."

"Good." Talon nodded his approval. "No doubt he's heading for Nicosia, where he has a large garrison. Apparently, he didn't want to fight it out with the French, who arrived in ships a few hours ago."

"A fleet? The French arrived with a fleet?" Rostam gasped.

"The King of France himself, if that banner is to be believed," Talon told him. "Now all we have to do is to await Richard and tell him the good news."

Talon was not at all sure it would be good news to the English king.

*****

Talon and his men mounted horses and set out. Several hours later when the gates had been closed on the remainder of the citizens they sighted King Richard riding at the fore of his cavalry, on the road that lead to the gates of Famagusta. A few stragglers were still to be seen on the road that led off to Nicosia, to the north of the highway that Richard had taken. The Norman army had swelled to many more than twice its former number, and most of the knights were now mounted, albeit on horses that had seen better days. All the same, by Talon's estimate, they could have given the Greeks a good fight, after all.

As Richard and his men approached, Talon rode forward with Rostam, Junayd, and Dar'an alongside. The Normans halted and King Richard greeted Talon in a friendly fashion.

"Well met, Lord Talon. I see you received my message."

"Greetings, Your Majesty," Talon responded, "But you have arrived a little late to catch the emperor."

Richard looked startled. "What are you talking about?" he demanded, then looked up to stare at the walls of the city, where sentries were standing, staring back at him. They looked strangely familiar; many were dressed quite like his own Normans, in fact. Then he noticed a very familiar banner floating above the gates.

Richard swore. "What the hell is going on?" he muttered and rode past Talon to get a closer look. "By the saint's toes, those fucking people up there are Frenchmen!" he bellowed, loud enough for everyone to hear.

"I think I like this man," Brandt grinned when he heard Richard's booming voice.

Talon nodded. "Yes, I am afraid they are, my lord." He glanced at Lord D'Onston, who grimaced, and then Talon gestured toward the city.

"King Philip brought his fleet in this morning. The emperor left in somewhat of a hurry. The French sentries won't let my men in because they think we are Greeks, but I had a look inside earlier, and one of the people in there really is the King of France. Another is Guy de Lusignan. I had hoped to never meet him again."

D'Onston gave him a look and seemed about to speak, but Richard was taking center stage, setting his horse, given to him by Talon, to cavort and surge ahead.

Richard waved his men forward and rode directly up to the gates of the city, dangerously within crossbow range, where he halted his horse and bellowed up at the silent men on the walls above. "Open up these gates now! Or I shall cut off your balls and chop you all up for gull meat!"

He became aware of the executed bodies propped against the wall at the side of the gates, still with arrows protruding from the blood-caked, naked corpses. He swiped at the flies that attacked him almost the moment he approached the gruesome scene, and grimaced in disgust.

A slender man in very rich clothing, wearing a bright orange cloak fastened to his expensive chainmail and a slim, gold crown on his blond locks, strode to the parapet.

"Why, Richard, it really is you! I could barely believe it when my men told me that a tiny army was coming to invest the city! But here you are, a little late, as usual. Alas, the fox has run, and we have the city." He didn't wait for an answer. Instead, he turned and directed the men below to open the gates, which, a few minutes later, began to creak open.

Talon, who had ridden closer to the English king, thought he could hear teeth grinding. Richard's jaw was clenched, but he said nothing, merely gripped his reins harder as he rode into the city, to find Philip of France standing next to the former king of Jerusalem, Guy de Lusignan.

"Why, Cousin," he finally rasped, "where in God's name did you pop up from?"

Talon, who was just behind the king and next to D'Onston and the other lords, glared at Guy and Guy's brother, Geoffrey, Duke of Lusignan. Talon felt his own anger beginning to mount.

"Look, there!" he muttered to Rostam, who was a pace behind him. "If ever I wished ill upon a man, it is he, Lusignan."

Rostam gave him a startled look, but before he could say anything, Richard bellowed, "I'll ask again. Where the hell did you come from, Philip?"

The slim French king shrugged. "Across the ocean, just like you. But I sailed directly here, because it seemed the simplest thing to do."

"Did you perpetrate those foul murders out there?" Richard called up.

"No, Cousin. I just lop off people's heads when they upset me. This is the work of our usurper." Philip gave a dry chuckle. "Quite the barbarian, isn't he?"

"Just remember that this is *my* island!" Richard snarled. "*My* men perished in the taking of it, and while you might have this *city,* I have the *island!*" His face was tight and red with anger, which he barely managed to keep under control. He dismounted and threw his reins at a squire, then marched up to stand in front of Philip. Richard wasn't a very tall man, but he towered over Philip as he put both fists on his hips and looked threatening. Philip didn't appear to be very intimidated by this posture.

"God's will, Cousin. I came to remind you of the true purpose of the Crusade we set out upon. This is just an island and it is all yours, but we have bigger fish to fry, and it is not here, it is the Holy Land!" This last was delivered in a louder tone, to ensure that all heard him. Neither was it lost upon Richard, who was about to answer, but Philip was not finished.

"By my reckoning, you do not have the island as of yet. The usurper is still at large and, from what I hear, still capable. What do you intend to do? Stay here and chase him all over the place, or fulfill your oath to God and complete the Crusade?"

Talon heard the intake of some breaths nearby at this open display of ill manners, but Richard had, by now, brought himself under control. "I shall do both, Cousin. First, I shall teach this usurper a lesson, and then I shall come and assist you in taking Acre. Have no fear," he added sweetly, "it will not take very long, in either case."

Philip's lips curled, and he stared past Richard at the men with him. But it was Geoffrey de Lusignan who pointed to Talon. "We know you," he said with some puzzlement. "Yes, now I have it, you are Talon de Gilles, the Templar knight!" His tone was accusatory, but not malicious. It had not been Geoffrey who led the ill-founded campaign that culminated in Hattin.

Talon bowed and smiled ironically. "Your servant, my lord."

King Philip glanced up at Talon, as though evaluating him, but then greeted Lord D'Onston. "My lord, I am right glad to see you. We have heard terrible rumors of shipwrecks and worse. I send my thanks to God that you are with us."

D'Onston bowed from the saddle. "My lord, praise be to God. I am right glad to see you, too. My survival is, in no small way, due to Lord Talon here, who saved myself and many others from a dreadful fate."

Philip's eyes widened, and he again looked over at Talon, but held his peace. There were clearly other things on his mind, and Richard was at the forefront.

"Ah, but forgive me, I almost forgot my manners." Philip pretended to remember the men standing next to him. "Richard of England, this is Guy de Lusignan, *king* of Jerusalem, and his brother, Lord Geoffrey de Lusignan." He gave Richard a sardonic smile. Then he bowed mockingly, and in a tone dripping with irony said, "Why don't *we three kings* avail ourselves of the legendary hospitality of the Greeks and take our ease at the palace, which is not far from here? It is teeming with eunuchs and, from what I have heard, the harem is still full of the usurper's wives. He forgot to take them with him! Ha! Ha!"

His jocular tone eased the tense atmosphere. Richard had a less forbidding expression on his face as he strode past Philip, ignoring Guy and his brother as he brushed by them.

"I do not think he is much interested in us," remarked Guy to his brother. He was smarting at the lack of respect shown by the king of England. "I am a king, too!" he muttered.

Chapter 18

Philip King of France

Yours, Lord, is the greatness and the power and
  the glory
The splendor and the majesty.
Yours, Lord, is the kingdom exalted over all.
—Gabirol

Talon had observed the exchange of pleasantries, and drew his own conclusions. So while the kings retired to the abandoned palace, and the French Normans and their English-Norman counterparts sought billets within the captured city, Talon gave thought to staying clear of possible altercations. He decided to take some of his Companions with him to the house where Dimitri lived. Brandt quickly understood that, with the English in close proximity to the French, there was likely to be trouble. As Talon wanted none of that, Brandt agreed to oversee an encampment within the cover of the olive trees. As Talon pointed out, "It is unlikely that the kings will want to spend much time together, Brandt. A few days, at most. They appear to detest one another and have just demonstrated that, to the world at large. But be on your guard, my friend."

"Is the French king able to order Richard to abandon his conquest of the island, Lord?"

Talon thought about that, but then shook his head. "No, I don't think so. Richard has the bit between his teeth, in that regard. He will stay on the island and chase after Isaac. But I expect Philip will be leaving soon. He is eager to take Acre before Richard gets there, and to humiliate the English in the process." Privately, Talon wondered how and where the Crusade would end.

*****

The inhabitants of Famagusta who had remained were soon busy making money out of the newcomers. The Greeks knew just how to relieve unwitting soldiers from distant lands of their last coins, as knights and men at arms alike sampled the liquid refreshment that was provided, at a price. There being no beer or mead such as the European men were used to, wine became the drink of choice, but arak, a very fierce, clear alcohol, was also available.

As darkness descended, soldiers gathered in groups on street corners around flaming braziers, drinking, singing, and brawling. With the music came some daring women, who mixed with the soldiers. While some wandered off along the narrow and darkened streets with their would-be lovers, others picked fights and flailed about with their swords. The noise grew to the point where both kings found it necessary to send out patrols to calm things down.

One patrol was marching along the street that Talon, his son, and Dar'an were taking as they tried to reach Dimitri's house. Dar'an carried a satchel, which he clutched close to his chest, and all three wore their swords. The three of them regarded the approaching patrol warily. A single knight was the leader, accompanied by some ten spearmen and a squire. They were unmounted and striding along, kicking aside the drunks lying in the middle of the road. Talon and his two men didn't get out of the way quickly enough for the knight, who called a halt and demanded who they were.

"He is Lord Talon de Gilles," Rostam responded, because he was in front at the time.

"Likely story," the knight snapped. "You don't look anything like one of us. Get out of my way or it will be the worse for you. You cowardly Greeks think you can invent all kinds of lies."

"Do we look like footpads or cutthroats, sir? I am Talon de Gilles. *Lord* Talon, to you."

The squire recognized Talon, and reached forward to touch the knight's arm. "Sir Fayolle, I think we should believe these people," he said hesitantly.

But Fayolle was angry that he had been assigned this work when he could have been enjoying himself at one of the whore houses and getting drunk like his compatriots, and this small group of insolent men standing in front of him appeared to be more like Greeks, or worse, Saracens. He shook off the squire's hand and growled, "I'll show you better manners," and reached for his sword.

His hand had only just reached the pommel of his weapon when Rostam's sword tip was at the side of his neck. He froze. There were audible gasps from a few onlookers nearby. Quite abruptly, there was a menace in the air.

"Do you want me to kill him, Father?" Rostam asked Talon in French, while holding his opponent's gaze, with his blade touching the now-rigid knight's neck.

Talon sucked at his teeth and pretended to think about it. Fayolle's eyes were wide open, and real fear was beginning to show on his features.

"Well, I'd like to cut his head off for his insolence, but we'll allow his king to do that, should he so wish," Talon replied in the same language. "But for now, his belt, if you please, Dar'an."

In one swift move, Dar'an slipped his blade out of its scabbard and sliced through the belt that held the bewildered knight's still-sheathed sword. The sword fell away, to be caught in a deft motion by Dar'an, who stepped forward to retrieve it. Rostam removed his blade and stepped back. Talon nodded approvingly and watched the spearmen for any move that might precipitate a fight, but they were standing back, unsure what to do. Ordinary townsmen were easily intimidated; but ordinary townsmen did not draw swords, nor did any of the Greeks they'd encountered speak French. Was it possible this man was indeed who he said he was?

The knight lunged forward to grab Dar'an, only to feel a sharp and very painful blow to his nose, administered by Talon. He had not seen that coming either, but this time he sat down hard on the ground, holding his face with both hands while blood began to pour through his fingers.

"Courtesy is always a good rule to observe when meeting with strangers," Talon reminded him, then he and his two men left the shocked and bewildered people to stare after them as they disappeared around a corner.

"That went well, Master," Dar'an remarked in his usual dry tone.

"Hmm," Talon responded. "But at least they can't accuse *you* of striking him. I did that, and the king can deal with me, should the need arise."

"I think we have to make ourselves scarce, Father," Rostam remarked, glancing back into the dusk. "They seem to be recovering and are now coming after us. That fellow doesn't appear to have learned very much."

Talon sighed with exasperation. "Dar'an, do you have those noise makers with you? How quickly can you light one?"

"A few moments, Lord."

"Good, then do so. They look eager to close with us."

Talon and Rostam drew their swords and waited for the spearmen who ran toward them. The knight was shouting at them from behind. He looked enraged.

Talon heard the strike of flint and an exasperated grunt from Dar'an, then he heard sparks and this time, there was a distinct hissing sound and a flare of light from behind.

"Throw it, now!" Talon called.

The string of hissing and flaming fire-crackers soared over his and Rostam's heads, leaving a trail of pungent-smelling smoke, to land ten paces ahead of them, almost at the feet of the oncoming spearmen, who hesitated, startled and unnerved. The crackers began to explode with loud bangs, making a deafening noise in the close confines of the street. Talon was unable to resist the opportunity.

He struck a pose as though he himself had loosed this terrifying spectacle directly at the petrified men. His sword pointed at the flash bangs as they went off as though they had come from its magical tip. The flashes and the bangs, accompanied by dense, sulfurous smoke, sufficed to scare them out of their wits.

With cries of dismay, they turned and ran back the way they had come, crossing themselves and wailing as they fled. The knight was left standing alone for a long moment, staring at the place where there had been three men. They had vanished behind the cloud of smoke, but the awful flashes and bangs continued for a while longer. His eyes bugged, and he, too, turned and fled, sure that the devil himself had arrived.

*****

The next morning, Talon and his son, still accompanied by Dar'an, were halted at the entrance to the palace by French guards, who eyed them up suspiciously. "You cannot come here," one of the pikemen stated rudely. "You look like Saracens."

"Find Lord D'Onston and tell him Lord Talon is being kept waiting at the door," Talon retorted impatiently. "None of these people are civil to anyone," he remarked, as one of the guards reluctantly departed. Lord D'Onston arrived a few minutes later, somewhat out of breath.

"Ah, Lord Talon, welcome," he said with a smile. "These men are with me. Show them due respect!" he snapped at the guards. The spearmen came to rigid attention, their expressions wooden. Talon noticed that Lord D'Onston sported a very long peacock feather from his leather cap, which had not been there the day before.

"Come with me. King Philip expressed a wish to see you in private. Did you come for that reason?" D'Onston asked.

"No, Lord D'Onston. I came because this is the palace, and I thought I should pay my respects to the king, I mean King Richard, and ask him what he might need from me."

"Ah, of course you did." D'Onston frowned, looked a little distracted, and then took Talon by the arm. "Come with me for a moment before you do," he said quietly. He looked askance at Rostam and Dar'an, who were hovering just behind Talon.

"They come with me, sir," Talon said, and gestured for the two to follow him. "Rostam is my son, and Dar'an is a companion of long standing."

D'Onston, nodding his comprehension, smiled. "Very well, but first, we go to see the King of France."

The main hallway, with which Talon had become familiar over his years of quiet, unannounced visits, was now crowded with a quite different collection of people. Whereas formerly the Greek nobles and merchants in their gaudy attire had been paying groveling homage to their tyrant, there were now Latin soldiers, knights, and nobles with their attendants. These people were clad in a wide variety of once-colorful—but now-faded, patched and dirty—hose, tunics and mended chainmail hauberks. Everyone was talking loudly, and the air was heavy with the stink of unwashed bodies and foul breath. Talon glimpsed the occasional palace servant creeping about, providing wine in expensive glass beakers to some of the nobles. Some of the beakers had already been broken, and there were shards of glass on the elaborately tiled floor and the once colorful carpets were stained and marked with spilled drinks. It might have been early in the day, but some were already in their cups. The wine was a heady concoction compared to the thin beer they had become used to on ship.

It proved difficult to find a quiet place to talk, so Talon suggested that they go into the gardens and led the way outside, where it was indeed much quieter. Reflexively, Talon looked over toward the cage where he had, on a memorable occasion, encountered two leopards. To his surprise, they were still there, tails snapping back and forth, snarling at a cluster of Normans, who were gawking at them.

He heard some yells and laughter, and a shard of tile fell to the stone pathway, not a few paces in front of them, which made him jerk his head up. High up on the orange variegated tiles of the roofs of the palace, the two peacocks were squawking hysterically and darting away from some of the more daring squires, who were cackling with laughter as they scrambled noisily over the tiles, dislodging some, as they tried to seize hold of the poor birds' tail feathers. These exotic birds could not fly, having had their wings clipped, but they tried for the highest places on the roofs, only to be followed by the foolhardy squires, who were enjoying themselves enormously.

"They had better not slip in the wrong place," Dar'an observed in a dry tone. "The leopards will have an early noontime meal if they do!"

"Perhaps that would cure some of their exuberance," Talon commented, his tone just as dry. "I see your squires have been busy, my lord," he said to D'Onston. "I am amazed that you have not tripped over the feather in your cap thus far." D'Onston laughed self-consciously and said, "I have seen these birds before, but few of my countrymen have, so the feathers are proving very popular. At least chasing the birds keeps the young men out of other trouble."

Talon shook his head to dismiss the image of the beautiful birds wandering around on the roofs with bare bottoms.

"It would ease my concern, Lord D'Onston, if you could persuade those men over there to stop prodding the leopards, which have done them no harm. I have a soft spot for the animals. In fact, unless they desist, the leopards might find themselves on the loose tonight and that, my friend, would not be pretty for anyone."

D'Onston paused and looked hard at Talon. "I do believe you mean that," he said. "Very well; I shall tell them to stop immediately."

"You!" he called out in his most authoritative voice to the raucous group. "You are to stand back, and no one is to provoke those animals any more. They belong to the king of England, and he will have something to say if you do not!"

The baiting ceased at once, and the men stood back, looking somewhat shamefaced. Clearly, none of the Englishmen had encountered beasts of the leopard kind before. Before D'Onston had spoken, one of them had even poked his sword through the bars, trying to goad the unhappy animals, one of which growled menacingly and showed its teeth.

Talon wondered what might happen if he once again released the cats to terrorize these new conquerors. He noticed that both Dar'an and Rostam took a keen interest in the cats. He shook his head at them, knowing full well what they were thinking. "Not today," he murmured, with a glare from under his brows. They just grinned and looked shifty.

D'Onston turned to Talon when they were, more or less, alone and said, "The two kings have been quarreling furiously, Talon, and are now sulking in their respective audience chambers. Philip is enraged about the lawlessness that went on last night, and when he is angry, he can be very disagreeable."

"I saw some of that lawlessness myself, Lord D'Onston. In fact, my men and I were accosted by a very unpleasant group. They didn't realize who we were, and I had to make a point."

D'Onston raised an eyebrow. "It wasn't with a knight called Fayolle, was it?" he asked, an amused expression forming on his bearded face.

"I believe so, yes. I left him intact, albeit somewhat bruised," Talon responded.

D'Onston grinned. "Yes, we have all noticed his broken nose. And strangely, his sword was found by one of those eunuch people in the palace hall last night. He had to come and collect it this morning. No one knows how it got here. There was much laughter at his expense. Some even said that it was magic that you used."

"No, just skill, and it wasn't me, either. I simply watched." Talon told Lord D'Onston what had happened, omitting the part about the flaming crackers, and the lord slapped his thigh and laughed.

"You and your people continue to surprise me, Talon," he exclaimed. "I suspect that even the King of France will feel that the man received his just desserts. Sir Fayolle is overly aggressive; useful in a battle, but not much good anywhere else. However, be careful of Philip. He is a bit of a snollygoster and is good at getting people to say what he wants to hear from them."

"Snollygoster?" Talon asked, sounding surprised.

"Yes, he is clever with words. He is much more of a politician than Richard, which frustrates the King of England no end when they are in the middle of an argument, which is often, because he gets confused and Philip keeps playing him."

Talon decided to bear this in mind.

They were ushered into a chamber where Philip of France had ensconced himself for the duration of the occupation. It was, without doubt, the best chamber in the palace, other than the audience chamber, which he had rejected out of hand, because it had been reduced to a shabby reflection of its former glory by marauding Normans.

There were a number of people in the room, among them several of Philip's closest advisers, Lords Bruglie and Guise, and a bishop, dressed in his best finery and fingering his rosary, who made the sign of the cross when Talon was announced. Fayolle was also there, standing off to Philip's left with a small cluster of other knights. Talon realized there were no Normans from England in the chamber, which he found a little odd, but then, he was beginning to realize that the alliance between these two nations and their followers did not extend to social engagements, unless it was absolutely necessary. He sighed inwardly as he saw the two Lusignan brothers standing to the right of the king.

Walking deliberately, with Rostam and Dar'an just behind him, he approached the French king, then bowed from the waist, after which he stood silently. He didn't fail to notice that the bishop was not the only one to cross himself, and he wondered, a trifle sardonically, if the king would, as well.

Philip, however, appeared to be made of sterner stuff. He watched as Talon approached, and there was a gleam in his eye when he began to speak.

"Lord Talon, you *are* a lord, are you not?" he asked with a quizzical expression, but it was not unfriendly. "I have heard conflicting stories about you from all corners."

"I am known as a lord these days, Your Highness," Talon responded in an even tone.

"Very well, then, Lord Talon. My knight here informs me that you assaulted him without provocation last evening and injured him, to boot. What say you to that?"

Talon flicked a glance at the glowering knight, who still had dried blood on his face, and smiled, but not with his eyes. "He was bullying his way along the street when we met, Sire. His appalling lack of manners toward myself led to a very light punishment. It could have been much worse."

Philip, who had been leaning forward on his chair, the one vacated by Isaac only a few days before, leaned back in his throne and waved his hand casually at Sir Fayolle.

"He claims that it was you who attacked him. He was doing his duty and keeping the peace at the time, so he claims." Philip gave a cool smile and flicked his fingers again at the angry man.

"Furthermore, he claims that you used magic and created much noise and thunderbolts with the stink of sulfur. He told me that it stank as though the Devil himself had farted." Philip gave Talon a quizzical look. "Are you, then, in the employ of the Devil, Lord Talon? It wasn't you who broke wind, was it, my lord?"

Talon couldn't help but laugh, "No, but it might have been Sir Fayolle, Sire. He certainly looked as though he had passed something." He heard several of the lords nearby snicker. Neither they nor King Philip appeared to have much sympathy for the errant knight.

Philip gave a snort of amusement. Talon realized that Philip was playing with him, but he went along and made himself sound just a trifle indignant. "I have no idea what he can be talking about, Sire! I am no Devil's spawn and, besides, he was drunk. He threw his sword right at me! I was flabbergasted, my liege, at such behavior. So, I punished him, left the scene, taking the sword with me, delivered it to the palace, and then returned home."

"He lies!" Fayolle called out, forgetting where he was for a moment, which he quickly regretted.

"You do not speak unless I allow you to!" Philip barked. The entire room fell silent.

"I hear the sword did show up here, which is a mystery resolved, now that Lord Talon de Gilles has explained."

Talon realized that, while Philip might not be as dominating a person physically as was Richard of England, he nonetheless was firmly in charge here, and no man gainsaid him. His respect for the king went up several notches.

"My lord, that man is a wizard and a heretic. We know of him! The whole island is fearful of him, and his name is cursed in the Holy Land." Guy de Lusignan spoke up.

The bishop, Eugene, was furiously counting his beads, but he bobbed his head like a puppet. "We of the Church know of him, my liege. He was charged with wizardry in Acre before the fall."

Men all about the room began to cross themselves, and some looked apprehensive, but Philip looked intrigued. "Is this true, Lord Talon?" he asked.

"The charges were brought by a false witness in Acre, Sire. This was with the sole purpose of stealing my property and my ships, because I was living too well for the bishop of Acre to tolerate at the time."

There was a low murmur, along with a gasp of indignation from the bishop, who now glared daggers at Talon. Philip, however, seemed to be enjoying himself. He sat upright.

"Leave us. I want to talk to Lord Talon de Gilles, alone. And send for wine and refreshments."

"But my liege!" the bishop protested, along with other murmurs of concern from the lords and knights.

"Lord D'Onston, We thank you for bringing Lord Talon to us, today." It was a dismissal, and D'Onston shot Talon a warning glance before he bowed himself out.

"You will be well advised to keep your council around Lord D'Onston, Lord Talon; he belongs to Richard from his bit to his saddle," Philip murmured as he watched the Englishman depart. "Lord Guise, you shall remain, just in case Lord Talon transforms himself into a goblin," Philip said with a smirk. "The rest of you, leave Us at once! Your men can stay, Lord Talon."

In the pause, after his attendants had reluctantly departed, Philip gestured around him at the beautiful frescoes on the walls, which were marred by large blank spaces, where gold halos had once decorated the icons of saints.

"Those barbarian Normans and English, from their king on down, are so bereft of gold that they think that the tiles on the saints' halos on these walls were made of it," he commented. There was contempt in his tone, accompanied by a shake of his head. "Richard is here for the loot as much as for any holy crusade, I'll warrant. They will leave this island looking as though a host of locusts came by, when they finally depart."

Talon didn't disagree with that observation. He was going to have to tread carefully with both kings, especially Richard. That much had already become evident.

For the next two hours, Philip asked Talon many a question that covered how he had come to live in Cyprus, to his understanding of Isaac—now a declared enemy of Richard—and his knowledge of the Holy Land. Inevitably, Guy and his brother, Geoffrey, came under discussion.

"Those two do not like you, Lord Talon," he remarked at that point.

"They might have good reason, Sire," Talon responded, with wry shake of his head.

"Why is that?"

"Guy listened to an imbecile called Ridefort, then the Grand Master of the Templars, and proceeded to march our entire army into a trap set by Salah ad-Din. And that, despite the entreaties from my lord of Tripoli. Hattin, my liege."

"Ah, yes, of course, Hattin. It has been on everyone's lips." Philip responded dryly. "Which is why we are here, I suppose. Geoffrey doesn't seem as weak as Guy, to my mind."

"Geoffrey is the better man, and he is a brave warrior, my lord. But he stays close to Guy, despite their misfortunes."

"Well then, he is loyal. That, in of itself, is rare enough these days." Philip observed, sounding approving. "They left a brother behind in Palestine to guard the approaches to Acre, along with my own Duke of Burgundy. I am impatient to return, because I cannot be sure that Salah ad-Din will not take advantage of my absence. Burgundy, while a good fighter, has very much his own agenda, and I need to keep him on a tight rein. As for Guy's brother, he is an unknown quantity. Do you know of him?"

"Salah ad-Din is limited by his smaller forces at present, my lord. However, the time rapidly approaches when he will have many more men at his disposal, and that time is not far off. Guy's brother is somewhere in between him and Geoffrey, with regards to reliability."

Philip looked hard at Talon. "So, you have met this man, Salah ad-Din?" he demanded.

"I have met him," Talon replied. "I went to see him in Damascus to try to persuade him not to invade the country. But his anger was too great at the foul deed perpetrated by Raynald de Châtillon." Talon gave a grimace of disgust. "He was not to be persuaded otherwise, no matter what the Duke of Tripoli had to say."

"Do you know Lord Conrad?" Philip asked.

Talon smiled. "I know him and admire him, my lord! Now, there is a man who should be the king of Jerusalem."

"Then I must persuade him to come out of Tyre and meet him," Philip said. "I dare say that Richard will want to appoint Guy back to his former place as the king."

Talon merely nodded. "I heard that Conrad turned him away from Tyre my Lord, just as he did Lusignan."

Just at that moment the palace servants appeared, bringing wine in pitchers and beakers, which they filled and offered to both men.

Philip swallowed, appreciatively. "This is good wine!" he commented. "Where does this come from, I wonder?"

Talon smiled. "From my lands, Sire," he said. "The emperor—I mean, the usurper—didn't know the source; had he, I suspect it might have upset him."

Philip laughed. But then he looked straight at Talon. "Is it true that you have sworn allegiance to the English king?"

"It seemed prudent at the time, Sire," Talon said, and watched Philip, who narrowed his eyes. "So, you are pragmatic, as well." It was a statement. "I could have had use for one like you."

"I shall attempt to assist you whenever I am able, within the bounds of my oath, Sire," Talon responded.

"This island, and that barren land over there," Philip made another of his gestures, "The Holy Land, are not places where I wish to linger. We are builders in my land, Lord Talon. We know how to build beautiful places for the glory of God. I have seen little of that here, so far. Have you ever been to France?"

"Not to France, my lord. To Languedoc, Albi, where my family lives, and Aigues-Mortes when I was younger."

"Is that where you met Richard?" Philip asked.

Talon blinked. How did the king know of that meeting? His respect for the French king rose another notch. Here was a man who had his finger on the finer points of ruling. He had knowledge and intelligence, both of which Talon regarded as essential for survival.

He nodded. "Er... yes, my lord. We met under difficult circumstances."

"Yes, I believe he was trying to steal some of his father's kingdom right from under his nose." Philip laughed without much humor at the uncomfortable expression on Talon's face.

"Richard and I used to be close friends, but times change, and we must change to survive. He has not made much of an effort in that regard. He is still a brawler, but I intend to make France great, as did Charlemagne, my ancestor, so we have agreed not to... agree." His bark of laugher caused Talon to smile in response.

"It is a pity that you have not been to Paris, Lord Talon," Philip commented. "I would be proud to show you the Church of San Martin, its beautiful windows, and the growing edifice of Notre Dame. A magnificent building, which will be dedicated to Mary, that is, even now, unmatched in any country, to the best of my knowledge. The masons and metal-smiths had nearly completed it when I left for this scanty place. I know in my soul that God will regard it as His house, when it is finally done. If you are ever to come to my land, then I shall make you my guest," Philip promised.

"Thank you, my lord." Talon thought of the Hagia Sophia in Constantinople and wondered if the king was right about this Notre Dame. If so, the church had to be truly impressive.

Then Philip abruptly changed the subject.

"We hear many rumors about you, not least that you are indeed a magician. Tell me, are the rumors true? People fear you, especially the church bishops, priests, and such alike," he added with a malicious smirk. "And what of those who serve you?" His glance rested speculatively on Rostam and

Dar'an, who had been standing quietly just behind Talon as the two men spoke. He was assessing, and did not fail to note their quiet, alert stance.

"People mistake skills, especially unfamiliar skills, for magic, Sire. The Latin Church is especially prone to suspect anyone who has talents outside their comprehension as being a servant of the Devil, or some such nonsense. I and my people are simply trained in unfamiliar skills, some of which we learned in China."

This set them off in another direction, during which Talon reevaluated this king of France. Philip, known as Philip August, was nobody's fool; his questions and remarks made that very plain. It was with some regret on Talon's part, and apparently on the part of the king, that they were finally interrupted by a messenger, who said that Richard needed to talk to Philip.

"Before I go, Lord Talon de Gilles," Philip murmured, "I say you should watch your back with Richard. He betrayed my trust in the matter of the marriage to my sister Alys. Easily making treaties but just as easily dissuaded from keeping those that do not suit him. He has no loyalty to anyone but himself. Be careful."

Talon chose to remain silent rather than say something he might regret; it was very clear to him that there were serious issues between the two kings. He wondered how they were going to accomplish a Crusade while in this state of affairs. It did not bode well.

"I hope very much that we can continue this discussion before too long, Lord Talon," the king told him. "But now, I have to go back to politics with my cousin Richard, and I doubt that it will be as enjoyable as this meeting."

"I am honored, and wish you good health and God's good will, my liege." Talon and his companions bowed themselves out.

Chapter 19

Nicosia, The Battle for Cyprus

Sword, how fair and bright thou art.
Come thou forth and view the light,
Long as I can wield thee here
Charles my Emperor shall not say
That I die alone, unwept.
—from *The Legend of Roland*

The two kings were quarreling again, and this time, it sounded quite serious. The knights and lords from both armies were crowded into the main audience hall, where the kings were standing, glaring at one another. Princess Joanna was also present and on her feet, though Berengaria, the new queen of England, was still seated at the table recently vacated by the monarchs as their tempers boiled over. Talon was there, along with Lord D'Onston, both keeping back from the fierce tempers on display.

"You know perfectly well why I must get back to the siege, Cousin. The Saracens are growing in numbers, and my men, as well as those of Lord Guy, are very worried. You should be, too." Philip said with some heat. "If this siege continues into the summer, we might find ourselves a nut to be cracked between the walls of Acre and the host that Salah ad-Din is going to pull together. In other words, Cousin," his voice took on a sarcastic note, "our backs will be threatened, and not even you will be able to fight on that front *and* take Acre!" Philip began to shout in an agitated manner as he waved his hands to emphasize his point.

"Then take your pitiful little army, get back on those ships of yours, and go to Palestine, Philip. I shall be along very soon. In the meantime, I want them out of this city. They are causing too much damage and trouble."

"Damage?" Philip snarled. "*Your* people are the ones who get drunk, pick fights, loot churches and destroy murals! My patrols were even attacked, and several of my knights nearly killed!" He paused. "But yes, you are right. I shall leave and go about the real business of our Crusade, as we swore to God... *both* of us!" He glared at Richard.

"You can go about conquering little islands which are Christian, rather than face the wrath of Salah ad-Din, who could probably make mincemeat of your bold and brave soldiers," Philip continued. "Stay, by all means, in this pitiful little palace. I gift it to you! I could fit it into one of my stables, it is so miserably poor." With that, he turned away and strode towards the doors, followed by his knights and their attendants, leaving a scowling Richard and his apprehensive, wide-eyed followers. Even the bishop looked sheepishly embarrassed.

"Good riddance," Richard managed to mutter.

Talon noted that neither Guy nor his brother, Geoffrey, moved to follow the French. Philip had paused near Geoffrey.

"Stay here, and do your best to persuade him to come as soon as he has finished with this fool's errand. We still have need of him, I regret to say," he murmured. Then he was gone, and the room was silent, as everyone contemplated the consequences of the quarrel.

"Muster the army. We leave tomorrow for Nicosia," Richard called out when the last of the French were gone.

"I'll deal with this usurper and be in Palestine before Philip's captains have figured out how to get there." He grinned at his sister, who shook her head but said nothing, not wanting to provoke yet another outburst from her brother. He was so enraged with Philip, he could start a quarrel with anyone close by.

*****

Three days later, on the plain to the east of the walled city of Nicosia, the self-appointed Emperor of Cyprus, Isaac Komnenos, stared out at an army arrayed against him and felt the chill of uncertainty once again gnawing at his vitals.

The day before, at council, the cacophony of voices around him, led by that of General Gôsakos, had presented him with only confusion, bordering on panic, as they vied for attention from their leader. In the past, as a malicious game, he had always set his advisers and officers against one another, in order to keep them off balance while he assessed their loyalty; so now, when the stakes were at their highest, for him in particular, they were capable of neither resolution nor cooperation.

The man who understood the situation better than most, Gôsakos, finally left the council in exasperation without showing any respect for Isaac, not even acknowledging his half-hearted demand to remain. The other advisors, who included several of the administrative eunuchs who had accompanied the emperor from Famagusta, finally dispersed, aimless and frightened. It was telling that Isaac didn't throw one of his famous tantrums and send men off to execute Gôsakos. He was out of options and had no other effective commanders. Eventually, Isaac sent for Gôsakos and asked the grizzled warrior—almost pleaded with him—to form up the army outside the gates of Nicosia, to confront the invaders, who were camped on the plain in front of his city.

*****

Talon and his men stood in three loose lines, set in the middle of the, by now, respectable army that Richard of England had mustered before Nicosia. It was hot and dry, and Talon suspected it would become hotter as the day progressed. There were almost no clouds in the azure blue sky above, and the sun blazed down upon the two armies, facing one another across a gap of about three hundred paces. Talon wiped his eyes and brow with a rag where he could around the constricting cheek guards of his helmet. He wondered how the people from England were faring in this heat and glanced to his right, where King Richard sat on his destrier, recovered enough from the sea journey to be useable in a battle. The king appeared calm enough and held in his fractious mount with a tight rein. His lords were scattered about, some nearby, while others were placed with the several rows of mounted knights on the two wings of the army.

It had taken Talon some time to persuade the king to deploy his troops in the formation that they now stood. "The mercenaries we will face are not good infantrymen, my lord, but they are excellent cavalrymen. They have learned hard lessons from the Arabs, and will, no doubt, use the same tactics that they and the Turks developed against the Franks in Palestine."

Richard had fidgeted but listened. "Go on; what tactics?" he demanded.

"They will try to draw your horsemen into a center well, where there will be hazards and pits to break up your charge; and then, while you are trying to extricate yourself from these hazards, they will cut your army to pieces from the wings. They sometimes call it the horns of the bull," Talon had explained.

"We have bigger horses and could easily take them on!" Guy de Lusignan ventured, and others had muttered agreement. Talon rounded on Guy, his anger reignited by the memories of Hattin. It felt very odd to be in his present role, almost as though he were standing in Raymond of Tripoli's boots when a similar heated argument had taken place, in the days before the ill-fated battle. He shook his head vehemently.

"It is because of you and Ridefort," he snarled, "that we lost Hattin! So many perished because you refused to listen to the better man then! Do you want to repeat those mistakes, my lord? Have you learned *nothing*?" His scathing tone in the presence of the king of England made many a man blink with surprise. The equally surprised English king seemed only just now to realize how much Hattin had affected Talon. Talon turned his back on Guy de Lusignan and his brother with contempt, ignoring the red-faced king of Jerusalem, who was about to shout a reply.

Richard held up his hand for silence. "I would hear Lord Talon out," he stated. "I shall also hear the opinion of others and make up my *own* mind as to how I shall deploy my army. Lord Talon, continue."

"They will place their infantry in the middle of their army, who will be prepared for a charge from your horsemen, Sire. The infantry will retreat, as planned, and may well leave traps, trenches, and spikes to injure the horsemen, but if my men, the Saxons and my other shield men, are in the middle, we can advance at a very deliberate pace. The best place for your cavalry with be on the wings, opposing the usurper's horsemen. Any ground that is safe for them to cover will be safe for your horses as well. If you ever notice their horsemen avoiding an area, it will be well for your cavalry to avoid the area also."

He continued in this vein for a few more minutes, and then stood back and waited. It amused him to listen to the

Normans, who had never fought in these climes, advocating a charge that would solve everything, and in this they had support from Guy de Lusignan, who glared at Talon while urging this approach.

Finally, after an hour of arguments, Richard held up his hand for silence and said, "I have listened to all of you, but I have decided upon the method put before me by Lord Talon. While I would like simply to get this over with, we have another obligation, and that is to bring as many men as possible to Palestine at the end of this venture. If Lord Talon is right, I stand to lose horses, which I cannot afford to chance; and if he and his men are willing to initially take the brunt of this battle, I shall conclude it with my horsemen from the wings."

Now, here they were. Talon glanced at Brandt and his men, who were standing patiently, leaning on their shields and talking together, waiting for the order to advance. The other Kantara men were somewhat less relaxed, but Brandt had placed several of his lieutenants in charge of them to stiffen their resolve. Talon, his Companions and the archers were mounted just behind them on either side of the shield wall. Talon had Rostam alongside him, while Khuzaymah rode on the other wing of the shield wall with Dar'an. They were there to support and use their bows, to inflict as much damage as they could, until the shield wall could close and begin its bloody work.

He stared across the stony ground before him, which was almost bare of grass other than clumps of already dried weeds, at the seemingly formidable army of Greeks forming up before them, easily discerning where the emperor was placed on a low mound—well-guarded, Talon noted sardonically. Isaac was some way behind the mob of milling footmen, who were being whipped and prodded into place by his mercenaries and harangued by a man whom, Talon supposed, was their latest leader, Gôsakos. Dimitri had told

Talon about the general while they were in Famagusta. Talon decided that this man was his, unless, of course, he could capture the emperor before that.

"He's a brutal mercenary who used to be in the Byzantine army, Talon. Knows a lot about fighting, but I'm not so sure about his ability to keep the emperor on track, if you see what I mean."

Talon had listened carefully as his spy told him much about the emperor's latest general. Now he stared across the flat land toward the Greek cavalry, which was crowding the wings of the footmen, almost as though they were there to prevent those worthies from running away before the battle even commenced. Talon was fairly sure that the reputation of the Saxons had preceded them, and now the infantry of the emperor was to be pitted, very reluctantly, against these dreadful warriors. This was just as he wanted it to be. There would be fear in their ranks, and this would make them weak.

There would be even more terror among the Greek forces if Talon ordered Dar'an to use his Chinese flaming crackers, but that would only be necessary should the fight go against the Kantara men. Talon wanted to keep his secrets, if he could. Staring hard at the enemy force, Talon was confident that, if Richard played this game of chess carefully and forcefully, he could win it with few casualties, and the island could belong to the King of England. That would be something to ponder when the battle was over.

While the noise of shouting and insults grew from the Greek side, the silence of the Norman army was, in its own way, more menacing. Richard waited just long enough, then lifted his right arm and dropped it. Trumpets sounded. The signal to advance had been given. Brandt shouted an order, and the Saxons, along with their Kantara shield men, closed ranks into a solid pack of overlapping shields that bristled with spears. Brandt and his lieutenants shouldered their long axes, and he glanced over at his leader. Talon and his Companions moved their horses closer to the wings. Talon waved at Brandt to begin.

"Move!" Brandt shouted, and the warriors commenced, shouting their battle songs and marching deliberately toward the emperor's men. The dreaded sound of their stamping boots reverberated through the warm air. Richard nodded to Talon and then waved his cavalry forward to keep pace with the shield wall. Their orders had been made very clear. Only when Talon's men were fully engaged were they to charge and break the wings. Trumpets were sounded from among the English cavalry, and colorful banners flapped in the light breeze. Talon didn't use trumpeters. He didn't feel the need.

To the clashing of swords on shields and loud battle shouts by the Kantara men, the distance closed to within forty paces. The Kantara longbow archers were taking their toll of mercenary lives, whose own crossbowmen returned the fire, but against the shield wall their bolts were ineffective. As his small but solid phalanx of warriors approached the enemy, Talon could see the uncertainty beginning to undermine the emperor's side. However, the mercenaries who worked for Isaac knew full well that they had no future if they gave up now, and their own trumpets blared and their drums pounded. Banners were waved while they responded to the Saxons with yells of their own, and drove their reluctant men forward at the point of spear and sword.

The Greeks braved the hail of arrows sent at them from Talon and his men, and moved forward. Talon could not decide whether it was because they were courageous or because they had nowhere to run. Either way, it was to be hard on them. The two sides met with a crash, but to Talon and his men alongside the Saxons, it was clear from the onset that the men of the shield wall had the upper hand. The spears of the shield wall drove in and out while the long axes of Brandt and his Saxons rose and fell, taking their deadly toll. The Saxon battle roar almost drowned out the screams and cries of the wounded and dying. Stamping forward with a shout one pace at a time, they appeared to shrug off the desperate attempts by the frantic mercenaries to break their wall. Their stabbing spears could not be stopped, and all those who stood before them soon died or were mortally wounded as the wall drove over them.

The mass of Greeks, most of whom were unused to this form of deadly fighting machine, began to fall back.

"Beware of traps, Brandt!" Talon roared over the din. Brandt heard him and called out warnings to his men. Indeed, the warning was timely; the Greeks had left stakes and covered pits full of sharp wooden spikes, which Brandt and the Kantara footmen carefully evaded. This terrain would have been a disaster for Richard's horsemen.

Soon Talon and his archers, still shooting their bows almost at point-blank range, were riding over bodies left behind by the Kantara shield wall; the stony ground was stained with the blood of their enemies, but there were also some of his own men who were wounded. At a signal from Talon, one of the Companions, Nasuh, dismounted and went to their aid.

With perfect timing, Richard, who had been closely watching the battle, galloped to one side, chased by his attendants, and rode straight to the front of his men. With a shout that could be heard across the field, he swirled his axe above his head and pricked his mount into a gallop. His men gave a great roar and charged after him, straight into the massed ranks of the Greek cavalry. For one brief moment, Talon wondered whether the Greeks would hold, but as the heavier horses slammed into the lighter animals, they broke apart. Richard, roaring, "For God and England!" plunged into their midst and attacked with gusto any rider unfortunate enough to encounter him. His men used lances and the weight of their mounts to overpower the enemy, who simply ceased to be a cohesive unit. When the lances broke or stuck in the armor of their victims, swords came out, along with maces and battle axes, and the Normans pressed forward. The mercenaries lacked the discipline needed to withstand even a ragged charge of this kind, and soon the taller and heavier destriers began to show their true worth in battle.

A man with a mace or an axe leaning over a lightly armed man on a smaller horse has a distinct advantage in an engagement, unless the smaller horse is very nimble. Talon had little time to contemplate the success of the Normans, however, as he himself engaged with the enemy to his front. Both wings of the Greek army began to collapse, and the Normans, led by their ferocious warrior king, began to close the horns of the bull. But this time it was an English bull.

Very soon after the Norman charge, the Greek infantry men were fleeing for their lives, while the Greek cavalry tried desperately to prevent the attackers from reaching their emperor. Talon searched in vain for Isaac, but he did see Gôsakos, who was riding just behind the mass of infantry towards the mountains to the north, in the direction of Kyrenia. He had evidently given up on the battle.

He must have hoped to take a boat and escape the island, Talon surmised. He shouted for Rostam and the other Companions to follow him, and drove his horse through the fleeing infantry enemy, who paid him scant attention, other than to give him room and to cower away from the flashing swords of his men.

"Gôsakos!" Talon bellowed, as he galloped toward the general and his small group of riders. "Where are you going? Are you then a coward?" Talon fully intended to provoke the man, who heard him over the din and pulled up his mount. He was bloodied, but didn't look as though he himself was wounded. Talon thought sardonically that it might be the blood of the commander's own people whom he had pricked into the battle.

"The Magician!" he called back and sneered. "I should have known! It has been you all along who has brought this about, curse you!" His features were distorted with frustration and impotent rage.

Without indicating what he was going to do, even to his own men, he put spurs to his horse and charged straight at Talon, who barely had time to collect his own mount before Gôsakos was upon him. Talon managed to drive his animal sideways to avoid a head-on collision, and parried a wild slash at his head. The steel shrieked and sparks flew, then the mercenary was past. Talon spun his willing mount around on its haunches and drove it hard at Gôsakos's horse, hammering it on the off-side rump just before the man could fully turn his sweating animal. It was a move straight out of chogan. Talon's first sword strike was aimed at Gôsakos's helmet. He intended to knock him off his animal and then capture him, but he just missed, nicking the bronze shoulder plate. However, the impact of the two horses made Gôsakos's horse stumble. Talon wasted no time; this time he struck for the neck. The man flailed back with his sword to parry the blow, but the end of Talon's blade went in deep, making Gôsakos gasp. His sword flew out of his hands and he slid sideways off his horse to tumble to the ground, where he lay in a bloody heap.

Talon reined in his own animal, intending to dismount and finish it, but Rostam was very quick. He dived off his own horse and stood over the fallen man with his sword ready. He looked up at the mounted men.

"He is dead, Father," he stated and dropped the point of his weapon. "That was very quick, Father," he called out in an awed tone.

"Chogan is a useful sport, my boy. I'll teach you how to play it one day!" Talon called back, as he wiped his blade and sheathed it. Rostam shook his head and laughed with the others, who had gathered around them. His father knew perfectly well how good a player his son had become.

They waited in a tight group until the exuberant Saxons and Kantara men marched up and joined them. They were still counting their wounded and losses, passing the water skins around, when Dar'an gestured toward a group of men riding toward them. The banner that flew over them told its own story.

"Here comes the king," he called out.

King Richard arrived with his men to halt their tired, sweating horses in front of the little Kantara army. Richard was disheveled, covered with other people's blood, and clearly exuberant, as were the men accompanying him.

"That was good work, Lord Talon!" he called out, his voice hoarse from shouting. He gestured to the area where the center of the battle had been fought. "I now see what you meant about traps and suchlike, Lord Talon. It could have gone badly for us." He waved his hand at the bloody corpse on the ground. "Is this the usurper?"

Talon shook his head. "No, Sire, Isaac has slipped away. This was his commander, Gôsakos. The usurper has run from the field."

He glanced past the king to see Guy de Lusignan and his brother seated among the group. He wondered cynically if Guy had sheltered from the dangers of battle behind the axe-wielding monarch. But while Guy didn't look as disheveled as the rest of the men with the king, it was clear that Geoffrey had gone into the battle with some enthusiasm. He was as bloody as Richard from the fighting, and his mount sported a light wound on its shoulder.

"Damn the villain!" Richard exclaimed in an exasperated tone. "Now we have to hunt for him, and that will be no easy task, even on this island. There must be many a bolt hole for him to crawl into." He took a long swallow of the water skin that Dar'an held up to him. "Thank you, I needed that," he said, and wiped his mouth. "Saint's balls, but that was hot work," he chuckled.

Talon gestured toward the north. "It is true, he will have to be hunted, Sire. But I have heard that his daughter might be in Kyrenia," he called out. "He could have gone that way."

Richard lifted his head from contemplating the dead general.

"Very well," he stated with some reluctance. "We will have to go there and find out."

"My lord," Guy interjected, "I and my brother can go and look for him there. We can take our own men and save you some trouble. You have the city to deal with, now that the battle is won." His ingratiating tone irked Talon, but he saw the logic in Guy's words and shrugged.

Richard looked relieved. "I wish to take my men and go back to Famagusta as soon as we are done here," he stated. "Go, then, Guy, and see if there is a scent of him. I'd like to have this man either dead or my prisoner before I leave for Palestine. Philip will become impossible if I delay much longer."

"At your command, Lord," Guy said, with a venomous glance at Talon. He wheeled his horse and rode away. Geoffrey nodded to Talon, as though implying some respect, and followed his brother, to gather their men together. Richard watched them leave with an expression of mild contempt.

"I shall be glad to be rid of those two, even if it is for a short while," he muttered to his nearby lords, who grinned agreement. Richard turned back to Talon.

"We owe you much for your contribution to this battle, Lord Talon. I must now invest this city; do you come with me?"

Talon gestured to his men. "I have to take my wounded home and bury our dead. Will you give me leave to return there for a short while?"

Richard nodded. "Come to Famagusta when you are done with these things. I shall be there, Lord Talon. Go with God."

He turned his horse and rode slowly with his men toward the gates of Nicosia, which were now open. Merchants and administrators, mostly the eunuchs who ran the place, along with humbler inhabitants lined up on either side of the road. Banners flew and trumpets sounded while citizens cheered nervously from the crowded battlements.

Sadly, other citizens were coming onto the field, looking for lost or wounded members of their families. A sound different from the battle shouts of the Saxons and other warriors began to be heard all over the field: the wailing of relatives and wives for the wounded and dead.

Talon noted with a grimace that scavengers were there too, surreptitiously plundering the dead.

"Come," he called. "We are going home!"

While King Richard and his English army rode into Nicosia in triumph, Talon and his army slipped away. Lord D'Onston glanced back in the direction he had last seen them, just as he rode into the city with the king. There was no sign of the men from Kantara. He felt a light chill down his back, and he made the sign of the cross on his breast.

Chapter 20

Kantara Receives a Visitor

He may be clearing you out
for some new delight.
The dark thought, the shame, the malice,
meet them at the door laughing and invite them in.
Be grateful for whatever comes,
because each has been sent
as a guide from beyond.
—Jalaluddin Rumi

For a time the castle settled into its established routines, and the weary warriors were able to recuperate. Talon, who wanted a little time with his family before becoming immersed in the pressing duties of the estates, went hawking with Rostam, taking Cristofo with them. The merchant was very happy to be able to ride out, as he was chaffing at the time he had been forced to remain within the castle walls. His minders came along to make sure that he did nothing stupid, but Talon was by now comfortable with the young man and felt that he could be trusted to behave, and they were still in the middle of their discussion about what cargo was to be shipped to Venice. The ride out also enabled Talon to check on the condition of the fields, the crops and the herds, while their birds of prey soared high in the sky, looking for victims.

The huntsman, Evanthis, who had remained along with some of the grooms and servants when Talon's predecessor had departed, called sharply to the hounds that accompanied them. They had brought them along, much to the animals' delight, although Evanthis kept them on a short leash.

"Just in case we should start a small deer, my lord," he told Talon with a grin.

Talon smiled back at the huntsman, who had proved to be very reliable and knowledgeable about the animals in his care. Talon had had no reason to regret keeping him on.

"I hope that neither Dimitri nor Boethius has sent any pigeons today, or it will be the worse for them, I fear," Rostam remarked. He gazed after his own red-footed falcon as it lifted into an air current and almost disappeared from sight.

Talon hoped the same; the air had been busy of late with message pigeons flying to and fro. But today their falcons were looking for rabbits and hares, which would go into the pot. He glanced up the hillside toward the caves where some of the villagers were working and noticed that one of the hounds had disturbed a large hare, which had broken cover. Evanthis, ever sharp-eyed, called the hound firmly to heel. It came reluctantly to stand near him, its ears pricked and a low whine in its throat. Talon's own hawk had clearly noticed the hare, for it stooped and closed its wings to begin its dive.

"Look, Rostam!" Talon called out, gesturing toward the plummeting bird. They all watched as the falcon sped like an arrow for its prey. However, the hare must have realized its peril because it began to flee for the cover of some bushes and rocks, a few hundred paces away. The hawk made a slight change of course and skimmed the ground with a cry. The hare was almost at its cover when the sharp claws of the large bird seized it, and the pair of them crash-landed in the weeds just before the rocks. Talon shook his head.

"That was close," he remarked.

"It's a good hunter, that bird of yours," Cristofo called out. "I've not been on a hunt like this before," he confessed to Rostam, who rode alongside.

"Have you not?" Rostam asked, somewhat surprised. He had grown up with the birds of prey and could not imagine life without them to hunt small game.

"I come from a city where creatures of this kind are rare, although I dare say the doge and his kind might have them," Cristofo told him.

"It is a city like no other in the world, young lord, waterways linking islands. Our merchants bring in so much wealth that we are able to build wonders. Our harbor welcomes us home with her great stone arms, and the Basilica of Saint Mark is more magnificent than Hagia Sophia! And wealth is creating a new order of nobility." He smirked. "Great families seek to marry their sons and daughter to the daughters and sons of merchants. Even they envy our wealth. And our women are the most beautiful in the world!" he boasted.

Privately, Rostam thought this must be an exaggeration. Besides, he was more interested in other matters than the looks of the daughters of Venice. "Are you plagued by fools and usurpers like Isaac?" he asked.

"Ah, well," Cristofo said deprecatingly, "it is said two types of men always rise to the top: the worst and the best, the scum and the cream. For many years we elected our doges, thinking that the men who wanted power would realize that there would be mutual benefit between rulers and ruled when the ruled had a say in the choosing. But now we are a Republic and have a Great Council." He nodded with an air of satisfaction.

"And what of learning?" Rostam inquired. "My father has told me of the schools in Constantinople; have you such places in Venice?"

"What need? Our craftsmen learn from their fathers, and we merchants can buy the skills we do not have ourselves." Cristofo shrugged. What matters is urbanity, and mother wit to make a profit, and family alliances. Once I know how to keep the accounts, of what use is more schooling?"

"Then tell me a joke of your people," Rostam said, "so I may better understand Venetian urbanity."

"Very well. It will be a good return for the tales your father has told us of chogan matches and the pranks of Greek islanders," Cristofo said with good cheer. So, why do you never invite a Genoan or Pisan to supper?"

Rostam shook his head with a smile.

"Because the Pisan will drink the finger bath water and the Genoan will comb his beard with the fork—and then pocket the fork. Ha ha! "

"Oh! And here is another. So, a Pisan and a Genoan were trying to strike a business bargain. Now the Genoan's father had warned him, "Never make a deal with a man who has withered balls." Of course the Genoan wanted to heed his father's advice, but how could he find out? It's not like Pisans ever bathe, so meeting at the bath house is out of the question. Suddenly, the Genoan gets an idea.

"He tells the Pisan, "Did you know, if you go into a church when it is empty, and climb the lectern, and extend your arms to heaven, the Holy Spirit will enter you and you will be absolved of all sins without having to pay the indulgence fee?"

Well, the Pisan was all for that! So they went to a church. The Pisan started to climb the lectern, while the Genoan tried to peer up his robe to see if his balls were withered. But he couldn't quite see. "Reach to Heaven, reach higher!" he urged the Pisan.

Just as he saw what he wanted to see, a stinky fart blasted the Genoan in the face, and the Pisan cried out, "I feel the Holy Spirit passing through me like a wind!"

Rostam choked on a laugh. Indeed, he thought a visit to the city built on water would prove an adventure. He resolved to spend some time in the company of the ship's pilot to see if he might learn how the merchant ships were conned into the harbor, and of the sea hazards Venetian sailors faced. Perhaps it would be well to do as his father had done with Cristofo, and drink arak to loosen the pilot's tongue.

By now the others had all ridden ahead, and Rostam thought it was time to rejoin them. "While I am curious to see for myself what your city is like, I would miss hunting sorely," Rostam told Cristofo. They cantered up the slope to where the hawk was perched on the very dead hare.

They made several more kills that day, and it was a tired but contented group of men who reentered the castle to hand off their spoils to the servants, and then to make their way up to the living quarters.

Talon had observed the two young men talking together and was pleased that they seemed to get along well. He was almost decided that he would give Rostam the responsibility for the eventual journey to Venice, as a form of ambassador, but perhaps not this time.

*****

Three days later, they bade farewell to Cristofo and his sister when they set sail for their home, their ship laden with goods that Talon and Cristofo had decided upon. As the ship was rowed out of the harbor, the two Venetians waved at the small crowd assembled on the wharf to see them off.

"I hope we can trust them to come back and continue to trade with us," Rav'an remarked to Talon, as they stood together, watching the pilot negotiate the entrance.

"God's will, my lady, but if there is only one thing on this earth that one can be sure of with a Venetian, and it is that they are traders; and as these two will arrive home with riches, I think we will see them again."

"Rostam!" he called. "Is there not to be a game of chogan today?"

"Indeed, there is, Father. Why? Do you want to play? It's a dangerous game, you know!" Rostam laughed and pretended to run as his father lunged for him. Talon was content and gave a surprised Rav'an a kiss, just to show all and sundry that he was in good spirits. A game of chogan was just what he needed. They all mounted up and started out for the castle on the mountain.

*****

Four days after the Venetians had departed, word that a small party of men were making their way along the coast toward the harbor was relayed to Talon. The goat herders were an established part of the spy system for just that reason. They were always well paid for their trouble. A breathless boy was admitted by the guards at the gates, and then interrogated by Palladius, who promptly sent a guard to call Talon.

He arrived to see the boy being given water and a large chunk of bread by one of the guards, while Palladius towered over him with his hands on his hips. Talon smiled to himself. Palladius was intimidating at the best of times, but here he was, unsuccessfully trying to sound kind, but the boy cringed away, clearly frightened, as the sergeant barked questions at him.

"He brings word of strangers coming from the west, Lord," Palladium growled to Talon as he walked up. Talon paused and then leaned over toward the boy with his hands on his knees and gave him a reassuring smile.

"Tell me what you have seen," he said, with a calming voice.

"The... there is a party of men riding along the coast tracks toward the harbor, Lord," the boy stammered. "They don't look like pirates. They have pretty clothes and their armor is shiny," he finished. "May I go back to the herd now, Lord?"

Talon chuckled. "You may go. But first, tell me. How pretty are their clothes?"

"Very pretty, Lord. They have grand-lookin' horses, too," the boy volunteered in an authoritative tone.

"You know horses, then, boy?"

"Love them, Lord. Seen you and your men playing chogan, Lord. Wish I could do that!" the boy said wistfully with an eager nod. "Good horses those men are riding."

"What's your name?" Talon asked him.

"It is Diondre, Lord," the boy drew himself up proudly.

"A good name. We shall see about bringing you to our stables. Would you like that? We could always do with an extra groom."

Talon thought the boy was going to burst with pride; then he asked, "How far from the harbor are these visitors of ours?"

Diondre thought for a minute. "Perhaps three leagues from the harbor, Lord."

Talon reached into his purse and drew out a silver coin and pressed it into the grubby hand of the boy. "You have done very well to bring this news, Diondre," he told him, and placed a hand on his skinny shoulder. "Here is a coin for your trouble, and now you should go back to the herd, and make sure you avoid the intruders. We will be dealing with them from here on."

The boy's eyes widened as he looked at the coin. It was a handsome reward for his efforts.

He grinned cheekily up at Talon, and then knuckled his forehead. "Thank you, Lord." Then he scampered off, clutching the coin and the loaf of bread. He dove out through the postern gate, which had been opened by one of the grinning guards, while Talon and Palladius watched him. They looked at one another thoughtfully.

Junayd appeared at Talon's elbow. "The Companions are ready to go any time you give the order, Lord," he said quietly.

"Yes, go, Junayd. Shadow them. I do not want them to be allowed into the village or the harbor. If they try to go there, stop them and if possible, bring them here instead. If they give trouble then you know what to do."

Junayd nodded. "As you wish, Lord."

"Wait, Junayd," Talon said, raising his hand. Something the boy had said was nagging at his mind. "Send some scouts across the ridge, just in case there is a ruse from the other side of the hills."

Junayd nodded. "Very well, Lord." He called out two of the Companions and sent them with their bows, hurrying off out of the castle to check the south side of the ridge for intruders.

Rostam wanted to go with Junayd, but Talon said, "Stay here with me, Rostam. Junayd can deal with it. Something doesn't fit here, and I want you and the other senior Companions with me."

Within minutes, the small group of Companions led by Junayd were exiting the castle and riding hard down toward the harbor, while the two other Companions had vanished into the woods.

"Sergeant, send the men to their stations," Talon ordered.

Henry, alerted by goatherds, would already be taking steps to protect the village and the harbor. Talon and Brandt made preparations to send a contingent of Saxons down to the harbor to help brace the villagers as quickly as possible, while Palladius bellowed orders to the garrison and sent more men to the walls of the castle.

Then Talon, Brandt, and Rostam climbed to the topmost point of the keep, where they could have a good view of the road leading down to the harbor, as well as of the walls, and the ships in the distance. There they were joined by Rav'an and Dar'an. For a moment, with the wind blowing about his head, Talon felt as though he were one of the hawks balancing on the high currents in the air.

"It is a strange direction to come from, if they are not of the merchant kind. Our herder boy said they were in rich clothes and rode expensive animals. I have a feeling..." his voice trailed off as he stared northwards. "I wonder..." he added, and this provoked a question from Rav'an.

"You wonder what, Talon?" she inquired with a frown.

Talon turned to Rostam. "The emperor left toward the north, did he not, Rostam?" he asked.

Rostam nodded. "That is what we heard, but no one can confirm it, Father. He disappeared completely, not long after the battle began!" He shook his head in disgust.

"Hmm. I think we should prepare for some interesting visitors," Talon told them. "My dear, please dress in your best, and Rostam, try to look a little less like a vagabond. I think important visitors are about to arrive."

*****

Talon stood on the battlements of the gate tower, with Rostam and Dar'an beside him, and waited for the small procession that was riding up the steep road up to the castle. The scouts had established that these were the only people approaching the lands held by Talon; there were no other forces approaching. Junayd and his men were now acting as outriders to prevent any one of them from trying to escape.

All three men were dressed in their best armor, which had been cleaned and polished to a shine. Down in the courtyard were assembled the Saxons, with Brandt standing at their front and the remaining Companions mounted and armed with bows and swords. There was complete silence down in the courtyard while everyone waited for the visitors to appear. Rav'an and Jannat, attended by senior servants of the keep, were on the steps to the bailey, should the visitors be made welcome; but until he was certain as to who they might be, Talon judged it prudent for them to be away from the battlements. Talon prayed that he had been right; otherwise, he would look a little foolish.

As the group ascended track that led to the gates, he peered down at the riders. He gave a start. "God help me, but I *was* right!"

"What is it, Father?" Rostam was also staring down at the foremost figures. He stepped back with an astonished look on his face. "It's him, isn't it?"

"Yes, my son, it is," Talon replied. "Come, Junayd has him safely in hand, and it doesn't appear that there will be any trouble. But we should be there to greet the Emperor of Cyprus."

Down in the courtyard, Talon ordered the gates to be thrown open and took his place in front of his men, with Rostam and Dar'an to either side. Every Kantara man in the yard had his face covered, lending a very sinister aspect to the assembly. The Saxons wore their helmets, which obscured their faces as well. Talon alone was uncovered, but the men who had escorted the emperor were also covered. Junayd led the way in. Close behind him came two strangers, followed by the unmistakable figure of the emperor on his white horse. Just behind him came four other horsemen, who looked like the emperor's guards. Following these riders came the four Companions, with Andreas among them. One of the emperor's guards had his arm bandaged and in a sling.

Junayd rode off to the side with a nod to Talon. Then Isaac rode forward, to stop his animal five paces in front of Talon, who motioned the guards to shut the gates. They closed with a crash that reverberated throughout the enclosed space; at the same time, all around the encircling walls men appeared, carrying bows and spears. The silence was profound. Caradog, Dewy, and their archers were poised with arrows at their strings, clearly ready for any sign of treachery.

Isaac looked at the men behind Talon, and then glanced apprehensively up at the archers.

"I come in peace," he said, fingering his reins. He looked tired and distinctly worried, with deep lines etched into his visage.

The former emperor looked bedraggled and worn out. Gone was the haughty expression he was so accustomed to wearing, and his dark, slightly protuberant eyes were even somewhat sunken. He had lost weight, and had also mislaid his hat or helmet, leaving his greying hair in tangled disarray. His formerly beautifully tailored clothes, from his collar down to his dust-covered and scuffed boots, were stained and filthy, as were those of his men, who looked exhausted. Even their horses looked tired, and were covered with old cuts, perhaps garnered from the battle. Men and horses alike wore a thin layer of dust from the road, mixed with dried sweat. None of the men in front of Talon looked as though they were ready for anything but a rest. There was no defiance here, certainly not with the kind of reception assembled to meet them.

"Welcome to my home, sir," Talon said. He lifted his hand and servants walked forward, taking hold of the listless horses. Isaac and his men looked apprehensive.

"Please, do not be concerned, Your Majesty," Talon said with just a trace of irony at using the title. "We will see to the horses and make sure they are well looked after. You will be treated as an honored guest in my house."

"You are Lord... er, Lord Talon?" Isaac stammered.

"I am indeed."

Isaac appeared to be wrestling with the emotions that flitted across his dark features, but finally he said again, "I come in peace, and only wish to rest for a little while. I wish to take ship and leave this pestilent isle."

"You shall be my guest," Talon stated firmly, and watched the emperor dismount.

"I see that one of your men is injured. We will attend to his wound. In the meantime, please, come with me, Your Majesty. You can bathe and take refreshments, and then we can talk."

Isaac finally dismounted and tossed his reins to the servant, in much the same manner as he would have in his own palace. But then he had to lean on his horse for a moment, as though he were too tired to walk. His men followed suit, albeit reluctantly. None knew what their fate was to be in this sinister castle, with its menacing people arrayed around them. Isaac walked stiffly toward Talon.

"I would like to rest, and I am very hungry," he said. Talon gestured toward the postern door and then followed him through. "You and your servants will be taken care of, my lord," he told the emperor, who was barely listening.

"I want to bathe and receive refreshments for myself and my men," Isaac said with more authority, as though he had not heard Talon. Talon merely smiled. He nodded to Brandt, Dar'an, and Junayd. They had discussed the eventuality of dealing with their visitors. The men would indeed be well cared for, but first they would have their swords and other weapons removed, and later would find themselves in the cells, down in the bowels of the castle. The only person who would be free, and under very limited conditions, would be Isaac. Talon would take care of him.

He glanced behind him as he stepped through the narrow postern and saw that Isaac's followers were already being disarmed by his men, with the archers looking on. He motioned to Rostam and Dar'an to come with him.

"We will allow him to bathe and clean himself up," he told them. "That is when his sword and any other weapons will be removed."

The Kantara men escorted the former emperor of Cyprus to the base of the steps leading up to the bailey, where Rav'an and Jannat stood looking down on him.

If Isaac expected them to genuflect before him, he was disappointed. The two beautiful women, dressed in their best for the occasion, did not so much as incline their heads, but only stood aside while Rostam and Dar'an escorted the bemused and bedraggled ex-emperor past them toward the bathing area. He hesitated, as though to stop and address them, and swiveled his head from side to side to stare at them. The women returned his stare with glacial looks of their own. Isaac, unused to this behavior, looked surprised, but Dar'an took his arm and murmured something in a low tone, tugging at his arm gently but insistently. Isaac finally ducked his head submissively and continued with them. Not a single word had been exchanged.

Talon ascended the steps and paused in front of the women.

"So, that is the vaunted emperor of Cyprus!" Rav'an said with some scorn in her tone.

"He doesn't look very regal to me," Jannat offered, staring after the departing men. "You've bested him on every occasion, Talon. So why would he come here at all?"

"He could have gone to Paphos, but the journey over the foothills of Trudos would have been perilous. I suspect that he and his men had hoped to commandeer a ship from our harbor and flee," Talon said. "Henry and Junayd denied them entrance and Junayd brought him here instead. I don't think he planned to be here of his own accord."

"Oh, yes, I can just see Henry giving him the ship, and even offering to sail it for him!" chortled Jannat, with a toss of her head.

"I cannot think why he thought he could get away with it. Without an army at his back he cannot command obedience, and he certainly inspires no loyalty. Isaac is responsible for heinous crimes against many, many people on this island," Talon said with a grimace. "We will treat with him as we would any guest, but then I will take him to Famagusta, where Richard can deal with him as he pleases," he added.

"I don't know why you have not already cast him into the cells below," Rav'an glared after the departing emperor. "After all he has tried to do to us. There would never have been a shred of mercy shown by him, had it gone his way."

"Come ladies, I do not wish him to leave us with a bad taste in *our* mouths when he has gone. We live here, and not he. Tonight, we will have him at the table and then tomorrow he goes to his fate. I doubt if Richard will be kind to him," Talon replied.

"That's *if* he arrives there," Rav'an said, without moving her lips. "How am I going to prevent the cook from poisoning him?"

*****

Early the next day, word arrived that a large band of Normans had attacked Kyrenia, and that Richard's men were roaming the island at will. News of this sort travels very fast. People who had come up the same track, along the coast from Kyrenia that Isaac had taken, arrived at the gates of the harbor village and told Henry lurid tales of rapine and burnings. Kyrenia was the home of Theodora, the emperor's daughter. Henry sent a messenger post haste, up to the castle, informing Talon that Theodora had been captured.

Talon wasted no time in bringing Isaac out from his confinement in a locked room to tell him of this event. Even after a day's rest and a bath, the emperor was disheveled. His once elegantly curled locks were lank, and the dye he used to color his hair a dark black all over had faded. His beard was untrimmed, though Talon had offered to provide him with a servant to shave him. Talon knew it would be hard to find anyone who would be willing to do that job with any intent other than regicide, for Isaac was universally despised by the population. Fortunately, Isaac, in a fit of rage, had refused the offer and had sulked in his lofty chamber thereafter.

Now he stood before Talon and Rostam and vented his feelings.

"You have not provided me with the hospitality I am due as your emperor!" he shouted, his face distorted with anger. His eyes bulged and glared balefully at his captor. "I shall have you punished for this, see that I don't. Where are my followers? I have not seen them since we arrived in this pestilential place!" A deep crease had formed between his dark eyes, and his full, petulant lips were pursed in a tight grimace. There was something else that Talon noticed, however, and that lurked in the back of the former emperor's eyes. Cruelty and brutality were now replaced by uncertainty, and Talon was content to see it.

He calmly held up his hand to stop Isaac and said, "You might wish to know that your daughter, Theodora, if that is her name, has been captured by the Normans."

Isaac stopped mid-sentence and looked stunned. "My... my daughter, you say?" he asked. His entire being altered and Talon watched as his expression changed from one of a man who still believed he was absolute master of his subjects to one of slowly dawning defeat, followed by despair. His arms fell to his sides and his shoulders slumped. His head dropped so that his chin almost touched his chest, and he muttered, "Then all is lost. I am done in. My treasure is a captive." He began to cry.

Talon felt little compassion for the man in his sorrow. He gestured to the two guards to find Isaac a chair, which he fell into.

Isaac sniffed loudly and dashed the tears from his eyes, but remained slumped in the chair. He looked up at Talon with fear and despair in his eyes. "What would you have of me?" he now pleaded. "Will they harm her?"

Talon shook his head. "They just want you to surrender to the king of England. That is why they have captured her, as a hostage to your good behavior. She will not be harmed unless you refuse to surrender, my lord." Talon knew very well that no harm would come to the girl, but he wasn't going to tell Isaac that. Guy de Lusignan wanted a lever with Richard to persuade him to leave Cyprus at the earliest opportunity and help with the siege of Acre. No harm would come to the girl.

The erstwhile emperor would have done cruel things to anyone whom he had captured.

Bleakly, Isaac nodded his comprehension. "I then surrender myself to you. I ask only that you do not place me in irons."

Talon understood the custom but it did not disturb him to agree. "Very well, but we will depart tomorrow, so I suggest that you prepare yourself, my lord." Talon's voice was cold. He wanted to be rid of the emperor.

Later, when Isaac had been taken away, Talon brought his family and close Companions together to discuss the news. Brandt was also there.

"It is important that I deliver him to Richard in Famagusta before Guy de Lusignan arrives. I want to take some of the glory away from that arrogant man, so we leave tomorrow at dawn," he told them.

"I heard that Isaac was weeping, Talon. What did you say to him?" Jannat asked.

"That his daughter was taken hostage," Talon told them.

"You sound as though you were waiting for this to happen, Talon," Rav'an said with a knowing look.

Talon paused before answering slowly. "Yes, perhaps. We heard that there was a possibility his daughter might be in Kyrenia. Guy de Lusignan told the king that he was going there to find out if she was. Apparently she was there, and he now holds her as a bargaining piece with the king of England. Anything to hasten Richard's departure from the island and get him to Acre, I suppose."

"Will the king's sister be brought to Famagusta? I'd like to meet her and to see the daughter of this man," Rav'an said. "He weeps for his daughter, but the crimes he has committed against his own people are truly terrible."

"I think we can arrange that you can come, my dear," Talon nodded, but his tone was grim. "This *guest* of ours would have granted us no mercy whatsoever, had he taken this castle or had any of us within his power. He has been brutal to anyone who dared to cross him in the past. I feel nothing for him at all. He goes to meet his just desserts in my opinion."

No one in the room gainsaid him, so they then began to plan for the eminent departure for Famagusta, at dawn the next day.

Chapter 21

The Princesses and the Kings

If you can dream—and not make dreams your master;
If you can think—and not make thoughts your aim;
If you can meet with Triumph and Disaster
And treat those two impostors just the same;
—Rudyard Kipling

Isaac's arrival with Talon and his escort created a sensation. Word went out faster than the wind that the hated tyrant had been captured and was about to be brought in front of the English king. No sooner had the gates to Famagusta been opened than a crowd formed of angry, shouting, and cursing citizens. Some even dared the menace of the Kantara escort and tried to rush past and strike or beat the cowering former emperor, whose horse had to be held in tight control by its guards.

They were admitted past the palace gates by astonished Norman guards, and rode into the courtyard, where Isaac was dragged off his horse and handed over to the not so kindly hands of soldiers. He was placed in one of his own cells below ground, to await the pleasure of the king—the same cells to which he had sent many an unfortunate in the past.

Talon had taken the precaution of bringing along a small chest full of Byzantine gold coins, some of the ones Yosef had looted from Isaac's camp, to present to the English king. Richard was shocked when Talon strode forward with his men who, after bowing politely, placed the chest before the king, and raised the lid to reveal its contents. People gasped and craned their necks to get a glimpse of the glittering gold coins. Few in the room had ever seen so much gold coin in one place before. It had not been lost on Talon that Richard's entire entourage seemed desperate to find plunder, and he'd concluded that the king might need some financial help.

His other motive was to ensure that Richard would allow him to remain undisturbed in his mountain aerie while the king left for his Crusade with his now-quite-respectable army. It was not clear, as yet, whom Richard would appoint as the regent to govern the island in his absence, but Talon wanted to make sure that the king of England was conscious of a debt to him, and would ensure that he was left in peace.

"This gold is much needed for our cause, Lord Talon," Richard told him, with a stunned look on his bearded face.

"My very sincere thanks. God bless you. How can I reward you in return?" he asked, shaking his head as he stared down at the fortune in front of him.

"You have already rewarded me, and the people of this island, by your very courage and actions, Sire. They, too, will be thankful once they realize what you have accomplished, and I need no further reward than to see Isaac as your prisoner."

Talon had not finished. "I have another gift for you, my lord," he said, as his men brought forward yet another small chest and placed it on the floor in front of the king.

Talon opened the chest and waved his hand at the silver bars, packed tight inside. "Isaac asked that he not be put in *iron* chains, Sire," Talon informed the king, who gave him a sharp, puzzled look from under his brows; then his features cleared, to be followed by a bellow of laughter.

"Then let them be made of silver!" he laughed. "I want a chain made from these bars immediately," he told the attendants, who hurried it away to find a smithy.

*****

The island of Cyprus, including the palace of Famagusta, was now firmly in the possession of Richard, the king of England, and his Norman followers. The town of Famagusta had not been taken by assault and fire, but simply because Isaac had deserted it for Nicosia. Now all the players were back in its plundered, depleted palace. The audience room was a mere shadow of its former glory, having been stripped of its rich hangings and carpets and many of the beautiful tiles that had once adorned its walls and floors. Richard held court in the bare room, seated on the throne previously occupied by Isaac.

During the gathering that followed and the luckless appearance of Isaac in his silver chains, Talon felt that he was being watched by someone. He turned and saw that Princess Joanna was observing him. She motioned with her head. It was clear that she wanted to talk to him. Earlier she had been seated next to Richard, but now Berengaria was in the place of honor, and Joanna was standing just below the dais, surrounded by attendants.

Talon touched Rav'an on the arm. "Come with me, my Rav'an, I am wanted by Queen Joanna."

"The lady over there is Joanna?" Rav'an inquired in Farsi. "The one giving you the eye?" She smiled and batted her eyelids. "Be careful, my knight. That lady is danger."

"Not as dangerous as her brother," Talon grinned. "But we shall go together and you can protect me," he added, and made a path for Rav'an through the throngs of Norman nobles and knights towards the king's sister. There was a dearth of females in the company. The Normans stared rudely, and many were the whispered comments. Rav'an appeared to ignore them, but it annoyed Talon and this might have shown on his face, for when he stared at the offenders they dropped their eyes and pretended not to see him. Talon did notice that the assembled lords, knights, and the few ladies were now somewhat better clad. The tailors in Famagusta had been busy, he surmised.

"Your Majesty, I would like to present my wife, Lady Rav'an de Gilles," Talon said with a deep bow to Joanna, who smiled at them both.

"I am pleased to see you again, Lord Talon. But I am no longer a queen since my husband died," she told them. She glanced appraisingly toward Rav'an. "You are a very fortunate man to have such a beautiful wife, Lord Talon." she said. "I am delighted to meet you, Lady de Gilles," she added with another smile for Rav'an, who curtsied and replied, "I am honored, my lady."

"Thank you, my lady. What may I do for you?" Talon replied.

"You have lived on this island for some time, I understand, and you therefore know the emperor well?" Joanna asked with an arched eyebrow.

Talon shook his head with a rueful smile. "No, Your Majesty, not very well. I... er, we had never actually met formally, that is until recently. He would rather I had perished in one of his dungeons, I suspect."

Joanna gave a low chuckle. "Yet you have had the better of him, and he is now destined for a dungeon himself."

They glanced over at the disconsolate man seated on a plain wooden stool on the raised dais, not far from where the king was seated on his new-won throne for all to see. Isaac's silver chains gleamed in the candlelight; he was bowed under their weight and stared fixedly at the floor, looking very forlorn. Suddenly, there was a small commotion at the main entrance to the great hall. Talon removed his gaze from his former enemy to look that way.

"We were just in time," he observed to Rav'an.

Guy de Lusignan made a grand entrance. A handsome man, he was now dressed in all the finery of a rich lord at court, from his ermine-lined cloak to his expensive sword belt and scabbard. To Talon, who had not seen him since the battle of Nicosia, he looked refreshed, but foppishly clad in his expensive silks and red satin doublet that gleamed with jewels. A golden chain hung from his neck. Talon wondered, sardonically, if the arrogant man might have wanted to wear his former crown, to make the point to the assembled crusaders. If he had, then Geoffrey, his far more sensible brother, had done well to deter him. Richard would not have responded well, had Guy flaunted that crown in this palace.

Guy walked—or rather minced—toward Richard, leaving a trail of perfume. Talon observed his progress with a sense of irony and not a little scorn. Here was the man who had been responsible for the loss of the kingdom, and he was still the arrogant upstart. His brother was dressed in a more practical manner. Geoffrey was a far better commander of troops and was a good warrior and worthy of some respect.

Guy de Lusignan held his head cocked high, but he nonetheless glanced about him, and at onc point his gaze fell upon Talon. They locked eyes, and in that moment the mutual dislike between the two men glowed white hot. Guy walked on, but he had been surprised to see Talon again, that much was clear, and his step had faltered briefly. His glance had changed from one of surprise to one of venom, while that which Talon sent back was full of contempt.

"You appear to know one another," Joanna remarked. She had not spent many a year in the English royal world and lived as queen in the Sicilian court to not recognize animosity when she beheld it.

"There goes the man who lost the Kingdom of Jerusalem, my lady," Talon said, trying to keep his voice neutral.

Rav'an exclaimed, "So that is the man! My husband was very nearly killed because of his foolishness. Your brother would be wise to regard him with some reserve, my lady."

Joanna nodded her head slowly. "He has not impressed me thus far, nor my brother, from his own account," she stated, "and it's very clear that you dislike one another," she remarked to Talon, with dry amusement in her tone. "But he certainly shows extravagance with the use of perfume!" Her nose wrinkled with distaste.

Talon turned to look straight at Joanna, his face grim. "No, my lady. I don't dislike that man. I despise him, and wish that he, too, had died at Hattin."

Her eyes widened. "You were at Hattin?" she asked with a look of surprise.

"I was, my lady." Talon's response was brief.

"All the world knows of Hattin; that awful tragedy," she responded with a new note of respect in her voice. "You must tell me what led to that fatal outcome, Lord Talon."

"Perhaps, in time, my lady. He is here, no doubt, to beg for haste and a departure for Acre," Talon finished, with a gesture in the direction of Guy, who had moved on.

"Hmm. Perhaps for some other reason," she replied. "Look over there."

Some twenty paces behind Guy and Geoffrey there came a small group of women guarded by a couple of spearmen, and in their midst was someone that all eyes rested upon. Talon could not help staring. He had thought that Guy de Lusignan had made his entrance for effect, but only for himself. Now he saw it had served a double purpose, calling all attention to himself—and what he had brought with him. For walking demurely, not far behind him, was his prize. A beautiful woman with blue eyes set within a pale, perfect oval face and long, lustrous black hair that fell to her waist walked slowly toward the king of England, escorted by four ladies-in-waiting and one eunuch servant. There was an audible gasp of surprise and an excited murmur of interest as she made her way through the packed hall.

Talon had the eerie feeling that he might have seen the woman before.

*****

Joanna watched the reaction of the crowd and that of her brother. Here was a woman who was, without doubt, one of the more beautiful in the hall, certainly more voluptuous than most, and she was Guy de Lusignan's prize! The daughter of the once emperor of Cyprus was now being displayed as a trophy. She knew her brother and watched with sardonic amusement as he appraised the woman, the lust in his eyes barely hidden. The woman, who held her head high, although her eyes were downcast as she approached the throne, now knelt in front of him and then looked up. The girl must have sensed something emanating from the king, because her former expression of trepidation softened, and a tiny smile appeared on her curving lips, although she said not a word.

Guy de Lusignan didn't waste any time. "My lord, Your Majesty, I wish to present Princess Theodora, the daughter of your prisoner Komnenos," he stated loudly with an elaborate wave towards the disconsolate prisoner, for all to hear in the now-hushed hall. All eyes turned first to Isaac, who sat up and stared at the woman intently, and then to his daughter. Isaac opened his mouth, but words didn't come. Neither did his daughter say anything, but ignored him as she knelt demurely in front of the king. She lowered her head submissively.

Guy continued, ignoring this exchange. "My lord, I trust to God that the arrival of this lady, whom my brother and I risked great perils to find and secure, will now persuade you to come with us to Acre. Her name is Theodora. I pray her arrival and the surrender of her father will please you and finally bring to an end the campaign in this island, so that we may all proceed to Palestine and fulfill our commitments to the Crusade for God and the True Cross."

Richard nodded, but took his time responding. His gaze flicked from Isaac to linger for some time on the former despot's daughter. He glanced up and eventually noticed Joanna, who stared back at him with a look askance, her lips set in a thin line. She suspected that she knew what he was going to say.

Then he smiled. There was a mischievous look in his eyes, which were now hooded. To Joanna, it was an all too familiar expression and boded no good. "It is time to set the record straight," Richard declared. "I declare the erstwhile usurper, Komnenos, a prisoner of the realm, and he will be escorted to a prison under the control of the Knights Templar. The island of Cyprus is now under the protection of the crown of England. The girl I give to the care of Princess Joanna."

*****

Above the rising babble of the crowd, Talon heard a thin sigh come from Joanna, and glanced at her set features. She clearly didn't approve of the latter edict, but was powerless to change her brother's mind. Behind her, Talon could make out the face of Berengaria, who looked distressed at hearing the order. The new queen could not have liked the idea at all, but no one wanted to contradict the king publicly, nor even perhaps in private. His intent was clear to anyone who was paying attention.

Rav'an, whose hand was on Talon's arm, tightened her fingers in a brief pressure. "This is not a popular command, I suspect," she murmured in Farsi.

"No, indeed, it does not appear to be," he murmured back.

Talon did notice something interesting, however. The girl had risen to her feet and was being guided down the steps, away from the king, by an attendant, yet she stared over her shoulder at Isaac, and Talon was sure that they exchanged an intense look, whereby a message of some sort was sent and received. Isaac's already haggard face dissolved, and he began to weep, paying no attention to the throng of lords and ladies. He held his hands out toward Theodora, but her guards hastened her away toward her new life.

"Lord Talon, I must go and attend to the princess. She appears to be my new ward," Joanna said to Rav'an and Talon. The sarcasm was easy enough to detect. "I trust we shall meet again, as I wish to discuss the siege of Acre and much else with you. And Lady de Gilles, I am pleased to have met you." She held out her hand to be kissed, and then she turned away. Talon bowed to her retreating back. She met Theodora midway, and then both of them, along with Queen Berengaria, left the assembly, which began to buzz aloud with speculation. It had not been lost on many present that the king had been very interested in the new arrival. Isaac was also led away, clinking in his chains. He was weeping copiously while murmuring something to himself in Greek. Talon thought he understood just a couple of words. They sounded like, "God protect you, Tam...."

At that moment, Rostam materialized at Talon's elbow. Talon remarked approvingly how easily his son could move through crowds, but as he turned his head to greet him, he saw Rostam was visibly put out.

Rav'an, who was quick to notice her son's frame of mind, asked, "Rostam! Is everything all right?"

"Mother, Father, is that supposed to be the emperor's—I mean the usurper's -- daughter?" Rostam asked in Farsi, speaking in a hoarse whisper.

"Indeed, it is," his mother responded, her tone a trifle tart. It had not been lost on Rav'an how alluring the woman was, nor how almost all of the men were displaying visible signs of lust toward her. She shot a glance at Talon, but he wore an expression of bland indifference. She fleetingly wondered if that was for her benefit.

"Well, no.... it... er... it isn't, Mother," Rostam whispered.

Both Talon and Rav'an looked startled. "It isn't?" Talon asked stupidly.

"No, Father, it's not," their son replied, "I am sure."

"How would you know this?" Rav'an asked a little sharply, although she was already coming to some conclusions.

"Well, um, that woman is a concubine of the emperor."

Talon and Rav'an stared at him. Rostam hastened on, "I met her once and, well, um.... She's changed the color of her hair. It was blonde before."

"Are you telling us that she might not be his—" Talon gestured toward the weeping Isaac, "his daughter?"

"No, Father, she's not. Not unless she could be in two places at once over the last couple of years. Dimitri knows her. She is the spy we have had in the palace all this time, while the daughter was living in Kyrenia."

Rav'an's eyes snapped open wide. "Talon," she said, "do I want to hear what our son is about to tell us?"

"I fear not, my dear," Talon murmured. "But what on earth has happened?" he wondered out loud. "If you are not mistaken, then where is the real princess?" His brow furrowed.

"I shall make some enquiries," he stated, "but it is important that no one—I mean *no one*—hears of this," he told his son. "There will be all hell to pay if the deceit is discovered. The woman, whosoever she is, will be in grave danger. These Normans would not be amused at all by the substitution. The self-righteous bishops would be the first to demand reprisals, and they would be upon the girl. Mark my words!" Talon clenched his fist. "Guy couldn't even get this mission right!" he muttered angrily, but then his lips twitched with amusement.

Rostam nodded. "Not a word, Father," he said. He wore the all too familiar look he used to wear when his mother caught him in the act of doing something he should not.

"Rostam, what on earth have you been up to?" Rav'an demanded.

"You have some explaining to do, young man," Talon told his son, but he was having trouble keeping his amusement out of his voice. *Wait until Reza and Jannat hear about this,* he told himself.

Talon glanced back at Richard, who had risen to his feet to bring the royal audience to an end. Talon had much to reflect upon. The entire island was now in the possession of the king of England.

Chapter 22

Kyrenia

Gall when it helps is good,
Even if it's bitter;
But sweetness when it starts
To harm will soon devour.
—Yosef Ibn Zabara

Tamura, once the prized concubine of Emperor Isaac Komnenos, was nothing if not a survivor.

A month ago she had been the *de facto* queen of the island. Then there had been the arrival of ships, and Isaac had been gleeful at the prospect of prisoners, slaves, and plunder. But these had not been merchants, easily cowed by a band of mercenaries, and Isaac had returned to his luxurious palace in Famagusta in terror for his life. Days later, he'd ordered an undignified, desperate, and rapid remove, to the decrepit palace in the middle of Nicosia.

He had rarely visited the town in the past because, as he said disparagingly, it was really just a marketplace with walls around it. As he rarely came to visit, the palace had deteriorated, and the eunuchs had done little to maintain it, beyond the very basics needed to make it habitable. The funds that had been designated for its upkeep had disappeared into their various pockets.

When frantic messengers warned the emperor that the invaders were massing in preparation for an assault on Nicosia, Isaac had sent for Tamura. On her arrival at the chamber, she noted that Isaac did not look well. Deep lines of worry furrowed his brow, and his black eyes bulged even more than usual. He stared at her for a long while from his seat on the bed, and then began to weep.

She rushed over to him and held her arms out to him. "Oh, my lord. What can I do to help?" she cried, as he seized her around her waist and cried into her breast. Isaac said something, but it was muffled.

"My lord?" she asked.

He took his head away and sniffled. "You must leave, my jewel!" His dark face was streaked with tears.

"Leave? To where? I cannot leave you, my lord!" she exclaimed, concerned about what he meant. Isaac gulped and then spoke. This time, his voice was more steady.

"You should leave today and travel to Kyrenia, where my daughter is living. I shall provide horses, guards. I—I think you will be safe there. I cannot trust anyone here in Nicosia. They are like vultures; they think I shall lose. But I shall not, and afterward, I will exact vengeance!" He glanced up at her, trying to look fierce. "But in the meantime, I cannot protect you as I would wish, while I am repulsing these invaders. Do not worry, I shall send for you when we have rid our island of these Normans."

Tamura had a brief moment of intense relief at the prospect of leaving. Life during the last few days had been harrowing and anything but pleasant. The eunuchs were terrified, and Isaac's attendants displayed a mixture of fright and concern. However, some were now displaying a certain satisfaction at the turn of events. It manifested itself in their attitude, and even in their behavior toward her. The power she had wielded in Famagusta was precarious in Nicosia.

However, she wanted to be sure that Isaac meant what he said.

"Are you very sure, my lord?" she whispered. He nodded, as more tears coursed down his cheeks. "You and my daughter are the only ones I treasure in the world." He dashed his tears away. "No one else matters to me," he murmured back at her. "I intend to wait for them here in Nicosia, and here I shall destroy them, you will see!"

Tamura had not meant it to happen, but her breast brushed his face and he looked up at her with a change of expression. She knew that look.

"I want you before you go," he murmured. Tamura sighed inwardly. A small price for her liberty, although this session might take a while. She had run out of the aphrodisiacs that had helped the emperor regain, temporarily, his former vigor.

*****

Kyrenia was a tiny fishing town north of Cyprus, huddled at the base of the steep rocky ridges that ran east to west on this large island, and formerly it had not been disturbed very much by the predations of the emperor, who preferred to visit the richer towns, like Paphos and Limassol, or Larnaca. There was, however, a well-guarded villa perched among the rocky outcroppings to the east of the harbor.

The reception Tamura met with was cold, bordering on hostile from the beginning, to the point where Tamura wondered if her life might be in danger.

Paradoxically, Theodora had not driven her off, but had kept Tamura as a guest and had spent much time interrogating her about life in the palace in Famagusta. Her interrogations went so far as to demand that Tamura tell her, in lascivious detail, her encounters with the emperor. Tamura found this disconcerting, and confided in her two servants, Siranos and Martina, who had accompanied her to

Kyrenia and who both warned her about telling the girl too much.

Theodora was an attractive girl, having inherited most of her deceased mother's features, with blue eyes and a cascade of dark hair, but she was as unpleasant as her father. The emperor's only daughter considered herself exiled in this miserable, out-of-the-way fishing village, and over the years her frustration with her isolated circumstances had grown. She was rude and dictatorial towards the guards, harsh and vindictive toward the servants. However, much as she wanted to get rid of this young and attractive woman who sought sanctuary in Kyrenia—for she viewed Tamura as a rival—she yearned for the company of another woman to share her pent up feelings.

Tamura quickly took an active dislike to Theodora and considered moving on. She might, if Siranos could pull it off, be able to go over the foothills of the tall mountain of Trudos and make it to Paphos, or even try for that enigmatic castle, Kantara, which lay in the opposite direction. However, events were to force her to take another path.

Only two days ago, all the young men in the township had been ordered by the garrison commander to assemble with whatever weapons they had in the town square, which opened onto the small fishing harbor. There they had been harangued by the mercenary commander for half an hour before being marched out of the town—herded, more accurately—by a number of the emperor's mercenaries, who saw to it that they didn't escape while on their way up the steep hillside behind the town, then to disappear over the pass that cut though the ridge of the knifelike mountains behind Kyrenia, heading in the direction of Nicosia.

Their departure had been followed by the wails and tears, along with the beating of breasts, by mothers and wives, who were convinced they would never see their loved ones again. The new recruits were, according to rumor, meant to reinforce the emperor's forces against the invading Norman forces, led by King Richard of England. There were other even more sinister rumors, that the magician who lived in the castle of Kantara had joined the invading forces, which spelled doom for the emperor's army from the onset.

Since that fateful day, the news that arrived from the other side of the mountains had been sporadic, and none of it good.

As news of yet another defeat of Isaac's forces trickled in, some of the young men who had pressed into military duty returned, looking scared, filthy, and ragged. Some bore poorly dressed wounds. All were frightened and exhausted. If any had shown bravado beforehand, none of that was on display now. They slunk back to the town and were quickly reunited with their families, who made them disappear, in case those dreaded mercenaries showed up again to drag them off to yet another lost cause. Loud were the wails and tears of grief for those who did not return.

Theodora, with her usual arrogance, demanded of her few servants to go and silence the grief-stricken families, or she would deal with them directly. How dared they disturb her peace? It did not occur to her that she had only four guards left in the entire villa, and only five cowed servants, which meant that she could do little to affect anything going on in the now-grieving little town of Kyrenia.

The other problem was that food was beginning to run out, with little hope of resupply until the chaos initiated by the invaders subsided. That evening, Theodora and Tamura ate a small supper of wild mushrooms, which had been gleaned from the woods and cooked in oil, then served with bread. Some black olives were at hand that had been preserved in oil, and thin slices of lamb that had been marinated in an indifferent wine and garnished with herbs, also from the mountain slopes.

Later in the night Siranos woke Tamura. "My lady! My lady! Wake up!" he wailed as he shook her. Tamura struggled to wake up from a deep sleep. "What is it, Siri?" she demanded grumpily.

"You must come at once, my lady. Her Highness is very ill!" he cried.

Tamura became wide awake immediately. She scrambled out of bed, pulled on a silk gown, and followed the gibbering Siranos and hand-wringing Martina, who had been woken by the commotion, along darkened narrow corridors to the room where Theodora slept.

They could hear retching sounds and groans of agony as they rushed into the room, to find her thrashing on the bed amid a tangle of bedclothes. Theodora was in obvious pain and the three newcomers could see that this was no normal illness. The girl was panting for breath and her face was streaked with perspiration.

Siranos shot Tamura a meaningful glance, but she shook her head. "No," she told him and Marina. "Not I!"

"Then who?" Marina quavered. "She appears to have been poisoned. This is not a simple illness!"

"We all ate wild mushrooms this evening, did we not?" Tamura demanded of Siranos. As realization dawned, his eyes opened wide. "Oh, God help us, she ate a bad one!" he cried. "Or one of the servants did this to her! I wouldn't be surprised if they have. She is such a bitch!" he muttered, grimacing as he did so.

They moved closer and stared down at the shivering girl, who had kicked off the remaining bedclothes and was lying on her back, gasping for air with a small froth forming at the corner of her mouth. Her eyes were wide and pleading. "Help me!" she croaked, reaching out a clawing hand to grasp Tamura, who leaned over her and wiped her sweat-drenched forehead with a cloth Marina handed her.

"Call the physician, at once!" Tamura snapped at Siranos, before turning back to the dying girl.

He didn't move. "It's... it's too late for any help, my lady," he responded in a frightened whisper. As though she had heard him, Theodora gave one last convulsion and her grip on Tamura's wrist slackened. Her eyes became blank and then, with one last shudder, she went limp and slowly relaxed into death.

There was complete silence in the room as the three of them contemplated the enormity of what had just happened. The emperor's daughter had died of poisoning of some kind, and while it might have been an accident, the emperor would insist on holding someone responsible. The first to recover was Siranos, who had witnessed more than one death of this kind. He shook his head, as though to banish the event, then went to the door and listened carefully to the night. Hearing nothing, he turned back toward Tamura, who was still leaning over the dead body, shocked at what she had witnessed. "This cannot be happening!" she whispered. Her eyes were wide with fear and alarm.

"My lady, no one appears to have heard. The servants are still asleep, and the guards are not showing any interest." There was relief in his voice.

"Dear God! What shall we do now?" Martina whimpered. She wrung her hands and looked ready to have a bout of hysterics.

"Be quiet, Martina, or I shall slap you!" Tamura snarled, her own self-control threatening to disintegrate. "Let me *think*!"

Siranos quietly closed the door and bolted it, then came to stand next to Tamura. He looked very thoughtful.

"There is one thing we must do immediately," Siranos stated.

Tamura looked at him.

"We must dispose of the body," he said, indicating the princess lying sprawled on the bed.

Tamura was recovering slowly. She looked at him long and hard, then nodded her head. "How?" she asked.

"I must find out where the guards are, first," he told her.

Tamura looked puzzled, but agreed. "Find them, and come back here as quickly as you can," she told him, with a plea in her tone.

Siranos slipped out of the room and roamed all over the villa. To his surprise, he encountered no one at all. He went outside the building to see if the guards might be loafing in the darkness, but there were none to be found. On an impulse, he went to the kitchen, expecting to find the maids or laborers sleeping on the floor or in a closet. Again, silence and no one to be seen. Where was everyone?

A very perturbed Siranos let himself back into the bed chamber of the dead princess, to find that Tamura and Martina had occupied themselves by cleaning the body and wrapping it in sheets pulled from the bed. The body was wound tightly from head to toe in several silk sheets, awaiting the next phase of its journey.

Siranos looked very somber. "There is no one, no one at all in the villa, my lady!" he stammered, not bothering to keep his voice down anymore. "They have all deserted and gone!"

"The guards? The servants? Where have they all gone?" a bewildered Tamura demanded.

Siranos looked thoughtful. "We heard today that a great battle was fought yesterday and lost by the emperor to that Norman king outside Nicosia. I suspect that the rats have left the ship." He sounded smug at having used that odd expression, but the meaning was clear enough to Tamura.

"So, they have deserted the princess," she observed, "and so has the emperor, because he did not send anyone here to protect her. The swine!" she exclaimed. "Not even Theodora deserved this," she muttered angrily. Siranos, who had heard stories from the other servants, looked as though he disagreed.

Martina indicated the body lying swathed in sheets on the bed. "What—what do we do about her, now?" she asked timidly.

Tamura thought for a minute, and then said, "We will put her in another room, one of the back rooms, where one of the servant women lived, and tidy this one up while I think upon it," she said. "Then we must see what the morning brings."

However, later that night she decided that the princess should disappear. Her reason being that if the princess could not be found, it would be assumed she must have departed for destinations unknown. Siranos was delegated to dig a grave, which he carried out in a surly manner, but he too realized that, should the body be discovered, they could be implicated in her death. There would be no trial, only a summary execution, despite their innocence.

In the very early hours they struggled to bring the body to the grave, which was located in the vegetable garden where Siranos had found some already-turned earth. As they lowered the sheet-bound corpse, it made a noise. All three of them froze, but it remained inert. After that, any decorum which might have been observed vanished, and they dumped it unceremoniously into the hole. Siranos feverishly filled it in and trampled the earth around to make it look like the rest of the vegetable garden. He even decorated the mound with some cabbage plants.

Tamura went back to bed exhausted and full of trepidation, tossing and turning in the humid night air, unable to banish the image of the dying princess from her mind. Eventually the first streaks of dawn crossed the sky, and with the light came noises from the street below.

*****

Tamura awoke to hear the clatter of iron hooves on the streets. The sound of horses on the road grew as many mounted men entered the village.

Siranos appeared like a djinn from somewhere and answered her unspoken question.

"The Franks have arrived, my lady." He looked panic-stricken, and she knew why.

The conqueror usually took what he wanted when he won, and that included plunder and women. Tamura knew, with a sense of dread, that she was going to become a victim, and for the briefest time, she thought about taking her own life. But then Siranos was joined by Martina, who wore an interesting expression.

'My lady..." she began.

"What is it, Martina?" Tamura sighed. Her nerves were raw from the previous night's exertions, lack of sleep, and now the arrival of the Normans.

"The princess is dead, my lady..." Martina stammered.

"Well, yes! You silly girl, were you not there when we buried her?" Tamura's exasperation was beginning to show.

"But the princess would be held as a hostage, not taken prisoner, and you, you look—" she got no further. Siranos's eyes lit up. "Oh! She is right!" he exclaimed.

"Right about what?" Tamura snapped, her patience almost at the end of its tether.

"My lady, you look very much like the princess!" Siranos crowed. Martina was nodding her head furiously as they both stared at Tamura. "They all said so down in the servant's quarters; the likeness is very real. We just have to do something about the color of your hair, my lady."

*****

King Guy de Lusignan, his brother Geoffrey, and some fifty of Guy's men had ridden hard along the road from

Nicosia toward Kyrenia. There was a prize to be had in that coastal village which might bring the campaign to an end, and the shorter their stay in Cyprus, the better. Then he and his men could bring Richard to Palestine and lift the siege of Acre.

They crested the narrow pass that led down to the town laid out below them. It didn't look like a very prepossessing place. Guy began to wonder if there was going to be anything at all worth his while in such a small town. Was the rumor of Isaac's daughter a mere ruse to divert him so his rivals could take for themselves all the wealth of Nicosia?

"I can scarcely believe that Isaac's daughter lives there, Brother," Geoffrey remarked, as they put their horses to the slope. Their followers, all fresh from the victory of Nicosia and eager for plunder, chased after the two men.

They entered the outskirts of Kyrenia at dawn and clattered along dark, empty streets. Dismounting in the tiny square, the riders warily looked around them. This town might have been small, but it was compact, and not as poor as it had seemed from up at the pass. The plaza, which was now crowded to capacity with armed Normans and their horses, was overlooked by a Greek church. Some men were already stamping their way up the steps, looking for loot. There was little respect showed to the Greek Church by the Normans, whose allegiance was to the Latin Pope.

"No one about!" grunted the king. "Flush some of them out and then we can ask where this mythical woman lives, if she does at all."

His men needed no urging. Doors were soon opened in response to the hammering of sword pommels, and reluctant people were dragged in front of the two brothers.

Only one of the knights spoke basic Greek. "Is there a princess in this town?" he asked one old man, who had been found inside the church and dragged without any ceremony to face Guy. He shook his head and cocked an ear as though he was hard of hearing.

"Is there a princess living in this town?" bellowed the knight in bad Greek.

The old man clutched his ear and muttered something, but then he nodded reluctantly and pointed off to the east, where a road was just visible that led to a villa partly concealed by trees. His action might well have saved the town from destruction, for Guy was primarily interested in getting Richard off the island. He and Geoffrey rose to their feet and Guy said, "Bring him along. We'll see if he is telling the truth. If not, gut him like a fish. Otherwise, he might live."

"Keep an open eye for any problems here. No looting," Geoffrey called out to his men. "At least not yet," he amended. "Four of you, come with us," he ordered as he swung back into the saddle.

It was a short ride to the entrance to the walled compound. One of the knights dismounted and kicked the iron gates open, then remounted. The small group of armed men rode through the gates toward a large, one-storied villa that hardly looked like any sort of palace, but the old man was insistent. There had been no guards at the gates, and the entire place appeared to be deserted.

Dismounting at the base of the four wide flagstone steps that led up to a terrace, Guy, Geoffrey, and three of their soldiers stamped up the steps, then Geoffrey hammered on the tall wooden doors. Still there was no sound, just a hollow echo which died away to silence. He pounded again. Just when Geoffrey was about to tell his men to break down the doors, they heard slow footsteps on the other side. There was the sound of a latch being lifted, bolts grated, and slowly the right-hand door creaked open.

They were greeted by a youngish-looking slave who appeared to be shaking with fear. "My lords," he stammered in poor French, "what may I do for you?"

"You can tell me if this is the house of the daughter of the usurper, Komnenos!" Guy snapped.

"Y...Yes, this is the house. Do you wish to see Lady Theodora?" Siranos quivered. He was genuinely scared of these large, hairy, scarred, chain-mailed warriors standing aggressively in the entrance. He stared in surprise at the old man, clearly recognizing him.

The old man smiled, a somewhat toothless smile, and unobserved by the Normans, placed a finger in front of his lips.

"Yes, we do, right now. Stand aside," snarled the leader. Siranos detected a waft of scent hanging about him.

"Who shall I say is come?" he asked timidly.

'The king of Jerusalem, His Majesty, King Guy de Lusignan," said the larger man to the king's right. "Now get out of our way."

The Normans shoved past the cringing Siranos and barged into the main room, where a vision greeted them.

"How dare you come into my house like this! Who are you? What is it that you want?" demanded the woman who stood before them. She stood quite alone in the spacious and well-appointed room.

Geoffrey had to reach out and seize his brother by the upper arm. Guy's reaction was all too familiar. He had lurched forward like a tiger ready to spring. Geoffrey himself had felt a similar impulse. She was very beautiful, he had to admit, but the very last thing he wanted was for his brother to spoil the goods, as it were.

"Let's not be hasty, Brother. We should consider the *value* of this asset before we rush in," he growled. "Who are you?" he demanded without answering her questions.

There was the briefest hesitation, but then she lifted her chin and spoke. "I am Theodora, daughter of the emperor. You are intruding, sir. I demand to know why you are here!"

Guy let out a sigh. "Ah," he said, and shook off his brother's hand. He strode up to the princess and bowed low. "We are here to protect you, my lady," he oozed.

A small, puzzled frown appeared on her brow. "Protect me from whom?" she asked. Both men liked the modulation of her voice, and neither could take his eyes off her. The men who had followed them into the building were gaping stupidly, while the short-sighted old man pointed at her with a shaking finger and babbled that indeed it was Theodora.

"From—from bandits and... vagabonds, my lady," Geoffrey stated, glancing around him. He was puzzled by the absence of servants and attendants. There were certainly riches here for the taking. He'd leave guards and come back, but now he exulted. They had a bargaining piece to provide to the king of England.

"Well, you certainly scared away my servants," she stated with some asperity. "They have all gone."

"I had noticed that, my lady," Geoffrey replied.

He turned to his brother and said, "We really must protect her, Brother. The king will want to see her, and once the usurper hears of this, he might surrender."

Guy nodded, never taking his eyes off the young woman. But then he shook his head, as though he was coming out of a dream, and smiled his most ingratiating smile. He removed his gloves, held out his hand to take hers, and kissed the back of it.

"My lady, do you know where your father might be at this time?" he inquired silkily.

"My fath—you mean the emperor?" Tamura stammered, but then recovered. Her tone turned haughty. "We hear very little here in Kyrenia, sir. I know there was a battle, and I am to suppose that he did not win it, because you are here. Other than that, I do not know of his whereabouts."

At that moment, they began to hear distant screams and shouts coming from the center of the town. One of the men at arms rushed out of the building. He came back a short while later.

"Well, what is going on?" Geoffrey demanded.

"There seems to be a disturbance in the town and... a fire, my lord," the man said.

Geoffrey cursed. "They have found an excuse to plunder the town," he rasped. "Guy, we need to get the princess out of here and safely on the road to Famagusta, as soon as we can."

"I want my two servants to come with me!" the princess called out loudly. A young woman dressed as a servant appeared at the door that led into the interior, looking very frightened.

"Yes, yes, all right. We must hurry." Geoffrey was worried that their men, starved of plunder and probably drunk on Church wine by now, might soon be here at the villa, and then it would be difficult to get these people away without trouble.

"Hurry! Take only what you need for the road and then come with us," he told her, and then turned to his men at the door. "Find horses for these people, and hurry up about it!"

Within half an hour, during which the noise in the town became a clamor and much more smoke went up into the cloudless sky, they left the villa behind and took a back path that the manservant showed them. This brought them out above the town, where pandemonium had erupted.

Geoffrey was angry. Turning to one of his men he called out, "Find a way to stop that mess down there. If necessary, place any of our men in irons who have taken a life. My command was to keep order, not to sack the damned place. Tell the men to mount up and follow me or, by God, there will be trouble. Go!" he shouted. One of their escorts reluctantly peeled away from the group and trotted his horse back down the hill toward the chaos that had been Kyrenia before the Normans had come. Guy and his entourage waited on the hillside.

*****

It took a little time to return order to the town and to get the men back into some semblance of a useful force, but Geoffrey was a stern man, and his men hastened to obey. Before long, Tamura was seated on a palfrey that had been obtained from some luckless owner and was escorted by Guy and the other Normans up the track, toward the split in the hills that would eventually take them back to Nicosia. Even at this distance she could smell the foul breath that his perfume did little to hide, and the stink of old sweat all around her. Being unused to soldiers and their various unwashed states, even those of kings, she felt nauseated.

"Where are you taking me?" she demanded in her haughtiest manner.

"We are going to meet with the king of England," Guy retorted in his poor Greek. He glanced back at the subsiding mayhem below them. He could see people running around trying to put fires out, even as the indifferent Normans departed.

"It was Diocles who brought them to you, my lady," Siranos muttered. "He knows, of that I am sure, but will say nothing."

Tamura cast a look over her shoulder and shuddered. She hoped that Diocles, the former chief of Isaac's palace affairs, would survive this latest crisis. She had become fond of him before he retired, and had not known he was here in Kyrenia. If not for Martina and Siranos, she would still be back in that village. Perhaps they had made the right decision. Not that she knew where this would end for her.

Chapter 23

Departures and Arrival

Then came to him the King Tafur,
   and with him fifty score
Of men-at-arms, not one of them but
   hunger gnawed him sore.
"Thou holy Hermit, counsel us, and
   help us at our need;
Help, for God's grace, these starving
   men with wherewithal to feed."
— from "The Leaguer of Antioch"

Not long after the return of Guy de Lusignan, King Richard and his knights did indeed sail for Acre, taking Isaac with them. He was destined for a dungeon on one of the bleak Templar castles in Palestine. Richard himself departed after making certain arrangements and issuing orders. Perhaps he felt anxious to prove to King Philip that the campaign in Cyprus had not been a mere self-indulgent distraction, for he commanded Talon and the other lords of the island to gather their forces and follow him to Acre within a couple of weeks.

Richard had plundered the cities of Cyprus, in particular Famagusta, Nicosia, Larnaca, and Limassol, leaving the northern cities of Paphos and Kyrenia because they were too remote to access and he had run out of time. Besides, Kyrenia had already been pillaged by Guy de Lusignan and his men, leaving only Paphos relatively untouched, even though it was, as Talon knew, one of the richer cities of the island. Talon had been glad that Paphos was spared, as it left his friend and spy, Boethius, untouched. But one of his ships in Limassol had been commandeered by Richard, along with the entire crew and its contents. It was a loss, but not one to lament over too hard.

Now the lords of the island had assembled in Limassol, supposedly to plan their departure, but there was very little in the way or planning going on. The lords and their attendants were scattered around one of the halls of the vacated palace; some were sitting, others stood grouped in animated discussions, accompanied by much waving of hands and the shaking of heads. Boethius and Dimitri, Talon's senior spies, were also at this gathering at his behest; Talon wanted them both to be fully aware of the rapidly changing situation on the island, and any plans that might affect them.

Now, as he listened to the angry, apprehensive, and loud arguments, Talon was reminded of a nest of hornets, buzzing furiously all around him. It was fortunate, he decided, that none of the Greek nobles possessed a sting, or it might end badly. They were all, without any doubt, glad that Isaac was deposed, but unsure as to who now actually ruled the island. Was it the English king, or was it the dour group of Templars who were housed in a stronghold, not far from the harbor?

Lord Tefkros, one of the more assertive Greek nobles, who owned land and a tower near Nicosia, threw his cloak behind him and turned toward Talon. His dark, bearded features were distorted by a scowl.

"Lord Talon de Gilles!" he called out. "You know the king better than any of us. It was you and your men who joined the king the day he arrived. What do you make of him? What do you make of our situation today?" he demanded.

Talon glanced at Junayd, who raised an eyebrow. He was clearly unimpressed, while the other Companions, standing nearby and listening to the noisy gathering, wore stolid expressions that told Talon that they too were impatient to be done with this seemingly endless debate. Talon turned his attention back to Lord Tefkros.

"My lord," he replied, "the situation is plain enough."

Lord Tefkros raised his voice. "Quiet!" he bellowed. "We should hear from Lord Talon de Gilles."

Talon rose to his feet. "My lords, I have heard many of your plans for what we should do with Cyprus, now that the usurper is deposed. Allow me to remind you, in case any of you had forgotten, that Richard, the king of England, conquered this island and then sold it to the Knights Templars."

This was true. People were still incredulous at how cavalier the king of England had been with the island's fate. One of the Greeks snickered. "Who are now cowering in a tower, not far from here. Are they really the new owners of this island, Lord Talon? Why should we bow down to them?" He looked around at his fellow lords and knights with a smirk and gave an elaborate shrug before continuing.

"I, for one, will be going home to my peaceful estate, free of Isaac, and these foreigners can fend for themselves. They have no power over us, now that the king of the English has left."

Talon's tone turned glacial. "Lord Victoros, the king of England has left orders that we assemble men and ships and join him in Acre—each of us to furnish a hundred men and to ensure that they are well armed and ready to support him. Have you so soon forgotten your pledge of loyalty?" he inquired in a clear tone that could be heard all across the room.

There was an uncomfortable silence as the Greek nobles and their attendants digested these words.

"You know him, this Richard. Would he come back?" Lord Tefkros asked in a quiet voice.

"Yes, I believe he would, if we fail to honor our side of the bargain." Talon paused. "He is a fierce leader of men. He is somewhat governed more by his emotions than by his reason, and should he feel slighted, there is every reason to believe he would return, just to wreak more havoc, and believe me, there would be no mercy for anyone. We should consider ourselves lucky that he did not stay to take more than he did."

"Take more than he did?" called out someone from the back of the crowd. "Why, they even pried the tiles off the walls of this palace; it looks like a horde of tile-eating moths has been by, and God alone knows what he left behind in Famagusta and Nicosia!"

"They are barbarians. Their churchmen hounded our own priests and banished them from our churches, which they then plundered," another called out.

"What do we owe to this king, who demands that we shed our blood in front of Acre?" Victoros called out.

Talon raised his hand for silence. Somewhat to his surprise, the general muttering and grumbles subsided. He had been given a lot of respect when he appeared with a contingent of his Saxons, whose reputation was now known all around the island, and his Companions, who were viewed with great wariness by all the men in the room. He had not failed to notice the fresh corpses dangling from the walls near the gates as he entered. Revenge was being melted out by the Cypriots upon those who had overtly supported Isaac during his appalling rule.

"This man, Richard, is a taker," he warned them, "but lest you have already forgotten, Isaac was a monster who took more than just your wealth. He took your daughters, and in some cases, even your wives. That brutal man has gone to his just desserts, thanks to King Richard. Make no mistake, this is not a weak king who has gone to the Crusade. Richard is known far and wide for his courage and determination. Whether we like his methods is not for us to dispute at this time. As he has commanded, we are here to prepare our own forces, and to leave before the summer is upon us, to assist him, as promised. Should we fail in that duty, then the consequences could be dire. If he comes back, who will be able to oppose him?"

"You could, Lord Talon," Lord Tefkros muttered under his breath. Talon heard him and gave him a hard look. "What could I gain by acting as a traitor, Lord Tefkros? You should banish thoughts of that kind and help me to take our army to Acre instead." His tone would tolerate no further discussion on that matter.

Lord Tefkros looked only somewhat contrite, but he nodded his shaggy head and pulled on his beard. He raised his voice for all to hear. "Very well. Lord Talon is right, we must assemble our men post haste and obtain whatever ships we can for their transport."

"There is one last thing," Talon called out. The conversations that had already started up again subsided, for the most part. "I think I can say in this place without fear of contradiction that most of us, while we carry titles, are really of the merchant kind."

He paused. Heads nodded somewhat reluctantly, so he continued, "I, too am, a merchant, so all of us should give some thought to the fact that the island of Cyprus is the only place in the entire region where the Latins can come for supplies, with the knowledge that they can buy supplies in safety."

Now they were all listening. "They cannot go to Egypt; there is nothing inland from Acre that they can obtain, nor the Duchy of Tripoli. Beirut belongs to a pirate at present, and not even the Byzantine ports are open to their ships. This means either Sicily, which is a *long* way off or... Cyprus." He let that word linger. 'We, the merchants, have access to the ports all along this side of the Inner Sea, and we can provide supplies to their quartermasters at reasonable prices for reasonable profit."

There was complete silence when he had finished, but then Tefkros gave a bark of laughter and slapped his thigh.

"Lord Talon, you are a fox. What was taken can all come back, with interest!" Before long, the whole room was laughing, and the atmosphere had changed from one of gloom and contention to one of cooperation, as the merchants of Cyprus gave thought to the profits to be had from the Third Crusade.

Watching them, Talon smiled to himself. Greed was one of the most basic of instincts.

Talon however was barely listening to the animated discussions going on in the hall. His thoughts were back at the castle of Kantara, wherein lived the family he had been forced to leave yet again. In the recent years it had been one thing to voyage on a merchant's endeavor, but now after four years, it was again for a cause founded in war. This time because the new king of Cyprus, Richard had ordered it.

Rav'an had been standing on the roof of the keep, staring out to sea, when he had arrived to bid her goodbye. Ever since the order to leave had come from the King she had been distant and tight lipped. He knew why, full well.

He exited the steps and saw her standing by the parapet and his heart felt as though it had stopped for a brief moment. His love for her was deep, but now he had to try and put not only his own fears to rest but hers as well.

She heard him come up to her but didn't turn. Instead she said, "Why do you go where this fickle king wants you? Back to that miserable, blood soaked land across the sea which has never been kind to you?"

"Because I have been ordered to by the king, my love." He murmured.

"Have you not done enough for these people! On this island and for that foreign king who cares not a whit for you nor yours!" She exclaimed turning to glare at him.

"I know I have," Talon sighed, "but this king is very much more dangerous than Isaac ever was, and I have to protect all of us from his fickle moods."

He put his arms around her but she was not compliant, although she didn't pull away either. She put a hand on his cheek. "Oh Talon, why is it that when that bloody, conflicted land calls, you go? It is like a siren call... as though you cannot resist it."

He shook his head vehemently. "No Rav'an... it is not the land that calls. I hate the country and all its sour memories. I had to swear fealty to this king. Had I not, I do believe he would have ravaged the island even more, and then our villages and our harbor would have been plundered, before he attempted to storm our castle. Richard is a quarrelsome man but no one should dismiss his determination, should he wish to demonstrate it."

"But you did so much for him!" She exclaimed with some anguish in her voice. "Is he then so ungrateful as to not allow you to live in peace here while he goes off on his wretched Crusade?"

"My assessment of this man is that he is one move away from disowning his allies, should they annoy him and we are a ripe prize; there is no gainsaying that. No I do not trust the man at all." Talon said and tightened his arms around his wife.

"So you have no choice in this, my Talon," she whispered with a catch in her voice. "I shall live in dread until you are home again," she informed him with tears welling in her huge grey eyes.

"No choice at all, from what I can see," He told her; his tone was bleak. But his embrace tightened as she buried her face in his shoulder.

"Then be safe and may God bring you home without injury," she told him.

He held her at arm's length and then gently pulled her back so that he could kiss away her tears.

"I love you my Rav'an. I shall come home as soon as I can," he whispered to her.

"I love you too, my Talon. Come home soon and in good health?" she beseeched him, as she reached up to kiss him.

*****

Talon was met on the beach to the south of Acre by several of the lords who attended Richard. They looked much the worse for the wear after their voyage from Cyprus and the rigors of camp life. The first thing that had greeted the newly arrived Greeks and men from Kantara was the smell.

"Ah, God, but what is that?" Lord Tefkros exclaimed, as he, along with everyone on the after deck of the ship were assailed by the putrid smell of death and excrement that pervaded the entire encampment. Men were holding their noses and some had placed kerchiefs over theirs. Talon did what he and his men did often enough; he wrapped his *shemaugh* around the lower part of his face.

To nostrils used to the clean air of the open sea it was an assault upon their senses, and decided Talon immediately to camp near the beach, as far from the other Christian camps as possible.

"Get used to it," he said, his own nostrils twitching with disgust. "That smell is the stink of pestilence and disease. We must be more careful than the Normans and the English, or we, too, will perish before we ever get to the gates of that unfortunate city."

His gaze moved to the all-too-familiar distant grey walls of the besieged city of Acre. There he could see faded banners of the Moslem design flying defiantly from every tower, and the two main towers of the gatehouse facing the plain and the crusader armies. He thought he recognized some of the banners of Arab nobles trapped within the city. It had now been under siege, in one form or another, for just under two years. He shuddered to think of the squalor this had engendered within its streets and open spaces. The starving inhabitants had withstood much before, but now worse was to come from the newly arrived English and French troops.

The Cypriot galleys were anchored well away from the cluster of Latin ships guarding the approaches of the harbor of Acre, and the Greeks unloaded their men and horses on the beach almost half a league away from the other sprawled encampments. Under the supervision of the physician who told them where to dig the latrines and where to pitch the hospital tents, everyone was put to work. It was late in the evening by the time they were settled in.

Besides Evanthis, who was one of the younger, as yet uninitiated Companions, Talon had another servant, the very same shepherd boy who had warned him about the arrival of the emperor on his lands. Diondre's father had come to the gates of the castle with the boy in tow and had almost begged Talon to take the lad off his hands, saying, "Please, Lord, make him into more than a shepherd boy. Bring him back a man."

Talon had stared at the boy and thought about it. "Do you not need him then, for the shepherding?"

"He has two older brothers who do the work. He is restless and has no inclination for tending sheep."

"Very well," he said, "I shall take him. Does he aspire to become a Companion?"

"The little wretch talks of nothing else, Lord. He lives to be a horseman. Take him, I beg you, I can do nothing more for him."

Diondre, while apprehensive, was eager to hear that he could go with Talon and his attendants. Talon had nodded his agreement, liking what he heard, and then he told the boy, "You obey me without question. But see that man over there?" he pointed to Junayd, who was hovering nearby. "He is also to be obeyed, and he is going to teach you, but you must listen. Fail to do so and you will be returned home in disgrace. My other man, Evanthis, will teach you what you have to do around the camp."

The boy had nodded mutely.

Talon had then pointed to Brandt, who was standing nearby and watching the exchange. "If you do not do as you are told, I shall give you to him and his Saxons, who will probably eat you. Certainly those Welsh bowmen will." Brandt and the Welsh heard this and they grinned ferociously, baring their teeth at the boy, who now looked really scared.

"Junayd, take the boy and give him a bath. That should be one of his first experiences. Evanthis, keep him busy and out from underfoot." Talon smiled and left the boy to the not-so-tender care of his men. They would ensure that he was kept safe, but they would also teach him much.

Now Evanthis and Diondre had a fire going and his armor laid out inside the tent, with a pallet prepared for sleeping. Talon heard the low murmur of voices behind him as he stood by the small fire upon which a small pot of tea was being prepared, staring out at the plain to his north, deep in thought.

D'Onston had been among the first to greet him when he landed, and the two had left the bustle of the unloading to the commanders and walked slowly toward a deserted patch of the beach, where they sat on the low sand banks overlooking the waves. D'Onston's squire and two of Talon's Companions kept a wary eye on them from a distance. It was clear that D'Onston wanted to talk in private.

"You are looking thin and definitely needing a bath," Talon commented when they had settled themselves and listened for a while to the surge and hiss of the sea as it advanced and retreated. D'Onston grimaced his agreement. He looked tired, and his once-bright clothing and chain were rent and filthy.

"You and your men look sleek and well fed, but the good Lord will see to it that you are reduced to my humble state before too long, I dare say," he retorted with a rueful grin. He looked at Talon and then down at himself with some disgust.

"I'm right glad to see you, though, Talon."

"If you look like this, then I can only imagine what the poor souls inside the city look like. They must have finished off all the rats by now," Talon said with a wave of his hand at the beleaguered walled city in the distance.

"I have no truck with them. They are the Saracen and should receive whatever the good Lord metes out to them. Curse them for not surrendering a long time ago. Then we could all go home," D'Onston said with some venom. "We perish more from pestilence and disease than from actual battle, and our wounds never seem to heal in this foul place."

"That could be for a number of reasons, and the first is that your leeches are insensible to reason and don't know anything about medicine, let alone wounds," Talon's tone was tart.

They were gazing out over the shimmering waters of the sea at the ships anchored in clusters offshore. There were quite a number of vessels, and that, Talon assumed, was what prevented any supplies from getting to the city.

"So, how are our lords and masters managing since they arrived here?" he asked.

"D'Onston sighed and plucked a dry stem of grass from the sand. He picked at his teeth ruminatively before he answered.

"They bicker, Talon. They bicker endlessly and do very little about coordinating assaults on the city." He shook his head in a bleak way. "Philip sees himself as a siege engineer and has begun to tunnel toward the tower known as The Accursed Tower. That will take weeks."

Talon barked a laugh. "Months, more likely. Does he know how deep run the foundations of that city and that tower? The people who built Acre knew what they were about."

D'Onston gave him a sharp look. "You know this city, Talon?" he demanded.

"I lived here once, before I traveled to the East. I came back to find my possessions seized by the church and my best friend imprisoned by the Templars," he sounded bitter to his own ears. "We have been on cool terms ever since, but I should be glad that they, and not the church, imprisoned my friend, as he would not have survived long enough in the church's kind hands for me to rescue him."

D'Onston grunted. "Philip is not well; the physicians think it is something called *leonardie,* or *arnaldia.*" It was Talon's turn to give him a sharp glance.

"I suspect it is because he, like all of you, refuses to eat green vegetables and insists on eating meat even when it is putrid," he said.

"We also eat bread, Talon," D'Onston sounded defensive. "That is surely not a bad thing to do? The Templars, after all, live on this diet, and they live out here in this pestilent place."

Talon gave a shrug. "The life span of a Templar is generally short! The Duke of Tripoli used to say that no one could teach those stubborn people anything, and their former Grand Master Ridefort was a good example." He paused, and then said, "I have brought fresh food and vegetables with me. I shall share that with you tonight if you wish, and tomorrow I will take some to the king of France and the princesses."

"Thank you, I will be honored," D'Onston said. "The food here isn't anything I would recommend to anyone."

"How, then, is our king of England?" Talon inquired.

"Ah, we come to it now. Our king is a restless man, and not really cut out to endure sieges from either perspective. He frets over the inaction and wants to storm the walls, but he will not aid Philip in that regard, and neither will Philip assist him, so it is something of an impasse." D'Onston shrugged. "The feud between him and Philip has not abated, and they quarrel every time they meet."

"How are his sister and his queen, and the daughter of our former emperor?" Talon asked with a half-smile. "These are not the conditions I would want to subject a woman to, least of all my queen and family."

"I so wish he had left them in Cyprus, perhaps even in your care, my friend. But our King Richard does not think of others in the same way as most of us do. They are here and enduring it, although I fear for their health. Did you know that queen Sibylla, Guy's wife, and her daughter, died here of some plague or other?"

"I had heard," Talon's response was dry. "Guy was never one to think of others, either."

"He is living up to his reputation for idleness. But I respect his brother, Geoffrey," D'Onston said. "He has been in the forefront of a couple of assaults, while Guy tends to stay back." Talon didn't miss the derisive tone.

"I am also here to tell you that King Richard wishes to see you tomorrow once you have settled in, Talon." He got to his feet. "I shall come back this evening to enjoy your hospitality."

They parted and Talon walked back to join his men, who had been very busy erecting tents and following Epiktitos's orders to dig trenches for their latrines. The wind changed direction, bringing with it the stench of the other camps.

*****

The following day, Talon and Lord Tefkros made their way with their guards to the king of England's tents, which were prominently placed on a mound overlooking the English encampment.

Their route took them along passageways between tents and horse lines, and Talon had time to remark on the condition of the army laying siege to Acre. He was not impressed. The streets, if they could be called that, were ankle-deep with mud in some places. The rain, when it came, drained into small lakes in the depressions of the land, and so did the effluence from many thousands of soldiers and their attendants, leaving a purple-green sheen on the stagnant water that he knew spelled disaster. He had seen Cholera before, under similar conditions of neglect and overcrowding.

As they passed the tents, they could hear raised voices as bored men argued and quarreled, and from many came the groans of those wounded in clashes with the defenders of Acre, or by the predatory incursions from the Arab army, which never let the crusaders forget that their presence did not go unchallenged.

"We have come to a sad place, I fear," commented Tefkros to Talon, as they sloshed across yet another huge foul-smelling puddle, just before they walked up the slope to the king's tents. There were several tents that Talon assumed were the accommodations belonging to Princess Joanna and Queen Berengaria. Talon wondered if Princess Theodora was also living nearby. He still had not been able to find out more about that young woman.

They were announced and then admitted through a wooden doorway, which impressed Talon, as did the rich furnishings of the king's tent itself. Made of silk and with many sections, it resembled a small fabric palace. Richard continued to surprise him.

The king was seated at a long, wooden table covered with some not-so-white linen and loaded with silver plate. The two visitors bowed to the king, and then to the attending ladies. Princess Joanna was there, as was Berengaria, but Isaac's daughter was not.

"You are welcome to our humble abode," King Richard called to them. He didn't rise to greet them, but merely waved them to some chairs in front of him. "I trust you had a speedy journey, Lord Talon. Who is this?" He stared at Tefkros.

"My liege, thank you, we had an uneventful voyage," Talon responded coolly. "May I present Lord Tefkros, whose allegiance you accepted at Limassol before you left."

"Oh, yes, yes; I remember now. You were one of the usurper's people beforehand, isn't that right, Lord Tef...close?" Richard responded.

"Lord Tefkros, dear Brother," murmured Joanna, who had an ear for Greek names.

"Yes, yes, I know," he waved his hand impatiently. He didn't look well, to Talon. While it was stuffy in the tent, he appeared to be sweating more than would be accounted for by the closeness, and his face was flushed.

"You look more like a Saracen every time I see you, Lord Talon," he observed. "I hope that is only an appearance. We have one of your countrymen, Lord Sidon, who is in bed with the Saracens."

He was referring to Lord Reginald Sidon, who had been on the verge of giving up Tyre to Salah ad-Din four years back, and was now ingratiating himself with the Arab forces in order to keep his lands.

Talon stiffened but held his peace. "To quote our lord and savior Jesus Christ, 'When in Rome, do as the Romans,' Lord. The climate is not a friend of the woolen cloth, especially as summer is well upon us," he replied evenly. "As for Lord Sidon, he has chosen his bed and must lie in it. I do not think he will last very much longer."

"You and your men are a welcome addition, Lord Talon," Princess Joanna spoke up. It did not pass her notice just how insulting her brother had been. Richard was already demonstrating how tactless he could be with allies—all of them, by the sound of it. "We have need of your knowledge of these parts and will take council from your good advice." Her tone was mollifying.

"My lady, I am glad to see you. I trust you are in good health?" Talon smiled at her and gave a small bow. "And you, my lady queen," he addressed the hitherto silent queen, who looked strained.

She inclined her head but remained silent, as Richard clearly wanted to talk.

"Since you have just arrived, I should bring you up on the situation here in Acre," he told them when they were seated. "Want any wine?" he asked abruptly.

Talon could only imagine how awful the wine here might be, but he politely accepted a silver goblet, which could have been pillaged from Isaac's palace, and both he and Tefkros tilted their cups to the king and his ladies, then sipped the wine. The aroma coming from his cup made Talon's eyes water, so he merely pretended to sip his, but Tefkros was not so cautious.

Talon rather enjoyed watching his Cypriot colleague from the corner of his eye, as he looked about to choke. Tefkros appeared to be looking around for some place to spit out the awful beverage, but clearly dared not, and finally swallowed his wine, but then he placed his cup very carefully on the table and sat back with a polite look on his bearded face. Talon nearly burst out laughing and then noticed that Joanna was observing his expression and was also looking amused. He tucked that away in his estimation of this sister of the king.

Richard was already talking again. "My cousin, Philip, fancies himself as a siege master and has had his sappers begun to dig under the Accursed Tower. The fool! That is where the Saracens will concentrate their forces, leaving the south end of the city to me."

D'Onston had already told Talon of Philip's aborted attempt to take the walls with siege towers and what a disaster that had been. D'Onston had been embarrassed and disturbed at the refusal of his own king to provide any help during that assault. The Knights Hospitalier and the Duke of Burgundy's men had had to go it alone, without the help of the English, and their casualties had been severe. This had only furthered the animosity that prevailed between the two camps.

"The Accursed Tower will be a very hard nut to crack, my liege." Talon said carefully. "It will take a very long time to bring that down, if it can be done at all."

"My thoughts exactly! Well, I don't have the time to wait for Philip and his people to complete that fruitless endeavor, Lord Talon. It will be either his tower collapsing, or the French giving up, or *me* taking the walls, which I have every intention of doing, and very soon."

Talon waited with some trepidation as to what Richard had in mind for him and the Cypriots.

Richard proceeded to outline his idea to the two visitors with enthusiasm. "I am in the process of building two assault towers, one of which will be manned by my men, but I want you and your Saxons and Greeks to man the other, further south of the gates." Richard paused and looked hard at

Talon. "Your men are amongst the best we have. They are also fresh, and none are sick. I want that rampart taken, Lord Talon. You, then, need to get those gates opened. We need to get that task done so that that the bulk of the troops led by me and the Templars can storm in by horse and take the streets."

Again, the pause, as though for emphasis. Talon began to realize that, despite his propensity for quarrels with just about everyone, Richard was a keen tactician. He continued, after taking a gulp of the foul wine.

"Very quickly after that, we can storm the Templar stronghold and the palace, in which case, it will be all over." He chuckled unpleasantly. "Philip will be left holding a shovel in his hand, and we will be in control of the city."

Talon asked, "Who will be in the second tower, my liege?"

Richard paused for just a moment before answering. "It will be Guy de Lusignan's men, led by Lord Gifford. I will need all my horsemen and the Templars for the assault when the gates are opened." He sounded evasive to Talon, who frowned, but he knew the king well enough by now to hold his peace.

He noticed Princess Joanna was watching him, perhaps for a reaction, but he refused to meet her eyes and kept his own on the king, simply nodding his head as though he was accepting of the unsavory fact that Guy was to support a somewhat suicidal venture. That didn't bode well.

Richard continued to expound his thoughts to his captive audience, but Princess Joanna appeared to be tired, so she stood up and said, "I shall leave you men to decide the fate of the city. Berengaria, come along, we must see to the preparations for the meal with King Philip, who is visiting this evening."

Richard gave a theatrical sigh of resignation, but both Talon and Tefkros immediately stood up.

"My lady, my lord, I have brought fresh provisions, vegetables, and the like, which I shall send to you when I get back to my own camp," he told her, and was rewarded with a bright smile.

Richard grunted. "I hope there was some beef or mutton in amongst your provisions. What we have is spoiling in the heat, and there is little enough to be had when hunted."

Princess Joanna smiled ruefully. "We are sorely in need of good food. Vegetables and fruit will do nicely, Lord Talon. We will welcome whatever you can provide. I bid you good day.

Talon felt it was time for him and Tefkros to leave soon after, as Richard appeared to be tired. Talon wondered about this, as he collected his attendant Companions and returned the way they had come to their own encampment.

Tefkros took a deep breath. "Ah, but I am glad you decided to camp here on the beach, Talon. That king, he shows no respect for us visitors."

Talon, who was seething, could only agree with him. The English king was utterly lacking in even the most basic kind of diplomacy. He didn't like the idea of working with Guy's choice of commander, either.

*****

Two nights later, a shadow slipped into the tent of Princess Theodora and crouched in the darkness by her pallet. For a long moment, the form, covered from head to foot in dark cloth that covered the face up to the eyes, listened to the slow breathing and contemplated the sleeping form. Finally, with a quiet sigh, he gently woke the princess with a firm hand over her mouth, and a hissed a warning not to do nor say anything, or she would die. A sharp knife was held against her throat to add emphasis to the words. When the assassin had assured himself that the princess was not going to do anything to jeopardize his presence, he released his hand from her mouth, but kept his knife blade just touching her neck, near her jugular.

"My master would like to know your real name, my lady... please," he added, almost as an afterthought.

Tamura had been rigid with terror at finding this ghost looming over her, and it took a few long moments for her to recover even a fraction of her normal composure. Dear God protect her, but how had this person managed to get into her chamber in the tent? Past the guards, and then Siranos and Martina? However, he had done it and here he was, and furthermore, he knew!

"Tell... tell him that I am Theodora, daughter of Isaac the emperor," she whispered hoarsely, trying but failing dismally to sound haughty. She was still frozen with fear, but there had been a question that demanded an answer.

"Please do not waste my time, my lady. Who are you?" The knife blade pressed a little harder onto her throat, and she never doubted that the dark menacing figure would use it.

"Tamura. I am Tamura, the concubine of the emperor," she gasped.

"Ah." There was a long pause. "Then, where is the daughter of Isaac?"

"She—she died; someone poisoned her, wild mushrooms, we think, and—and then the Normans came, and I was taken."

The figure stirred, as though listening, but then returned to the questions.

"Did you murder her?"

"No! Of course not!" she hissed indignantly. "One of her servants might have done so. I do not know. They all hated her!"

Another long silence.

"Why did you say you were the daughter of Isaac?" the figure demanded.

"The Normans mistook me for her, and by then, it was too late. They told the king I was she," she stammered.

"You have been very convincing," the figure observed.

"I spent many years in the palace at Famagusta with Isaac! I learned how to be *convincing*," she retorted.

Had the figure given a quiet chuckle? "My master and his son both wish you good fortune, my lady. I am leaving now, but do not move nor raise an alarm because that would be a big mistake. Now, close your eyes and count to fifty without opening them. You *can* count to fifty?"

Tamura nodded speechlessly, closed her eyes and began counting. The pressure on her throat went away and there was the quietest rustle, after which, she sensed that the intruder was gone. Nevertheless, she continued to count to fifty before she opened her eyes.

Tamura didn't sleep a wink after that, and appeared at the breakfast table hollow-eyed and tired. Joanna, who noticed most things, observed.

"God's blessings. Did you not sleep well, Princess Theodora?" she asked, with a concerned look from under her brows, matched by the pursed lips of mild disapproval.

"God's blessings, I did not sleep well, my lady," she replied evenly. "It must be the heat, or a bad dream."

"Where did you get that?" Joanna pointed to a thin red line along the left side of Tamura's throat.

"I—I don't know, my lady," Tamura stammered. Her fingers touched the slightly painful welt. She stared at her fingers, expecting to see some blood. There was none. "This wretched place is infested with insects. Perhaps one bit me?"

Berengaria gave her a glare. It was clear to Tamura that she thought Tamura had spent a long night with her husband.

"I can only imagine what *insect* did that!" she muttered balefully.

Tamura didn't care. A small sack of gold left on her bed had helped a great deal to calm her shattered nerves.

Part III
Acre

Against the walls of Acre

"They'll drink every hour of the daylight
*   and poach every hour of the dark.*
It's the sport not the rabbits they're after
*   (we've plenty of game in the park).*
Don't hang them or cut off their fingers.
*   That's wasteful as well as unkind,*
For a hard-bitten, South-country poacher
*   makes the best man-at-arms you can find."*
—Rudyard Kipling

"Are you ready?" Talon called out to his men, who were braced for the last two-hundred-pace dash for the dubious shelter of the tall walls of the city of Acre.

"Ready, Lord!" Brandt bellowed from off to his left. The Saxons were clustered in a loose shield wall formation, while to Talon's right were some of the Kantara men, led by Cynemaer and Hrodulf, who were there to tighten them up. Their shield walls were serving another purpose today; they protected the warriors from the stones and arrows being shot down at them by the defenders.

They were not here to attack another enemy on foot. Their objective was the tall, daunting walls facing them, which were, at this time, crowded with Arabs and Turks, who were waiting for them. Trumpets blared on both sides, and banners waved in the light sea breeze on the walls, while the grim-faced men on the ground contemplated, yet again, the almost-impossible task of storming the walls.

Talon sighed inwardly. The king had ordered this action. His brand new towers—the long-delayed construction of which was finally complete—were grinding and swaying their way slowly toward the fortifications, pushed and hauled by slaves and soldiers, sheltering however they could, under wet skins and layered shields. The man in charge of the apparatus and the task of getting them to the walls had wanted to use Talon's burly Saxons, but Talon had refused, and told him that his men were for the fighting that would follow and were not draft horses. Brandt had heard the lively exchange and had told his men, who had cheered derisively as the thwarted, angry man rode off. Talon ignored him and turned back to his own men.

"Dewy and Caradog. Prepare yourselves!' he called. "And you men who are to guard them, make sure the wooden panels are in place to protect them, and do as they say. Make sure they can shoot without being endangered, and bring them arrows. Never stop until they tell you."

He wiped his already-sweating brow with a cotton cloth. His precious archers were going to be right up there in the forefront of danger, but the distance might be to their advantage. The enemy could not reach them easily with either a crossbow or one of their ordinary bows.

"We're ready, Lord," Dewy stated, and he hefted his longbow. Both he and Caradog were grim-faced and tense, as were the other ten longbow-men, their students. Everyone was on edge, fidgeting with their equipment or praying, but all eager to be done with the waiting, which was in some ways the worst part of an assault.

Talon glanced over to the other side of the massive, trundling tower nearest to him. Both would be rammed against the walls, just to the south of the gates. King Richard, ever to the fore, was one of the few mounted men facing the enemy today. His lords and retainers had all made it clear that he could not be part of the assault on the walls. All the knights taking part in the attack were on foot. Their horses were useless for this kind of fight. Further off to the right of the English were the Germans and a motley mass of other nationals who had joined the Crusade. The French were not there.

Due to the interminable quarreling of the two kings, Philip had declared that his men would not take part in this attack. Talon wished the two kings would stop their bickering. Richard had denied his help in the last assault made by the French, so now Philip retaliated.

"They are like two spoiled boys who have never grown up," he had confided in Brandt the day before, when they learned that they were the spearhead of the attack. Now he looked over at Richard, drew his sword, and waited for the signal.

Richard drew his own sword and raised it. The towers were now within twenty paces of the walls and coming under an intense barrage of arrows, boiling hot water, and even some oil, as they edged ever closer. Chillingly, Greek fire was also in evidence. The defenders must also be deploying some small mangonels because stones were flying through the air and bouncing along the plain, doing little in the way of damage. Such missiles were difficult to aim, more effective against walls or massed forces than small clusters.

"Go now, archers!" Talon yelled. "Strike at the defenders facing the towers, as many as you can. God protect you!" he called out. The archers scampered forward, accompanied by men who lugged huge, flat shields, as tall as men and twice as wide, behind which the archers could stand and shoot. Talon was determined to protect his men where he was able.

They arrived at the one hundred pace marker, and the wide boards, which could absorb arrows, were propped upright. Caradog and Dewy, along with their men, had already loosed arrows into the clusters of men on the walls when Richard gave a great shout and waved his sword around his head as a signal for the main assault to begin.

Trumpets blared their brassy shriek, drums rattled and men roared. Swords clashed on shields, and the army of Christians began to surge forward, making for the walls. Many carried ladders, as did some of Talon's men. Talon and his Saxons and Companions shouted their own battle cries and went with them. The few trebuchets the Christians possessed went to work, tossing large rocks over the walls to distract the men on the parapet, but also to wreak destruction within the city. The swish of the rocks flying overhead and the distant crashes heralded the beginning of another desperate attempt to take the city by storm.

But it was the towers that would make the difference, if anything could. These behemoth structures were taller than the massive walls of Acre and provided a fast, sheltered way for men, some of them in heavy armor, to get to the top of the walls. A few archers and crossbowmen were already inside the towers, which made them heavier and harder to push forward.

It was one of those hot, dry days of early summer, and very soon the dust churned up by the running men had created a light, choking haze. At least it was better than mud, which had hampered them the last time, Talon thought, as he tried his best to keep pace with the eager Saxons and Kantara men. His knee, ever a nuisance since Hattin, was stiff, and he was sweating like everyone else as they ran forward. Their objective was to arrive at just the same time as the towers were rammed against the walls by their luckless crews, many of whom were already lying scattered along the trail left by the towers, wounded or dead, attesting to the skill of the enemy archers.

Talon's own archers had been busy. Dewy and Caradog were pointing out targets to their men, who systematically killed off many defenders on the walls directly in front of the towers, which now had only a few more paces to go.

The few archers who were already inside the towers were at the same height as the parapet and could do much damage from behind their cover. Their task was to make sure the towers were not destroyed by some brave enemy throwing fire onto them.

Talon and his men endured the hail of arrows that came from the walls and arrived in a rush at the base, right next to one tower, with only a couple of casualties. Here, however, there was little cover; stones and rocks were now being tossed down at them, forcing them to hold their shields high and hope that no one would kill them ignominiously at the very base of their objective.

Brandt and his men filed hurriedly into the base of the tower and began the arduous dash up the steps within the framework, which shuddered and rattled as men went pounding up the crude steps. They arrived on the platform at the very top, huffing and panting. There was to be no respite. The tower archers stood aside to let the warriors assemble.

One of them gave a yell and, with a short sword, slashed down at the rope that held the gangway upright. The rope parted with a twang and the gangway fell with a crash onto the stone parapet, its heavy planks crushing an unwary defender, who gave a shriek and lay screaming and bleeding, as the first of the big blond men, roaring and yelling and brandishing long swords, huge axes and big shields, thundered across the precarious wooden platform, which shook and trembled under their weight.

Talon had been slow to reach the top, assisted by one of the Kantara men. When he arrived he could see that it was going to be a hard fight. He limped across the gangway with more of his men crowding behind him and glanced off to his right, to see the other tower spewing King Guy's Normans onto the walls, a hundred paces away. He shook his head. They might have gained the walls, but the large numbers of defenders were far too many, unless they could win some space along the walls and drive down to the gates of the city, which were a few hundred paces away. But they must gain that precious space, so he charged, with Brandt at his side, into the crowded mass of howling enemy soldiers, waiting to greet them with spear, ax, and sword.

From this moment on Talon could not remember very much, other than what was taking place to his very front. The desperate battle for control of the wall was engaged. His small band of men, Saxon and Greeks combined, fought for control of their section of the wall against a bristling mass of defenders, who fought with the desperation of those who had everything to lose. Hacking and stabbing over the tiny shield wall that Brandt put together on both sides of the tower, the Saxons slowly managed to clear some space on either side, to allow other men, Greeks with Tefkros at their head, to clamber up the inside of the tower and join them. Men fell screaming, to be trampled, regardless of who they were. His own men began to fall, as archers from buildings and towers within the city began to shoot at them. Talon's archers could no longer protect them; the press was too thick.

Shoulder to shoulder with his men on the ramparts, he stabbed or hacked at whatever target presented itself, be it shield or arm or leg; his sword, still sharp and hard as that special steel from Nippon, could do much damage, and he used it to good effect. Brandt was roaring and hacking with his huge ax, so that before long they all looked like people in an abattoir. The hideous noise of men shrieking their lives away—or crying as they died—filled the air, and they screamed imprecations into each other's faces in several different languages while trying to hack each other to pieces.

It appeared to be going better than he had expected and the space was widening, but Talon sensed that all was not going well further along the parapet. During one tiny pause in the desperate fight, he lifted his head to glance along the wall toward where the other tower was located and saw, to his horror, that it was on fire. The men who had climbed it tried to escape down its stairs but the flames must have consumed them, because their comrades, harried by jubilant defenders, either jumped or were overwhelmed by flames. He noticed with a sinking feeling that all along the line, the defenders had rallied and were driving the crusaders off the walls!

Talon slammed his hand onto Brandt's shoulder to get his attention and pointed mutely at the flaming tower. Brandt finished off a luckless man in rags, who had had the reckless temerity to engage him, and looked up, his ax dripped gore.

"Bugger!" he exclaimed. "What do you want to do, Lord? We cannot hold this place without their help."

"We will perish if we continue. We must disengage, Brandt. Call off the hounds!" Talon shouted resignedly. "We will take our wounded with us."

Brandt turned and bellowed, "Aedwald! We go back! Grab the wounded and our dead and get back down the tower. Now!" His anger at having to abandon the hard-won space was demonstrated when he hacked viciously at yet another victim, sending him screaming back into the mass of men below the parapet on the inside of the city. "Fuck all of you bastards!" he roared.

Where was the help they should have had from the other nations, who were supposed to have taken their share of the walls? Talon wondered angrily. But he knew, only too well, how difficult it was to assault a city so well defended; Tyre came to mind, and the desperate fights that had occurred on its walls. There, he had been a defender. Unless the walls had been demolished to rubble, the defender always had the advantage, he thought ruefully.

He had no time for further reflection, for now they were being driven back, as more and more men from the enemy ranks rushed to attack the only Christians left on the walls of Acre. Their shouts of victory rang in Talon's ears as he and his men retreated to the gangway in ferocious fighting that left bodies strewn along the route. Talon struck and stabbed at anyone foolish enough to come near him, but he had a bitter taste in his mouth as he glanced hurriedly behind him.

He prayed that their tower was not going to burst into flames, but there were ominous signs that it was going to be on fire before long. Someone had been able to throw a torch or a Greek fire pot into the construction. Smoke was beginning to pour out of the exit at the top, right where they were trying to escape.

Finally, he and Brandt, Oswine, Wembar, and Aedwald, were the only men left on the parapet. Brandt grabbed Talon by the shoulder. "Go, Lord. Go now!" He shoved Talon along the gangway, using his shield to protect him from the long spears that reached out for him. Talon stepped across the gangway and then tore the bow from the hands of one of the archers—not one of his own men—who had remained. He looked very uncertain as to what he should do. Talon snatched up the man's quiver and shoved him toward the steps.

"Get out of here," he shouted above the din. The youth needed no further encouragement and vanished. Talon tore an arrow from the quiver and knocked it hurriedly. From here, he could shoot at anyone across the gap and at close range.

"Get over here, Brandt. You, too, Aedwald, and—" At that moment, Oswine stumbled and began to fall. He had an arrow embedded in his chest. Aedwald seized him by his hauberk collar just before he could fall to the ground below and hauled him unceremoniously across the gangway. Brandt and Wembar, standing on the wooden platform, backed off slowly, fending off the screaming and yelling defenders. Talon grabbed Brandt by the arm and pulled him to the side without ceremony.

"Get going, Brandt. I have a bow." Talon loosed another arrow into the mob.

"Wembar, come on! Get over here!" Talon bawled over the din.

Brandt joined in. "Get back, Wembar. It is time to fucking leave!"

Wembar had just dismembered someone with his ax and glanced back at them, his blonde braids whirling around him. He was covered with other men's blood and his blue eyes had the madness of a berserker as he glared around, but he heard them.

He almost danced across the bridge, then he lifted his ax on high and smashed it down upon the leather hinges, severing one set. The bridge sagged crazily to one side, dropping two overeager warriors from the city. One tumbled with a scream, to land on the ground with a sickening thump, only to be skewered to death by one of Talon's men while he lay groaning. The other slipped and grabbed onto the remaining framework and lost his spear and shield as he tried desperately to get back up. However, Wembar was not done yet. Pushing Talon roughly aside and shouting, "Go, Lord. Go!" he hacked at the other thick leather hinge, then stooped and lifted the entire end of the bridge, with all his enormous strength, and dropped it and its screaming passenger over the side, to fall with a crash at the base of the tower.

Talon was breathing smoke by now and glanced down the steps. Several arrows, thumped into the wood nearby. He tugged at Wembar's sleeve urgently, but Wembar turned slowly to give him a hopeless look, then coughed. A small stream of blood poured from his mouth. He tried to speak but choked again, then bared his blood-stained teeth in a snarl. His eyes glazed over, and he fell backwards with a crash to the wooden floor. His chest was bristling with arrows that had been shot at close range.

Talon knew without doubt that he was dead, but he still seized Wembar by his collar and dragged him through the smoke that was boiling up from the well of the tower. He could barely see, and the smoke caused him to choke and retch as he staggered down the steps, without much idea as to how much further he had to go, dragging the inert and very heavy body, which thumped along behind him. Just as he was about to fall, a huge form lumbered up next to him and shouted.

"I shall take him, Lord. Go now!" Brandt called and gave him a rough shove in a downward direction.

Talon dived down the last of the steps, through the now-flaming base, and out of the tower. He took a huge breath of air and bent over, retching. Someone stood over him with a shield. It was Andreas. Talon nodded his thanks, then looked back to watch, with a sense of profound relief, as Brandt staggered out with Wembar over his broad shoulders. Men were all around them, shouting and waving their shields high and calling urgently for him and Brandt to run to safety. Talon staggered away, surrounded by his own men, who formed a protective wall around him, deflecting the many arrows that were being shot at them from high above.

The tower, as though it had been waiting for this moment, suddenly began to pour flames from the entrance at the bottom, and a column of flame reached out from the top like a huge chimney. But this tower was made of wood and hide, not stone. Very soon it burst its seams and, in a shower of sparks, the entire framework was engulfed in flame and smoke. The heat could be felt even a hundred paces away as the tower became a bonfire, keeping company with the first, which was still ablaze.

*****

With his men, Talon limped back toward the safety of the encampment. They were accompanied by scores of others in large and small groups, dejected men who had experienced similar disappointments all along the walls. They were followed by the jeers and obscene gestures from the joyful defenders. Richard had wanted a full-on assault in the vain hope that they might simply overcome the determined defenders, but it had failed. Talon could not but help thinking that if these two petulant kings could only agree on a strategy, they might have succeeded.

Richard, still mounted and now joined by King Philip, surrounded by their retainers, watched in glowering silence as Talon and his men came abreast. Richard said nothing, but Philip raised his hand in silent acknowledgement. Talon only nodded and plodded on. He was too exhausted and too bitter, at this moment, to say anything.

The recriminations and finger pointing would come later. He noted that Guy de Lusignan was seated on a horse nearby. There was no sign of Geoffrey. He had probably been at the forefront of the attack; but Guy, of course, considered himself above the fray. Guy didn't even acknowledge the men dragging themselves past the two kings. He simply fidgeted with his reins and stared at the burning ruins of the towers.

Talon and his men, carrying their dead and supporting their wounded, those who needed it, made for their encampment near the beach and within easy distance of their ship, whenever it was at the port. There were going to be some hurried burials that night and a funeral pyre the next day for the dead Saxons, but first, there would be men to patch up this evening.

Talon wondered, sardonically, how many of the Norman wounded would survive their treatment at the hands of their leeches. Talon trusted his physician, Epiktitos, to do his best to keep his men alive, and to recommend the more seriously wounded be sent home to Cyprus, where Rav'an and her assistants would certainly take care of them. He wondered vaguely if Theodora was back yet, but was too tired to continue with that train of thought.

He was still seething with rage when he arrived at his tent. Evanthis was there to greet him, but Talon brushed past him and tossed his shield into a corner. He threw off his helmet and sat down with a thump, swearing quietly to himself. He swore again, but beckoned the two nervous boys in, and turned to have them untie his pesky straps and other cords to allow him to shrug off the heavy chainmail hauberk.

Evanthis presented him with a mug of herbal tea, for which Talon thanked him more gracefully. It wasn't the fault of the boys that he'd almost had his head handed to him, he told himself. He sipped the hot fluid gratefully, although he was more than ready for a heavy gulp of arak. He thought better of it when he considered that his work assisting Epiktitos was just about to begin.

*****

Hours later, Epiktitos finished stitching up the last of Talon's wounded men. Talon looked on with approval. His physician was doing his job well and Talon was pleased with his work. The doctor had intercepted him at the tent doorway earlier and examined the big bruise and the cut on his temple. "You need to have that attended to, Lord Talon," he had insisted. Right away he sat Talon down, bathed the wound, and wrapped it with a clean linen bandage.

The patient was Julian, a member of the Kantara shield wall crew. Julian was a brave man who didn't shrink from danger, and that was probably why he had received this wound. It was a gaping slash to his thigh. Epiktitos's assistant, along with Evanthis, helped by Diondre, completed the task of washing caked blood off the area and bandaged the man's leg with clean linen torn from sheets that had been provided by Rav'an, who had said dryly, as she handed them to Talon, "These may prove useful."

"I shall come and see you every day, Julian," Epiktitos told the wounded warrior. "The wound has to be kept clean or you will suffer badly. If I am not here, Evanthis will see to it in my stead. Meanwhile, you will rest and allow it to heal. No moving about."

"You'll do as he says, or I'll come along and remind you, Julian," Talon threatened the man, as he clapped him on his shoulder.

"Yes, Lord. I understand," Julian said meekly, and gave them a wan smile.

"We are going to send you home on the ship with the other four within the week." Talon added.

"God bless you, Lord," Julian said. "I'm sorry we could not get past them to the gates."

"I am too, Julian. I am too," Talon sighed.

Some of Julian's comrades, who had been waiting nearby, came to assist him out of the medical tent and off to his own tent.

The fight had been very hard, and Talon had lost several good men. Given the size of his little army, he could not sustain these losses for very long.

Richard had put him in charge of the Greeks from Cyprus; reluctant footmen and riders from all the towns of the island were here with Talon and his Kantara men, alongside a mixed bag of others.

Talon had noted that the Christians were from just about anywhere, including a small contingent of *Pullani,* men who had been born here in Palestine, but who had lost their strongholds or homes, one by one, as Salah ad-Din had systematically besieged them and captured or even destroyed their holdings. Some of these now-leaderless men, none of whom wanted to serve either Philip or Richard, had joined Talon's little army, and he had welcomed them, although he had exacted oaths of allegiance from them. Some had died today in the frenzy that had taken place on the ramparts. Time to morn later, he decided, pushing the memories aside into the dark recesses of his mind, while he worked with Epiktitos and the two boys to set the tent to rights.

"You have done good work today, Master Physician," he told the doctor, whose features lit up in a smile at the praise. Epiktitos was not quite like the run-of-the-mill physicians. He hailed from Constantinople and knew a great deal about wounds. Before they had arrived at Acre he had been somewhat rotund, for he enjoyed his food and wine. Weeks of sparse food and less wine had reduced some of the weight he had carried around his middle. However, his good nature had remained firmly intact, and his smiles and words of encouragement to the wounded carried weight, especially as Lord Talon stood firmly behind him with regard to his ministrations and medicines.

The Christian leeches in the other segments of the vast encampment did not receive the glow of praise the men from Cyprus sent his way.

"Don't go around pretending you are big men with open wounds who don't need treatment. Big idiots die of infected wounds just like anyone else, and I should know," Talon had admonished the men time and again as he watched Epiktitos stitching wounds, while they groaned and grit their teeth, and then bandaging them up. "Besides, if I tell Lady Rav'an and she gets hold of you, you will be in deep trouble!" he had assured them. After this lecture, anyone who had even a slight wound came to see him.

Hereward, ever the joker, had left just as Brandt had arrived at the entrance of the tent. "What's wrong with him, Lord?" he asked as he looked back at the departing Saxon with suspicious eye. "I didn't know he was wounded."

"Silly bugger—to use your terminology, Brandt—he said he had cut his middle finger and showed it to the physician," Talon told him with a grin. "I told Epiktitos to bandage it, but I threatened to break it, and was about to put my boot up his arse for being rude, just before you came along. All the same, in this pestilent place it's better to be safe than sorry. Infections are rife at present in the other camps, and it's killing them."

"You are right there, Lord. People are dying of the smallest wound in the other camps. Thank the Lord we have Epiktitos and you to keep us going. I'll take care of Hereward," Brandt threatened. "Furthermore, I will really put my boot up his arse for being cheeky. Don't worry on that account." Brandt grinned apologetically.

*****

The sun began to set in the west in a blaze of crimson, which splashed across the sky, the red and orange colors smeared dark by the dense smoke from the still-smoldering towers. As evening settled over the Christian encampments and the beleaguered city of Acre, the world of men seemed to pause in its activities and, for a brief time, there was quiet in the encampments.

Talon, Brandt, the Companions, and the two Welsh archers crowded into his tent. The four Companions who had accompanied him and his precious Saxons, wore bandages of clean linen strips almost as badges of honor. Epiktitos was finicky about these things. Everyone who had survived the parapets had taken heavy bruising and minor cuts. Talon provided wine from his limited stock, which they all took gratefully. Talon noted the glum atmosphere.

While still fuming at how it had ended, he wanted to understand what might have gone wrong, that had left him and his men so isolated on their portion of the walls.

The men settled in, clutching the beakers of wine that Talon had provided, and for a while there was a silence, broken only by the sound of the boys cleaning equipment in the back section of the tent.

Maymun finally spoke up. "No one else gained a foothold this time around, Lord. We were out on a limb with no help forthcoming... from anywhere." He sounded resentful.

"We could not sup'port you once you were on the parapet, Lord," Dewy said, sounding defensive. "Big risk for hitting our own, see you?" Now he sounded apologetic.

"Dewy, I did not mean you or your archers!" Maymun protested. "You did your part before we got there, and that made a huge difference. No, it was the other companies who should have pressed harder. But that's just my opinion." He looked at the others, as though wanting confirmation.

Brandt nodded his agreement. "I hate to have to say it, but you Welsh did us proud today. Don't let that go to your fat, ugly heads." He smiled his wolfish smile at them, but then his demeanor changed. "There is something else about today, Lord."

"Will you listen to that Saxon. Ugly, now, is it?" Caradog protested.

"What is it Brandt?" Talon swiped at an fly that had taken an interest in the wound on his face. They were everywhere and very annoying.

"The enemy, the people we were fighting today."

Khuzaymah slapped his thigh. "Yes, that's it, Lord!" He nodded vigorously toward Brandt. "Those were not normal citizens of the town. These were real warriors, and there were many of them!"

Talon squinted at his men. They all had the sunken-eyed look of men who were exhausted and had just had a taste of hell. These men of his were unused to failure and probably felt as mauled as he. He silently cursed the two kings, who could not even unite to take the walls.

"Well, they certainly gave the citizens some backbone, and we suffered for it! So how did they get in there without anyone knowing?" he asked. "They were not there a week ago. There is a whole fleet out there that is supposed to be preventing just this kind of thing from happening."

His men shrugged and stared back at him. "They must have slipped past the Frans during the night. They could not have gained entrance any other way," Khuzaymah muttered reluctantly, and Talon was forced to agree. Many of the men they had encountered during those frantic minutes on the parapets had been seasoned warriors, not the usual rag tag of desperate citizens trying to defend themselves.

"Very well, I shall point this out to the king, should he ask, but in the meantime, Maymun, I want you and Nasuh to prepare for Henry's arrival and make sure the wounded, who are to go home, are made ready. Go and get some rest," he told them. "There is nothing more we can do now."

He watched as his despondent men filed out of the tent. Brandt lingered, obviously wanting to say something.

"What is on your mind, Brandt?" Talons asked his Saxon commander.

"You risked your life to bring Wembar back, Lord. I and all the others will remember that."

"I only did what any of you would have done, Brandt," Talon told him with a wry smile. He didn't add that he was not prepared to see Wembar's corpse at the base of the city walls, mutilated beyond recognition by the defenders. Both sides carried out atrocities. He would, if he could, bring his dead home. "Any one of you would have done the same for me. Here, have some more wine. Not much left, but Henry will be bringing more before too long, so we can indulge ourselves a little."

Brandt gratefully accepted the full beaker of wine that Talon pressed on him.

He took an appreciative sip, then said, "We cannot continue to be in the lead, only to find that no one is there to protect our flanks or even our backs, Lord. I won't be seen dead telling them so, but our Welsh are fantastic at long range, but even they cannot help us when we are over the top of those fucking walls."

Talon swilled some of the wine around in his mouth before swallowing. It took some of the bitter taste of the engagement away.

"There won't be many of us left if this goes on. I'll talk to the king, and we will see."

"You know what I miss most lately?" Brandt said.

"Tell me," Talon said.

"I miss the music your lady wife plays. It's as though an angel is playing." Brandt was clearly embarrassed at this display of confidence, but Talon smiled.

"I agree with you. I, too, miss the music, Brandt," he assured his friend.

They talked some more as old comrades, then Brandt finished off the remnants of his wine, heaved himself stiffly to his feet, and with a nod to his chief, left to get some much-earned rest. Talon was too tired to go to bed and spent some time thinking about the way the new warriors had managed to get into the town. He needed some eyes and ears inside the city, he decided.

He remembered that he had not cleaned his sword since he sheathed it, just before leaving the tower. He reached for it and tried to draw the blade, but it stuck in the scabbard. Talon cursed quietly to himself. He'd learned a good many swear words from Brandt. Finally, he managed to tug the blade free. He stared at the dried blood caked along its length and sighed. Not much had gone right this day, he decided, and he berated himself for not seeing to it before. Fang, the swordsman who had taught him, would have been beside himself at the lack of respect for the deadly weapon. Talon wouldn't let Evanthis clean his sword. The boy and Diondre had busied themselves with the other weapons and his armor, as soon as Talon handed it off to them.

Chapter 24

Spies

There are no leaders to lead us to honour, and yet
*   without leaders we sally,*
Each man reporting for duty alone, out of sight,
*   out of reach, of his fellow.*
There are no bugles to call the battalions, and yet
*   without bugle we rally*
From the ends of the earth to the ends of the earth,
*   to follow the Standard of Yellow!*
Fall in! O fall in! O fall in!
—Rudyard Kipling

Talon decided that he needed eyes and ears inside the city, so he talked it over with Junayd and the other Companions.

"Both Reza and I have gotten in and out of that place at night by climbing the city walls," he told them. "The stones are not as tightly mortared on the seaward side and, in any case, the weather and the sea salt have created deep recesses."

He left it hanging there and waited, with a sideways glance at Junayd, for the youths to consider. He wanted a couple of volunteers.

Maymun put up his hand. "Once we are in there, Lord, where will we hide? We have to have a safe place to stay while we look around."

"I'm thinking we will be able to find a place in the city. There must be deserted houses we can get into," Khuzaymah commented.

Talon was pleased that it didn't seem to occur to the Companions that climbing the outer walls would be a problem. Instead, they were thinking ahead.

Before he could say anything else, Nasuh spoke up. "If Maymun goes, then so do I, Lord," he stated, with a grin at his friend.

"That's settled, then." Talon nodded his approval. "Now listen carefully, as this is what you must do. Firstly, I should remind you both that capture is not an option. Not at all, so be very careful."

The two volunteers nodded their understanding. No one had any illusions as to how dangerous the mission was.

Two days later, during the darkest hours, a small, low rowboat pulled slowly alongside the rocks at the base of the city walls. Talon was in the boat and directed it with hand signals toward where he remembered climbing into the city, up what appeared to be a sheer stone wall.

As soon as the boat ground quietly onto the sand between some boulders, where its dark silhouette would not be so obvious, the two Companions leapt off silently and hugged the dark weed-and-slime-covered walls. They carried a small bag each, which held food enough for four days, their bows and their swords. They wore no armor, but they each carried a rolled-up chain vest, within which was a small helmet that they could wear to make them look like the ragtag inhabitants within the city. Talon worried that they didn't look starved enough!

He scanned the battlements high above with great care, as did the rowers. But no one appeared to have noticed either the boat or the arrival of its passengers. No word was spoken. Talon signaled to the rowers to pull away. He was prepared to create a diversion, should it be necessary, but the city slept, and the only sound was that of the sea lapping and hissing quietly against the rocks they had just left behind. He stared hard at the place where his two young Companions had landed, but could see nothing. They had vanished, just as they knew how. All he could do now was hope that they would be able, in four days, to return to the exact same place to be picked up. The boat left as silently as it had come. The rowlocks were wrapped in sacking and made no noise, and the rowers were very careful not to miss the water and make an unwelcome splash.

*****

Maymun and Nasuh climbed the wall without too much difficulty. Master Reza had trained them well and the mortar, eroded over time from wind and weather, provided nice, deep, hand and toe holds most of the way up the stone edifice to the parapet. However, there was slime in places, and their fingers and feet slipped on occasion, causing intakes of breath and a desperate scrabble for a safer hold.

Their equipment was heavy and sometimes hindered them, so that it was with profound relief that they eventually arrived near to the top without discovery or accident, where they paused and listened, even while their fingertips pleaded to let them rest. Maymun inched his way to the gap in the battlements to see if there was anyone nearby.

There was no one to be seen, so he slipped all the way over and slid into a dark recess where a tower joined the battlements. No one challenged him, either from the top of the tower or from along the walkway. Nasuh observed the movements of his companion and did likewise. Both youths huddled in the darkness with their ears wide open and listened intently to the night. In the distance, on the east side, they did hear the faint calls of sentries, but no noise was to be heard at this end at all.

"They expect an attack from that quarter, not from here," Nasuh whispered. "We could have brought our Lord and even the Saxons with us!"

Maymun nudged him. "Perhaps not," he whispered. "Someone is coming,"

They huddled even deeper into the shadows and listened as someone approached. Both youths had slipped their knives out, just in case. It was a sentry carrying a spear, but he was walking almost as though he was lame. When he drew near, the two men crouched in the darkness could make out gaunt features under a helmet that looked too large for his head. He was not only starving but appeared to be sick. They let him pass in the hope that he wouldn't notice them, and were relieved to see the back of him.

Without more ado, they rose from their crouch and hurried down into the silent streets of the city, making for their objective. Talon had told them that their best chance of hiding might be in the old Jewish quarter.

Pausing in the darker shadows whenever they heard someone coming, which was not often, they found the street, a very narrow one, with even less light from the stars. They then located a broken door, which led them into a small courtyard surrounded by a group of dwellings that had certainly known better days. Even in the darkness they could see that one of the houses was wrecked, its roof caved in and broken beams lying on the ground, perhaps destroyed by one of the random rocks tossed into the city by King Philip's trebuchet. Cautiously they navigated the yard and found the door that Talon had described to them. Opening it as quietly as possible, they slipped into the darkness and closed the creaking door behind them.

Maymun nearly jumped out of his skin when something stirred in the darkness. He could just make out a small form that rolled over and sat up. His hand had moved to his knife reflexively, and he heard the hiss of Nasuh's blade leaving its sheath. Both men froze where they stood and watched as the form squeaked something in a small voice and then began to get up. Maymun decided to act. He slipped across the floor, and with one hand he seized the shoulder of his intended victim, while with the other, he readied his knife for the throat. But Nasuh was also very fast. His hand came and held Maymun's wrist.

"No!" he whispered urgently. "We don't have to kill him! Remember what Lord Talon said. We should find out more before we do that."

Maymun got over his surprise, but the figure didn't. It gave a feeble squawk of surprise and fear, then froze. Nasuh took his hand away and Maymun relaxed his grip and shifted his knife to rest the blade on the child's throat. It was a child, they could tell that, but girl or boy, they could not tell.

"Salam, little one. You will not move, nor cry out, or you die," Nasuh offered in polite Arabic. "Nod if you understand."

The creature nodded, then gasped, "Who—who are you? I have nothing!"

Both men stared at the dark small shape. Now they knew. "You are a girl?" Maymun asked stupidly. The figure nodded, emanating fear; there was a tiny sob.

"We don't have time for this," Maymun muttered. "Should have done it."

"What are you doing here?" Nasuh demanded, ignoring his companion.

"My father and mother have died." The child whimpered now. There was another small sob, and she put her forearm over her face.

Both men looked at one another in the dark. They had not expected this. "Don't you have a home?" Maymun demanded, perhaps more harshly than he intended.

"They took it and I ran away," she told them.

"Who took it?"

"The new soldiers, who came a week ago. They wanted the house for themselves, and one of them would not leave me alone." In the silence that followed both men shook their heads, then Nasuh said firmly, "We are not here to harm you. Do you understand? What is your name?"

"I am Naida bint i Mohammad al-Haddad," she stated, with an element of pride in her voice.

Maymun sat back on his heels and contemplated the girl. "Saint's balls!" he said out loud. He didn't even know what the curse meant, but he had heard Brandt swearing so often that he used it.

"Maymun, don't swear in front of the child!" Nasuh, who was somewhat more prudish in his behavior, admonished him. "You know Lord Talon would not like it."

"Lord Talon is not here, and besides, he allows Brandt to curse all the time!"

"That's because Brandt is a crazy man," Nasuh reminded him. "Lord Talon puts up with his cursing because he is a demon in a fight."

"You have to admit that this is not what we expected, nor do we need it!" Maymun shot back.

"No, but now it's here, and we have to deal with it. Master Reza always told us to think on our feet."

"You are right, but at this moment, we are on our arses, and this little pest is in our way!" Maymun snapped. But then he changed his tone. "We need some light. Is it safe to have light here, Naida?" he asked the mute but wide-eyed girl.

She nodded. "I think it is. I have a candle with me," she offered.

"Good, then we can talk some more. Find the candle and light it."

She leaned away from her bed and reached for something in the dark. Both men's hands rested on their knives. There was a snapping sound, and a small stream of sparks was soon followed by a tiny flame that grew. The candle lit up their surroundings, and it was not at all comforting. Now the two men could clearly see where they had arrived.

They were in some kind of low-arched brick tunnel entrance with walls made of mud brick, bare except for cobwebs, while the floor was composed of dirt, with bits of bone and other rubbish. The further reaches of the tunnel, which Talon had told them led to other streets, were completely blocked with more rubbish, sand, and mortar. Naida was seated on a thin, filthy quilt that was threadbare and full of holes. She looked dirty and starved, her once long, dark hair was matted and tangled. All three people in the small chamber stared at one another. Naida now could see her captors, and it must have been intimidating. She shrank away and asked in a quaver, "Who are you?"

"We are just visiting. Don't be frightened, we will not harm you. I swear to God." Nasuh put his hand on his heart as he said this, and the child relaxed a little.

'I am Nasuh, and that ugly person over there," he indicated Maymun with a dismissive gesture, "is Maymun. Be nice to him and all will be well." Nasuh smiled.

Maymun scowled, but then relented and tried to smile reassuringly at the girl. Both men stared thoughtfully at the little creature crouched in front of them. This was totally unexpected. There was a long silence, but finally, Nasuh asked, "How long since you've eaten anything?"

"A day, perhaps two," she responded, her eyes wide. She looked starved, her cheek bones stood out and she was as skinny as a stick.

"Then eat this, but eat it slowly," Maymun said, and rummaged in his bag for some of the cheese and bread he carried with him. "Is there any clean water nearby, from a well?" Nasuh asked.

"I have some here," she offered, gesturing toward a small jug in the corner.

While they watched Naida stuff the food into her elfin face, they instinctively listened to the night. All was still but for the rustle of small creatures in this subterranean chamber, so they began to relax. "Tell us more about these people who took your house," Maymun asked eventually.

She swallowed the last of the cheese and bread, then picked the crumbs of the blanket with great care and put them in her mouth before she spoke. "What do you want to know about them?" she asked in her small voice.

There was much they wanted to know, and the questions and answers went back and forth. It turned out that Naida was an observant child, and she told them much. Dawn was beginning to filter into the chamber by this time, and they were all ready for some sleep. Reluctantly, the men decided to take shifts to keep an eye on the orphan, whose head was falling onto her chest by this time.

"Go to sleep and we will be on guard. No one will harm you. We will see to that," Nasuh told her. Naida needed no further persuasion. Wary though she might have been of these two strange men, she was too exhausted to worry and fell asleep almost immediately, curled into a tiny ball.

Maymun reached over and covered the child with the shreds of the blanket she had pushed aside when they arrived.

"Now what do we do?" he grumped. "We don't know if we can trust her not to betray us, and we have to complete our mission."

"I've been thinking," Nasuh said in a low tone.

"Have you, indeed?" came the somewhat caustic reply.

"Yes. She sees things, and knows what is going on, and if we throw the bones right she can help us," Nasuh remarked. "Lord Talon has told us often enough about beggars seeing but not being seen. Besides, we have something she needs badly."

"Hmm? Food? Well, we'll see."

They talked for another few minutes and then Nasuh went to sleep, wrapped in his cloak and with his dagger and sword nearby, while a yawning Maymun took the first watch.

They stayed in the cover of their den until the following afternoon, by which time Naida had eaten again, as had the Companions, and they were all getting on somewhat better, even if it was still uneasily. Nasuh explained to Naida what they hoped for, and she nodded her shaggy head, appearing eager to please.

When the afternoon was well advanced, they ventured out. Her task was to lead them to certain areas, where they could look around and assess the mood and the condition of the city and its inhabitants. The streets remained almost empty. People hurried by, ignoring the little girl who would call out and ask for food. They passed other starving creatures, crouched in doorways and on street corners. It soon became clear that no one was going to help a starving orphan, nor any of the small army of other beggars dotted about the city. These were desperate times indeed.

There was a dry, musty smell about the town. Everything was dilapidated and there was extensive damage caused by the huge stones hurled into the city by the catapult of the Knights Hospitalier. In fact, they were at it again this afternoon; all three of them heard the loud crash of a rock as it fell into a house nearby. There were screams, frightened calls, and a lot of dust. They hurried on.

Maymun and Nasuh were trained to observe and remain out of sight, so it was merely a matter of following Naida. She led them to the first location near the huge gate towers. There were many more armed men here, and not a few looked a good deal better fed than the citizenry they had encountered on the way. Motioning for Naida to crouch by a doorway with her bowl at the ready, the two assassins slipped in among the groups of armed men, who were taking their ease for the time being. It was not hard to blend with these men. They all bore spears and bows and a patchwork of armor and helmets. No one reacted as Maymun and Nasuh joined one group or another, listening and assessing.

It was while thus occupied that they discovered something interesting. The men grouped here were going to be part of a diversion. They were going to sally forth the following night, on foot— horses were a rarity within the city bay now—and they were to attack the nearest camp. While they were doing this, Salah ad-Din's cavalry was going to attack in force from the rear.

"How do we know if they will really attack when we leave the safety of the city?" one man demanded.

"Because our swimmer has told them it is tomorrow night, and they have agreed. He is back with us now. He was picked up last night by our boat."

There were many conversations of this nature. Maymun and Nasuh's ears were wide open. An hour later, Maymun tipped his hooded head and Nasuh sauntered over to join him. They casually strolled away to blend into the dusk, leaving the armed men to continue gossiping. A little to Maymun's surprise, they found Naida still where they had left her. She jumped as they appeared silently in front of her, but recovered and climbed to her feet. Despite the food they had given her, she still looked very shaky on her feet.

"Come along, little one," Nasuh told her. "We are going to have supper, and then do some planning."

Back in their den, they left her on her makeshift bed, gnawing on some cheese and dried meat, oblivious of anything else while they talked.

Lord Talon told us that we should write a letter and shoot it over the walls at a certain place, so we had better get to work," Maymun muttered. "You write it, Nasuh; you're better at that than I am."

"We have to leave her here while we go and shoot the arrow. D'you think it is safe to do so?" Nasuh asked.

"She could have denounced us at the gates if she was inclined to do so. We should not tarry. There could be others creeping about in this area, and Lord Talon needs this information as soon as possible.

*****

Talon and Junayd waited in the dark, crouched against the rocks that bordered on a thin stretch of beach. With them were several of the other Companions, watching the dark silhouette of the walls that loomed over them intently. They were not far from the corner tower of the eastern reaches of the city, where the sea met the land.

"You are sure that they can get to a place where they can send an arrow, Lord?" Junayd muttered for the second time since they had arrived.

"Quite sure, if they have not run into any trouble," said his leader, who was just as tense.

A good two hours past sunset, Junayd, who had sharp ears, gripped Talon by the arm. "Something—yes, that's it! An arrow! They have shot an arrow!" he exclaimed in a hoarse whisper. They all heard a light clatter of something maybe twenty paces behind them, as it landed in the rocks.

"Now all we have to do is to find it!" Talon muttered as he got carefully to his feet.

It did not take very long for Junayd to find it, and before long, they were all in Talon's tent, eagerly watching him unroll the message that had been bound to the haft of an arrow.

Talon peered at the message written in hurried scrawl by Nasuh. "It says they are well, but they have a very small problem they will have to deal with. There is to be an attack on the English camp by the army of Salah ad-Din tomorrow night. A diversion is to be mounted from the city just beforehand, and flares lit to tell the Arab army they have commenced their attack," Talon told his men.

"Then we shall be ready for them!" Brandt grunted, and his eyes glinted.

"That is not all. According to this, there is talk of a man who swims past the ships and delivers messages between the sultan and the city."

"We should see if we can catch him, Lord," suggested Junayd with a wolfish smile.

"Firstly, we need to alert the French and the Knights Hospitalier, and then King Richard, so that he too can be ready when the time comes," Talon stated. "I wish we had a way to let our lads know we have the message."

"They will know when they see our counter measures, Lord," Junayd told him in a matter-of-fact manner.

*****

Nasuh slipped into the den later the next day, having been out looking around, as he put it, and making sure that no one had taken an unwelcome interest in their area.

"We had best lie low for the rest of the day," he stated as he squatted in front of Naida, who was gnawing at some dried meat. "If you keep feeding her like this, we won't have anything left for ourselves," he commented, shaking his head at the little creature, who regarded him with huge, solemn eyes that were still somewhat wary.

"It keeps her from asking endless questions. Why should we be more careful than we are already?" Maymun demanded with a frown.

"There are patrols on the streets, and I get the feeling that they are looking for, and perhaps sweeping up, volunteers for the evening's entertainment." Nasuh gave him a look. "No one here can be eager to come to grips with the Normans."

"You are probably right. But I want to witness the attack, if it does happen. It's the only way we will know that our message was received."

Nasuh agreed, and later that evening they made their way cautiously along the streets of the beleaguered city. They noticed, as they drew closer, that there was furtive activity nearer to the gates. The leaders of the venture were determined not to give the Normans any clues as to what was to come before the gates were opened. Close-packed, nervous soldiers by the gates were tense and ready for the signal to attack. When the order came, the guards rushed to the gates, unbarred them and push them open. Another order was shouted, and they began to crowd the entrance and rush out of the opening. Several fires were lit in large iron braziers on the ramparts, presumably to signal Salah ad-Din and his people.

However, the advantage of surprise was not to be theirs this night. Almost as soon as they exited the city, torches flared a few hundred paces away, and they heard, to their horror, a roar from the Franks who had been waiting for them.

The shouts of alarm that rose in the night were not from the Franks but from the now-frantic guards, who rushed to close the gates, even if it meant that they would leave many of their army helpless and unable to get back into the city.

The men who had been left tried desperately to push through before the gate closed, and the Franks, having charged furiously, tried to press forward to hold them open for others to pour into the city and take it.

In the panic and desperate fight many were wounded and even killed, as they obstructed the action of closing the huge portals by the defenders. Torches were thrown down on the outside for archers to find targets, and they were not very discriminating; men fell on both sides to their arrows. An answering hail of arrows flew in from the darkness from the Frankish side, to further add to the panic and terror.

With much pushing, shoving and shouting, the gates were finally closed and their bars dropped in place by panting and frightened guards. Outside, the screaming men who had been left behind were butchered by the angry Franks and Normans, who took their frustration out on the luckless victims and took no prisoners. Maymun and Nasuh watched from the darkness as the fierce battle played out; then, as men staggered away from the gates and began to filter back along toward their hiding place, they slipped away. There was no mistake about where their arrow had ended up. Lord Talon had been busy.

Acre was a disconsolate city as its citizens awoke the next day and gave thought to its bleak future. Down in their lair, Naida, eager to help because she now had a food supply, found out that there had been much in the way of alarms and torchlight in the eastern side of the crusader camp, but no one could tell what had actually happened. She had kept her ears open and reported excitedly that the swimmer had returned.

"One might be forgiven for wondering why they don't use pigeons like everyone else. They must have run out of them, or perhaps they ate them!" Maymun snickered. "I can just imagine that little thing over there, if she caught one." He gestured with his chin. "She'd eat the whole thing, feathers, feet, and beak!"

Maymun and Nasuh gave much thought as to what point along the seaward walls the swimmer might have landed. They decided to pay the walls a visit on the third night. Although Naida was not able to articulate her every observation, she noticed much, and listening to her halting descriptions, the two Companions came to the conclusion that morale, already very low, had plummeted even further into the pit of despair. The question everywhere she had been with her begging bowl was, how had the infidels been able to anticipate their plan? There was widespread speculation of a traitor somewhere in their ranks. Many wondered why Salah ad-Din did not relieve them, or feared that he no longer intended to. Nasuh and Maymun decided that this was worthy news to pass along. First, however, their imperative was to find that swimmer.

No one on the streets knew the details of who he was and how he did it, and no one in the upper echelons of the city rulers was about to explain it to them, but this brave man was coming and going and slipping past the infidel ships as though he was a porpoise. He alone sustained their morale and they saw him as their hero.

With that in mind, the two assassins prowled around the walls, avoiding the sleepy and exhausted sentries while they searched for any clues. But it wasn't until late that night that they found something. Tucked into a recess along the parapet, facing the sea, was a rope. It was a long rope, easily long enough to allow someone to descend to the rocks and the water below the walls.

"Now we know, or think we know, where he comes and goes," Nasuh stated. "It is enough; we send an arrow."

*****

When the message was delivered to Talon, he decided it was time to act. "I want people to be in a boat close enough to that place to intercept whomsoever is doing the swimming, but not too close to be discovered," he told Junayd.

"If you will permit me, Lord, I will send Andreas and Khuzaymah with some others to patrol the waters. The ships are anchored all around, but our clever man evades them. Perhaps if we have people nearer to the water and his entry point we'll be able to catch this mystery man," Junayd stated. "I do admire him, whoever he is. It is no mean feat to swim so far!"

Talon agreed. "It is regrettable, but he must be stopped. The harder we can make the siege the sooner it will come to an end, and messengers to and fro are not something we can permit. They appear to have run out of pigeons."

*****

Andreas and his men paddled very quietly in the dark, oily waters of the bay, avoiding the ships that were anchored all around. Their watches were lax, and the men rowing quietly by could often hear shouts of drunken laughter as the sailors made free with their drink. It no longer surprised them that fit men and warriors could evade them and make it to the city to assist the beleaguered inhabitants.

Andreas supposed that the swimmer would try to avoid the largest assemblies of ships and try for the quieter areas of the waters. In the dark of the night the watchers frequently thought they had seen something, hence there were many false alarms. Junayd had counseled patience, but it was not easy to stare endlessly out at the sometimes calm and sometimes not so calm choppy waters.

On the following night the waters were agitated because a storm had swept in, carrying rain over the whole area, accompanied by a strong wind which had whipped up the waves in the bay. It was all the crew of the rowboat could do not to toss their suppers over the side while they bailed, trying to prevent their boat from becoming swamped, let alone find a swimmer in the dark. Nonetheless, Junayd insisted that they keep patrolling. If he were the swimmer, these were the very conditions he would take advantage of.

*****

Maymun and Nasuh traversed windblown streets, pelted by a stinging rain, and arrived at the place where the rope had been stored only to find that it had disappeared. "Now what do we do?" Maymun asked in an annoyed tone.

"We look for it. They might have let him down the wall in a different place. But I would not want to be in these waters tonight."

"Ugh, no," Maymun agreed, shivering.

They found the rope, but it was guarded by an alert, lone sentry huddling in a cloak, his attention fixed on the roiling dark waters below. The two assassins had little choice; they didn't even discuss the options. The sentry died from a broken neck and his body was tossed over the walls, then the assassins settled down and waited to see if the swimmer would return that night.

Out in the bay, with the gusty wind causing small waves to splash over the sides of the boat, the cold and unhappy men huddled under their cloaks and waited and watched. Finally, even Khuzaymah had had enough.

"I cannot believe that anyone could survive in this,' he told his crew. "Turn around; we are going back to the beach." Just as he said this, one of the others noticed a splashing quite close by. "Wait!" he called out. "Row over there. Quickly! Row hard," he instructed; his tone was urgent now.

The closer they came, the more sure they were that there was a swimmer in the water, but something was wrong. Andreas finally saw their objective when he was only a few lengths away. A man was struggling weakly against the waves and making little progress.

"Hey!" Khuzaymah called out. "Stop, you!" Then, "Row harder, men, he's trying to get away!"

The swimmer was indeed trying to get away, but from Khuzaymah's perspective he was losing his battle with the agitated water. Khuzaymah was surprised that the swimmer had even made it this far.

They came alongside the man, but he shook his head at the outstretched hands and pulled away from them with a cry. "No, by God, I shall not be a prisoner!" he gurgled as he swallowed some water. He sank, and they thought he might have drowned, but he surfaced a few strokes away. This time he looked back at them and called, "I curse you, Frans! I go to my judgment!" With that he sank out of sight again, and no matter where they rowed for the next half hour, calling all the while, there was no sign of him.

People on the ships nearest to them were beginning to take an unwelcome interest in their activities, so they pulled for shore. It was a disconsolate, cold, and wet group that reported to Talon in his tent.

"We could not catch him, nor persuade him to surrender to us, Lord," Khuzaymah told him unhappily. "He seemed to prefer a watery grave to our company. I saw him go down. He died of exhaustion, it seemed to me." The others nodded their agreement.

"Well, at least we know that avenue of information is shut off. I think it is time for our spies to come out of the city."

*****

366

As if he had read Talon's mind, Nasuh mentioned that they were on day five of their intended stay in the city, and it was time to leave, as he would be expecting them that evening. They were crouched in the musty hideout again and it was dark outside.

"What do we do about her?" Maymun asked the question that had been haunting both of them for some time now. "We cannot take her with us."

"She has no family and will starve if we leave her," Nasuh remarked with a scowl. He was unhappy with the situation. "Could we not take her?" He glanced over at their small charge, who was asleep at this time, looking very thin and vulnerable.

"How would we do that? Toss her into the sea, and then climb down and pick her up?" Maymun was just as unhappy about the situation.

"You might be forgetting something, my brother," Nasuh remarked thoughtfully. "The rope."

There was a pause before Maymun spoke. "Ah, yes, I'd forgotten that. But also, there is a chance that we might be waiting a long time at the base of the walls. If we have a rope, perhaps we can climb down the land side nearer to the beach?"

"Lord Talon isn't going to be pleased," Nasuh mumbled, but he had decided that they could not leave the child behind. Somehow, the little waif had won them over, once she had recovered from her initial fright, and she had provided them with genuinely useful information. "We'll make our peace with Lord Talon when that time comes," Nasuh told his companion.

"It's agreed, then, we try for the beach?"

"Better tell her what we intend, I suppose."

They woke her and told her what they intended.

"What will happen to me when you bring me to your friends?" was all she asked, with her huge luminous eyes frightened and questioning.

"Lord Talon will work something out, Naida. He is very wise." Nasuh attempted to reassure her.

"The first thing he is going to do is to make sure the little monkey has a bath!" Maymun murmured." We'd best hope that Brandt and his flesh-eating Saxons don't get to her before Lord Talon does!"

Nasuh snorted with amusement, then frowned and admonished his companion. "She has ears, Brother, don't frighten her before we have even started. She will be scared out of her wits when she sees them anyway."

Somewhat mollified, but clearly apprehensive, Naida nodded her head and agreed.

So it was that, close to midnight, all three were crouched near the parapet overlooking the rocky beach. They had no idea as to whether the boat had arrived or not; the weather had deteriorated to such an extent that both counted it as unlikely. They, however, could not wait any longer. Their food had run out, and they were very hungry. It was time to leave, no matter what.

Their biggest problem was not the rope. They found that easily enough, coiled in its old location, waiting for the swimmer to materialize. The citizens of the city were still waiting for their hero to return, with, perhaps, good news.

Their problem was that the guards appeared to be much more vigilant. Not one but two sentries were patrolling the length of wall. Some kind of distraction would be needed, but in the end they were prepared to take drastic action.

Naida provided an answer, "Are you frightened of those men up there?" she whispered. They were on the ground looking up at the battlements where men patrolled.

There were indignant intakes of breath. "No, you little scarecrow!" Maymun snapped back, "but we need them out of the way so that we can get down the rope."

"I could yell something from down here and distract them, perhaps?" she suggested.

'How, then, would you be able to join us up there?" came the skeptical reply.

"I know my way about. I can lead them off and then get back to you. You won't leave me?" she demanded of them, sounding fearful.

"No, but you need to be very careful. We don't want to leave a trail of bodies," muttered Maymun.

The sentries met again and were exchanging gossip when things changed abruptly. Neither of the two sentries in question was prepared for the scream that came from just below their feet in the darkness, near some stone steps. Both whirled and one pointed.

"That was a child!" one of them called to the other. The two men rushed down the steps to find out what had happened. Despite the fact that the screaming continued, it appeared to be moving. Bewildered, they peered around them, standing at the base of the steps, wondering which way to run.

At the top on the battlements, two dark shadows raced to the parapet and tied the rope off, letting it fall loosely to the rocks below. One of them waved in the general direction of the screams, and then crouched, waiting. It was only a minute later that a skinny form came scampering hard along the ramparts to run full tilt into the arms of the waiting Nasuh, who grasped her and then growled urgently, "Climb onto my back and hang on!"

She scrambled onto his back and clung tightly, almost choking him with her desperate grip as he hastened to seize the rope and clamber over the parapet. He slid down as fast as he could, with Maymun standing guard and watching for the two sentries, who were on their way back. Before Nasuh had even reached the ground, Maymun seized the rope and, without ceremony, slid down after him. Nasuh landed heavily, with Naida clinging to his neck, and headed rapidly for the shelter of the rocks and the deeper darkness.

He shook the child off and pressed her down into cover, and they waited for Maymun to join them.

"Time to get to the camp. Come along, little one," Nasuh told her, and took her hand to guide her over the rocks as they headed for safety.

They arrived at the camp to find that people were still awake. They were challenged by alert guards, who expressed delight at their arrival, and word was sent to Lord Talon to expect them. He was at the entrance of his candlelit tent to greet the new arrivals, and was as surprised as everyone else to see the little girl with his two assassins.

"I don't remember telling you to take hostages," he remarked with a smile, as he scrutinized the two tired men and their young ward. "Who is this?"

"An orphan who helped us, who we could not leave behind, Lord," Maymun said, carefully. "We could not leave her to starve to death," he added in an even more defensive tone.

"No, I suppose not," Talon remarked. "Well, she is here now, so we need to get her taken care of by some of the women, and then we can decide what to do with her."

He sent Diondre running off to find one of the Greek women who had come with them from Kantara. The child was staring around fearfully as she clutched at Nasuh's tunic, as though to prevent him from disappearing.

"It's all right, Naida," he patted her on her thin shoulder. "You are safe now, and a woman is coming to take care of you. And she will see to it that you are fed." Nasuh's stomach growled.

After Naida was led away, the men turned their attention to food that Talon ordered for them and the latest events. For nearly two hours Nasuh and Maymun described what they had learned and what they had found out about the swimmer. "And they are still waiting for his return," Maymun added.

"I can put your minds at rest about that," Talon told them. "He drowned while trying to escape our people in the bay."

Chapter 25

Raiders

Who soars through air without being stricken
Is a fly soon crushed in a net or prison;
And the ant lifting it limb is a sign;
Its fall is near, for an arrow will strike him.
—Eli Ben Josef

During the next few weeks, the defenders took their ease behind the high stone walls of Acre, where they starved while the besiegers licked their wounds, died of them, and squabbled. There was one thing that irritated Talon more than anything else: inactivity when there was really much that could be done.

Salah ad-Din and his army made sure that the Christians did not become complacent; their sallies from the mountains to attack the rear of the crusader army increased in frequency and ferocity. It was after one such skirmish that a disgruntled, harried Lord D'Onston paid a visit Talon one evening.

"I'm always a little nervous as to whether I shall leave this place in one piece," he confessed to Talon with a sideways look at Junayd. "You and your people have a reputation for being dangerous. People think you might even be cannibals and you a magician," he laughed but just a little bit nervously.

"Well you are right about one thing Lord D'Onstan. If Junayd thinks you have offended me in any way you will know, because a group of Saxons will appear accompanied by two Welsh archers, all of them sharpening their eating knives. It is hungry work being at a siege!"

D'Onstan chuckled but still glanced about him. The Saxons were nowhere to be seen. However he did notice something that baffled him.

"What is that you are chewing on?" he demanded. His curiosity was piqued because while they were speaking Talon and Junayd were crunching down on something long and fibrous, and evidently enjoying it.

"It's sugar cane," Talon told him. "Here, take some. Don't swallow its pith, just chew on it. You'll like it."

D'Onston tentatively chewed on the stick that Junayd proffered. His expression changed to one of bliss. "Oh, God! Where did this come from?" he demanded. "It is sooo sweet!"

"It has just come into season. My people bring it with them from Cyprus for us poor, suffering, and starving soldiers here in the midst of battle."

D'Onston was too busy enjoying his stick to comment, but the skeptical look he gave Talon from under brows was eloquent. He finally stopped chewing and wiped his mouth with a contented sigh. His blue eyes twinkled with amusement.

He looked over at Junayd who was watching him with his dark eyes. "Your man looks as though he is ready to stick a knife in me, Talon."He murmured. "Does he dislike me so?"

"If he disliked you, Lord D'Onston he would have asked me if he could kill you, but he has not so you are perfectly safe," Talon assured him. "For the time being anyway..." He smiled.

D'Onston's eyes flicked back and forth between the two men seated in front of him. He looked somewhat relieved but then added. "None of you look very starved, Talon. You appear to look after your men very well certainly as compared to anywhere else in this pestilent place." His eyes strayed to a ripe-looking melon that was also on the table. It had been cut open by Junayd in preparation for their meal and the inside looked enticing. A light aroma drifted to D'Onstan's nostrils which caused him to salivate. Talon noticed and said, "Would you like some melon? It is known by the Arabs as *easal al-batikh*."

Lord D'Onston nodded hungrily. "Why, yes, if it pleases you, Talon. But after this, this sugar cane as you call it, I'd believe it if someone told me that you and your men dine better than the kings!"

"Don't tell them that, at least not until the next ship comes in," Talon laughed. "Now, what brings you here? You didn't come here just to chew on our sugar cane... or did you?"

D'Onston chuckled. "No, but please allow me to take some of the cane and that fruit over there to the princesses, and perhaps even the king?" he begged.

Talon looked thoughtful. "I'm not so sure about that king of yours. He quarrels with everyone!" he said, the corners of his mouth downturned in a lugubrious expression. "There will be a price for some of this melon of course," he added almost as an afterthought.

D'Onston sighed. "He's your king now, Talon, and there's no getting away from it. But I shall give more to the princesses. They do seem to be in need of some comforting food, and this would be perfect for them. The mood is glum in the royal tent at present," he said. Then, as Talon's words sunk in, he looked startled.

"What price?" he demanded, realizing there had been a caveat.

"The price is that you tell me what is going on in the royal pavilion, and then you receive a slice of melon."

"But that's—that's bribery, Talon!" D'Onston sounded indignant.

"Hmm, yes, it is. A slice?"

D'Onston was almost drooling. Pride fought with need across his face.

Junayd cut himself a slice of the melon and started to eat it, the sweet juice dribbling down his short beard. He closed his eyes in apparent ecstasy as he chewed, then he opened them and stared wide eyed at D'Onston, who glared back reproachfully. Junayd didn't even bother to wipe the juice off his chin.

"He comes here to eat our food and to spy on you for that king, Master," Junayd stated, as he finished the slice of melon.

"I know, but I somehow doubt that the king pays much attention. It's more likely to be the queen who listens. But no matter, I quite like him," Talon told his assassin. They both looked at D'Onston.

"These are our last fruits before the ship comes in, my friend, and we intend to eat them with or without your help," Talon murmured, pretending to look disinterested in the expressions playing across D'Onston's face.

"You are a wretch, Talon!" D'Onston shouted. "Please don't do this to me!" he begged, but then, "Oh, very well, I will tell you what I can, but it must not be bandied about like any old gossip. These are the royals! God help me, but what have I been reduced to?" he lamented ruefully.

Talon pretended to look hurt. "You know perfectly well, my friend, that nothing goes further than here when we talk. Junayd, stop that sloppy behavior, and give our poor friend a slice before he dies of envy from watching you," he ordered his now grinning Companion.

There was silence as D'Onston took a huge bite out of his slice of melon and closed his eyes in pure delight as he allowed the juice to slip down his throat. "Ah, me," he crooned. "Dear God, thank you for this bounty!" Some of the juice ran down his chin. He swiped it off and licked his fingers before continuing to eat.

"I think you should really be thanking my farmers," Talon murmured.

They watched in amused silence as D'Onston finished off two slices and wiped his beard with the back of his grubby sleeve. Then, with a cup of red wine placed in front of him, he brought Talon and Junayd up to speed on the activities going on in the royal pavilions. Notably, Princess Theodora was now Richard's concubine and Princess Berengaria was pining, while Princess Joanna, who could do nothing about the situation, was seething. His tone became somewhat sad as he recounted how much Princess Joanna had sacrificed for her brother, who treated both her and his wife with casual disregard.

"I heard that there was an attack on the rear of the army the other day," Talon commented.

"The king is very angry and frustrated. We cannot do very much about the attacks, Talon," D'Onston complained. "They appear so rapidly, with their yells and flying arrows, that we cannot counter them effectively; and before we rally they are gone, leaving some of our people dead or wounded and everyone out of sorts. Sometimes they actually get into our camp, and then it's mayhem until they are driven off!" He glanced up at Talon with a look of frustration on his face.

Talon cast a quick glance at Junayd, who was listening closely. "Quick and nimble, are they?" he asked, a thoughtful expression beginning to form.

"Well, they have these smaller horses, and yes, they're very nimble, a bit like yours," D'Onston told him. "Why? What are you thinking?" he demanded.

'I am thinking," Talon said slowly, "that two can play at this game. Tell our king that I shall do something about the raids."

As he watched D'Onston leaving that evening, Talon was not sure whether the cunning man had come to plant the idea in his head, or whether it might have already been there, waiting to be brought out into the open.

*****

Not long after this discussion, on a dry mid-afternoon, Talon was informed that one of his ships was approaching.

Excited men gathered to welcome one of their own vessels from Cyprus. It turned out to be Guy's galley that dropped anchor with a splash, and Talon, as he stood on the shoreline watching the final preparations, noticed someone on the deck who had been on his mind for quite a while. Loud greetings were exchanged between the crew and those on shore. Guy's voice was booming over everyone else.

"Look who I have brought with me!" he shouted, gesturing toward Reza, who waved at them. "Now they are doomed! They might as well surrender this very day!"

Reza took the first boat ride from the ship, jumped out of the boat before it had even grounded, and splashed his way eagerly to embrace the equally delighted Talon, who received him with open arms. "You old dog!" Talon shouted. "I didn't expect to see you any time soon!"

They held each other at arm's length and scrutinized one another. "You've lost weight again, Brother." Reza flashed his white teeth in a smile. "Are you well?"

"That's what happens during sieges, Brother. I am well, most of us are well, but you look as though you have gained weight! Loafing around in the flesh pots of the City! Was the food good in Constantinople?"

"Much to tell, Brother, but—"

"Theodora and her son. They are well, too?" Talon interrupted.

"I was about to tell you," Reza said. "They came back from that sorry place with me and are returned to Kantara."

He noticed how Talon's expression relaxed, and commented, "You've been worried about her, haven't you, Brother?"

"I have, Reza," Talon admitted. "Your tone implies that all was not well over there. I want to hear all about it, but first we have much to do before we can find a quiet place to talk. There are a few people here, not many, mind you, with short memories who might have forgotten who you are! But all will be glad to see you."

Reza laughed at his brother's teasing. A small, excited crowd was growing behind the joyful friends, led by the Companions, Brandt, and the archers. "Go on and speak to them while I talk to Guy, who is probably going to crush my ribs," Talon told him.

It wasn't long before Reza was surrounded by the Companions and many others who wanted to greet him. He disappeared among them, all of them talking at once. Talon smiled to himself. Reza's appearance would improve morale enormously.

Then Talon found himself in one of Guy's famous embraces. He struggled for breath. "Guy! Put me down this minute! I am your Lord and I'm supposed to possess some dignity!" he gasped. He landed unsteadily back on his feet as the giant released him, still exuberantly shouting his delight at seeing his chief. "Bugger the dignity, Talon! I am glad to see you are still alive in this stink hole!"

"It's always good to see you too, Guy." Talon grinned, adjusting his disheveled tunic. "I'm happy that you brought Reza with you."

"He only managed to come along because his wife and the Lady Rav'an permitted it, and only then if he swore a dreadful oath to come back with me on the return trip." Guy gave Talon one of his ferocious grins. "They were very clear about it, too. No one wants either of you here, to begin with, least of all the Ladies Rav'an and Jannat, but they understand that you are under the king's command and cannot gainsay him. Reza, on the other hand, is at *their* command, just like the rest of us."

"Ah," Talon murmured with a smile. "I do understand. But tell me, my old friend, you brought the lady Theodora back with you, so there were problems in Constantinople?"

Guy sobered quickly and cast a glance in the direction Reza had taken. Reza and his Companions had disappeared, but all around the two men there was much bustle as crewmen and soldiers, pressed into labor by Brandt and his commanders, brought the precious supplies ashore.

"There were problems, Talon. But, from what I understand from Yosef and Reza, and the little imparted by Her Ladyship Theodora, those two dealt with them effectively enough. I shall leave it to Reza to tell you the rest, as he can do so better than I. However, to put your mind at ease on their account, they are safe and back with the family, and we even managed to bring her brother out of that unhappy place. The City has changed, and not, from my observations, for the better."

Talon nodded his head slowly. "Very well, Guy. We will talk later, as you are going to be busy here for a while. Remember the physician, Epiktitos?"

Guy shook his head. "No, I don't know him."

"No matter, this man has saved the lives of many of our men here, and while I would put the lady Theodora ahead of any physician alive, he has proved his worth these last months. I shall introduce you to him, as he will have instructions for you."

Guy clapped Talon on the shoulder. "God be praised you are well, Talon. News is very sparse, and it is good for you to have someone like that who knows what he is about. I shall deal with all this" — he waved his arm at the activity all around — "then we shall talk." He gave a wink. "I have a letter for you from Her Ladyship. I also have some of the precious wine and arak to ease the pain of being here. Dear God Almighty, but you can smell this place leagues out to sea! Perhaps not so much *here*," he continued pointedly, glancing around at the well-ordered tents and the lack of fetid puddles that existed in the other encampments.

Talon sighed. "Not today, as it is dry, but we will be having some rain in a couple of days, so tie the boat down well, Guy. After a downpour the sun comes up, but so does just about every stinking object buried in the mud, if you know what I mean."

*****

Guy was obliged to sail within the week, as he was to take the badly wounded back with him to Kantara. Talon was very pleased that the wounded would now have the benefit of Theodora's skill, combined with the nursing skills of Rav'an and Jannat. Despite the competence of Epiktitos, some of the more seriously wounded were suffering from infections, which were the slow killers of this siege. Talon knew, only too well, how hellish conditions were in some of the other armies' sick areas. He had visited the English infirmary to see for himself, but had been forced to leave, unable to stomach the stink of suppurating flesh, the filth and the despair that had assaulted him.

He wanted to read the letter from Rav'an, so went off to sit on a sand bank overlooking the sea and the clustered ships. There, with the sounds of his camp behind him that had become just a murmur, along with the lapping of the small waves, he broke the seal of Rav'an's letter.

My Talon,

I pray that God is treating you well in that unhappy place. I can only hope you have been protected from the horrors, about which we hear rumors and those few truths via pigeons from Boethius and Dimitri. You are badly missed, by myself of course, my love, but also by Fariba, who misses the evening stories. Her command to you is that you stop whatever you are doing and come back at once to carry out your bounded duties here on her behalf. I am shedding tears as I write this, my Talon, because I am so worried that you are in danger.

Thus far, all is quiet in our land. The castle is well guarded by Palladius, who is to be commended for his diligence and attention to duty. Perhaps he is a little too enthusiastic, but he has taken your admonishment to guard us all very earnestly, and for that he has my gratitude. The Companions, under the ever-watchful eyes of Dar'an, are active in all manner of secretive ways. They spend much time out in the forests, meeting with the goat herders, boys and men, to ensure that no one can approach our land without our knowing long before they could perpetrate any mischief. For that, I rest more easily.

The best news of all is that our sister, Theodora, is back with us, with her son, Damion, and her brother, Alexios. Jannat and I are truly delighted to have her back, but Alexios is a very frail man. Although close in age to you, my Prince, he appears to be many years older. I shall allow Reza to tell you that story, as he is bringing this letter with him. Rostam is doing very well as the commander, under the discreet guidance of Dar'an. While I know Dar'an is chaffing at the lack of excitement and would much rather be with you, I have felt bound to keep him here with me, while I allowed Yosef to go with Reza, for Dar'an is the only person amongst the Companions who can manipulate the catapult, and even the dragon in the courtyard, should things come to that desperate point, so he must stay. However, he has taken Rostam under his wing and is teaching him all about that infernal Chinese powder and how to make it. A mixed blessing, because he also shows him how to test it. Jannat and I now have to listen to the crash and bang of the catapult, and the booms at the base of the mountain, which is a weekly exercise, as they practice what Rostam has learned in the dark recesses of this castle. Their jubilation is just as noisy. I hope to God that he learns well and does not blow us all to heaven before our time. I can only imagine what the villagers think of it all, and what mischievous stories they tell others about the terrible magician in the castle.

The servants, Palladius, and the soldiers who guard us, who already consider Dar'an one of your magical circle, are now treating Rostam in the same manner. I trust it will not go to his head. Dar'an says our boy is a quick learner. I have brought Rostam with myself and Henry to attend the magistrate's court. While you know only too well what a trial that can be, he is respectful and intuitive during the sessions. Or is this just a mother's pride talking?

The villagers are generally behaving and keeping the peace between themselves, while the crops are thus far doing well. Perhaps a little more rain would help, as this is a dry year.

You will be glad to know that the towers at the harbor entrance are now fully completed. Henry has expressed confidence that they can sink any vessel that is unwelcome well before it comes close to the entrance. Henry has installed the braziers on the top of the towers, which, if alight, can be seen from the castle. He has assumed the village governance and our remaining Saxons are assisting him whenever there is a need for restraint of anyone who becomes unruly.

The news on the rest of the island is composed of rumor, clarified by occasional facts from Dimitri and Boethius and our other spies, who do their best to provide real information, even if very brief. Boethius sent his daughter, Irene, to stay with us, as the times are somewhat uncertain and he knows full well that this is a safe haven. That girl is turning into something of a beauty, and I may have to keep an eye on our own boy. The two of them are as thick as thieves whenever he is free of his duties with Dar'an. Jannat and I are keeping our eyes on them.

Famagusta appears to be quiet. Dimitri says the palace is a ghost of its former glory, having been first pillaged by the English king, and then by the citizens who rushed in there when the last of the English had departed. The governance of the island is apparently still in the hands of the twelve or so Knights Templar, who keep to their castle outside Limassol, leaving the island very much to its own devices. There is trouble brewing in that area, according to Boethius, as the islanders, seeing their new king has abandoned them, do not feel the need to pay any taxes to these surly Templar overlords. Irene says that no one wants to get downwind of them, as they stink, despite the availability of fresh water and baths!

It remains for me to tell you that my hopes and my love stay with you, and my fervent prayer that you can come home to me, to us, before too long. I fret that you will find yourself in a similar situation as the last time, and I dread what might happen. I *shall demand a full report from our brother when he returns. He was no sooner home than he expressed a wish to join you! You can just imagine how annoyed Jannat was, but at the same time, while we do not understand why, you men always want to be in harm's way, and Reza would have been like an angry badger if he had to remain. She finally agreed. He is under oath to be on the return voyage with Guy. I am trusting you to ensure that even if you cannot be on that ship yourself, then he will be.*

As ever, you have my eternal love. You are greatly missed, my Talon.

Rav'an.

Talon smiled to himself when he came to the end of the letter and stared out to sea. His thoughts were interrupted by the arrival of Reza, who dropped down to sit on the sand next to him.

*****

They were still talking hours later, when the sun began to set, in a flare of reds and deep ochre colors, turning the clouds in the west crimson. The sea was as calm as a bronze mirror as the two men stood up and dusted sand off their clothes.

"Come with me, Brother," Talon said. "I know why you came, but none of this sad play here is what you came for." He waved his arm in the general direction of the city and the haphazard encampments. Reza glanced up at him. "What do you mean, Brother?" he asked.

Talon turned and looked at him. "I have a plan, and you are the perfect fellow to share it with."

"This sounds interesting," Reza commented with a grin. "You do know that I am bound on oath to return with Guy?"

Talon nodded. "Yes, hmm, I do, and if you don't want to do this, I shall quite understand. You do remember how to play tent pegs, don't you?" he asked.

"Now you are being really insulting, my brother! You know perfectly well I know that game and, in fact, I beat you the last time we played it!" He had noticed the twinkle in Talon's eyes, so he pretended indignation.

"Well, I have been thinking about conducting a raid of our own, turning trick against Salah al-Din's men, who are so fond of playing it on the Franks and Normans. I know you are getting old and Jannat would not approve, but—" He got no further. Reza almost jumped on him, pummeling his shoulder. "You know perfectly well I want to go on this... this raid!" Reza shouted in Farsi. "How could you think otherwise, Brother?" He stomped around pretending rage.

A laughing Talon had to dodge his flailing fist. "Ouch, that's my sword arm you are disabling!" He rubbed his shoulder with a rueful laugh.

They had drawn a little crowd of amused spectators by now with their antics. "Yosef, will you keep this barbarian off me!" Talon called out to Yosef, who was at the forefront of the group, grinning from ear to ear.

"Serves you right for being... for being foxy!" Reza snapped.

"Well, now that we have established that you want to come along, if you can promise me that you will not get killed or wounded, then this is what I want to do," Talon told his excited brother. "Yosef, would you want to come along, too?" he addressed their equally excited friend.

"Just try to stop me, Lord!" Yosef said happily.

That evening was a merry one. The Companions were very happy to see their comrades and their Master Reza after the long, dreary weeks of the siege; but also, the prospect of some action galvanized them. Brandt was there, and Talon allowed the two senior archers a place at the rough-hewn table where the fresh food was stacked.

They drank the good wine of Kantara and ate fresh food delivered from Kantara that very day, supplemented by fish the soldiers had drawn with nets and lines from the sea nearby. The flour had been put to good use and was now part of the pies that dotted the table, filled with chunks of fresh meat or foul over which the cook had poured a dark, tasty gravy that made more than one man roll his eyes and look to the heavens. The fresh fruit was there for all, as the physician Epiktitos had insisted that everyone eat that, too, telling Talon that a diet of meat alone would lead to the same sickness the kings were suffering from. No one wanted that so they did as they were told.

The men and their lords plotted while they ate.

"We must accomplish this raid before the rain, which I suspect is going to arrive in the next couple of days," Talon told them. "You know how sticky and impossible it can be during and just after. So we go in hard while it is still dry and get out quickly, and then, hopefully, it will rain all over what we have left behind."

Reza snickered. "So we wait for your knee to start hurting, then we go and play at tent pegs!"

*****

Two mornings later, a few hours before dawn, Talon awoke to a nudge of his boot. No one would dare to wake him any other way. He was awake in an instant and on his feet a moment later. He spent the next few minutes checking on his weapons and preparing to mount his horse. All around him in the predawn darkness, his men were doing the same as he, looking to their weapons and horses. All of them moving like ghosts. Their position was just on the edge of a neglected olive grove, within a league of the Arab army.

Salah ad-Din might not have been able to dislodge the Christians from their siege of Acre with his still-depleted forces, but he could and did send his light cavalry to harass them. It had proved to be an effective strategy, and as a result the Christians were constantly on edge with yet another peril to unsettle their minds, along with plagues, illness, and gangrenous wounds that refused to heal.

Yesterday Talon had gone to King Richard and told him what he planned. The king was sickening from some unknown disease which utterly baffled the leeches, but which the Greek physicians were calling *arnaldia*. Richard had nodded weakly and agreed that retaliation was needed. "Your speedy mounts should be able to deliver a sting, Lord Talon. Go with God and hurt them as much as you can."

Talon needed no further encouragement and wasted no time. He and Reza had gathered their Companions and several of the Greek riders who came from the villages of Kantara, to number a good score of excellent riders skilled with lances, swords, and bows.

"We are going to play a game of tent pegging, which in some ways is like chogan," he had told his happy men, who were itching for some excitement. Sieges were not the most rewarding of occupations, and his bored men wanted some action.

Now they were all mounted, and the sky to the east was displaying the first streaks of light, heralding the dawn which was now very close.

"We go in silence softly until I give the signal," Talon said. "Then we ride hard, but in total silence. Not a shout from anyone! Do you understand?" he demanded in a hoarse whisper.

There were nods and sounds of acknowledgement from the dark figures in front of him. He lifted his hand and put his horse into a light canter, which brought him very quickly to the crest of the low hill overlooking the still-sleeping encampment below.

Talon, with Reza alongside, carried right on over the hill and down the other side, hearing only the muted pounding hooves of their men's mounts immediately behind him. They aimed for a gap in the defenses that hours of observation the previous day had shown them was a weak point. Their horses' hooves were covered with sacking so their presence would be known only at the last moment. It had been Reza's suggestion, and Talon was glad of it.

He raised his right hand with his lance held on high, which was the signal, then put his horse into a flat-out gallop, straight for the long, deep ditch that appeared before him. The two men cleared the ditch and then rode apart. It was a small hurdle to cross, and he knew his men were well able to do the same. Talon's eyes were darting about, looking for the small targets ahead of him. Of a sudden he heard frantic shouts of alarm from the sentries, who had only just become aware of the danger coming out of the north.

They rode past the bewildered sentries, who were taken down by a hail of arrows, and then Talon saw what he had been looking for. The tents were held by ropes, tied to pegs made of wood, which had been hammered into the ground. He lowered his lance and aimed it at the base of the first peg. He knew that if he missed Junayd would catch it while he focused on another.

His horse was galloping hard and crouched over its neck with his lance point lowered so that the sharp tip went directly into the base of the first peg. He felt the shock of its impact, and then he was past, with his lance rotated sharply behind him. The peg that he had captured was dragged out of the ground by the lance but then flew off the point, jerked off by the securing rope, whereupon the tent began to sag. He twirled the lance forward, looking for another tent. He rode past the next one, confident that Junayd would snag it, and if he missed then Khuzaymah behind him would manage. His band of men was in two lines, galloping along the strip between the enemy tents. Talon led one column, Reza the other with Yosef right behind him.

A man ran out of the tent directly in front of Talon and whirled to face him, sword in hand, but it was too late for him to defend himself. Talon's lance struck him in the middle of his chest and threw him backward. Talon again allowed the lance to rotate behind him, then felt a hard tug as he rode on. He just managed to hang onto the deadly weapon, swing it forward with a scattering of a light stream of blood, and again focus on finding another tent peg to lift.

All around him alarms were being sounded as trumpets blared and sleepy men shouted and called to one another. But Talon and his men were well practiced at this art. On the other side of the tent Talon and Junayd had just passed, the same action had been carried out by Reza, Yosef, and other Companions. Right behind the two teams of tent peggers were the remainder of the group of riders, and they were spearing and shooting arrows at close range into the struggling occupants of the collapsed tents as the raiders rode deeper into the camp.

Talon watched for any coordinated resistance, which would form as they penetrated deeper into the enemy encampment. After the fifth large tent had been dropped onto its unfortunate occupants, he shouted one command loud enough for Reza and his riders to hear and hauled his sweating horse to a halt, while behind him his men, alerted to this signal, carried out the same maneuver. Their nimble animals spun around, almost as one.

All the bowmen among them, including the Companions, Talon and Reza, now loosed arrow after arrow at anyone rash enough to approach. Resuming a gallop, they tipped braziers over to cause fires, slashed at ropes that held still-standing tents, and toppled racks of spears. One or two riders managed to seize torches, which they tossed into the openings of even more tents. As an added distraction, Khuzaymah tossed a small grass-woven bucket of the Chinese powder over one tent that he passed, covering a bunch of struggling men; one of the other men threw a torch at it. The tent blazed alight with a suddenness that stunned the enemy witnesses.

It was not to go all the way in the raider's favor, however. On Reza's side, Maymun, who was right behind Yosef, ran into a flying tent peg and a rope, which promptly wrapped itself around his horse's front legs. The horse gave a frightened whinny and went down, while Maymun gave a desperate shout as he threw himself clear. Yosef reacted very quickly; he spun his horse on its haunches and jumped it back toward the Companion, who was scrambling to his feet. Another of their men lanced a would-be attacker who tried to seize the opportunity to strike at Maymun. Yosef hooked his elbow and leaned over as he rode flat out toward Maymun. Maymun leapt for Yosef's arm and was hauled round, onto the back of Yosef's mount, which he spurred hard for their exit route. No one else interfered with their escape, much to Talon's relief. He had only just observed the latter part of the incident.

The entire action had taken but a few long minutes. Talon and his men departed, leaving behind chaos and frantic activity. There were a few bold souls who were very quick to respond to the attack and followed the raiders, but Talon and Reza had prepared for this and fled with their pack of bandits through a small defile. Here Dewy and Caradog were waiting with several of their own archers, and brought down all the pursuers.

When he was sure they were clear of the camp and all pursuit, Talon halted his blowing animal and cocked an ear at the distant chaos that still reigned in the Arab camp.

"A good day's work," he commented to a jubilant Reza and their men. Just as he said this, a large drop of rain fell on his shoulder. He waved to Dewy and Caradog, and the archers scurried off to mount their own horses. They would have to be shepherded back to the camp, none of them being as good horsemen as the Companions.

"We must ride away before the hornets rally and come after us," Talon called to them, and wheeled his horse to lead the way back at a canter toward the hills as the rain intensified. Then they turned sharply west toward their own lines, where they were greeted by English guards, who at first didn't recognize the now-soaked and bedraggled band. An exasperated Talon had to shout at them in bad English over the noise of the downpour, with thunder raging overhead. It wasn't until Brandt arrived and told the guards to stand down that they could advance, after the barriers were dragged aside to allow the raiders to trot their horses through.

"How did it go, Lord?" Brandt called, swiping rain from his beard as he peered up at Talon.

"Much as we planned, Brandt. Come along with us and we shall tell you all about it. Thank you for greeting us. The rain came exactly on time, too. But those fellows are not very friendly—or grateful." Talon jerked a thumb at the glowering sentries as he and his horsemen splashed their way toward their own camp.

"Fucking idiots from that English king's army. They think anyone who doesn't look like them must be Saracens, Lord." Brandt grinned at Reza. "You appear to have enjoyed yourself, Master Reza," he commented, as he stood aside for the horses to go by.

Reza barked a laugh. "I would not have missed it for the world, Brandt!" he told the huge Saxon, who slapped his thigh with glee. "Very happy to see you are all safe, Master Reza."

"I am not only happy that you came with us, Brother, and added your wisdom to the effort, but that you can now go home safely," Talon told Reza, pretending to sound solemn. "Not a word of this to the ladies when you get back!"

Reza winked. "Not a word. Those women made me promise to return, Brother. I wish I could stay," Reza replied, his tone sounding rueful.

"I, too, Brother, I too. Well, we managed to send a little message to the sultan. But they will be wiser to us the next time, I fear." Talon smiled to himself as he heard Dewy and Caradog bragging to Brandt.

"Des'perate it was out there! You sitting back here in com'fort while we was risking our very *lives,* we was, Bach!"

"Terri'fy-ing it was, Bach!" Called out the other.

"Bollocks!" Came the loud rejoinder from Brandt.

*****

Several hours later, a light drizzle still fell over the encampment of Salah ad-Din, and the sultan listened to the reports from the soaked men who had been in the middle of the recent attack. One of them had his left arm in a bloody sling.

"They came out of the north, Your Highness. Not a sound until they were almost upon us, in the camp itself!"

"Not the west where the Frans are? What do you mean, not a sound?" the sultan demanded. He sounded skeptical.

"Total silence, Lord. As God is my witness, they were like phantoms. They did not shout at all, they just galloped out of the darkness. It is as though even their horses fly on the air, they make so little noise!" the man with the wounded arm elaborated. "Then they took down the tents and killed whomsoever was unfortunate to be within, and those who stood in front of them."

"They surprised the sentries? They did all this in silence?"

392

"The surviving sentries had said all was well, but then suddenly there they were, Lord." There was quiet in the tent when the man, who was a low-level commander, finished.

The other man, who had come with him to make his report, continued. "They are *very* skilled at picking up tent pegs, Lord. They killed and destroyed everything in their path, and then they were gone, Lord."

"Why did our people not know to follow them and bring them to battle? Surely we were not that unprepared?" demanded Al-Adil, the Sultan's brother. He sounded angry, incredulous, and frustrated.

"Some brave souls did follow them, but none returned, Lord. We are still out looking for them. We... we lost them in the rain; their tracks have been obliterated." The two soaked officers were clearly upset. To Salah ad-Din's perceptive gaze, they were also fearful. Who was it that was using similar tactics to his own light cavalry, but even more effectively? A sharp, deadly attack that was not pressed home, but which nonetheless achieved its objective, instilling fear and uncertainty. This was the first such occurrence that had been reported to him. He was sure that none of the Christians he had encountered hitherto were capable of this kind of tactic. Who, then, was responsible?

"What do they look like, these riders?" he demanded. He rubbed his side. The pain was a real distraction, and had moved to almost encircle his midriff. Now it kept him awake at night. His physicians had recommended that he eat fruit and vegetables, as much as he could, to keep the illness at bay. He had woken from a restless doze that morning to hear the distant alarms.

"They dress as do we, Lord. I mean, more like the Turks and Kurds. They wear loose turbans, like the tribes, except that their turbans and robes are one color, dark, almost blue. They are covered all over, with only their eyes visible, and their horses are very agile. They are as quick and deadly as... as our own people," the man said reluctantly.

"So, they do not wear the clothes of the Christians?" Al-Adil said, with surprise in his tone.

"Do we have a quarrel with our Turks and Kurds?" Salah ad-Din asked with a thin, wry smile at his brother.

Al-Adil shrugged and grimaced, as though to say, there are always squabbles. But then he shook his head emphatically. "We do not have anyone within our ranks with that measure of a grudge, my lord," he told the sultan. "Least of all the Kurds, who are very loyal to you," he added.

The sultan agreed. The Kurds, while they had wanted to go home with the other tribes, had remained to see him through the winter. He had been very happy to have them. These men were superb horsemen, surely a match for whoever was trying to cause fear and uncertainty within the ranks of his army.

"Could it have been the Bedu who come up from the Sinai?" he queried, but then answered his own question. "No, they are only ever after booty. They would confine themselves to raids of caravans. *Anyone's* caravan," he said with a trace of bitterness. He relied upon the caravans to supply his much-needed equipment, grain, and salt from Egypt and Damascus, but the Bedu respected no one. Then who? Neither did he suspect the Nabateans who lived in the deserts to the east. They kept very much to themselves.

"It must then be from the ranks of the Christians. Perhaps the English king has men similar to ours, although I find that idea unlikely. All the same, our spies in the Christian camp should keep us better informed," he told his brother with some asperity, who nodded his head in agreement.

"I shall notify whomsoever we have to be more vigilant," he told the sultan. In fact, the spies for the Arab army were keeping the sultan well informed. The news had been passed along that King Philip of France and Richard of England were both sick with the *arnaldia*, an illness that caused fever, and the hair and the fingernails to fall out. It gave Salah ad-Din small comfort to know that his enemies were becoming as sick as he. Some days he could barely get out of bed. Meanwhile, there was this new threat to his peace of mind.

"They are very bold to attack us like this. We must anticipate these people. To start with, mount more guards in all corners. Double the patrols in our vicinity, and I want prisoners," he told his captains.

But as the days and nights went by, they would find sentries in the mornings leaning on their spears, quite dead. Men who bivouacked on the outskirts of the army began to wear haunted looks and moved their tents closer to one another. But then, even further into the encampment, tents would inexplicably catch fire, causing much distress as the crowded conditions allowed fires to spread quickly.

Chapter 26

Reza's Tale

Here from my Window I at once survey
The crowded City & resounding Sea,
In distant Views see Assian Mountains rise
And Lose their Snowy Summits in ye Skies.
Above those Mountains high Olympus Tow'rs
The Parliamental Seat of Heavenly Powers.

—"Overlooking Constantinople" by Mary Wortley Montagu

Reza stood on the after deck of the ship with Guy at the helm as the galley sailed north up the Hellespont, the southern seaway highway to Constantinople, two weeks after they had left Cyprus. When they arrived off the coast of the city called Abydos, Guy informed him this was the Byzantine city that guarded the entrance to the sea of Marmar at the other end of the Hellespont.

"We must stop at the city to replenish our water, but otherwise we don't have to tarry," the captain told him.

Guy took them unerringly through the gap in the rocks while Reza looked on with his heart in his mouth. He shook his head with awe at the seamanship his seafaring friend displayed.

"I have always been impressed by your navigation, Guy, but I did not know your skills went as far as this kind of thing," he told the captain when they were busy tying up alongside the quay.

"Henry took me through the first time, but since then, I've done this many times," Guy responded.

They went through the usual tedious process of bribing a petty official for docking rights, and then paid an exorbitant price for the water barrels. "They have stuck us for twice the real cost of the water and the privilege of docking, the swine," Guy told Reza, "but at least we can leave this pot hole and make our way to the city now."

*****

Reza, for one of the times in his life, was dumbstruck when he first saw the city in the distance. It loomed out of the early dawn like some magical creation from a glowing legend.

He could not believe that such a beautiful place could exist, rivaling his personal favorite of cities, Isfahan. He went forward to see better from the bows, while Guy stayed on the back deck and made sure they sailed around the peninsular without mishap or collision with any of the multitude of large and small ships plying in all directions.

Reza could only stare. The massive fortifications encircling the city seemed to go on forever and to rise straight out of the sea. Behind the fortifications, he could see a row of low, uneven hills, upon which were dense clusters of buildings of every shape and size. There were enormous, square-looking constructions with many pillars, and lesser buildings planted all over the green wooded hillsides. In the distance, he could see the domes of numerous churches rising among the red-tiled housing, denoting a pious population. What dominated the entire city, however, was an enormous complex of domes and towers that one of the sailors pointed out to him.

"There! See Master Reza? The Great Palace and the Hagia Sophia." There was reverence in his voice as he spoke.

These buildings were built on the highest point of the peninsular ridge to the right of the harbor, and the Hagia was, without doubt, the most magnificent building Reza had ever beheld. Apart from its general size, he could tell that the width of its dome was immense, and he wondered how men could build such a structure. Its dome dominated all, yet, clustered about the round, central building were several other smaller structures, each with a lesser dome. Reza gazed in awe at the most enormous and beautiful city in the world, which sprawled over a long tongue of land, jutting out into the Marmar Sea. He pointed to a huge construction with many arches near them. "What is that building over there, Alexios?"

"That is the Hippodrome, where they race chariots," the knowledgeable sailor replied. He began to point out many other places, from palaces to barracks, as they drew near the walls of the city. After three weeks of traveling, all the men were ready to step onto dry land and stay for a while.

*****

Two men made their way swiftly up the crowded hill, past vendors and market stalls that lines the streets, toward the entrance to the villa they sought. It was late afternoon, and Guy had warned them that the Greek administration didn't like people wandering the streets after dark. Because they were obviously foreigners, they would get short shrift from the night patrols, should they be intercepted.

Guy had been forced to stay on the ship because at any moment the customs official might appear, and it would go badly for the ship and its crew if there was no one in authority to greet him.

"We have time to see the place and to let Theo know we are here," Reza had said, "but we should probably stay on the ship tonight." And so Reza and Yosef had been rowed to the shore and sent on their way.

They came within sight of the gates belonging to the estate, but Yosef noticed something and held up his hand as a warning. Reza noticed it at the same time. Soldiers were hanging around the main gate, as though waiting for someone to appear from the villa.

Reza and Yosef melted into the darker shadows cast by the old cotton trees that lined the narrow street. They watched the soldiers for a while, then Reza nudged Yosef and whispered, "We are alongside the walls to the property. Have you heard any dogs?"

"No," responded Yosef. "Nor guards, other than that rabble up there."

"It's getting dark, and I, for one, do not wish to be found by any of these night patrols, nor those men, so why don't we go over the wall and then decide what to do," Reza whispered.

They scaled the wall and lay along its top, assessing the grounds and the villa, which was a jumble of attached buildings about a hundred paces away on a rise above the gardens. Reza noted that there had once been a vineyard in the area just to the north of their location. It looked run down and neglected. In fact, even in the darkness, he could tell there was an aura of neglect about the place. His gaze was drawn to the buildings and he could just see that a small procession was departing the main building; a box-like litter was being carried by some slaves, and there were other men carrying torches. The two Companions lay as still as stones on the top of the wall and watched the procession move slowly toward the gates, where the group of soldiers was assembled. The litter was carried out of the gates and disappeared up the hill. The men at the gate lounged about, seemingly on guard.

"Well, now we know that someone lives here and has just departed, so we will go and take a look," Reza whispered.

The two men slid off the wall and vanished into the nearest clump of unkempt bushes, where they paused. Dogs were uppermost in their minds. Talon and Guy had talked about huge creatures that the Greeks used as guard dogs, and neither of them wanted to encounter one. However, all was quiet, other than the crickets and the occasional low boom of a bullfrog in a pond somewhere nearby.

Like two phantoms, they slipped across the open ground and paused again, close to the house. There was a faint glow from one of the windows, which Reza pointed to. Slowly, and listening very hard, they slid along the side of the house until they were on the flags of the loggia and right under the shutters of the window. Reza peered in. There was an oil lamp burning low on a table next to a bed, which was occupied by a sleeping form. He found it a little odd that there were spears and a sword leaning against the wall. He motioned for Yosef to come with him and slid along the wall until they came to another pair of shutters, behind which all was dark. Very carefully, Yosef slid his knife up until he had lifted the latch, and then eased the shutters open.

The two men slipped over the sill like eels and discovered that, while the one man was asleep and snoring loudly, there were several others who were not, and they were drinking and playing dice games in the large room that overlooked the sea and the harbor. This was unexpected and not at all what Reza had expected.

By the time the two ghosts had explored the entire house, Reza was profoundly disturbed. There was no sign of Theodora, nor her son Damion. He began to worry that he had come to the wrong house. They crept around the kitchens and what appeared to be the servants' quarters and found maids and manservants asleep in various corners, but still no sign of Theodora. Reza decided to leave the house and try to come to grips with the odd situation.

As they left the large villa, it was at this point that Yosef brought Reza's attention to a dim light in the area of the stables. They decided to investigate, and found a couple of well-bred horses munching on their hay. Reza realized that there was a living accommodation at the back of the stables, which was where the light had come from. Determined not to leave before he had checked everything and every possible place for Theodora, he nodded to Yosef and they headed for the light. Once again they decided to slip into the house via a shuttered window. They were about to climb into the darkened space when the door opened and a figure walked in, carrying a lamp. It was Theodora. She was dressed in a simple shift and appeared to be ready to go to her bed, which they could now see to the left of the window. What was the Senator's daughter doing sleeping in the stable?

"Psst!"

She whirled. Reza lifted his head above the window sill and waved his hand. Theodora was so surprised she nearly dropped the lamp. The very first thing she did was to snatch a linen sheet from a chair to cover herself, and next, to stare wide-eyed, with her mouth half open and in silence, as Reza slipped over the window sill, followed by a grinning Yosef.

"It's us, Theo! Me and Yosef!"

"Oh, dear God, is it really you, Reza? You gave me such a fright!" Theo gasped. "I thought for a moment...!" She didn't finish. She put the lamp down with great care on the table, but then, without warning, she threw herself into Reza's arms. He grasped her in a tight embrace, but he was somewhat alarmed. This was not the normally calm and unruffled Theo he knew, who rarely showed much emotion.

She clung to him and reached for Yosef's hand and gripped it hard while tears flowed. Yosef closed both hands on hers and squeezed.

"Hey, hey, Theo. It's alright, we are here with you now. God be praised you are alive," Reza told her softly, and pushed her gently back, still holding her arms so that he could see her. "Nothing to fear."

She was crying. 'You have... you have *no* idea how happy I am to see you," she babbled in a hoarse whisper. Then she collected herself and put a finger to her lips. "It is very dangerous for you to be here, but I am so happy that you are."

"Come now, Theo. What is happening? Yosef and I saw a procession leaving and decided to come in the back way."

She laughed as she wiped her tears and stared at the two dark, slender men standing in front of her, lithe as cats, for whom she had so much affection. "I would not have expected you to come in the front door to begin with, Reza! Yosef, it is so good to see you," she told the embarrassed Companion. "I... I have missed you all so very much."

"I am happy to see you, too, Lady Theo. But why are you not living in the main house?" Yosef asked. They were all whispering because of her former gesture.

"We went all over that place over there," Reza jerked a thumb at the main house, "and it was only by luck and Yosef's sharp eye that we came here at all. What is going on?"

"Why am I not surprised that you did that!" Theodora snuffled with amusement, but then looked serious. "I cannot trust the servants, Reza, nor those men, so I live here," she told them.

Reza guided her gently to sit down on the bed, and then he and Yosef stood waiting. Reza noted the lines of worry and tension on her handsome face that had not been there before.

"Tell us what is going on, Theo. Clearly Talon and Rav'an were right to worry. They sent us here. There is something going on, and I don't like the look of it thus far."

Theodora shivered. "Yosef, could you please give me that wrap over there?" she asked him. Yosef retrieved the wrap and handed it to her. She pulled over her shoulders and shook herself. Theodora was not one to dwell on emotions very much, so it was not long before she had calmed down enough to be able to explain what had happened since she had arrived back at the villa in Constantinople.

"I should have known you would be concerned, and I thank God that you came, but there is real danger, and I have to confess, I have been afraid."

"Tell us from the beginning, Theo. There is time," Reza prompted her. "Yosef, keep an ear open for trouble, but you should hear this, too," he told his friend.

*****

Theodora had arrived in Constantinople to find it a changed city from what she remembered, and not in ways for which she might have hoped. This concern was eclipsed by the joy and the excitement of seeing her brother Alex, whom she had thought killed. News of his survival had galvanized her to leave Kantara and all her friends to come and find Alexios.

In that regard, she had not been disappointed, but she saw immediately that her brother was not in good health. The vicissitudes of the dungeons and the neglect of his physical health as he lived in the virtually abandoned villa, which had once been a vibrant place of parties and meetings for important people, were very evident to her professional perspective. She was appalled at his condition, but was equally sure that, with some time and nursing, she could repair much of the physical damage, if not some of the damage to his mind.

The reunion with her brother had been joyous and for a brief time very satisfying for Theodora, and Damion was also happy to be in the city. Theodora was very thankful for the gold provided by Talon, as it had paid for food and warm clothing, which were in short supply. They had spent a happy week together; despite the run-down condition of the garden. She and her brother sat on the bench next to the grave of her mother, who had been buried in the garden before she had fled to Cyprus. They shared memories and simply enjoyed each other's company. She told him in detail about her life in the lands of Kantara, and about Talon and his beautiful wife, Rav'an, about Reza and Jannat and their children. And how the emperor had tried and failed to take back Kantara after Talon had stolen it from him. Alexios was delighted to hear of this.

"Now he is a lord? Well-deserved, I suspect. And they were good to you! For that, I am eternally grateful. Do you still carry a torch for him?" he asked with a chuckle as she pretended to glower at him.

"He is a brother, like you," she told him firmly, but he smiled to himself, and he noticed the blush that appeared on her cheeks.

However, it was not long before Theodora realized that there was another more pressing problem than the reduced conditions of the estate, which could not be solved by gold alone. She had hesitated to ask what the issue might be, but one evening, when Alexios had invited over his friend, an equally emaciated man named Stephan, while they were all together and sharing wine, her brother finally told her.

"You have come at a bad time, my sister," he told her. He and Stephan exchanged looks. "You should tell her," Stephan said with a nod towards Theodora.

"How so?" she asked.

"Because we are to be evicted within a few days, my darling sister," Alex told her, and he took another swig of the wine while shaking his head.

"It's about the taxes, or rather, the back taxes, that are owed on the property, Lady," Stephan interjected.

"Taxes? Back taxes? I'm confused, please explain what you mean," she had asked.

So they had told her that the trouble had started with a man called Aeneas, who was now a powerful man in the Treasury and enjoyed a high position because he had come up with a scheme to keep the emperor in money.

"You might remember Andronikos was notorious for his hatred of the upper class, and in particular the senatorial class, Sister. Us, in other words," Alex said bitterly. "Initially, we all thought his successor would be the better man. In some ways he was, because the crazed bloodbath in the palace dungeons was stopped, but... this one, Isaac Angelos, is a big spender, and he inherited an empty treasury.

"The story goes that this pig, Aeneas, was sent on a mission to find the gold stolen by our dear *former* friend, Pantoleon. He failed in that endeavor, for which he should have been executed, or at the very least banished to some hole on the border. But somehow or another he managed to convince the emperor and his minions that he could still be of service."

"Hence, the tax upon wealth," Stephan joined in. "It was a brilliant idea for an abacus flicker. I mean, the man was a mere accountant, but this idea, once put into motion, began to bring in the money. He redeemed himself with the Office of the Treasury, and certainly with the emperor. The wealthy, and those with land, are being soaked for the money they would otherwise hide from the state. A tax in itself is not unjust, but the taxes are very heavy, and the price for being unable to pay them is also very high."

Theodora felt a lump grow in her throat. "What... what does this mean for us? We have no money, only the remains of Papa's estate, which is ruined. It will take much time to heal this land, yet surely, given time we can do that. But there is no income to be had here at present!" She waved her arm about at the dilapidated floor, the paint peeling off the walls and the scratched and faded murals, which had once been the pride and joy of her mother.

Both men looked at one another and, after a small silence, Alex spoke up. "They decide the tax which is owed, you see, Theo. Then if it cannot be paid, they take land, or the entire estate, in payment and give it to others, who can generate money from the property. It is very corrupt, but the emperor, Isaac," his lips curled in disgust, "is not only indifferent to our suffering but happy, for he has coin to pay for his lavish lifestyle. I can tell you, Sister, that many of our former friends are out on the streets of Constantinople because of this tax and his avarice!"

Theodora shook her head. Their family and their friends had been very wealthy; but the torture, imprisonment, and outright murders of the senatorial class under Andronikos had thinned their ranks. And now this.

"So we owe taxes on this property, which we cannot pay?" she said in a resigned tone. Her mind on the gold given to her by Talon, she asked, "How much do we owe? And what about our estates in the north?"

Alex gave a bark of laughter. "They're gone! To pay for what was owed on *this* house. Now they are coming for our home." He looked worn out and her heart went out to him. Time in prison and worry had made him very thin. His once-aristocratic nose was now a thin, long beak in a gaunt face.

"Oh, Alex. I'm so sorry, but I have some gold. Perhaps...?"

"Do you have enough to buy a ship, or even two? The amount that crook wants is up there. We don't have enough to buy even a horse at present. No, my sister, we are destitute and will have to leave before very long. I am only heartbroken because we will have to leave Mama here, and that you have had to witness this."

Chapter 27

The Reckoning

What course of life should wretched mortals take?
In courts hard questions large contention make.
Care dwells in houses, labor in the field,
Tumultuous seas affrighting dangers yield.
In foreign lands thou never canst be blessed;
If rich, thou art in fear; if poor, distressed.
—Posidippus

Theodora woke the next day with a heavy heart and prepared as best she could for a visit that Alex had warned her would be exacting; they were expecting the man called Aeneas from the Treasury. Something about that name bothered her; she wondered where she might have heard it before. In any case, she needed to put on a brave face and see what she could do to enable them to keep the estate. She and Alexios, with Stephan and Damion in attendance, waited apprehensively.

The Treasury Secretary arrived in a litter carried by four stalwart slaves, who placed the sedan carefully down on its four legs and stood to attention. A corpulent man extricated himself, with the help of a rough-looking man in a coat of the plate armor favored by the Byzantine army. The escorts accompanying them were also armed.

Aeneas stood and adjusted his senatorial toga-like dress, looking about him with approval. He liked having an escort of soldiers. He had asked for them some time before because of the nature of his new role, which was the eviction of people from their houses and estates for not paying their taxes. There had been violence before, and he abhorred violence, especially when it was directed against himself. After he had surveyed the dilapidated gardens with some satisfaction, he walked toward the entrance of the once-resplendent villa. This was soon to be his, and he intended to enjoy every moment. Stephan, the surly companion of the senator, was there to open the door, while Alexios Kalothesos, son of the deceased senator Damian Kalothesos, greeted him in the shabby and unkempt foyer, which had once featured beautiful murals and stunning mosaic images on the walls.

Aeneas barely glanced at Alexios and didn't acknowledge his polite greeting. Instead, his gaze fastened upon the vision before him. Theodora knew how to make an impression when she wanted; Rav'an and Jannat had taught her much in that regard, so she had spent some time that morning on her appearance. She had wanted to evoke the former greatness of their home, as a sign that it would be restored.

Aeneas saw a slim, beautiful woman with a halo of copper red hair, whose eyes were huge and whose mouth formed a sensual, rose-colored bow. He longed to kiss that mouth!

Theo held her hand out to him to kiss. He virtually devoured her fingers with his wet lips, leaving her with a feeling of disgust.

"My lady?" he drooled.

"My lord of the Treasury, may I present my sister, Lady Theodora Kalothesos." Alexios had observed the reaction, and his tone was only just less than sardonic.

"Had I known you existed before today, my lady, I would not have been such a stranger!" Aeneas murmured as his eyes swept all over Theodora, who endured his avid gaze and waved him in. "You will forgive us for not providing you with the best of hospitality, my lord, but please come in, you are welcome," she just managed.

Aeneas preened at the title, although it was not his to brandish about. The formalities had to be gone through before they could get down to business, but eventually his own impatience and the reticence of his host prompted him to open the conversation in the direction he wished it to take. He addressed Alexios as the head of the household, although he could barely take his eyes off Theodora, who had adopted a demure pose, quite unlike her usual forthright and inquisitive manner, for the benefit of their guest.

"I am desolated, Senator but I must press you for a response to the Office of the Treasury for payment of the back taxes owed. I, of course, deplore the severity of these taxes, but I am merely the messenger here. I beg you to understand that."

Alexios drew a deep breath, sighed then he said. "You know perfectly well that we cannot pay the amount you are demanding. I only ask that you give me more time to find the coin to pay this exorbitant fee," his tone was polite but resigned.

Aeneas's brain had been swirling since he arrived. His original objective had been to give an ultimatum, and upon hearing it rejected, to eject the two men from the villa. He had even brought a gang of rough men, who were waiting at the gates, to do just that. He had been looking forward to this day for weeks, no, months! The entire scheme of imposing exorbitant taxes on senators he had formulated with this object in mind, of securing this estate for himself. However, with the appearance of the lovely sister of the senator, a better option presented itself.

"I would like to discuss something alone with you, Senator," he told Alexios, and stood up, waving his hand toward the verandah that overlooked the harbor. He nodded to Theodora and walked outside. It was a sunny day and there was not much of a breeze. There he waited, staring out over the magnificent view, for Alexios to come and join him.

Alexios shuffled out onto the verandah and Aeneas turned to him. "I think I might be able to provide a solution for both you and for myself," he said without preamble.

The senator was still in possession of his faculties and had already guessed what was on the portly man's mind. He stared back without comment.

"Is... is your sister a married woman?" came the expected question.

*****

Later, when the secretary had left and they were all gathered in the main room, Alexios told his sister about the proposal.

Theodora recoiled. This was not quite what she had expected, but upon reflection, she realized that she should have seen it coming.

"He wants to marry me, which would give him access to the estate *and* a title?" she asked. Her tone was both incredulous and outraged.

"It's the title he craves, I am sure of that," Stephan told them. "He can already lay claim to the land, but only Theodora can provide him with the family status. Now there's a man with ambition!"

Alexios shrugged. "He was perfectly clear about that, and equally clear about the consequences, should we refuse his offer."

"So, it is now a threat?" she demanded.

"He will be back for his answer in a month, as he has to go north for a while. To check on the other estates the emperor has confiscated, no doubt," Alexios said in a bitter tone.

"Do you wish it that I should marry this... this bloated abacus shifter?" she said with an expression of disgust on her face.

"No, my precious sister, I do not," Alexios exclaimed with emphasis, " but we can be sure of one thing. If we refuse him, he will throw us out with nothing."

Her tone was equally bitter. "What have I come back to?" she asked out loud. "Truly, this city has become a sad, sad place to live! We must find a way to escape!"

Alexios nodded his agreement. "Yes, but how? I did ask him if we could move into the back building, should he want to occupy the main house while we discussed the other issue," Alexios ventured. "I took the liberty of saying that we could at least pay for that. He agreed and said to make the arrangements and move before he comes back. I think he wants to make a point."

Theodora snorted with disgust. The secretary was oozing into their lives, slowly but inexorably. She would rather die than submit to his *other* option.

Her mind went back to the life she had lived with Rav'an, Talon, and their friends. There had been companionship, music, and laughter much of the time. She had practiced medicine, her first passion in life, and then there had been the closeness of the family itself, which had effortlessly included her and Damion. 'Their bonds were so strong,' she reflected. They were drawn together by the shared hardships and adventures they had lived through. "But I cannot leave without my brother!" she lamented to herself, "and what ship is there to take us?"

The rumors were that it was less safe than ever to travel the seas around Cyprus. In fact, there were rumors aplenty in the city that an English king and a French king had embarked on a Crusade and were taking ships and their crews prisoners, or confiscating all their cargos. Now she was worried about how her dear friends might be faring. Word was that Sicily had been conquered, which had pleased the inhabitants of the city of Constantinople very much, for the Normans were unpopular since their failed attempt to take the city and the sacking of Dalmatia. Now, however, according to Stephan, the Crusaders, almost all Normans themselves, were all over the place and creating mayhem in the eastern seas. War, which had been simmering for years, was going to break out in Palestine yet again. Unsettling times, and that meant she was trapped, with very few options available to her.

The one thing she was quite sure of was that she was not going to marry this corpulent, hideous man from the palace. Her mind went back to another time when a family friend-turned-monster had tried to force her into marriage. She had escaped then. The gold she possessed might help, but one thing was clear: they could no longer live on this estate. Her overriding hope was that she and her brother could escape the new tentacles, which had reached out of the palace once again to poison their lives.

*****

It was late by the time she had finished telling her story to the two men from Kantara, who said very little while she talked. There was a long pause as they digested the information, but then Reza asked the question. "Could you not have just walked out of here, Theo? What was to stop you?"

"You ask a good question, Reza. I had thought we could, but that very day, after he made his outrageous proposal, we became prisoners! He is clever and might well have supposed we would try that option, for he posted the guards you now see at the gates and brought in men to stay at the house, along with some servants. We did try to leave, but when we reached the gates they sent us back under guard, and since then we have not been allowed even to walk in the gardens without a guard hovering over us. That was almost a month ago."

"Now I see how it is," said Reza with a grim look at Yosef. He glanced at the closed window. It was past time for them to be on the ship. Guy would be very worried by now.

"Theo, we must leave. Will you be all right while we are gone?"

She nodded silently, but then said, "I have prayed so hard for this moment, Reza. Thank you for coming and giving me hope. God bless you both."

"Where does he come from, this Aeneas fellow?" Yosef growled.

"From the great Palace of Blachernae, to the north, where the Treasury offices are located. He is due to come back here in about two days when the month is up."

"I need to see what he looks like." Reza told her.

"He comes and goes in a litter carried by four men. He came to inspect the house this evening and see that the servants are making all ready. I made a point of visiting the horses when he arrives," she told him, and smiled briefly. "He is afraid of horses." Then she added, "He is running out of patience. I have not dared refuse him, but I must give a definite answer before the end of the month."

"You just need a little more patience, my dear Theo, and then we will take you home. Don't speak of this to anyone. We will be back after this next sunset."

"You can leave via a small door at the end of the garden, which leads onto a narrow road which, in turn, will take you to the harbor, Reza," she told him. Unexpectedly, she gave them both a peck on the cheek. "That is for coming," she told them, through her tears.

Reza and Yosef exited via the small wooden gate and evaded the night patrols by keeping to the narrow paths intended for servants and messengers. They were safely on the ship with Guy well before dawn.

They held an immediate council of war down in the main cabin and told Guy everything they'd learned. Guy nodded his shaggy head at the end of the tale, took a swig of the arak which he kept for just such occasions, and tugged at his graying beard thoughtfully.

"So you want to bring her with Damion and her brother *and* his friend out of there, Reza? That we can take care of, but *when* is the question."

"I want to do more than that, Guy. I want to bring what remains of her family home. This is no longer their home, and there is nothing to be done about that, but I want to take what we can, and take care of this man, too." Reza's face was set.

Guy gave him a sharp look from under his bushy brows. He knew that expression. With a glance at Yosef, who wore a similar look, he nodded again. "Very well, Master Reza, you only have to ask, and I shall do all I can to help."

"We will have to take her away without any clues as to where she has gone, but first, I want to find a way to deal with this fellow, before he arrives at the villa."

"Why would that be? Why not just go in there and deal with them all, which I am sure you can both do, and then leave?" Guy demanded. He wasn't mocking them, either.

Reza heaved a sigh. Guy could be obtuse at times, but he loved the old captain. His heart was always in the right place.

"Because I don't want anyone to know how it happened, nor where she went, thus avoiding any chance of pursuit," he stated. "So I will need you to have the ship ready to sail and a boat to take us off when the time comes."

"Don't worry about that, Master Reza. Just tell me when. I shall clear for sailing within the next two days. Those damned customs people will want coin just to let us leave. My cargoes are almost all carried to the wharf-side. I'll deal with that. It will keep me busy all day to see the goods unloaded. You concentrate on getting Lady Theo out of there."

The two men made some special preparations, then slept through most of the following day. Later in the evening, when the sun had set, they appeared once again at the window of Theodora's bedroom. She was expecting them and, after a light tap, the lamp went out and shutters were eased open then she beckoned them in.

"I asked the others to wait in the kitchen because I wanted you to talk to them," she told Reza, as he slipped into the room as silent as a wraith, closely followed by Yosef. The shutters were closed, and they exited the room to appear soon after at the doorway of the kitchen, where Alexios, Stephan, and Damion were seated. The men were very surprised to see the two hooded men from Kantara, but Damion jumped up immediately and embraced them both. "I cannot believe it is you!" he exclaimed with tears in his eyes.

The introductions and explanations were made, and then they settled down to discuss the escape.

One of Reza's main concerns was dealt with more easily than expected. When he brought up the idea of intercepting the litter while on its way from the palace, Stephan volunteered.

"I have no idea what you are planning, Master Reza, but I can point it out, on the day we expect to see the pig. I think it is going to be tomorrow, because I heard one of the guards talking today." Stephan made his contempt for the official very clear.

"Good, then this is what we will be doing." Reza explained his plan to them. "We stay here tonight, and at dawn you, me and Yosef here leave together. After that, I have to take care of the people here.

"You don't intend to harm them? I mean, you are not going to kill them all , are you, Reza?" Theodora demanded. She knew full well what he and Yosef were capable of doing.

"No. No, Theo, just make them all feel a little queasy."

*****

The litter carrying Aeneas left the Blachernae Palace at about mid-morning when the bells of the churches began to ring. The light tones of the bells could be heard all over the peninsula at this time of day, but then there would be quiet until late noon, when they would begin again, competing with the normal everyday sounds of a large city. Aeneas was looking forward to this visit to the villa of Kalothesos. His imagination threatened to get the better of him as he thought about the lovely woman to whom he intended to be married, whether she liked it or not.

He was therefore totally unprepared for the terrific bang that went off next to the litter, which scared the two carriers into dropping it with a thud. The frame of the litter tilted over and fell on its side with a splintering crash. The carriers staggered about, holding their ears and staring stupidly at a column of yellow smoke that arose from its mysterious source, very close to the fallen litter.

The two outriding guards found themselves lying on the hard cobbles, dazed and bruised, while their horses galloped off, still bucking and whinnying with fright. People in the crowded stalls who had been close by when the explosion went off and who had been struck by the blast were crouched, cowering among the resulting trash and torn awnings. Others thought the devil had paid a smelly visit, and crossed themselves repeatedly while muttering feverish prayers. There was the strong stink of sulfur in the air, so it was reasonable to suppose that was what had happened.

The four soldiers who had been on foot were stunned, and three had even dropped their spears as they clutched at their ringing ears and staggered around, looking dazed. Aeneas, who had been tipped out of the sedan chair, crawled for a few paces, leaving his toga behind, before he staggered to his feet. But just as he did, he received a sting on the left-hand side of his exposed neck. He clapped a hand to the area, and it came away with a spot of blood on it— and a tiny little dart, which he stared at for a long moment before he began to feel very dizzy.

It dawned on him that he had been murdered, and for one desperate moment his dimming eyes searched for his killer. Among the people near him was an old man leaning on a stick that was about waist-high, and someone else whom he thought he might know from somewhere. The old man was watching him, and as Aeneas's life drained away, the man he thought he might know vanished, while the old man winked and gave him a smile.

The leader of his escort, which had been provided from the Palace of Blachernae, where all the administration for the Treasury took place, recovered enough to become alarmed when he saw his charge lying sprawled on the street. Shaking his head to clear the ringing in his ears, he knelt next to Aeneas and turned him over. The Treasury Secretary flopped over onto his back, his dead eyes staring up at the sky.

The centurion swore furiously and shook him, but it was clear his charge was quite dead. The centurion could not think what might have killed the Secretary; perhaps the blast itself? It had certainly knocked him off his feet. He shouted at the men to get the sedan back upright, and then they hauled Aeneas into the box, where he lay sprawled in an untidy heap.

"What in God's name just happened?" one of the still-dazed men demanded. "Was that a clap of thunder just now?"

The other men from the escort, who were now clustered around the sedan, just shook their heads. They could barely hear. No one knew what had happened, other than a dreadful noise and an unholy stink, but their passenger, an important man, was lying dead beside the litter. There was a growing crowd of curious and unwelcome onlookers. The centurion knew that something was dreadfully wrong, and that he would probably be held accountable, but there was no recourse.

"We have to go back to the palace and try to explain what happened," he muttered. How he was to do that he had no idea, but he was pretty sure he was going to be posted to the Bulgarian border for the rest of his career after this incident, and he cursed the dead man. He looked around him, but the old man he had noticed out of the corner of his eye had gone. He doubted if anyone would have been able to provide much useful information, anyway.

*****

"Now, all we have to do is to distract the men in the villa," Reza said to Yosef and Stephan, as they walked briskly down a small alley, away from the growing crowd on the main route, and he pulled the beard off his face. Yosef laughed at his chief.

"What's so funny?" Reza inquired.

"You have a white mustache, Reza, and it looks funny on you without the beard. I'm impressed as to how fast the poison worked, though."

"Humph," Reza snorted. "Is everything in place for tonight?"

Stephan was still shaking his head and trying to clear the ringing from his ears as they hurried along. "Are you some kind of magician?" he asked Reza. He was in awe of what had transpired.

"Yes, he is," Yosef answered, with a side smirk at the deadpan face of his leader. Stephan's eyes widened and he crossed himself.

They managed to reenter the villa grounds without detection and laid low until late evening. Stephan stayed as far away from Reza as he could.

"We need a distraction that is not going to leave any clues as to how you have left," Reza explained to Theodora. She looked interested.

"What I need you to do is to distract the cook for long enough to let me and Yosef get into the kitchen," he told her.

*****

Just before sunset, when the kitchen was at its busiest, Theodora appeared at the outside door and gestured for the cook with a show of urgency. The cook knew that she should not be here at the main house; the food for the family was always taken over by a couple of the new guards. However, this attractive woman was evidently in need of something, so he came outside, wiping his hands on his apron.

"What is it?" he asked. His tone was barely civil.

Ignoring the rude attitude, Theodora drew herself up and pointed to the storeroom behind her. "I was taking a walk when I saw a person stealing food. You should go and have a look," she told him. "Come with me and I will show you."

He was very reluctant to leave the kitchen, because the stew was almost ready and the bread was warming in an oven, but with a glance behind him, hastened to follow her to the small shed where much of the grain was stored. Brushing past her, he hauled the door open and saw that some sacks had fallen over and the grain was spreading over the floor. If he did nothing, the rats would get to it before the dawn, and it would spoil. With a curse, he ran in and hauled one of the two open sacks back upright, and then the other. He left the sacks like that, with the grain still scattered on the floor.

Theodora only just noticed the two figures come and go from the vicinity of the kitchen but then turned her attention back to the cook, who was staring with an exasperated expression on his face at the grain strewn about.

"I'll send the maid to clean it up later. I have supper to prepare!" he snapped at the woman, who turned her back on him and made her way up the slope toward the stables. He glowered after her. "Bitch!" he muttered. "That abacus flicker can have her, and good luck!"

He hastened back into the kitchen just in time to keep the stew from boiling over and to salvage the bread. Cursing, he dragged the slightly burned loaves out of the oven and hauled the large pot of fish stew off its hook over the fire.

The maid arrived in time to collect the bowls for the men, who were lounging in the main room while the cook sat down to eat his own supper. The people in the stables could wait for theirs. He was hungry.

The maid, who was no longer in her youth, set out the food on a long table, and then flounced off to join the cook and eat her own supper, but not before she had received some ribald invitations and one painful pinch on her ample behind. Neither she nor the cook were very concerned about the people living in the stables.

*****

An hour later, things had changed dramatically. When the men in the front room realized that something was badly wrong, their suspicion was directed at the supper they had all enjoyed, but by this time few of them were in any condition to follow up on this with punishment for the cook. Their guts were clamoring for relief; they felt dangerously sick. Several of them ran out of the house to head directly for the outhouses, where they found the two guards, who normally watched the stables, being sick into the bushes.

"Get out of there, woman!" one shouted at the closed door of one of the only two available toilets. "We need to go!"

"Go away!" the maid screamed back at them, and then there was a ghastly sound followed by groans and agonized moans.

"By the saints in the Hagia, I have to go, and I don't care where!" one of the men bellowed. He rushed for the bushes, where first he vomited and then, with a groan of desperation, squatted and voided his bowels. He was joined by several of the others, some of whom emptied their stomachs at the same time. They heard the cook cursing and discovered him lying in the bushes, in just as bad a condition as the angry men. They were unsympathetic.

"You've poisoned us, you bastard!" one yelled at the miserable man, who lay in his own vomit, and kicked him hard in the ribs.

"Ghaah!" he gasped, and rolled over to retch some more.

They left him moaning in the shrubs, to attend to their own problems.

Reza and Yosef, who had been watching the events taking place in the semi-darkness with some amusement, signaled the others. By this time the inhabitants of the main house were in no condition to pay any attention to a small group of dark figures who hastened down past the stables, then ran past the main house, and disappeared amongst the straggly rows of old vines. From here they scurried to the small, well-hidden door set into the garden wall. They exited onto the street and hastened down the hill to the waterfront, where they were met by a boat and taken out to the ship.

Just before they left the gardens, however, Alexios snapped off several of the twigs from the vines that had once produced his father's wine. "For you one day, Father," he muttered as he stuffed them into his tunic. "Goodbye, Mother," he said, as he left his birthplace and former home.

Within minutes of their arrival on board, with the greetings over, the ship drew up its anchor stones as quietly as possible and set sail. Guy could navigate in the darkness of the harbor, he had been here so often, and so it was that they rounded the peninsular without incident and glided into the Marmar Sea to the south of the city.

Dawn found them well out of sight of Constantinople and on their way to Cyprus. Theodora came on deck with the dawn and smiled at Guy and Reza and the imperturbable Yosef, who were standing on the upper deck.

"You are going home, Theo!" Reza called down to her, and she laughed. "Yes, Reza, we are!" she called back up, before mounting the steps to join them.

Chapter 28

Terms and Conditions

Ivory palaces built on earth
And mansions lined with galleries—
With marble columns on inlaid floors
In spacious halls that filled with parties:
In a flash I saw them all as rubble
And weathered ruins without a soul.
—Moshe Ibn Ezra

Acre finally surrendered to the Crusaders on July 12, 1191. They had held out for as long as they could, but Salah ad-Din could not penetrate the sea blockade—the dense clusters of Frankish and other European ships saw to that. Nor could his raiders, despite their determination, penetrate the land armies encircling the city. So, Acre had starved.

The news traveled around the various armies like wildfire. Talon and his Companions were aware, before almost everyone else, that something important was about to occur. So he was ready when the trumpets sounded on the walls near the city gates announcing either a sortie, which he didn't think was about to happen, or a delegation about to exit. The trumpets on the crusader side blared in response, and the entire encampment roused itself from the torpor brought on by the increasing heat that had settled over the entire area.

He donned his chainmail hauberk hurriedly, helped by his two young assistants, and strode out of his tent to be greeted by Junayd, who was already mounted, and the other Companions. Talon nodded his thanks as he took the reins to his horse and glanced back along the tent lines to see the Saxons making haste to be ready, in case of any conflict, along with the Cypriot Greeks, who were not quite in such a hurry.

"Come along, men, let's go and see what the fuss is about." As Talon nudged his mount forward, the city gates began to open and a small group of dignitaries began to walk out on foot. They carried only two banners: that of Salah ad-Din, depicting the eagle, and a large white flag of peace. Otherwise they were unarmed. They had a very small escort, and even from this distance Talon could see how hesitant they were to venture out from the relative security of their city walls.

"It seems they want to parley!" he exclaimed. He cantered with his Companions toward the space where the delegation had come to a halt. He and his men were among the first to arrive, and perhaps just as well. The rough men who had come from the crusader encampment in a hurry were not in the mood to pay full attention to the situation. Some wanted to kill the well-dressed but very gaunt representatives from the city, huddled in front of them.

"They come to parley! Do not dishonor the white flag!" Talon shouted at the eager bullies. "Wait for the kings. See, King Philip is coming, and King Richard is close. Wait!" he called, with all the authority he could muster.

His call was taken up by Lord D'Onston and other chiefs, who had now arrived and supported Talon's orders. Talon was somewhat relieved that Brandt had moved very fast to bring his contingent of Saxons to the meeting. He wondered briefly if he would have to use them to keep order. But that proved unnecessary as Philip, accompanied by his lords and attendants, arrived, closely followed by Richard. Both men looked tired, and it was clear that Philip was still quite ill. Richard appeared to be recovering. He rode up to where Talon and his men were waiting with D'Onston and stared at the small group of the enemy to their fore.

"What do they want?" he asked the world at large. He barely acknowledged his cousin or the other lords gathered nearby. His voice was gravelly and he had to clear his throat, after which he spat in their direction.

"I dare say they have come to parley again, Cousin. You do see the white flag, do you not? They certainly don't look as though they are here to do us harm," Philip answered sarcastically.

He turned to Talon. "Lord Talon, you speak their language. Ask them why they are here."

"Very well, my liege," Talon replied. "Lord D'Onston and that man over there," he pointed to one of the Templars who was riding just behind Richard, "you speak some Arabic. You should come with us." The Templar glanced at Richard for permission, who nodded, and moved his horse to come alongside that of Talon and D'Onston.

As they approached the men of the delegation, Talon remarked on their condition. It was pitiable. Despite the fact that they were clearly dressed in their very best for the occasion, they were physically in very poor condition, and this showed in their gaunt features and skeletal frames, which the clothes could not hide. Their expressions ranged from mild to genuine fear and actual defiance, resignation, and apathy.

"They are here to surrender," he remarked to his two companions.

"Dear God above, but I hope you are right, Talon. I, for one, have had enough of this siege," D'Onston returned.

They halted their animals in front of the group, but did not dismount. Talon raised his right hand.

"*As-salaam-alaikum,*" he intoned.

One of the men stepped forward. "*Wa-alaikum-salaam,*" he stated, and placed both hands together, as though in prayer.

"To whom do I have the honor of speaking?" Talon asked in Arabic.

"My name is Manqid al-Din. I am a representative of the Governor al-Kamil of the city, who would come himself, but he is ill. We have come to discuss terms. To whom do I have the honor of speaking?" he asked in turn.

"My name is Talon de Gilles," Talon responded.

Manqid nodded slowly. "Yes, I have heard of you, Lord Talon. Your name is spoken with respect."

Talon bowed from the saddle. "State your terms and I will convey them to the kings," he told them.

"Our lord Salah ad-Din is unwilling or unable to come to our aid. Hence we have no choice but to surrender. Eight days ago, we asked for fair terms and conditions for our people to go free if we give up the city to your kings. *Insha'Allah,* they will show compassion and allow us to leave with our families and something of our possessions. We have not heard anything for eight days." He paused, and then opened his hands in a gesture of submission.

"We are here again, to hear what terms the kings will give us."

It was clear to Talon that Manqid was struggling with his pride as he made this statement, but he appeared determined not to show how desperate he and his attendants really were. Talon knew how bad it was within the city. There probably was not a rat nor a mouse nor a green leaf of anything left to be eaten. They could not even fish because of the blockade. And Talon knew, only too well, that sickness follows starvation. Nasuh and Maymun had told him that there was no one to bury the dead in the city, so plague was rampant. Even leprosy was evident.

"We will speak to the kings immediately. Please wait here," Talon ordered, and turned his horse away.

"Did you understand what they were saying?" he asked the Templar, who nodded uncertainly. "They want to surrender; I did understand that much," he responded.

Talon rolled his eyes at D'Onston. "They are here for years on end, yet they speak barely a word of the people in this land," he muttered in disgust.

D'Onston nodded somewhat ruefully. They were one horse's length ahead of the Templar, who was giving them some space. "I shall make sure that the kings appoint you to be our negotiator and translator, Talon. We have to know what they are saying, down to the last word," he assured him.

Talon wondered if that was a role he really wanted, but with the lack of people able to talk to their enemies, he found himself in the unenviable position of negotiating on behalf of the two surly Latin kings. He wondered if they would be kind to their enemies. He doubted it; the siege had drawn out for a long time, enough for hatreds and frustrations to fester and boil.

They arrived in front of the kings and their-sweating attendants. Everyone was feeling the heat of the day, as it was close to noon.

"Well? What do they want?" Richard demanded, before Philip could speak.

"They are here to surrender, my lords," Talon told the kings and their attendants.

Those who were nearby and heard him began to cheer. Soon no words could be spoken, as the entire Christian army took up the roar of triumph and relief. All around them men were clapping each other on the back and tossing their caps into the air.

"What terms do they want this time?" King Philip demanded of Talon and D'Onston, when the noise had abated somewhat.

"Perhaps we should adjourn to some shade, my lord?" D'Onston suggested, ever solicitous of his king's comfort. Both the kings were perspiring heavily in the increased heat and looked decidedly uncomfortable.

"Yes, we shall go to my tent. Cousin, you will come with us?" Richard, for a change, showed some concern for his sick cousin. Indeed, he himself seemed to be in need of shade. "We can have some privacy at the same time."

"I shall tell the delegation to attend us, my lord?" Talon asked.

"No, by God! They can wait out in the sun until we come back with our terms, not theirs," Richard snarled.

Talon knew better than to argue. He watched the kings depart; he would follow when he had talked to the delegation. He turned back to the pathetic little group and told them to wait. Manqid al-Din nodded resignedly. He hadn't expected anything else by the look of it.

Talon turned to the Companions. "Junayd, come with me, but Khuzaymah, I want you to bring them clean water and some fruit, if we still have any, to keep them going, and perhaps some shade if you and the others can contrive something."

"As you wish, Lord," Khuzaymah responded, and turned his horse away, followed by Maymun. Talon then followed the hangers on who attended the two kings, to the distant royal tent, attended by Junayd and Andreas. His expression was grim.

He found the kings seated with a few select attendants in Richard's tent. It was already stuffy in there, and the addition of sweating, unwashed people didn't make it any less stifling. However, the mood was far better than Talon remembered it since the early days, when a sense of optimism had existed. That had subsequently been replaced by gloom and dissatisfaction with the way the siege had gone. Now Richard was in an expansive mood, and even Philip had cheered up. Duke Leopold was there, eager to hear the terms and to be present at the conclusion of the siege with the two kings.

"Ah, Lord Talon, I am informed by all and sundry, including my sister over there," Richard waved in the direction of Joanna, who was seated just a little apart from the men, "that because of your intimate knowledge of these people, you should be one of the emissaries to deal with them."

Talon bowed low to the princess, who gave him a wan smile. She had spent the last two weeks attending to her sick brother's needs and looked exhausted.

Talon was shown to a chair on one side of the table occupied by the two kings. A wine mug was placed in front of him and Richard raised his cup.

"To a speedy resolution to this tiresome siege, and then on to Jaffa!" Talon noted with wry amusement that none of the wine he had contributed was on offer. Richard was not one to share his bounty.

"And these," Richard leaned forward in his chair, "these will be our final conditions."

That didn't take long! Talon remarked to himself, as he composed his features in preparation for what he suspected might be coming. Richard glanced at Philip but barely acknowledged Leopold, who was ostensibly there to represent the Austrian and German contingents.

"The city will surrender all—and I mean *all*—its possessions to us. That includes every vessel and ship in the harbor, and all the properties within its walls." He paused, and for a moment Talon thought he might have finished, but he looked up at the emissaries-to-be and said, "Furthermore, two hundred thousand pieces of gold will be provided by the sultan, and a fragment of the True Cross that the infidels did not manage to destroy will be returned to us." Richard sat back as though content with that idea.

"You are forgetting the Christian prisoners that he still holds in his dungeons, Cousin," Philip murmured.

"Ah, yes, thank you, Cousin." Richard nodded. "Yes, we demand that the fifteen hundred Christian prisoners who are held captive by him are to be released. We shall name one hundred of them so that there are no mistakes. All this to be provided before we allow the citizens of Acre to go free, but he is not to delay. Our deadline expires on the twentieth of August. After that," he opened his hands and gave a sneer, "There will be reprisals. I have roughly twenty-five hundred hostages, so he should bear that in mind."

Talon sat rooted to his chair and stared for a long moment at the two kings. He was astonished at the severity of the terms and knew full well that the citizens of Acre could not possibly meet the terms.

"You seem to be unhappy, Lord Talon. Is there something you want to say?" Richard demanded with narrowed eyes.

"My lord," he nearly stammered, "these terms must be presented to Salah ad-Din himself. The city could never meet them! He must know of and agree to the conditions. He has the sole authority to meet your demands! For the sake of the people of Acre, could you not moderate them?"

Richard glared at him. "The conditions are reasonable and I shall not negotiate with them like this a second time. That is why you will be with the party who inform the sultan of them," he snapped. "I can just see his face when you do." He smirked at Philip, who gave a grimace of a smile in return.

"Who will come with me, my lord?"

"Lord D'Onston, Sir Jacques de Longes, the Templar knight who was with you today, and Lord Almond de Ais, our seneschal of the Knights Templar," Richard gestured toward the small group of standing knights of the Templar. "He also speaks Arabic. Then," Richard heaved a theatrical sigh, "we have Lord Garnier de Nablus, whom my *cousin*, Philip, wishes to attend the meeting you will have with the sultan."

Talon glanced at the other small group of the Knights Hospitalier, who were standing nearer to Philip. It came as no surprise to him that the two kings would insist upon having one of their own order represent them. Suspicion and distrust were pervasive.

"Lord D'Onston will be the leader of the mission," Richard concluded. "Know this, Lord Talon, that these are our terms and they are not negotiable. I intend to make the infidels pay for the misery they have put us through."

Talon could sense the mood in the tent had changed according to the royal temper. There was to be no compassion for the luckless inhabitants of the city here. Sensing that he was dismissed, Talon stood up, leaving his untasted wine on the table, and bowed to the two kings and the princess, and then turned on his heel and rejoined his Companions outside the tent.

However, he could not fail to overhear the comment made by King Richard as he left.

"Is he to be trusted? He is, after all, almost one of them... they call them *Pullani*, don't they? Keep an eye on him; I'm sending you, Lord Almond, to listen in carefully when he speaks with those Turks."

He also could not fail to hear the clear voice of Princess Joanna. "How many times must that man prove to you that he is loyal?"

"He is a *Pullani*, isn't he? Just like that weasel, Lord Sidon, who is in the Saracen nest. None of them can be fully trusted." Richard's tone was contemptuous. The princess retorted something, but the rest of her words were not for

Talon's ears. He heard steps and quietly left the area near the tent doors.

Talon paused by his men, his anger mounting, but then shrugged. It had been a pattern here during the siege. The Latins were suspicious of anyone who appeared to mimic the Saracen ways, let alone spoke their language. He took the reins from Junayd and mounted up, whereupon they rode back toward the small huddle of emissaries from the city in silence.

He noticed that Khuzaymah had provided the group with several carpets to sit on, and water was at hand, as were some empty plates. There was a crude cloth covering to protect them from the blazing sun. He nodded to himself with approval. He was not going to be accused of abusing the basic requirements of hospitality, even here upon this foul-smelling plain.

Talon dismounted and came to stand facing the group. His Companions hovered about to make sure that none of the inquisitive crusaders could come within earshot or to harm the group. The legation from Acre all stood up. The thunderous expression on his face must have warned them, as most of them looked apprehensive. Even so, the representatives were appalled when he told then of the king's demands. Manqid gasped, and in his weakened state nearly fell to the ground. His companions supported him as he cast anguished eyes up at Talon. "Allah, protect us!" he exclaimed. "Is there no discussion to be had, Lord Talon?" he asked in a pleading tone.

Talon kept his voice neutral. "I fear not, Manqid al-Din. The kings are adamant, and it is not for me to tell them how to make their demands. I am here purely as the messenger. *Insha'Allah,* we will be able to convince the sultan that it has to happen."

*****

Salah ad-Din was alerted to the presence of a delegation of Franks by his brother, Prince al-Adil.

"I do believe that it is Lord Talon, Brother, and he heads a delegation which includes Templars and Hospitaliers," Al-Adil ground out; his features were tight. "They carry a large white flag along with some royal banners."

Salah ad-Din had for some time known about the quarreling among the Christian camps, and that Hospitaliers had sided with Philip of France while the Templars were aligning themselves with King Richard.

"They have come to negotiate for both the kings," he remarked. "Lord Talon is going to speak for them, I suppose. They do come with a white flag of truce," he reminded his brother. "I—we shall not be guilty of abusing that right." He knew full well how much Al-Adil hated Talon, so he felt compelled to remind his brother of the rules of hospitality.

He received the delegation in his spacious tent with all the ceremony he could put together at such short notice. Fruit and cool water were provided, and a clean carpet of intricate weave was laid out upon several others for the delegation to sit upon.

Talon was the first to enter the tent, ahead of the contingent of lords and the knights.

Salah ad-Din noticed that Lord Talon wore the flowing robes that people wore who had spent their lifetime in the Palestinian world, despite their religious beliefs. The knights, on the other hand, wore their heavy hauberks and wool clothes, and suffered accordingly. He wondered, briefly, if being over-heated made men hot-tempered.

"*As-salaam-alaikum,* Lord Talon. We finally meet again." There was a genuine smile of welcome on Salah ad-Din's dark, aquiline features. "You honor me and are very welcome in my humble accommodations."

"*Wa-alaikum-salaam*, my lord. The honor is all mine," Talon responded with a sincere smile of his own.

"You will remember my brother, Prince al-Adil, Lord Talon," the sultan said, with a twitch of his lips.

Talon dipped his head to the stiff form of Al-Adil, who glared back, but nodded, nonetheless. "I am honored to meet you again, Prince," Talon said. His tone was cool.

"Please, be seated." The sultan covered his mouth with his hand for just a moment and his eyes gleamed with amusement, but then he gestured to the carpet, where, in the middle, were jugs of water and plates of fruit. "We shall have some refreshments and then talk." Salah ad-Din also derived some amusement from the expressions on the faces of his guests, other than Talon. They were unused to sitting on carpets, and their armor made it both difficult and uncomfortable. Talon, however, led the way and eased himself into a comfortable cross-legged position. Salah ad-Din made himself equally comfortable.

He waited patiently until they were all finally seated, with much clanking. Talon had already informed the group that to refuse the sultan's hospitality would result in no discussion at all, so they should accept it in good grace and leave the talking to him. D'Onston had agreed with Talon and had admonished the others. "Do as he says, my lords. Talon knows this man and his people better than any of us. I do not want this to fail before it has even begun." The small group of lords had reluctantly agreed, but there had been mutters of protest. They had been influenced by Richard and now they had become reflections of his attitude.

When the visitors had finally seated themselves and were uncomfortable enough, the sultan addressed them.

"You have honored my house, my lords. I wish to inquire as to the health of your kings." He looked from the Templar to the Hospitalier as he said this.

Talon translated for him, as it had become very clear to him that none of the men who had been sent with him into the lion's den, as he called it, were competent at the language.

D'Onston, having just taken a sip of the clean, clear water, nodded his head and licked his lips. The taste of untainted water was very pleasant to someone who had become used to the foul water in the crusader camp, with the consequent dysentery that accompanied it.

"Please inform His Majesty that it is we who are honored, and explain to him the reason we are here, Talon," he said.

Talon was not to be deflected just yet from the pleasantries, which he well knew were mandatory on an occasion like this. He in turn asked after the sultan's health, which he knew to be poor, although to look at the leader of the Moslem army one might not have thought so; he hid it well from the visitors.

"I am... recovering," Salah ad-Din replied with a half-smile. He knew very well the Franks were blunt people and wanted their tasks to be done, and done their way. But he appreciated the fact that Talon was insisting upon some decorum.

"I would inquire as to the health of yourself and that of your brother, Reza?" he asked in Persian. His eyes twinkled.

Talon was amused and almost laughed out loud, but the occasion was too serious for him to prolong the difficult subject of the mission.

"My lord, he is well, and I am sure that, were he here, he would wish you, as do I, a speedy recovery."

He paused, but then plunged with some reluctance. "But I— we are here for a very difficult task and I beg you to hear me out. I must speak Arabic for the benefit of a couple of my associates here, but I say this with great reluctance." He spoke in Farsi.

The sultan's eyes sharpened, and he glanced at the others. "Very well, then, Lord Talon. Please continue," he stated briefly. They were back in Arabic.

Talon nodded and then passed over a thick-rolled parchment affixed with large seals denoting the seals belonging to the Latin kings. It was bound with a wide silk ribbon. Salah ad-Din took it and put it aside while he focused on Talon, who then proceeded to tell the sultan the terms of the surrender.

When he finished, there was a very long silence. Talon watched the emotions flit across the face of the sultan, despite his efforts to conquer them. Finally, he said in a harsh voice, "I cannot possibly meet these conditions within the time frame your Richard has demanded!" he told Talon. He paused, as though searching his mind for more to say.

Just as the sultan was about to speak again, there was a disturbance at the entrance of the tent. All eyes turned to see what it was about. The sultan looked annoyed and Al-Adil called out angrily to know what was going on.

A well-dressed retainer of the sultan entered. He looked distraught and wrung his hands as he fell to his knees and then addressed the sultan.

"My lord, oh, my lord! The city is taken!" he called out. "Merciful Allah, but the city is lost!" He was weeping now, in front of the now standing sultan. All rose to their feet; even the clumsy Franks scrambled upright. Without ceremony, the sultan brushed past the still-weeping officer and strode out of the tent to join the mass of men staring toward the west, towards the city and the crusader camp.

While they could not hear the noise from that area, it was very clear that Christian banners were now flying from the towers of the city.

Salah ad-Din whirled upon the small group of Franks, his dark eyes blazing, "Did you know of this... this treachery, Lord Talon?"

"I knew it was about to happen, but not so soon, my lord. We were told to see you first, and then inform the kings as to what you had agreed to," Talon almost stammered. Richard had not even allowed him time to negotiate with the sultan. He felt betrayed.

The sultan was livid. "You, of all people, know that this is near to an impossible demand! I cannot find all these prisoners in less than a month, let alone acquire all the coin he is demanding!"

Talon nodded his head and stared back at the sultan. His features were bleak. "My lord, I do understand. The kings, in particular King Richard, are adamant, and now they are in possession of the city. I cannot say more."

"Tell your kings," Salah ad-Din ground out, his face a mask of rage, "that I shall do all within my power to meet these terms, *insha'Allah*!" He was about to turn away when a thought appeared to occur to him.

"I have had reason to learn that this King Richard is not such a trustworthy man. Do *you* swear that he in turn will keep *his* word?" He addressed this question directly to the seneschal of the Templars and the Grand Master of the Hospitaliers.

Talon watched the knights expressions once they were clear about the question. He knew the sultan loathed the Christian orders, but he could at least be sure that they would not lie to him. It was not reassuring that both men hesitated for a long moment and looked uncomfortable. They knew enough of the language to understand the words, and the meaning behind them, in this case, was not lost on them. The seneschal shook his head.

"I cannot swear to such a thing, my lord."

"I see," said Salah ad-Din, his voice dripping with scorn. He turned to Talon and shook his head.

"You serve a man whom not even his holy orders can trust, Lord Talon! I pity you, for I know you to be a man of honor. Tell your king that I will honor my word to the very best of my ability."

Chapter 29

A Congress of Kings

For thy sake yielding all I love and prize;
And O, how mighty must that influence be,
That steals me thus from all my cherished joys.
Here, ready, then, myself surrendering.
—Thibout

The incident with the Sultan had unsettled Talon more than he could have imagined. Upon his return to the Christian camp and his own lines he had spent a considerable time on the sand dunes staring out to sea, his mind in turmoil. How could there be honor when the king behaved as though nothing mattered but his own whims?

He confided in his senior commanders later that day. "We have to be very careful indeed with what comes from these people. They lack honor and as such there is little to trust about them. Be on your guard from this time onward," he told his men.

For some time Talon and his Greek associates had been aware of the seething undercurrents between the various Christian factions during the siege. Now that the siege was over, these began to bubble up to the surface, and they were not conducive to the peace and tranquility of the crusading condition.

In the first instance, the men of Leopold's army were furious because of the humiliation brought on by the disrespect shown to their flag by Richard. Many had left for home, not least because their own emperor had died, leaving a vacuum in the German states, and they were anxious to be home in case of a civil war.

The same day that Talon and the knights had gone to see Salah ad-Din, the city masters had opened the gates. Whether this was intentional and arranged by Richard, neither Talon nor D'Onston knew, but it had sealed the negotiations in Richard's favor, because now he owned the city.

Talon and D'Onston had ridden back to the camp with a sense of betrayal, but also some relief.

"I wonder if Richard would not have cared if we had lost our heads to the sultan? He must have known Salah ad-Din would be livid!" D'Onston remarked to Talon, as they arrived back at the now-busy encampment. Preparations were being made all around, for the army to move into the shelter of the city.

They were dismayed to hear of an incident that had taken place, just as the kings began to make their triumphant entry.

It was difficult to hear or understand the particulars as they rode through an excited, chattering crowd. Finally D'Onston leaned over, demanding to know what had occurred, aside from the parade into Acre.

The man who answered was English. He knuckled his forehead and pointed to the two large banners now placed on either side of the great gates of the city.

"The king, God bless 'im, saw the banner of the Austrians flying up thar' alongside his and got really angry, m'lord."

"Well, then? What about it?" D'Onston demanded impatiently.

"Well, 'e shouted wi' rage and told 'is knights to get it down, and then the king trampled it into the dirt!" the pikeman told them. "Serves them right! It's our king as has won this battle, not those damned furriners!"

D'Onston turned away and kicked his horse back into motion. "I sometimes despair of our king's lack of diplomacy. He is jealous and rude. He makes enemies of our friends at the slightest whim!"

"Why would he do something like that?" Talon demanded, as they continued to ride toward the now-open gates of the city.

"Because he has never had to show restraint and is ever jealous of his position. It's bad enough that he has to share the city and the victory with King Philip. The Germans and the Austrians are of no significance to him, despite their sacrifices. He may yet pay a price for his high-handedness, I fear." D'Onston sounded dismayed.

They were soon to find out that this act of arrogance led to simmering rage within the Leopold faction, punctuated by brawls within the city and even outside, as the troops from all the armies, already hostile because of the incident with the flag, grew bored, drunk, and then vented their anger upon each other. Fights became commonplace with deaths to follow and kept the guards appointed to keep the peace very busy.

The second issue that D'Onston made Talon aware of, and which further threatened the fragile peace between the kings, was the fact that, while Richard had taken for himself the palace of Acre, a once-sumptuous building, Philip had taken the Templar stronghold, where he had set up house.

The two men were seated outside Talon's tent, sipping some of Talon's wine, observing the activity taking place out in the bay. Ships were moving back and forth between the anchorage and the now-open harbor.

"You look glum, my friend," Talon remarked.

"Well, our mission was not one I shall remember with any pleasure, although I finally managed to meet our archenemy. I did not find him equipped with horns nor a tail, as the bishops would have us believe." D'Onston sighed. "That much I am glad to have done."

"You will find he is a very determined enemy, but he is a most honorable man, and will stand by his word," Talon stated. "But why is there all this discontent and squabbling going on, even now?"

D'Onston gave him an unhappy look.

"From the onset of this siege, the two great orders, the Templars and the Hospitaliers have taken sides, jealously abetted by both kings. The Templars, unsurprisingly, took up with Richard, while the Hospitaliers have sided with Philip."

Talon nodded. He already knew this. D'Onston continued. "This has meant that, while both kings have formidable armed forces working for them, they do not coordinate any activity, which might have brought the siege to an earlier conclusion. But that's just my opinion, and please don't share it with anyone."

Talon nodded his agreement. "I think you are perfectly right," he said. "Neither of those two orders has thus far distinguished themselves in any way, except by intrigue and complaint. If they would only combine their strengths, they could bring the whole war to an end, but, it's not just the orders, is it, that's bothering you?"

D'Onston nodded and looked somewhat relieved that he could unburden himself to Talon. He wiped his mouth with the back of his sleeve. He no longer looked as debonair as he had in Famagusta. His tunic was patched and dirty. The colors of red, yellow, and green were faded and washed out, and his woolen cloak was threadbare. His boots had given out some time ago, but Talon had provided replacements, of which he was justifiably proud. He wore a leather cap that had once been blue, with the feather stolen from the peacock in the Famagusta palace. The plume was tattered and only half its former length.

"Well now, the Templars have complained that the French king is occupying space in the city that rightfully belongs to them. Richard has agreed with them, and because Philip is too tired and sick to argue, he and his attendants have been displaced and forced to move into diminished quarters."

Talon saw little of the French king these days. It was rumored that he was very sick and was considering leaving for France. "Is the rumor true that he wants to leave for France?"

"More than a rumor, now. He awaits the arrival of Lord Conrad de Montferrat, and after that he will probably depart."

"Ah, Lord Conrad—I spent a little time with him in Tyre. We managed to see the sultan off on a number of occasions."

"I had heard that you were there. What sort of a man is Lord Conrad?" D'Onston brightened a little, but then he looked glum again. "You know he refused to allow Richard to land at the city? So, there is no friendship there."

"Then you already know a little of the man. Strong willed, brave, stubborn, and ambitious and he definitely does not like Guy de Lusignan."

"That much I had surmised, and Guy is firmly in Richard's camp, and Philip takes for Conrad."

"Is this about who will be king when Richard and Philip are gone?" Talon asked abruptly. He waved his attendant over for some more wine.

"I should have known you would divine the situation correctly. Yes, Philip is determined to have Conrad replace Guy."

"Better Conrad than that sack of horse manure, Guy."

D'Onston laughed. "Philip agrees with you, but it will come down to a vote, I suspect. Here is what makes the issue political, as opposed to merely contentious. Conrad, by fair means or foul, has managed to marry Isabella who, by blood, is the heir to the throne of Jerusalem. With Sibylla dead, Guy no longer holds any real rights to it. Ibelin would agree with that. Both he and Raymond of Tripoli were for that, right from the beginning."

"Hmm. But Conrad's investment will only happen if Richard agrees, am I right?"

D'Onston nodded his head reluctantly.

*****

After the events that led up to the surrender of the city, Talon and the Greek noble were not invited to be a part of the interminable conferences and squabbles that ensued over entitlements to the booty found in the city. It was not much. Talon informed the nobles that they should consider themselves lucky not to be drawn into the fray, because then new enmities would appear and they would suffer accordingly. Their discontent was mollified by the fact that nearly all of them had been making good coin from the supplies they provided the armies from Cyprus.

Things only became more complicated when Conrad made his appearance. King Philip was an advocate for Conrad, which promptly meant that Richard was not, and he made it plain that he was for setting Guy de Lusignan back on the throne of Jerusalem, something that not only Talon was vehemently opposed to. In one of their many discussions, D'Onston, who was a frequent visitor to Talon's tent, asked the question, "Is he not the rightful king, though, Talon? Richard is here to place him back on the throne he lost, not to change anything. Besides, they have become good friends."

"Lusignan lost his right to retake the crown when he lost Hattin," Talon replied in a sour tone. "Not only that, he no longer has legitimacy, since his wife Sibylla and her daughters died. It was she who put him on the throne in the first place; gave him the crown with her own hand, no less!"

"What should the king do, then? Find someone else, other than himself, of course?"

"If rumor is to be believed, your king is impatient to finish this Crusade."

" *Our* king, Talon. While I have not been privy to the letters from his mother, Queen Eleanor, that is correct. He must find someone to hold the crown when he regains Jerusalem."

"Well, then it should be Conrad. He is admired by all, for holding Tyre for four long years, against every effort by Salah ad-Din to take the city. The only place, by the way, that was left of the Christian strongholds after the fall of Acre. Even the Arabs respect him and call him *al-Markis*. He is greatly respected, whereas Lusignan is scorned."

"Richard was turned away from Tyre by Conrad when he visited the city on his way to Acre, and won't be in a generous mood, as to Conrad being an alternative to Lusignan," D'Onston remarked.

"Both men are pig-headed, but they are fierce warriors who are respected by the enemy and, if there is anyone who can hold onto Jerusalem *and* make peace with the Arabs, it is Conrad. The day Richard leaves for England, Lusignan would lose the kingdom all over again," Talon asserted.

Talon joined the other lords in the palace of Acre when Conrad made his appearance. Both kings were there, as was Guy de Lusignan, who looked grim and resentful. Conrad breezed into the palace, accompanied by several of his attendants, several of whom Talon knew and had fought alongside while he had been at Tyre. The Lord of Montferrat strode energetically into the great chamber full of curious nobility and lesser knights, most of whom only knew the count by his reputation, the man who had held Tyre against all odds.

He carried himself almost as though he owned the chamber, glancing around him from under his bushy, graying brows, and approached the throne that Richard had taken for himself. Neither Richard nor Philip looked well, but of the two, Philip was in worse condition, and it showed in his bloodshot eyes and shriveled appearance. However, Philip was determined to be present to show his preference for Conrad to be the king of Jerusalem, not Guy de Lusignan.

From Talon's perspective within the crowd, Conrad had not changed much since they had last met, which was only a year ago. Talon had provided what supplies he could from Cyprus, whether stolen or from his own resources, which had been very well received by the beleaguered fortress on the island.

The Count of Montferrat stopped in front of the two kings and dipped his head. It was a perfunctory gesture which, while acknowledging their ranks, also signaled to everyone in the room and the world at large that only he, Conrad de Montferrat, had held the most important city in the Holy Land next to Acre, against strong odds, while the rest of the country had fallen to the hated Saracen. Talon smiled to himself. While a good deal thinner than he had been when he'd first arrived, Conrad was still as feisty as ever and looked very much as though he was determined to be treated as an equal.

While not a very tall man, Conrad was stocky and presented an imposing figure. He was dressed in full chainmail with the cowl of his hauberk thrown back to expose his strong neck and hard jawline, with long, rather unkempt graying locks and his full, bearded face, from which glared his bright blue eyes that didn't appear to miss very much. His helmet was carried behind him by a squire, and the attendants with him all looked very much the seasoned warriors that they were.

Talon felt that the atmosphere in the crowded chamber altered in some subtle manner upon his arrival. Respect, perhaps? These men from Tyre had been combatting the Saracens successfully for longer than four long years, and everyone knew it. Conrad's keen glance had met that of Talon as he'd walked by, whereupon he'd nodded and smiled. It was a significant gesture from one seasoned warrior to another, nor was it lost on Philip, who while very sick, still noticed everything.

Richard appeared to be annoyed at the count's cavalier attitude, but Philip smiled and acknowledged the count with a feeble wave of his hand. He was clearly not going to be eclipsed by Richard on this occasion.

"We are pleased to see you, Lord Conrad. You are welcome," he began. "I see you have old acquaintances amongst our gathering."

"I have one to whom I owe much, my lord," Conrad replied in his rumbling voice. "Lord Talon, whom I am glad to see here, has been very supportive, shall we say?"

Philip chuckled. "Yes, we, too, have come to know Lord Talon. But the three of us should retire and discuss in private much that concerns us at present."

Without waiting for Richard to say anything, he rose a little unsteadily to his feet and, assisted by one of his attendants, led the way to a more private setting. Richard, with a glare at the chamber, beckoned to Guy de Lusignan to follow them, and then he, Conrad, and Guy disappeared, with their closest advisers right behind them. This included Lord D'Onston and Princess Joanna. Talon wondered how that meeting would go. He had little doubt as to what it would be about.

Later that evening, Talon was alerted that a small contingent of riders had exited the city of Acre and were heading toward his encampment. After scrutinizing the group as it cantered toward them, Talon exclaimed, "It's Conrad! We should prepare for high-ranking visitors. Brandt! Where are you?"

Brandt appeared with some of his Saxons in tow and grinned. "And you were doubting that he would remember you, Lord?" he teased.

"Yes, perhaps, Brandt, but now he is here, and we all look like scarecrows!" Talon was just a little flustered.

"I shall lay odds that, whether we look scruffy or not, we set a better table than the kings themselves, Lord."

"Not if those Welsh poachers get to it first. Where are they?"

"Here, Lord," Dewy called. "Did you mention food?" Caradog and Dewy laughed.

"Not for you two scoundrels! We have lordly visitors, and Lord Talon wants to be able to feed them without wondering what happened to the meat or the new pies when they left this kitchen tent," Brandt countered. "Watch it, or I'll set my men on you both!"

"Ooer!" Dewy cackled. "Which one of you Saxons wants to try your luck, eh?"

Talon laughed. Come along, all of you. Dewy and Caradog, put your bows aside. You have just been appointed "Servers of the food at the table," so that Brandt and I can keep an eye on you. Just behave, and we can all eat. And I need someone to bring Lord Tefkros to the meal."

*****

Talon greeted Lord Conrad on foot and with a smile of welcome. The count gave a shout and jumped off his mount to give Talon a bear hug.

"We meet again, Talon!" he shouted. "I could tell immediately that this was your camp," he added, as he looked about him approvingly.

"May I ask why, my lord?"

"Because it doesn't stink like shit!" the count laughed. "Everywhere else in this pestilence-ridden camp, and within the city, it reeks of filth and death, but here it smells a good deal cleaner."

"You will remember my commander, Brandt?" Talon introduced the burly Saxon, who had gone red with embarrassment and nearly took a knee, but Conrad forestalled that gesture and clapped him on both arms. "It has been a long time, Brandt, and you have been missed on the battlements of Tyre!"

"Remember the archers, Lord?" Talon asked, as he waved Dewy and Caradog over to greet the count.

"How could I forget you two rascals!" the count exclaimed delightedly. "Apart from your skill with the bow, which we also missed. We starved for a week after you had gone. I believe you even stole what rats were left when you departed with Lord Talon here!"

Both of the Welshmen shuffled their feet and looked embarrassed, but they were pleased with the offhand compliment.

"We still have some good wine, my lord. I want very much to hear how you have been faring," Talon told the count.

D'Onston, who had accompanied the count along with two attendants, had by this time dismounted and joined them. "I can vouch for the wine, my lord," he told the count.

"Lord D'Onston, how do you think I survived and maintained my resolve in Tyre all this time?" Conrad demanded. "I know this man has the best wine in this God forsaken corner of the world. He kept me supplied, just as he promised, those four years ago. Every time a ship came from Cyprus there were several barrels of wine, and even a weird kind of spirit, which I am suspect will send a man blind." Conrad slapped his thigh and laughed again. Clearly, he was pleased to be here.

"Now, Talon, I want to hear all about the unscheduled visit by these two kings to Cyprus. Richard does nothing but brag, while Philip is his usual reticent self. As for that wastrel, Lusignan, I doubt if he knows how to tell of anything without embellishing his own part in it."

"Come this way, my lord. We have prepared a modest meal for you, as best we were able," Talon told the count

They had a feast that evening. The main dish was of roasted wild antelope brought in by Junayd and his men that very day. This was accompanied by almost fresh bread and great chunks of cheese along with the usual olives, fish paste and roasted fish. The final dishes of apples and dates along with honeyed cakes completed the feast. The entire assembly was in a festive mood brought about by a man all admired, who in turn was not coy about his appreciation of the men and the food provided.

Talon brought the senior Companions and Brandt into the conversation, as well as the Greek lords and knights of the island. The count ate as though he had not been fed a decent meal for a year and at the very end he took a large swig from his beaker of wine and belched contentedly, then sighed.

"Ah, but a man could eat himself into a stupor at your table, Talon," he said, as he cast his looks around at the other guests. "It has been a long time since I ate so well, or with such company."

He pressed Talon and the Greeks for details from the day of the storm to the conclusion, when Isaac had been marched before King Richard in silver chains, and he nodded his head often in appreciation of the battles and scrapes they described. By the time they had concluded the story it was late in the evening. Candles were lit, and flickered as a light breeze ruffled the walls of the tent and brought some relief to the close space.

"He is an impulsive man, our King Richard," Conrad observed to D'Onstan at one point. "It could have gone very badly if you had not been there, I suspect, Talon." he looked thoughtful.

"No one can argue with his courage, however," Talon remarked, but then he changed the subject.

"Why did you come here to Acre, my lord?" he asked, his tone careful. The question had been on his mind for some time now.

"Why, to see the two kings and congratulate them on their victory here at Acre, Talon. Why else?" Conrad replied. His bright blue eyes looked innocent. Talon was not deceived. He smiled.

"I personally hope to God it was to make your case with the two kings for your elevation to the position of kingship of Jerusalem, Lord," he said.

"Ah, but what about Guy de Lusignan?" Conrad mocked gently.

"I suspect that you know full well how I feel about him, Lord," Talon said evenly.

"Yes, indeed, I do," the count responded, and took another swig.

"I did come for another reason, and that was to enjoin the kings to remember who it was who held Tyre all this time, and who was the better qualified for the position of king."

"How then did you fare, Lord?"

"As one might expect, with Guy in the room and virtually begging on his knees," the count snorted contemptuously. I was ready to stab Guy to death with a wooden spoon, the only weapon at hand! It was truly a stressful argument, and there was even a shouting match. Those two kings cannot agree upon the time of day. Richard behaves like some petulant child!" He shook his head. "It was Philip who summed it up. 'We are a congress of kings,' he told us all. 'We cannot agree upon anything!' Ha ha!"

"So, nothing was achieved?" Talon demanded. He was aghast. He looked over at D'Onston, who ruefully shook his head.

"Don't worry, Talon. There is a strong lobby in my favor from the orders and from your own kind, the *Pullani*, none of whom want to see Guy back in the kingship."

"So Richard would simply take Jerusalem, hand it over to Lusignan and then leave for England. Just like that?" Talon had not meant to sound quite so disgusted but it came out that way nonetheless.

Conrad glanced at D'Onston as though wondering how much he should say, then shrugged. "King Richard is constantly looking over his shoulder. His brother, John, is misbehaving. Mummy is writing letters to him every day, telling him to come home." Another swig. "God's blood, but this is good wine, Talon," he wiped his beard and continued.

"My problem is Philip. He looks sick and I am hearing rumors that he is going to die if he doesn't leave soon. Richard, while he detests him, doesn't want that, because Philip will take most of his army with him. But it's even worse for me, because it means I lose my strongest supporter should he go... or even die here."

"I pray to God that they do not appoint Guy," Talon grumbled. "But I hear that you had an interesting encounter on your way here from Tyre?"

Conrad laughed. "Yes, by God, we did. On our way here with my two ships we ran into an Arab galley that was in trouble for some reason, so he could not flee. I immediately decided to take the ship, and if possible add it to my small flotilla. You know how important ships are." He paused and sat up proudly.

"It turns out that this galley was loaded with treasure! By the saint's toes, it was *loaded*!" Conrad exclaimed. "To make a long story short, we boarded it. After a sharp engagement we tossed the crew overboard and then repaired the mast, which was damaged. It is now anchored alongside my own two ships in the harbor."

"Was it a merchant vessel, Lord?"

"No, that was the odd thing. It was manned by some very tough youths who fought to the death, even though it was clear that we were overwhelming them. They were all dressed in expensive-looking armor and wore red and white sashes."

Talon started. "Red and white sashes, Lord? Can you describe these youths more fully?"

Conrad peered at him. He had drunk a lot of wine. "Well, yes, they were youths. The older men were crewmen, but these were the real fighters. We threw them all overboard, anyway. So as far as treasure is concerned, I now have some and Guy has none!" Conrad chortled.

*****

Late that night, Junayd and Khuzaymah rode quietly back into Talon's encampment, exchanged quiet calls and passwords with the alert guards, and then made their way to where Talon was waiting for them in the darkness of his tent.

"Any problems?" Talon asked.

"None, Lord. They were all asleep, including the guards. No one was hurt." Junayd's tone implied contempt for the people on the ship that the two killers had visited. Talon had stipulated that he wanted there to be no trace of their presence while they were there or after they were gone from the vessel that Conrad had captured.

"What did you find?" he asked without preamble.

"We found these in the captain's cabin, Lord," Khuzaymah said, and handed him a long strip of cloth and a gold coin. Talon lit another couple of candles and scrutinized the objects that his Companions had gone to some lengths to obtain.

Talon heaved a deep sigh as he stared at the coin and the cloth. "This," he whispered, "belongs to the Batinis of Syria. It is just as I feared. They were Rashid's assassins on that ship. It was his treasure!"

"You are sure, Lord?" Junayd asked sharply in a tone of deep concern.

"Yes," said Talon reluctantly. "I am very sure, and I fear that Rashid ad-Din is going to be very angry. Conrad could not have taken from a worse enemy. The School Teacher will want revenge."

Chapter 30

A Parting of Kings

Sword, how fair and bright thou art.
Come thou forth and view the light,
Long as I can wield thee here
Charles my Emperor shall not say
That I die alone, unwept.
—from *The Legend of Roland*

The city of Acre, in the hands of the crusaders, lurched from one riot to another as the factions drank too much and brawled in the narrow streets. Talon paid a visit to the former Jewish area with some of his men, and Maymun showed him where they had stayed with Naida.

The tiny girl was being looked after by one of the Greek women who had come along with the small Cypriot army. Talon had made it clear that the child should be well-looked after and, indeed, the womenfolk had taken to the child, cleaned her up, and given her clean clothes. She now scampered about with some of the more friendly dogs and appeared to be filling out just a little from the skeletal creature who had escaped the city.

The captivity of her former people was, however, not something Talon could so readily redress. They were confined to their houses or herded into barns to await their fate, while Salah ad-Din scrambled to obtain the vast sum of coin demanded by the kings, and to find the prisoners on the list presented to him.

Talon noticed that the city streets were shabbier than when he had been there last. Despite the jubilation that had followed the surrender, the city was, to Talon, a sad place that could not rid itself of the despair that had permeated even the streets during the siege.

Lord Conrad lingered another week in Acre, but then, as he told Talon on one of his visits to the Cypriot camp, "I am tired of the endless barking of the English King and seek the relative quiet of Tyre. Guy and his brothers are nagging the kings to move out of Acre, but Richard wants the question of the ransom dealt with first." He looked disgusted. "More people have died of disease and wounds than in actual combat. This is a sorry place, Talon. I wish you good fortune with these two."

"My lord," Talon said, as his guest prepared to depart. .

"What is on your mind, Talon?" Conrad asked.

"You must take precautions when you arrive back in Tyre, my lord."

"Precautions? What sort of precautions?" Conrad sounded puzzled

"The ship that you captured belonged to Rashid ad-Din, the Old Man of the Mountains. He will seek revenge."

Conrad looked startled. "How do you know this?" he demanded, looking uncomfortable.

"Let us say that I have deduced it, and I pray I am wrong, Lord. However, I advise you to see that you are protected at all times, even and especially at night, because the Batinis are clever and Rashid will not be stopped from trying for revenge."

Conrad laughed. "He has to get into the city first, Talon. Don't worry about me. I've outwitted these Saracens on more than one occasion."

He departed with a wave of his hand as he and his retinue cantered off to begin preparations for departure. Talon waved, too, but he looked very somber when he turned back to his waiting men.

"You look worried, Lord," Brandt ventured.

"I am, Brandt, but there is nothing I can do about it now. We have to look to our own. With Henry arrived, we have to get the wounded and ill men aboard as soon as we can. Even our own camp is beginning to look like a swamp."

*****

A summons arrived for Talon the very next day at the behest of Philip of France. He went with his senior Companions and Brandt to see what the king wanted from him. They rode into the city and along almost-deserted streets. Drunken soldiers from both armies were to be seen lying in doorways and against walls, snoring or completely unconscious. Someone had come across a supply of wine the previous day, and the entire army was celebrating still.

They finally came to a house that Talon knew well. The house was not as pretentious as the palace, nor as forbidding as the Templar fortress, but it was nonetheless a wealthy man's dwelling. They handed off their horses and walked through the doorway to the main audience room, which Talon was unfamiliar with. The bishop had lived well in his day, he decided, with a sardonic shake of his head.

They were announced by the lord Chamberlain, who insisted upon decorum, there being little to hand in this conquered city. Philip was seated in a large, carved chair with a high back, and barely greeted them upon their marching forward and bowing to him. His pallid face was gaunt, and he looked exhausted. The *arnaldia* had ravaged him. His head was covered in a large hat to hide the loss of hair, and he kept his hands out of sight. The word was that the disease caused the hair and nails fall out, and the loosening of teeth.

"Ah, there you are, Lord Talon de Gilles! Welcome to my humble abode." His sarcasm was not lost on his visitors, but it was easy enough to judge that it was directed against Richard, who had imposed this humiliation on him.

"I am honored, my liege. I fear that I do not find you well. I can provide the services of my physician, should you wish. He is very skilled in the art of medicine."

Philip shook his head. "Be seated, Lord Talon. While I have heard good things about your Greek, I am intent upon one thing, and that is what I wish to discuss here today."

Talon seated himself while his attendants stood behind him. They must have presented a somewhat threatening aspect, as the bishop standing to Philip's right gave them a fearful look, crossed himself, and then busied himself with his rosary. A priest just behind him did the same, while the few lords clustered around the throne looked wary.

As though sensing this, Philip remarked in his usual caustic fashion, "You and your men are frightening my people by your mere presence, Lord Talon. Please tell them, especially that huge man, to stop glowering at us so that we can all relax." He chuckled as he spoke, and Talon's respect rose for the man.

He laughed with the king and told his men, "The king commands it; Brandt, and you, Junayd, are to look more pleasant. At least try!"

He didn't look behind him at his men, but he heard them shuffle about before he focused upon what the French king might have to say.

Philip gestured to a lord, who had been standing nearby. "You have already met the Duke of Burgundy," he said. "This concerns him as well, so we will proceed. I shall not insult you, Lord Talon, by asking if you would like some wine. We have only the swill that was discovered the other day and I, for one, cannot recommend it to anyone but, perhaps, an Englishman."

Talon smiled. "Forgive me, my liege, I did not know that you were in need. I shall send over a barrel for you, the moment I return to my camp."

"Yes, your camp. How do you manage that? It always looks clean, and I have heard that your sick people almost always recover, while there is little of the *arnaldia* to be seen there."

"God's will, but we do not have that particular sickness with us, my liege." Talon replied. "I fear that it comes about from the lack of green food and fruit. But we have not been let off completely. Fevers and sickness have struck us, too."

"Since you were kind enough to share some of your supplies with me, I cannot complain," Philip replied. "Now, Hugh, come closer." He beckoned the truculent-looking man, whom Talon knew only slightly. Hugh III of Burgundy was a heavyset man, whose broad shoulders and strong arms denoted a fighting lord. Burgundy nodded his shaggy head to Talon but didn't speak. Talon knew that Hugh's relationship with Philip was somewhat tense. Whereas Hugh had once had ambitions to be independent of France, Philip had quickly corrected that notion, and then forced the duke to come on the Third Crusade, as it was now called.

He was not coy about stating his rank, either, for he wore a large badge on his left breast next to the cross, depicting a mounted horseman brandishing a sword. The words embroidered around the image stated: ONIS.DUCIS BVRGVNDIE SIGILLUM. HVC. Talon, who didn't believe in trumpets because they made too much noise, or emblems because they said too much about the wearers, thought this to be ostentatious, but he was at an audience with the king of

France, so he kept his council and his expression neutral as he greeted the duke.

"I am honored to meet you again, my lord," he said evenly.

The duke nodded and replied, "You are a notable warrior, Lord Talon."

This was said grudgingly, but Talon wasn't paying him much attention. Philip was coughing and looking worse than ever. "My liege, I can ask my physician to come at once."

Philip shook his head impatiently. "No. Clear the room, Burgundy."

The duke waved to the men scattered in the room and gestured for them all to leave, except the bishop. After everyone had gone, including Talon's men, Philip continued.

"I am indebted to you, Lord Talon, for your offer of a physician, but there is no time for that. Now, listen. I am a sick man and I am also tired, exhausted by that cousin of mine who listens to no one and does just as he pleases. I am about to leave for France."

Hugh may have suspected this was coming, but he seemed surprised too.

"What will King Richard say, my liege. He is expecting you to accompany him to Jaffe, and then march to victory at Jerusalem, itself!"

"I don't doubt but that he will stamp his foot and demand that I stay," Philip replied sourly. "But I am, by my own physician's account, too sick to continue, and unlike my cousin I do not have a mother to run the country in my absence." He glanced over at the bishop and called to him. "Bishop Eugene, stop playing with your beads and come here."

Philip turned to Talon and said *sotto voce*, "It is known that you are not an overly pious man, Lord Talon, but sometimes it is good to have the church on your side." He looked up at the bishop as he stepped closer.

"Bishop Eugene, you and Burgundy will take the message to Richard, as I am not well enough to go and see him. Tell him simply that I am now very ill, and that I cannot go on anymore." He sighed. "Of one thing I am certain, and that is that I have no intention of dying in this awful place, no matter how holy it might be."

Philip took ship for France soon after this audience. He was a mere shadow of his former self as he stood on the deck of his ship, staring bleakly back at the city. He didn't wave farewell, and neither was he sent off with any enthusiasm. Richard had tried very hard to persuade him to stay, but Philip had been adamant. The angry crowd on the quayside jeered and raised their fists to him, calling him coward and other names. To the watching Talon, it was a wretched moment.

"I shall leave you with the Duke of Burgundy and the rest of the army. The duke is at your disposal," Philip told the angry English king. Burgundy had looked less than happy at this, but had agreed beforehand to this arrangement.

"I want your promise that you will not do anything untoward while I am away from home, Cousin," Richard had insisted, in a tactless and insulting manner, but Philip was too tired to care. "I will swear not to advance into any of the lands of Normandy, and I also swear not to communicate with your brother, Cousin." His tone was equally terse and unfriendly.

Richard had no choice but to leave it at that. "Go, then. I shall finish what we started, and the glory shall all be mine!"

*****

One morning, not long after Philip's departure, Talon was nudged awake by Junayd. It was stifling in the tent, as there was little in the way of a breeze that night.

"What is it, Junayd?" he demanded sleepily.

"We have news from Tyre, my lord," Junayd said. His tone was careful.

Talon was instantly awake. "Tell me," he ordered, as he swung off of his pallet and sat on the edge, pushing his fingers through his tousled hair.

Junayd hesitated, but Talon pressed him. "What is the news, Junayd?"

"Lord Conrad has been murdered, Lord."

Talon stared at him for a long moment. "How did it happen?" He rubbed his forehead pensively.

"The messengers are outside, Lord. Their leader said they came here first, because of your friendship with Lord Conrad."

"Bring them in; I must hear from them what happened. The king will need to know as soon as possible."

The messengers were men whom Talon had met before, Saxons and former comrades of Brandt. Talon recognized them immediately and greeted them. "Welcome, Radulfus. I understand you are the bearer of sad news?"

The leader of the three knelt in front of Talon and bowed his head.

"We came because our chief is dead; and I would pledge fealty to you, Lord Talon, I and my two comrades. We came to tell you what happened."

"Evanthis! Diondre!" Talon called.

"Yes, Lord?" Evanthis poked his head into the section of tent where Talon slept.

"Tea for our guests, Evanthis. Diondre, go and fetch Brandt. Tell him that some of his friends have arrived from Tyre," Talon told him.

Brandt arrived looking tousled but wide awake and concerned. His arrival, combined with that of the other Saxons, made the tent seem small and crowded. The greetings over and with tea at hand, Radulfus was encouraged to tell what he knew, which was only a small part of what had transpired.

*****

Conrad arrived back at the austere city of Tyre on its stronghold island a week after leaving the crusader armies in Acre. He was well pleased with events. He was now the designated king of Jerusalem, an ambition he had carried with him for a long time now. Eventually the English king had given way to pressure and called a vote. To Richard's evident astonishment and consternation the vote had been overwhelmingly in Conrad's favor, and while he had not accepted the vote graciously, Richard had finally agreed to the majority will of the barons and lords, many of whom were *Pullani* and had no wish to have Guy in the role of king again.

Now, all Conrad had to do was to prepare for the role of king, which meant that Richard himself would come to Tyre and oversee the crowning.

*****

High in the mountains to the east of Beirut, the man known far and wide as the School Master was seated at the window of his private chambers, watching some riders who were moving down the steep track that led away from his castle and down to the valley that would eventually join the caravan route, which in turn led to the city of Tyre. Two of his best *fida'iyin* warriors were on their way. Rashid ad-Din had high hopes that they would achieve what Salah ad-Din had not been able to do for four long years.

None of them would return and this was not what he had originally intended for them. He had spent much time and effort in training these particular assassins for an entirely different task. He had wanted them to be better even than the killers who served Reza and Talon and, to his mind, they were, but now there was an even more pressing task that had to be performed because his very reputation was at stake. He shrugged mentally; there was time.

Messengers had arrived a full three weeks before, their eyes wide with fear as to what the reaction of their master would be when he heard the news of the capture of one of his ships.

They had been right. The Master had listened in icy silence as the messengers poured out their tale, kneeling on the expensive carpets that were strewn about his upper chamber.

The ship had been carrying much in the way of gold bullion and some coin from Alexandria. It had run into some bad weather, which had damaged the ship and driven it closer to the eastern shores than the captain wished. None of the Arab ships wanted to come anywhere near Acre these days because of the predations of the Frankish ships, and which would not hesitate to stop and board one of theirs.

The repairs they had tried to complete at sea were insufficient to take them away from the hostile coastline. While wallowing in the water several leagues out to sea and south of Tyre, they were making repairs to the mast when disaster had appeared in the form of a couple of Latin ships sailing southward.

To the despair of the crew and its passengers, the Latin ships had altered course and borne down upon their master's ship to investigate. The crew and the passengers, who were *fida'iyin,* had prepared to fight to the death. The Latin ships had barely hesitated before they had maneuvered into positions enabling them to board the luckless vessel. The battle had opened with a hail of arrows and then the fighting had begun. Despite their ferocious courage, the youths—the *fida'iyin—* were overwhelmed when the Franks came charging on board to finish them off. No quarter was asked and none given during the desperate fight, but it was not long before the youths were all dead or maimed and lying on the bloody deck. The fighting subsided and the remaining defenders were rounded up and held in a huddle at spear point, while the man who had set the event in motion boarded the ship.

The messengers were very clear as to whom it had been. Count Conrad de Montferrat stepped aboard the ship and stared around him at the carnage. After speaking for a few minutes with his men, he gestured to the prisoners. "Throw them all overboard," he told his men. "I want the ship, not these vermin."

Within minutes, there was not a living man from the former crew or the *fida'iyin* still on board. The living and the dead were thrown into the sea for the fishes, while their ship was taken in tow by the Frankish ships.

There were only two survivors, sailors who were picked up by fishing boats three days later. Neither was very coherent, but the news spread, and the messengers picked up on it and investigated. The ship was long overdue in Beirut, which had been its destination. By the time the messengers learned where they were are and came to question them, one of the survivors had already died and the other was near death. He gasped out the story and made it clear that the attack was the count's doing. Soon after he died, the messengers set off on the long journey to inform their master.

The only reason the ship had been carrying so much gold was because their master had deemed the sea the safest route by which he could transport his treasure. The land route was more dangerous than ever. Interception by the roving cavalry of Salah ad-Din had been a real possibility. The sea had seemed, at the time, to be the better option. Now he had lost much, but revenge was still his to be had.

*****

Two youthful men in rich clothing arrived with a small caravan at the causeway that led to the city of Tyre. After showing their letters of introduction to the guards and explaining that they wished to see the Bishop of Beauvais, they were allowed into the city. Their arrival caused a small stir. It was highly unusual for persons of the Moslem kind to want to convert, but these two young merchants appeared to be quite serious. Not only that, they both spoke the Frankish tongue. Thus they were able to communicate easily enough with the Bishop of Beauvais, who was delighted to hear about their wish and not a little flattered that they should want to convert. He informed the count, who had recently returned from Acre, and the count paid the bishop a visit.

He, too, appeared to be pleased with the two young and very presentable men. They were clearly rich, and they spread their wealth around, which pleased the citizens of the fortressed city. No one had visited the city in this manner for a very long time, so they became something of a sensation. The bishop was totally beguiled by their polite but not servile behavior, and they made it plain they were serious about their conversion to the Roman Church.

Meanwhile, preparations were afoot to welcome Richard to the coronation, which was to take place in late April. The formerly grim city that had been under siege for so long began to take on a lively and festive air, as its citizens prepared for the pageant to come.

The count took his Saxon body guard with him, perhaps as a result of the warning from Talon, but he didn't really think there was any danger at hand. Nor did his bodyguard, as Radulfus admitted to Talon, with a look of genuine regret and sorrow on his broad features. "We went with him to the church, Lord Talon, where our master, Lord Conrad, spoke at length with the bishop." He wiped his face with a wide hand as though to banish the image from his mind. "Lord Conrad insisted upon walking back to the castle instead of riding, and we attended him." He fell silent, and no one spoke for a long interval.

"Go on, Radulfus, you must tell me what you know," Talon prompted the distressed man.

"We met the two men who had come to be converted, Lord. May their souls be cast in hell forever," Radulfus ground out. "The count greeted them amiably and walked closer to them. Then, without warning, one of them seized the Lord's sword wrist and held onto it with both hands in a tight grip, while the other drew his dagger and plunged it into the count's side!" The large Saxon almost wailed. "They were so very quick, Lord!

"I—we were taken completely by surprise, but as soon as we saw this treachery we leapt at the two men. I managed to kill one of them, but the other fled. We took hold of the count and feared him dead, but there was a flicker of life in him. He told us to take him to the church nearby."

A crowd was gathering and making it hard to help him, but we carried him to the church." Again, Radulfus paused, and the silence was heavy while he composed himself. "We thought he might be safe there, Lord Talon, but we were sadly mistaken. We placed the count, who was bleeding copiously, on a table, and before the monks could see to him, the other treacherous swine emerged from the shadows like a snake with a knife and struck the poor count again and again." Radulfus gave a huge sigh. "We managed to stop him, finally, but the count was gone by this time. We were so angry that we dragged the treacherous killer off and tortured him for information while the monks and priests attended to the body of the count. It took a long time, but the man finally confessed that the Old Man on the Mountain had ordered the killing, in return for the count having taken the ship."

Radulfus looked up at Talon and his eyes were wet. "I wish to God that they had killed me in his stead, Lord. We did not protect him when we should have, and I am desolated. We failed in our duty."

"Is that why you all three came here?" Talon asked, his tone was more curt than he had intended and the man looked apprehensive.

"We... we have nowhere to go, Lord." He stammered. " But I would understand if you do not wish to have us. We failed our master."

Talon and Brandt looked at one another for a long moment, and then he made a decision. "Swear fealty to me and then come under the command of Brandt, here," he told the three men. "You must also come with me tomorrow and tell the king all that you have told me."

Brandt looked relieved, as did the three Saxons, who promptly knelt and pledged their fealty to Talon, before Brandt took them away to join his own band of warriors.

Talon and Junayd and, later on after Brandt had joined them, stayed up late into the night discussing the event and its consequences.

"Richard might well be blamed for this, I fear," Talon remarked eventually. "It was widely known he preferred Lusignan over Lord Conrad, and he has made so many enemies that they would be ready to believe any form of treachery from him."

"But did not Radulfus tell the truth, Lord?" Junayd asked with a frown.

"I think so, and you think so, and some of the lords who are *Pullani* may understand. But others may find it unbelievable. And even I wonder if Count Sidon, being who he is, might have gone to the School Master and paid to have Conrad taken down." He shook his head. "Sidon hated Conrad, but I don't think even he could be behind this. No, I am sure it was the just revenge from the School Master."

Chapter 31

An Assault Upon Honor

The Rape of St Mary's
Where is the blitheness that has been:
Dancing, singing, game and play?
But weill I know nocht what they mean:
This was murder! All merriness is worn away.
—"Satire on the Age"

Talon was made aware that there was something momentous about to happen when he heard trumpets blaring from the top of the walls of the city of Acre. While the city had been occupied for almost a month now, he and his men had preferred to remain outside the walls near the beach where the air was clean, away from the foul smells that pervaded the city.

Talon had visited several times and then left in a saddened frame of mind. Where the Jews had once thrived, there were deserted, dusty streets that gave off all manner of unpleasant stinks, but above all, it was the cloying smell of apprehension and fear. The inhabitants, who had once defiantly opposed the Christians, were now cowering in their houses waiting for their fate to be decided.

He strode to the entrance of his tent and stared toward the city gates. The king's banner floated high on one tower, while the other sported King Philip of France's banner. Leopold had wanted his banner to fly up there with these two, but Richard had torn it down and thrown it into the mud. Talon had doubted that the remnants of King Leopold's army would ever forget that humiliation.

Now the gates were opening, and a sad procession began to exit Acre. The former inhabitants, men, women, and children, were being herded out of the city, driven by spear point and sword, toward the huge open space in front of the Christian lines. They kept coming out of the city in a long, dark line of wailing women and protesting men, most of them calling upon God for mercy.

Talon was joined by Junayd and Khuzaymah, then the ship's captains, Henry and Guy, and others came to watch with growing concern as the forlorn procession was herded onto a low rise and then surrounded by men at arms from the English and French armies. All the soldiers were armed, their spear points and swords leveled at the terrified prisoners, who began belatedly to realize what their fate was to be. The wailing intensified, but the soldiers wore expressions of stone.

A knight rode up and raised his arm, waiting until the frightened crowd was completely surrounded, and then he dropped his arm and the soldiers advanced. The slaughter began. Talon was wide-eyed with shock and horror, as were every one of his men, many of whom cried out at what they were now witnessing. The soldiers spared no one. The wails turned to shrieks of terror and agony as the soldiers butchered every living person on the field. Some of Talon's men were weeping at the awful spectacle.

The killing seemed to go on forever, but it was not very long before there were no longer any of the former citizens of Acre, either standing bravely to meet their fate, or kneeling and begging for their lives and those of their children. The soldiers were remorseless and indifferent to the screams and pleading. They stabbed and struck with savage glee, and even when there were only corpses lying on the bloody ground they continued to mutilate the dead. There were shouts that the victims had probably swallowed their fortunes, so soldiers disemboweled the corpses. To Talon, they looked like manic, bloody devils from hell. He felt like vomiting and turned away from the carnage.

"Get my sword," he told his orderly. "You stay here, all of you, except Junayd and Andreas. Wait here!" he called, as he strode off to confront the king of England, who had ordered the massacre.

"Dear God! Oh, Dear God, what has he done?" Talon muttered to himself as he strode purposefully up to the entrance to the king's tent, which was still standing, and where the king now stood witness to the killing. He brushed past the guards, who made a half-hearted attempt to stop him, and found himself in front of Richard, who was just finishing off a goblet of wine. He glanced over when he heard Talon approach, shouting.

"What have you done? This is a murder most terrible! In God's name, do you realize what the response from the Arabs will be?" Talon glared at the king. "I cannot serve a man who has committed such a heinous crime. I am no longer at your service! You should be called the Butcher of Ayyadieh, not Coeur de Lion!" Talon was too angry to address the king with any kind of respect.

The big man strode forward and, although he could have avoided it, Talon waited and was struck across the face with the back of Richard's mailed glove. It knocked Talon sideways, but he didn't fall. He felt that a tooth had been loosened, however, and there was blood on his hand when he wiped his face.

"You swore fealty to me, and by God, you will honor that oath!" Richard roared, and drew his arm back for another blow.

"Stop this at once!" Joanna shouted angrily. Her voice managed to penetrate the fog of rage. "Have you not done enough for one day?" she said, still speaking loudly. She had been watching Talon. His green eyes had blazed, but then she saw something that made her feel cold. His eyes went flat and almost dead, the eyes of a killer, and his hand was on his sword. Her hand went to her mouth in panic.

"Stop this at once!" she cried again, but this time with real panic in her voice. The king had no idea how much danger he had brought upon himself.

Richard, a fighting man himself, must have suddenly sensed what was about to happen and dropped his hand to his side, visibly trying to calm himself. The blood that had suffused his face slowly drained away to reveal pallor. The king, not being well, had lost much of the weathered tan he used to have.

"You are right, as usual, sister of mine," he finally drawled, with a glare at Talon. "Guards! To me," he roared.

"My liege?" one of them asked, his eyes flicking from the king to his sister, and back to Talon.

"Arrest this man," the king thundered. "He is a traitor, and you will escort him to the Templar dungeon. Immediately!" Richard snarled. "I shall decide what your fate should be at a later date. In the meantime, you can contemplate your folly and behavior in the quiet of a cell, in the care of the Templars!"

Talon threw a look at the princess, a look of thanks. Had the king struck him a second time he might have done something he would have seriously regretted. It was as though she understood, because she nodded in silence as he was seized by the arms and dragged away.

Talon's two Companions reacted predictably.

Junayd skipped forward and his sword slipped out of its sheath, while Andreas stepped sideways to attack the two spearmen from their flank.

"No!" Talon told them. "Let them take me. It is to be to the Templar dungeons. First take my sword, otherwise they will steal it. Go to the seaward side of the fortress and go over the walls there to find me."

Junayd held the tip of his own sword at the throat of the spearman to Talon's left side and speedily removed Talon's sword belt. As he was doing so, Talon muttered in Arabic.

"Get everyone—I mean *everyone*—onto the ships and be ready, Junayd. We are leaving. Come and get me tonight after midnight. I will be waiting."

Junayd stepped back and tossed the sword to Andreas, who caught it with his left hand and nodded vigorously. "It will be done, Lord. Everyone? The Greeks, too?"

"Yes," Talon called over his shoulder. "Them too. Everyone!"

Junayd and Andreas watched as the spearmen stamped off, with Talon marching between them. They watched as more men joined the spearmen, who were glancing apprehensively back at the two glowering Companions.

They made their way back toward the Cypriot encampment. They tried not to see the gristly remains scattered all around, but the plain and the low mounds were strewn with half naked and disemboweled corpses, and it was unavoidable.

"How could the king do such a thing?" Andreas asked Junayd. He was close to tears with anger.

"I suspect it was impatience and willful arrogance." Junayd responded. "Expediency maybe; he cannot afford to take prisoners with him, but there will be repercussions from the Arab side now, and it will go hard on any Christians in their dungeons, I suspect." He shook his head; he too was shocked. "Come along, my friend, we have much work to do before midnight."

"Why didn't Lord Talon make his escape while we were there? He could have done it!" Andreas demanded as they jogged along the beach path toward their lines.

"He wanted to give us time to prepare, I suspect," Junayd responded. Privately, he thought even Lord Talon would have found it hard to escape the king's reach in time to escape unscathed.

*****

Junayd was right. While Talon knew he could have easily broken free from his guards, he could not have escaped the king's army. He wanted, instead, to provide his men with enough time to alert the captains of his ships of their eminent departure and for the commanders to prepare their men to leave. Once Brandt had overcome his shock and horror at what had been done by Richard and his Norman allies, and subdued his anger at the arrest of his chief, he would go to work with his men and ensure that the escape went as smoothly and as unobtrusively as possible.

Talon was confident that his Companions would come back for him when all was ready, and he would be waiting for them. In the meantime, he would have time to think about how Richard would react to his leaving, and whether there would be any reprisals against the island of Cyprus. The twelve Templar knights who were now nominally in charge could not represent any kind of threat, but Richard himself might.

Talon was marched to the Templar stronghold and there he was relieved of his belt dagger by the guards, who, although rude and insulting, were still wary of him. "You didn't think we would forget this, did you, Magician?" One of them brandished the knife tip in his face. The man's breath was foul, his remaining teeth blackened and broken. Talon's expression must have reflected his disgust, because the man drew back his fist to strike him.

"Careful," Talon said evenly, staring straight into the man's eyes. The guard dropped his fist and instead led the way to the dungeons.

Talon's reputation as a sorcerer was known by all. He glanced up at the sky as they walked along the open passageway, just before they entered the tunnel that led to the dungeons. It was just before noon by his reckoning. Time enough, he thought, for his people to abandon their tents and get aboard the ships. The guards marched him down into the depths of the stronghold to a place that was familiar to him. These were the same cells where his friend, Max, had been incarcerated for so very long.

"Get in there and shut up," the jailer growled, and gave him a shove. As Talon stumbled into the cell, the barred door slammed behind him. The man made a ceremony of running the bolts and putting a huge padlock on the shaft, which locked the door at waist height. The jailer, his ring of keys jangling at his waist, and the guards appeared relieved that he had not placed some kind of spell on them. Nevertheless, they all crossed themselves, and one even spat onto the ground in front of him.

"Devil worshiper," the guard snarled. His companion took him by the arm and pulled him away.

"Leave him. Time to go. This fella is a goner," he said. "The king'll hang him tomorrow, and then we can leave for Jaffa, and not too soon for my reckoning."

They climbed the steps that curled up the wall to the doorway above his head, leaving one flaming torch in a sconce near the door. It hissed and smoked, shedding a flickering dim light on the floor nearby, but otherwise, very little light reached the depths.

As soon as the door above crashed shut and silence descended in the cavernous place, Talon got to work. He fished out his slim knife from the boot they had not thought to check. It took a little time for him to open the lock and allow it to fall; when at last he managed he gave a sigh of relief. It took a little longer to reach the top sliding bolt, but then he was free, and began to look around to see where he could get out of this cold, wet place. The doors above had bolts on the outside, and he had heard them being slammed closed.

He shivered in the dank, cold place. Here many people, Christian and Moslem, had been incarcerated, and many had died here of disease or simply of the cold, wet conditions. Talon knew that the dungeons were below the level of the harbor because the walls were dripping with water. He remembered a previous experience in Baghdad and shivered again.

Something stirred in another cell nearby. Talon had been too preoccupied to notice whether there were any other unfortunates buried here in the Templar dungeons. He started with surprise and gripped his knife harder.

"Who is that?" he demanded in a hoarse whisper.

"Just some poor souls who are keeping you company," came the response from the shadows. By now Talon could make out several dark forms in the two cells nearby. Several were crouched against the walls, while the one who had spoken and another were on their feet, gripping the bars and staring out at him.

"How did you do that?" the larger one asked. The tone of his voice was incredulous.

"Without too much difficulty. Who are you and what are you doing here?" Talon demanded.

"We are informed that we are guests of the king of England. We were captured when the city went under." They were speaking Arabic, but to Talon, there was just a trace of an accent that didn't fit with the language.

"But you are not from Damascus," he responded.

"And you, being a Frans, are not from Acre, I have to presume, although you speak our language well," the other countered. "We two are Kurds, from far away, and we wish we had remained there."

Talon grinned at that. "Ah, yes... of course. And the others?"

"Also from the army of His Most Exulted Sultan, Salah ad-Din. We came to help the citizens some time ago. I wish we had not come, but Allah, in his infinite wisdom, brought us here as reinforcements, just in time to be at the surrender of the city. Why are you here, Frans?"

"I am here because I displeased the king of England, more or less like you, and I, too wish I had not come here. Now I am trying to find a way out."

"Then you are even more foolish than we were. We are doomed to rot here until we die."

"This is indeed an unhappy place," Talon responded. Then he added, "Perhaps you have not heard, but the king of England ordered over two thousand of the citizens of this city to be killed today. I witnessed it, and I protested, and that is why I am here," Talon told the shadows.

There were exclamations of disbelief and horror. "In the prophet's good name! Why would he do such a thing?" someone called out one of the dark shadows, rising to his feet. All the others now crowded to the bars. Talon counted eight men. One or two looked like Nubians, and he remembered his friend, Panhsj, from Egypt. He shook his head. This was no time to be wandering down memory lane and gossiping, but he realized that he now had a dilemma.

"I think they might have forgotten you, for the time being," he told the agitated people. "They might be back to collect you... if they remember, that is."

"Allah protect us! He really did this?" murmured the first man.

"Yes, by God, he did, and I made the mistake of telling him what a crime it was," Talon remarked, as he studied the walls all around him and wondered how on earth he was going to get out of this hell hole. It was going to be a long afternoon, he surmised.

"Can you do your magic on our locks?" demanded the first man

"Tell me *your* name, and I shall see what I can do, but we have to wait. It is not time yet," he told them. I shall go back to my cell and wait."

"Wait for what? I am Hejar and this is Zarav. Who do we have the honor of talking to?" asked Hejar, with a trace of sarcasm in his voice.

"I wait for my people. They will come for me," Talon said. "My name is Talon de Gilles."

"I've heard of him!" one of the shadows muttered with surprise in his voice.

Talon had re-entered his cell and replaced the lock, although it was not fastened. He lifted his head to listen to the murmurs coming from the other cells.

"You have?" demanded Zarav. "How so?"

"He is the one who leads the assassins, those cursed phantoms, whatever you want to call them, who have attacked our lines for the last two months. They have wreaked havoc whenever they appeared, you all know that! His name and that of his companion, Reza the Ghost, are well known. He is a lord in his own right."

"Is this true?" Hejar called from is cell. "Are you the Lord Talon we have all heard of?"

"It is he," affirmed one of the other shadows. "I know it. How else could he get out of his cell so easily? He is known for his magical powers!"

Hejar laughed. "You must have upset the king of that England country very much indeed to be in here, then, Lord."

Talon nodded in the dark. "I imagine that I did," he told them. "Now leave me alone while I think about things."

Hejar sighed. "Yes, there is much to ponder. I shall pray to Allah for our deliverance, with perhaps a little help from a magician, of course."

The other inmates had an animated discussion about him and Reza after that. It provided them with something to talk about in their miserable condition, and it meant they left him alone for a while.

He began to wonder if his people might really be able to gain access to this almost-impregnable fortress in the middle of the city. He fervently hoped so.

"Hejar, how often do they come to check on you?" Talon called out.

"When they remember, Lord," Zarav answered for Hejar. "Sometimes they leave us alone for the whole day."

"So they don't feed you very often? You looked a little thin," Talon remarked. That drew a snicker from several of the prisoners. He continued looking all around him at the walls and the stone steps that led up to the doorway. Then he saw something which caused him to open his door again and almost run up to the torch that flared on its sconce near to the exit door.

He seized the torch and ran back down to the base of the steps, then walked slowly to where he could look at the darkness underneath the steps. It was very dark there, but when he raised the torch to shed light on the area he saw a very low archway beneath the steps, and set deep into the archway was a wooden door!

Talon gave an intake of breath. A door? Where could it possibly lead to, here in the depths of the Templar stronghold? But then he remembered some of the rumors that Max had talked about, of a labyrinth that had been built beneath the towers. He stared at the door and moved slowly toward it.

There was a lock on the right-hand side of the stout wooden door panels. It was iron-studded, and a large key would have been used to open it. He drew out his knife and probed the opening. After some shifting and pressing he felt, more than heard, a solid click. The last time the door had been opened had been some time ago, he surmised. It had not been easy to shift the bars inside the lock, but when he tried the handle lever, he felt it give. His heart was beating hard by this time. Could this be some way out of the stronghold, and the city?

He pushed harder and the door began to creak open. Its iron hinges resisted at first, but he pushed hard and opened it enough to slip through. Conscious by now that he had the full attention of the other prisoners, Talon gave the door one last shove that opened it enough for him to go through; he felt a blast of musty but salt-smelling air. He then turned to his new companions.

"I shall be back," he told them, and left the protesting and excited prisoners to exclaim and call to one another in the darkness. Some even called after him and rattled their bars with frustration, but Hejar told them to be silent.

"The magician will be back. I believe him. Wait!"

Talon wanted to find out where this mysterious tunnel went. The air that came to him smelt of the sea, which was reassuring. He had been wondering if all he had discovered was another layer of dungeon. He walked carefully along the very narrow tunnel, which gradually led upward instead of down, then widened just a little, and then split into two tunnels, both dark and forbidding. He took the one that continued to lead upward, escape being foremost in his mind. Rats fled the flickering light of the torch, squeaking with alarm and scuttling away into small recesses, while cobwebs clung to his face and arms as he walked slowly by. Then he heard a sound.

It was the unmistakable sound of the sea, and the smells of the water became even more pronounced. It was only another twenty paces further when the tunnel dropped abruptly into the heaving sea, leaving only a space above the water that was half the height of an average man, but the exit was blocked in a barred and locked gate. Talon wondered where on the walls of Acre this opening might be. He decided to wade into the water and try to find out. Time was running out because the pitch torch was beginning to gutter and smoke, indicating that it was about to go out.

He was exasperated. Why on earth would anyone build a tunnel that led to a barred grill if there was not a way beyond it? With a sigh of annoyance, he placed the torch in a recess and then hurriedly stripped down to his breeks. Wading into the filthy water that ebbed and flowed back and forth with the tide, he approached the bars and began to work on the lock. It was rusty and refused to give. He almost broke the blade when he tried too hard, but then he looked into the water below him and saw with surprise and delight that just below the water's surface the bars had rusted to ugly stumps and the stone and masonry had rotted and fallen away, to provide space.

He began to kick at the masonry and more fell away under his feet, with a cloud of mud forming. Finally, after much kicking, while trying not to splash a lot and at times holding his breath and leaning down into the filthy water to dislodge some larger stones by hand, he had created a space that was enough for a man to crawl through, albeit with some difficulty. Thoroughly soaked and chilled, he waded back to the pile of clothes and hurriedly donned them, shivering in the cool of the tunnel. Then he took up the torch, which was almost out, and raced back along the corridor toward the dungeons.

He approached the door with care, wondering if the jailer might have arrived and discovered his absence, but there was no one waiting for him and he slipped back through the door, closing it behind him, and then raced up the steps to place the torch back where he had found it. Then he trotted back down again to open his cell door and walked calmly back in, closing it with a clatter behind him.

The dungeon erupted in calls and even shouts as the other prisoners demanded what he had found. Hejar was particularly loud, and Talon surmised that he might be counted as a leader among the other prisoners.

Ignoring the agitated shouts, Talon called over to Hejar, "When can we expect to see the jailer again today?"

"Hejar hesitated and conferred with Zarav before answering. "Any time soon, if they come at all. It will be with our supper," he eventually called back.

"Then we wait," Talon told him.

"Give us some hope, for the love of Allah!" Zarav pleaded.

"Can you swim?" Talon asked him.

"I could swim to Cairo if it meant getting out of here alive," came the response.

"Then all of you be quiet when they come and wait until they are gone. Then we can talk, and perhaps even walk," Talon told them and settled down to wait. The torch, meanwhile, had gone out, leaving them all in darkness.

*****

The jailer arrived some time later. Talon had lost his sense of time in the absolute darkness of the dungeon and was dozing when the door above them rattled as the bolts were shot open, then a boot kicked the door open. Several men walked in, two of them carrying a pail and some wooden bowls. They humped the heavy-looking pail down the stone steps with a man leading, carrying a drawn sword and a torch that threw around dark shadows as he moved.

"Here, you heathens!" called out the jailer. "Soup from the Templar kitchens! Can't do better than that, now, can you?"

As none of the prisoners spoke his language, they were silent. The jailers stumbled along the row of cells, handing out bowls and slopping something that didn't smell very nice into them. They didn't provide spoons.

When they came abreast of Talon, the jailer smirked at him and said, "Eat up, Lord! This might be your very last meal. We hang traitors in the early hours and, by God, the king is good for that, as I hear it."

Talon took his bowl, and then watched as the jailers finished their chore and mounted the steps again. One of them replaced the torch that had been there, with the comment, "Now, don't run off. We're watching, you miserable lot." With a laugh, he and his companions left through the door at the top of the steps, and the bolts were again slammed closed.

"Will they be back tonight?" Talon demanded.

"No. This slop is supper, and we have a long night ahead of us," came the surly reply from Hejar. He had wanted to know where Talon had been, and was annoyed that Talon had not been forthcoming. "We are sure they put pork in the food, so we are truly in hell."

Talon ignored his supper and exited his cell. Then he proceeded to pick the locks of the other three cells and stood aside as the prisoners shuffled out to gather around him. He wrinkled his nose. They all stank from their long confinement and the filth that had accumulated around them. There were eight of them in various stages of raggedness.

"Follow me," he told them, "and *don't* make a sound."

He retrieved the torch, opened the door beneath the stone steps, and then led the way. When the last of the prisoners was through the opening, he closed the door and relocked it. That might confuse anyone who knew where the door was, he surmised, as he took the lead and went back along the narrow tunnel.

It did not seem to take as long for them to reach the grill as it had taken Talon the first time. He told Hejar to keep the others where they were and wait in the tunnel while he found out where they actually were with respect to the castle above.

"We have to negotiate that grill, but I don't want to be exposed at the base of the walls in broad daylight, with a watchful sentry above us." He warned them about talking and then he handed the torch to Hejar, stripped off his shirt, and waded back into the filthy water. He took a deep lungful of air, held his breath, and negotiated the gap between the bars and the stone floor. Surfacing on the other side, Talon kept his head low in the water to where he could just breathe. He flicked his eyes to his left and right, and then realized where he had arrived.

He was on the seaward side of the Templar stronghold, looking directly out to sea. To his left, some several hundred paces away, was a tower that guarded the entrance to the harbor. To his right was more wall, which fell away at one point. There was no beach; the walls rose almost straight up out of the rock base, so there was nowhere to hide if they escaped in daylight.

Then he noticed a fishing boat about two hundred paces out to sea. That in of itself was not strange. The city of Acre was coastal, and whether in Moslem or in Christian hands, men were out at sea trying to make a living as best they could. However, there was something he could not put a finger on about these men that made him stare. Then he realized that the men on board were scrutinizing the walls, and as he stared, he saw one of the men stand up and move toward the back of the boat. It was unmistakably Khuzaymah. He would recognize the way Khuzaymah carried himself anywhere. Hope washed over him, and he grinned.

His men were watching for an opportunity to climb into the stronghold and find their way to the dungeons, killing anyone they encountered on the way. It would be a bloodbath, and no guarantee that it would succeed. Glancing up at the sky, which was now crimson, with the setting sun just about to disappear below the horizon, Talon decided to take a chance.

Talon scanned walls above to see if there was any activity, and saw none. Moving very slowly, he stood up against the wall, and then waved his arms up and down.

Although it was some distance, the alert men in the boat noticed him almost immediately. They acknowledged his presence with some low hand movements, and Talon nodded and slipped back into the water. His men were not going to come to the walls until it was quite dark, but they knew he was there.

*****

In the boat, five of Talon's Companions stared at one another.

"That was Lord Talon, if I am not mistaken," Khuzaymah stated, wide-eyed with surprise. "How in the world he did it, God alone knows."

Andreas nodded his head. "I cannot think of it being anyone else. It will be dark within a short time. The sun is almost set. Then we can row in fast and scoop him up."

"Talon has disappeared," commented Khuzaymah, staring at the place where he had last seen his leader.

"We at least know where he disappeared into that wall," Andreas commented. "I didn't relish the prospect of scaling them and trying to find him, all in the dark. And now you see," he said sententiously for the benefit of the younger Companions, "the virtue of the arduous training our lord puts us through. A man with skills and a knife need not wait in a cell to be rescued; he can rescue himself."

Andreas snickered. "At least as far as getting to the ocean. After that, it is good to have friends with a boat who will pick you out of the water."

By way of reply, Khuzaymah swiped at his head, and Andreas ducked.

<h1 style="text-align:center">Chapter 32</h1>

<h2 style="text-align:center">Secrets and Escape</h2>

But never from thy golden bow
May I beneath the shaft expire!
Whose creeping venom, sure and slow,
Awakes an all-consuming fire:
Ye racking doubts! ye jealous fears!
With others wage internal war;
Repentance, source of future tears,
From me be ever distant far!
—Euripides

While the Companions were waiting for darkness and trying to contain their impatience, Talon went back to his new acquaintances.

"Help is on the way, but we must be patient," he informed them as he replaced his shirt. He shivered. It was going to be a cold night for him, he suspected. Then he sat up from his reclining position against the damp stones.

"I need to find something out," he told Hejar. He left the others staring after him as he took the sputtering torch and left them in the darkness.

Talon made his way back along the tunnel until he reached the junction. He continued back to the dungeons and eased the door slowly open. There was no one there, so he entered the cavernous chamber and locked every cell, after which, he retreated through the door under the stairs and locked that, as well. Now he felt free to investigate the other tunnel.

It led away at a level with the other tunnel, so he was surprised when it stopped, after a further hundred paces of dry tunnel, at yet another doorway. Intrigued, he ran his hands over the door and discovered another lock similar to that which he had picked earlier. Very carefully, he set about opening the lock and then, equally and carefully, he eased the door open. It, too, creaked with lack of use and grease to its hinges. Not knowing what might be on the other side, Talon was very cautious about how he opened this reluctant door.

The very first thing he noticed was light coming in from the other side. He eased the door open enough for him to peer into a dimly lit chamber. It was a chapel, but not an ordinary one. This chamber of worship was lit by four large candles, which were burned halfway down; the wax was dripping down huge brass candlesticks and onto a coarse wooden altar. The arched roof of the room was gray-with-age dark. The chamber was small, only about ten paces by twelve; other than the altar there was nothing in the way of furniture to be seen. This was where the initiations took place, he guessed. His eyes were drawn to a gleam in the dark recess of the chamber. Talon gasped.

The floor in the other half of the room was piled with treasure. He glanced at the other entrance, which was another heavy, solid-looking door, but it was closed and there was no one to be seen. There were no guards. Of course there weren't—they were, if there at all, he reasoned, on the outside of the closed door.

He slipped into the room and walked over to the chests of coin and plates. So, this was where the ransom had been stored. At least some of it, he surmised, as he stared at the gleaming trove of coin. The very ransom that Salah ad-Din had provided to Richard, and of which the Templars were now the custodians. Richard had killed the populace because the ransom had not been fully paid. Yet Talon felt that he had stumbled upon a king's ransom. Richard had been greedy.

There was something else of interest lying off to the side that caught his attention: a small box that contained rolls of papyrus and an old leather-bound book placed on a ledge nearby. Talon had a curious nature, in particular for the written word. Aware that time was short and the torch was sputtering, Talon investigated.

*****

The day after Talon was imprisoned by Richard, the king of England was preparing to leave for Jaffa, a good six leagues south of Acre. The army was assembled, sweating in the blazing sun of the late morning, and waiting for him to arrive and lead the way south.

As Richard exited the tent, he noticed that Lord D'Onston was waiting outside his tent, and with him was the new Grand Master of the Templars and the seneschal for the Templars. All three men looked very uncomfortable.

Richard was not the most perceptive man, but he could not fail to notice the discomfort of his lords. "What is it?" he demanded. "You all look as though you have swallowed horse shit."

"Er—" D'Onston began.

"Spit it out, man. We haven't got all day. We are leaving for Jaffa, in case you have forgotten, and I have had to learn to live in a tent again."

"Yes, my liege. Um... it's about Lord Talon de Gilles." The Grand Master didn't seem to know where to look, and the seneschal scraped his foot in the sand and looked down.

"What in the saint's bollocks name is this all about?" Richard almost shouted. "Cat got your tongue, D'Onston?"

"He is gone, my liege." D'Onston said, through gritted teeth. "Quite gone, Sire."

"What do you mean, gone?" Richard bellowed, and glared at the Grand Master. "Did I not place him in your care? Did you not place him in a dungeon, and why is he not hanging off the walls of the city at this very moment?"

"Vanished," the Grand Master mumbled. "Disappeared overnight, and we have no idea as to how he did it, nor when."

"Where the hell were the jailers!" Richard thundered. "Dame their hides, they can hang alongside him when he is caught. Can't have gone far," he raged. "Find him and hang him. Those were my orders to begin with."

"He is gone, Sire, and you might notice that his ships and all his men are gone, too."

"Bugger!" Richard shouted. "God's trews! Is this the truth?" The disconsolate lords nodded mutely. There was more that the seneschal knew about, but it would have to wait until he was calm enough to hear it, and that would be a good few days away from Acre. Everyone knew they needed to be at the walls of Jerusalem before winter to complete the final triumph of the Crusade.

"Give chase, man, and bring him back to me in chains. We have delayed long enough as it is. Do it!" he bellowed over his shoulder, as he climbed aboard his favorite mount and trotted off to join his army.

"No one saw anything!" The seneschal grunted. "He is a magician, just as they say. The cells were still locked, but none of the prisoners were anywhere to be found when the jailer went there this morning with the guards, to bring him to the gallows. No one at all!" He smashed his fist into his other hand. "How in God's name?" he asked the world in bewilderment.

It occurred to D'Onston that Talon's skills, whether magical or military, might bode ill for the king, if Talon harbored any revenge in his heart. Secretly, however, he was pleased that Talon had managed to disappear. He had not liked the idea of seeing the man who had saved his life hanging off the walls of Acre, no matter how much his king desired it.

"That dungeon has never lost its prisoners in the past, or so you tell me?" he posed the question.

The seneschal shook his head. What he didn't add was that he was sure he knew how Talon had left the stronghold, but at this point, he dared not tell D'Onston, nor even the Grand Master, what else had been discovered missing. The tiny chapel, where much of the treasure obtained from Salah ad-Din had been stored, was bare, except for a few coins lying on the stone floor in a neat row of five, almost as though the thieves, whoever they were, had wanted to taunt the knights. He was mortified and aghast. How would he ever be able to replace such a treasure? But there was more, and it was, to his mind, much worse. Within the chapel had been some very important documents, a manuscript and some rolls of ancient papyrus. These, too, had vanished.

Those among the council of knights, who were the only ones in the society who knew their contents, were going to be half mad with concern. Those who had survived the last tumultuous four years since the fall of the Kingdom of Jerusalem, that is. They were very few left, and they were scattered, so the seneschal was not even sure where a number of them were. These documents had been found almost twenty years before; no one could understand the writing except the Byzantine and Jewish scholars who had made themselves scarce once the Latin nations arrived. The church, in particular, the bishop, had wanted to burn the documents as heathen nonsense, but there were men within the Templar society, one of them a man called Sir Guy de Veres, who were curious. This man knew enough to know the rolls of paper were written in Hebrew, while the manuscript was in old Greek.

Sir Guy was a remarkable man who had spoken Arabic fluently, with a good knowledge of Latin and some Greek. In that respect alone he stood out from his peers, because few of the Latins, as the European Christians were known, troubled themselves to learn the languages of the people of Palestine and their neighbors, the Arab nations, let alone use the knowledge to divine the intent of their enemies. What Sir Guy had observed, while delving through the trove of papers without the knowledge of the bishops, was that the papers made references to Jesus and his association with his disciples, and one person in particular: Mary Magdalene.

His interest piqued, Sir Guy had found a Jewish man in the depths of the city of Acre who could read both Greek and ancient Hebrew. The old man had spent a good week with Sir Guy in Guy's chambers, helping him to sort through the small pile of rolled papyrus, and translating the one leather-bound manuscript. The more they read, the more interested the Jew became, and the more agitated Sir Guy became. If these papers were to be believed and were not forgeries, which he seriously doubted, then the Church of Rome was going to be very unhappy with what was stated within them.

Acting on his own initiative, and knowing that he was on very dangerous ground, Sir Guy had sworn the old man to silence, sweetened the agreement with some gold, and had not destroyed the papers as ordered. Instead, he had stored them well below the ground, in the tiny, well-hidden chapel where the Templar Order kept some of its treasure. Subsequently, Sir Guy had died in the debacle at Joshua's

Crossing, and the old man, too, had died before the Jews departed Acre, a year before it had fallen to Salah ad-Din.

The only person who knew that the papers were hugely important was the seneschal, and he was not about to reveal to anyone what he knew. King Richard was too unpredictable, and over time the seneschal had become wary of passing along information of real importance to the king, who seemed more intent upon pillage than reestablishing a Christian government in this region. It was common knowledge that his mother, Queen Eleanor of Aquitaine, as she was known, wanted him back in England, because his brother, John, was mismanaging the kingdom in his absence.

Sir Guy had considered these papers to be far too important to be simply burned on the whim of a bishop, and more important than any gold treasure. He, of course, had had to make his confession, as did all the knights. His confession had been to a previous seneschal, upon whom he had impressed the importance, and indeed the danger represented by the papers. It had become a ritual for each new seneschal to be notified as to their content; but then the treasure had been lost, due to the fall of Acre. The doors of the chapel had been sealed and covered, and there the writings had remained until the chapel was reopened by the Templars, when Acre had fallen to the Christians. The only person who knew what the missing papers were, was the seneschal, because the new Grand Master had not as yet been informed as to their content. Now the papers and the manuscript, along with the treasure, were gone, and with them the notorious magician, Talon de Gilles. The seneschal dreaded his coming confession, which would be to the new Grand Master, Robert de Sable.

*****

Talon stood on the afterdeck of his ship, captained by Henry, who, sensing he needed some space, had left that side of the ship to him, to be alone with his thoughts. There was much to think about, not least whether the infuriated king of England would give chase, and whether Kantara would be threatened yet again by some hostile king, or emperor, as the Greeks liked to call them. He glanced around him. On either side of his ship were four other ships, each jammed with men, all from Cyprus, and all glad to be going home, even if they might have wished for different circumstances.

Most had no idea as to why they had abandoned the Crusade, but few had any regrets, and almost all of them had been appalled at the slaughter ordered by the king of England. For most of the Greek nobles the fealty they had sworn was a tenuous affair, and this had been the final straw. The imprisonment and escape of Lord Talon de Gilles had provided the right excuse, so here they were, well on their way toward home.

He turned his gaze to the waist of his ship, and the small group of ex-prisoners who were clustered there. They didn't fully understand their situation at this moment, but he had plans for some of them, which he would share in due course.

His thoughts went back to the evening before. Soon after dark, he had collected the prisoners and asked for their help. They had hustled along the dark corridor to the small chapel, where he had pointed out the chests and the other findings. "I want you to carry those to the opening while we wait for the boat," he had told them.

"You don't tell us much, Lord," Hejar had grunted, as he and Zarav picked up one of the heavy chests.

"It's enough that you know there will be a boat arriving soon to pick us up," Talon told him. "In the meantime, we should hasten to remove these chests."

That had been the easy part. The wait for the boat, the apprehension that discovery was only a matter of moments away, had felt like an eternity to Talon, as he tried to set a calm example for the nervous prisoners. He set some of the more fidgety prisoners to work, widening the hole under the rusty grill. They set to with a will. Anything was better than the idleness of the wait. Finally the lookout, one of the burly Nubians, gave a hoarse whisper. 'They come! Someone comes in a boat!"

Talon had risen to his feet and joined the man at the opening.

"It is time," Talon said briefly.

He took off his shirt again and waded into the water, then slipped under the dangerous spikes of the rusty grill. Surfacing very carefully, he looked around. He noticed a dark shape only a few paces away. "I'm here," he whispered and received a grunt of acknowledgement from Khuzaymah, who was in the bows and reached down a hand to pull Talon aboard.

Talon, instead, reached up and held onto the side of the boat. "Thank God you are safe, Lord," Khuzaymah whispered. "We have been very worried."

"I have people with me and some cargo," Talon told him without preamble. He could almost see the surprise on his Companion's face in the dark. There was a moment of silence, and then Andreas asked in a hoarse whisper, "How many, Lord, and what is the cargo?"

"There are nine of us, altogether. Can we all get into the boat?"

"I think so, Lord, but it will be a tight thing."

"I have some chests to take with us as well."

Again, there was an astonished silence, but Khuzaymah whispered reluctantly, "We will have to see what can be done, Lord."

Thus, it had happened, but the business of bringing the chests out from under the grill proved difficult, and despite all their care, one of the chests jammed and fell apart, spilling its contents over the ledge, down to the bottom of the sea. The other challenge for Talon was to get the parchments to the men in the boat without soaking them. He impressed upon Hejar that it was vital that they did not get wet. Apart from a few splashes, the documents were handled with great care by the prisoners, who, while they did not understand why all the fuss over some paper, were all intent upon aiding this strange man who was helping them to escape. The documents having been transferred, each prisoner slipped under the grill and swam to the boat, where the Companions hauled them aboard without ceremony and shoved them into the waist of the boat, then hushed them, while keeping watch on the top of the walls, in case of discovery.

Talon made it last, and was hauled, dripping, aboard the boat by eager hands, even as Khuzaymah ordered his men to turn out to sea. Thankfully, no one on the parapets appeared to notice or remark on their departure, and before long they were a good half a league out to sea. The boat was dangerously overloaded, but Andreas was a fisherman's son, so he was able to guide them unerringly until they were parallel to the beach, well south of the city. Then, out of the darkness, loomed the hull of a ship.

"Who goes there?" demanded a voice that Talon recognized. "It is I, Talon," he called back, and immediately the ship came to life. No lamps were used, but ropes were dropped and figures lined the side to greet him. Henry was there to give him a bear hug and a back-slapping that took his breath away.

"I have been so worried, Talon!" Henry exclaimed, as he stood back and beamed in the dark.

"I was almost about to go to the church and pray! Imagine that? Me! Anyway, God must have heard my pleas, so you are here, and *we* are ready to sail on your command!"

"Then we must do so at once, Henry," Talon replied with a delighted grin of his own. "It will be light in a couple of hours, and we must be over the horizon before then."

Brandt was there -- the only person Talon knew who could combine a delighted grin with a scowl on his broad features, but he was hesitant, not sure what to do. Talon took care of that and embraced his commander hard.

"Good to see you, Brandt. It might be that we shall live to persuade the lady Rav'an to play some music for us, after all," he murmured.

"Fucking Normans," Brandt grunted. "I was getting ready to storm the city. So, did you use magic to escape, Lord?"

"Why do you ask?" Talon inquired. "Are the Welsh misbehaving?" he joked.

"This will be your opportunity to dump them both in the sea before we arrive back home, Lord," growled the happy giant. "Dewy said you would use magic and bet me my dinner on it. If you say yes I go hungry."

Talon laughed, and embraced in turn the two archers who had been standing right behind the Saxon. "What have you two been up to? Brandt sounds ready to throw you both into the sea," he inquired of the happy pair.

"Well, Lord, it goes like this..." Dewy began. "No, Bach, it was like this!" Caradog interrupted. Thus the argument was underway, while Henry took care of the ship's imminent departure.

Within a very short time, the ship was moving fast out to sea in a northwesterly direction, towing the fishing boat behind it; Talon wanted no evidence for his enemies to ponder. Further back, he could make out the dark shadows of the other ships, keeping pace with his vessel. Everyone was going home, but he hoped that he wasn't bringing even more trouble back with him from this seemingly cursed land.

Later, as the dawn was showing gray on the eastern horizon, Talon was still standing on the afterdeck when

Henry brought him a mug of something to drink. "You should get some rest, Talon," Henry admonished him. Talon smiled at his old friend of many years.

"I'm just glad that we are going in the right direction, Henry," he said, as he took the mug. He was cold, and almost downed it in one full swallow without thinking, then choked on the arak as it burned its way down to his empty stomach.

"Arrgh! Do we really make this stuff and then expect people to drink it, Henry?" he spluttered.

"Well, no, but the villagers down by the harbor do, and we sailors love it. But they start at the age of ten and have cast bronze stomachs," Henry laughed. "Should I give some to our passengers?"

"Hmm, maybe not, but give them something to warm them, and then we have to talk with them."

Henry departed and told one of the men to obtain some soup for the rescued prisoners. Talon walked over to gaze upon the emaciated men down in the waist. He understood their apprehension. They were uncertain of their future, and their freedom appeared to be receding over the horizon. Hejar noticed him first, and nudged Zarav awake, who had been dozing.

"Salam, Lord Talon. I thank God for our deliverance and your help in doing so," Hejar said cautiously. "You really are Lord Talon, and rule all these ships and men!" He sounded very impressed.

"Salam, Hejar. How is everyone?"

"We are slowly waking up to the fact that we are no longer prisoners of the Templars, but are we now your prisoners, Lord?"

Talon shook his head. "No, you are not. Where do you wish to go?" he asked.

"Back to the sultan, if at all possible, Lord," Hejar told him with surprise written on his gaunt face.

"Then it shall be so. All I ask is for your patience, as I have responsibility toward all these men." He waved his arm at the following ships. "I must see them safely to Cyprus, and then I shall have you taken to Beirut."

"We thank you, Lord, but why Beirut?" Zarav asked. "It is quite some way north of Acre. Besides, we have no clothes nor coin, how would we manage?"

"Ah," said Talon with a smile. "I am charging you with a small errand for the sultan, so you will have clothes, horses, and coin to see you on your way once we put you ashore. As for why Beirut, know that all along the coast, from Acre to Jaffa and beyond, the Frans, as you call us, will be intercepting ships of any kind, other than their own, and it will not go well for you, should you be caught at sea." He paused. "I want you to deliver a message to His Highness, the sultan, when you find him, as eventually you will."

All the prisoners had visibly brightened at this news. "We will honor that commitment, Lord," Zarav told him.

*****

In the unhappy land of Palestine, where so much blood had been shed, yet another tragedy was about to be etched into the annals of history. The day after, rumors of the massacre outside Acre traveled like the wind and reached the ears of the sultan, even though he was well to the east of the city and on his way south to confront Richard's army, when it made its way down the coast.

The exhausted messengers fell to their knees and bowed their heads to the ground as he stood to greet them. Salah ad-Din was in full armor, despite his worsening condition, and he suspected ill news. How had he known? Pigeons with coded messages had arrived within hours of the awful event, which no one yet could quite believe, but now the human messengers were here, and their very demeanor confirmed the worst.

It behooved him to be dressed thus to greet them. He was surrounded by his closest advisers and, in particular, his brother Al-Adil and his sons, as well as several high-ranking officers from his army. Some were Arab, others Turks and Kurds, all loyal to the death to this charismatic man who had led them back to the city of Jerusalem after one hundred years of Christian rule. Now they were confronted by a formidable enemy who did not scruple to slaughter their people for the vaguest of reasons.

The messengers stammered out their stories to the stunned assembly, which left almost every man in the tent weeping with rage and shock. Salah ad-Din himself, well known for his ability to control his emotions, was shocked into silence as the dreadful messages borne by the pigeons were confirmed.

When the messengers were done describing the horror, they too fell silent, not daring to look up at their leader. For a long time, the only sound within the tent was the buzzing of flies against the sunlit fabric of the walls, and the quiet sobbing of some of the attendants. Salah ad-Din took some time to bring himself under control, to an ice-cold calm. He finally spoke.

"This has been an assault upon *honor* itself!" Salah ad-Din ground out, his dark eyes blazing with anger. "The English king has broken his word, the most sacred commitment to which a king can possibly commit. I cannot now speak for the safety of any of the Christian prisoners that we have in our own dungeons."

That was when the attendants and his followers gave vent to their full emotions, and the rage and sorrow at this dreadful deed came out in full. Al-Adil smashed his fist into the cup of his other hand. All around him, the sultan heard his men weeping openly and swearing by all they knew, to revenge the slaughtered victims. The English king's actions would be revenged at every turn. Before long, the entire encampment was calling out its collective grief and rage to the heavens. The sultan, observing these demonstrations of grief and rage, hoped privately that they would turn their fury on the crusaders and drive them into the sea.

"Where is his army at present?" he finally demanded.

"They are preparing to leave the city, Lord," one of the messengers told him. "I am informed that his sister, Princess Joanna, tried to reason with the king and argued against the massacre, but was struck to the ground before the killing. She and her brother are no longer on speaking terms, and she is going to remain with the queen and Princess Komnenos in the city."

The sultan nodded as though to himself. The princess Joanna was known for her courage and honor, but up against her willful and arrogant brother she would have had no chance, and now he had dishonored her by striking her. Briefly, the sultan wondered if he could send men to snatch the three women from the city and hold them as ransom to the king. It was a tempting thought, but he dismissed it as being merely a dream. The pieces on the chess board were moving in another direction. He needed to be in position further south, to harry the Christians along every step of their march to Jaffa.

"There is one other somewhat odd occurrence, Your Highness," one of the messengers murmured over the conversations that had broken out.

"What is it? Speak!" Salah ad-Din snapped. He wanted nothing more than to close this meeting and be alone to collect his thoughts and to pray for the victims.

"There was one, a Lord Talon de Gilles, who went to the king to remonstrate with him over the killings, Lord."

Al-Adil and the sultan, as well as several of the attendant generals, stiffened at this remark. The messenger hurried on.

"We do not know what was said in the tent, Lord, but we do know that Lord Talon is now in prison, held within the Templar stronghold."

The sultan's men who knew Talon in person, like Prince al-Adil, and those who knew of him, exclaimed with surprise.

"I could not wish him to be anywhere else," Al-Adil stated frankly. "He is a most dangerous opponent. But I suspect it might be for very wrong reasons."

"I have to agree with you there, Brother. Perhaps he told the king what he didn't want to hear. This Lord Talon is what the Frans call a *Pullani,* as was Count Raymond. Born to this land, so he would know full well what the consequences would be, and perhaps he tried to tell the king," the sultan agreed.

Another man interjected. "This Lord Talon is an honorable man, my lord. He would be shocked at what has occurred and would speak out, of that I am sure."

"How do you know of him, General?" the sultan demanded with some surprise, and turned to look at his Turkish leader.

"I did not meet him personally, but my father did, my lord. It was many years ago, outside a Byzantine city called Dorylaeum, soon after a great battle which the Byzantine army had lost." The man known as General Burak smiled ruefully. "He spared my father, Yiğit, when it was well within his power to kill him. My father never forgot his name, and said he was truly a man of honor. That is how I remember the name today. I am sure it is the same man. I cannot believe he would condone such an act of barbarity."

"Which might explain why he is in prison," the sultan murmured with a nod of his head. "Yes, we certainly do know of this Talon, General."" His tone was dry. "But, I cannot do anything for him at this time. We have the city of Jerusalem to defend from a man who is utterly ruthless and will stop at nothing to achieve his ends."

Although now very tired, as much from the ill news as from his persistent ailment, Salah ad-Din set about arranging for his commanders to encourage his men to put Acre behind them for the time being, and to leave the area for the second stage of this war. He did so with a heavy heart, as he knew with some bitterness that, even if he gave personal orders for the protection of the numerous Christian prisoners held in many of his strongholds, these same unfortunates were probably doomed to die in acts of revenge. The awful deed carried out by the English king had made the struggle for this blood-soaked land more bitter than ever before. He would pray for all the souls lost, regardless of their faith.

He resolved one thing, and that was to make the march down to Jaffa as terrible an experience for the Franks as he could. While he was not going to be able to stop Richard easily, his Turkish cavalry and his Kurds would emulate the actions of the imprisoned Lord Talon, and deliver stings many times worse than hornets, all the way to Jaffa.

The End

It is not easy to put words into the mouths of kings and sultans. Yet historical novelists are expected to do so, if the story is to be at all entertaining, as well as plausible. However, we are entitled to some license in so doing. Not too much, though, or that in turn detracts from the recorded history.

In this particular case, most of the events in this novel did occur, although perhaps not in *quite* the chronological order that history has recorded.

While researching the times, and not just for this book, I have discovered that, while the Latin, Greek, and Arab chroniclers agree upon some of the most significant events that took place, they can rarely agree upon the details, or indeed, the motives for many of the actions that did take place in this violent and eventful period of history.

The men who recorded events on the side of the Latins, or Franks, as the Europeans were known, were for the most part bishops or their secretaries. These worthies demonstrate enormous bias, and manage to justify some of the most appalling misdeeds that took place in the Third Crusade, which by today's, or any standard for that matter, were reprehensible. These people considered the Saracen destined for hell by any means possible because of their differences, hence they could justify any action that accomplished that goal.

The Arab chroniclers and poets of the time were no less biased and peppered their prose with derogatory words against the infidels, and they, too, often muddled the facts. They credited the Latins with little in the way of human decency, hence the Frans, as they were known, were also destined for the deepest pits of hell. The more they feared them, the deeper the fiery pit to which they were consigned.

To hear them speak of Conrad de Montferrat, you would think that Hell opened all its gates specially to receive him.

The two cultures were irreconcilable in many ways. Both sides generated false information about one another to keep the negative emotions alive and their respective cultures at each another's throats. A cautionary tale for us in the 21st Century, as zealots rarely seem to rely upon the truth to gain their ends.

I have taken license, for the sake of the tale. However, Richard did indeed invade Cyprus, and for the reasons outlined. That is well recorded. Don't ask me how it was that Talon happened to be there when he arrived. Four books back, I could not have told you. Perhaps that is fate? A story, often as not, follows its own path, and this one is no exception.

As to how Richard actually managed to get ashore without having his head handed to him in this reckless endeavor is not well recorded, so this is where the tale begins. The events that followed were very much as told in the history books, except that I brought Philip of France into Cyprus when, in fact, he had gone directly to Acre. However, it is well known that the schism between him and Richard was legendary, and I simply could not resist bringing him in early to define their differences.

The two kings were so very unlike. Richard was, without doubt, a courageous but often reckless battle commander, and it is also a well-documented fact that he quarreled incessantly with Philip and many others who could have been staunch allies instead. Philip was, by comparison, physically a slight figure but not one to be underestimated. One might be forgiven for wondering how on earth the Third Crusade got as far as it did under the circumstances, but that is perhaps for another time.

Suffice it to say that Richard's arrival on Cyprus brought a long overdue end to Isaac Komnenos, who was a sadistic tyrant. Yes, he did surrender because he was told his daughter had been captured; and yes, he did, according to records, surrender to the Castilian in the Kantara Castle. And yes, King Richard promised not to place Isaac in iron chains, so instead placed him in silver chains. It seemed appropriate for Talon to have provided the silver. There wasn't much to be found on the island after Nicosia fell to the English.

The grim siege at Acre is, of course, well documented. There appears to have been a swimmer who swam to and fro from the city of Acre during the siege. A very brave man, who ran the gauntlet of the sea blockade for a while, carrying messages to Salah ad-Din (doubtless, the pigeons had all been cooked and eaten by this time). He died on one of his missions. It is thought he was intercepted fatally at sea. There was also an archer who sent arrows over the walls with messages for the Franks and frustrated sorties by the desperate city forces. I merely filled in some of those gaps. There is also much conjecture as to who might have actually been the daughter of Isaac, so perhaps that was a little mischief on my part.

After the surrender of the city to the combined English and French forces and the departure of King Philip, the frightful event that took place soon after was also a sad fact, although the numbers vary. At this point, Talon simply could not, in all conscience, remain with the Crusade. Being a *Pullani,* he knew only too well what the consequences would be and wanted no part of it. By any standards at all, this was a heinous act by King Richard, of which I was only dimly aware before I researched it. However, to hear the bishops tell it, the heavens trumpeted their approval! Somewhat at odds with the message that Jesus put out to the world. The Arab chroniclers were horrified. The Templars didn't approve either; they knew they too would have to deal with the aftermath.

The reprisals that followed the massacre at Acre were just as horrific, and so continued the bitter tale of the Third

Crusade, and indeed the history of the region, which has rarely known a lasting peace of any kind.

The English have quietly written this dark episode out of their schoolbooks, and Richard Coeur de Lion has been, wait for it... lionized down the ages. It is ironic that he spent less than a year of his entire life in the country over which he ruled, yet the English virtually bankrupted themselves to pay his exorbitant ransom to the vengeful Duke Ferdinand. Not only that, to hear the story from the English side, anyone could be forgiven for thinking that they were the *only* crusaders to have inhabited the Holy Land. Yet they actually arrived at the very end of one hundred years of occupation by the French and other nationals!

Meanwhile, at the time Talon left for Cyprus, the Third Crusade was not, by any means over, so there is, perhaps, more to this tale.

James Boschert

James Boschert grew up in the then colony of Malaya in the early fifties. He learned first-hand about terrorism while there, as the Communist insurgency was in full swing. His school was burnt down and the family, while traveling, narrowly survived an ambush, saved by a Gurkha patrol, which drove off the insurgents.

He went on to join the British army at the age of fifteen, serving in remote places like Borneo, Malaya and Oman. Later he spent five years in Iran and the Middle East before the revolution, where he played polo with the Iranian Army, developed a passion for the remote Assassin castles found in the high mountains to the North, and learned to understand and speak the Farsi language.

Escaping Iran during the revolution, he went on to become an engineer, and now lives in Arizona on a small ranch with his family and animals.

If You Enjoyed This Book

Please write a review.
This is important to the author and helps to get
the word out to others.

Visit

PENMORE PRESS
www.penmorepress.com

All Penmore Press books are available directly through
our website.

Storms of Retribution
By
James Boschert

The year 1187 is one of the most fateful for the Christian crusades in the Holy Land, and one of the most disastrous.

With an act of savage banditry, an infamous lord of the Kingdom of Jerusalem destroys the treaties that have made possible trade and a fragile peace. Led by Salah Ed Din, the armies of the Arab world converge on the borders of the Christian kingdom, seeking retribution. Duke Raymond, the Count of Tripoli, sends for Talon, reminding him of the promise he made: to return to Jerusalem after he completed his quest to find Ra'van. The Duke is confident that, with Talon's help, he can help prevent a disaster of enormous magnitude by negotiating directly with Salah Ed Din. But the King of Jerusalem and his advisers, who know little of the land and nothing of their opponents, refuse to honor the pact and ignore the warnings.

PENMORE PRESS
www.penmorepress.com

The Dragon's Breath

by

James Boschert

Talon stared wide-eyed at the devices, awed that they could make such an overwhelming, head-splitting noise. His ears rang and his eyes were burning from the drifting smoke that carried with it an evil stink. "That will show the bastards," Hsü told him with one of his rare smiles. "The General calls his weapons 'the Dragon's breath.' They certainly stink like it."

Talon, an assassin turned knight turned merchant, is restless. Enticed by tales of lucrative trade, he sets sail for the coasts of Africa and India. Traveling with him are his wife and son, eager to share in this new adventure, as well as Reza, his trusted comrade in arms. Treasures beckon at the ports, but Talon and Reza quickly learn that dangers attend every opportunity, and the chance rescue of a Chinese lord named Hsü changes their destination—and their fates.

Hsü introduces Talon to the intricacies of trading in China and the sophisticated wonders of Guangzhou, China's richest city. Here the companions discover wealth beyond their imagining. But Hsü is drawn into a political competition for the position of governor, and his opponents target everyone associated with him, including the foreign merchants he has welcomed into his home. When Hsü is sent on a dangerous mission to deliver the annual Tribute to the Mongols, no one is safe, not even the women and children of the household. As Talon and Reza are drawn into supporting Hsü's bid for power, their fighting skills are put to the test against new weapons and unfamiliar fighting styles. It will take their combined skills to navigate the treacherous waters of intrigue and violence if they hope to return to home.

PENMORE PRESS
www.penmorepress.com

Historical fiction and nonfiction
Paperback available for order on line
and as Ebook with all major distributers

Talon returns to Acre, the Crusader port, a rich man after more than a year in Byzantium. But riches bring enemies, and Talon's past is about to catch up with him: accusations of witchcraft have followed him from Languedoc. Everything is changed, however, when Talon travels to a small fort with Sir Guy de Veres, his Templar mentor, and learns stunning news about Rav'an.

Before he can act, the kingdom of Baldwin IV is threatened by none other than the Sultan of Egypt, Salah Ed Din, who is bringing a vast army through Sinai to retake Jerusalem from the Christians. Talon must take part in the ferocious battle at Montgisard before he can set out to rejoin Rav'an and honor his promise made six years ago.

The 'Assassins of Rashid Ed Din, the Old Man of the Mountain, have targeted Talon for death for obstructing their plans once too often. To avoid them, Talon must take a circuitous route through the loneliest reaches of the southern deserts on his way to Persia, but even so he risks betrayal, imprisonment, and execution.

His sole objective is to find Rav'an, but she is not where he had expected her to be.

PENMORE PRESS
www.penmorepress.com

Assassination

in

Al Qahira

James Boschert

Talon, a young Knight of the Order of Templars, is finally returning to the Holy Land to search for his lost love, but Fate as other plans for him.

He and his companions find themselves shipwrecked on Egypt's shore. In that hostile land they face the constant threat of imprisonment, slavery and execution.

When Talon thwarts a murder attempt, he finds out that a good deed can lead to even greater danger. Soon Talon becomes a pawn in a political game within a society that is seething with enmities, intrigues and treachery at the highest levels. To save the lives of the two children and a beautiful widow he is now oath-sworn to protect, he must call upon all of his skills as an assassin.

A page turner that grips you from the very beginning!

PENMORE PRESS
www.penmorepress.com

Penmore Press

Challenging, Intriguing, Adventurous, Historical and Imaginative

www.penmorepress.com